凱信企管

用對的方法充實自己，
讓人生變得更美好！

凱信企管

用對的方法充實自己，
讓人生變得更美好！

凱信企管

用對的方法充實自己，
讓人生變得更美好！

凱信企管

用對的方法充實自己，
讓人生變得更美好！

國中單字

2000

得分王

**會考、英檢初級必考單字全收錄，關連性記憶
取代背誦，答題快狠準！**

User's guide
使用說明

狠狠學一次！

用關鍵2000單字，扎根英文基礎，有效攻克「聽力」和「閱讀」測驗！

1 單字依主題、詞性分類

讓單字做相關性串聯、主題式學習記憶，而且想從哪一個單元開始學習都可以！

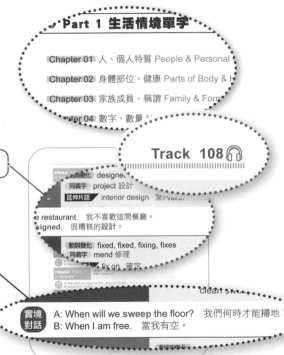

Part 1 生活情境單字

Chapter 01 人、個人特質 People & Personal
Chapter 02 身體部位、健康 Parts of Body & H
Chapter 03 家族成員、稱謂 Family & Form
...ter 04 數字、數量 N...

Track 108 🎧

clean ... 詞性變化 designe...
同義字 project 設計
延伸片語 interior design 室內...

e restaurant. 我不喜歡這間餐廳。
signed. 很糟糕的設計。

動詞變化 fixed, fixed, fixing, fixes
同義字 mend 修理
... fix on 確定

repair [ ]

2 相關單字的學習一網打盡

詞性、同反義字、延伸片語、道地口音，通通一起學，學習更全面。

clean sw...

實境對話 A: When will we sweep the floor? 我們何時才能掃地？
B: When I am free. 當我有空。

3 實境對話情境連結設計

將單字融入生活裡，不僅能真正理解單字用法，還能應用在日常對話中。

4 勤作課後練習當複習

讀寫並用，時時都能藉由練習題加深記憶、溫故知新，掌握學習成效。記憶更深刻。

練習試試看

用簡單的小測驗，驗收一下，單字記住了嗎？

( ) 1 mother   ( ) 11 daughter
( ) 2 twelve   ( ) 12 both
( ) 3 parent   ( ) 13 many
( ) 4 marry   ( ) 14 fifteen
( ) ... name   ( ) 1 ... eight
( ) 10 seven   ( ) 20 a few

A.母親 B.十五 C.兩個的 D.百萬 E.同意 F.女士 G.漂亮的
H.七 I.父子 J.男人 K.多字 L.兩個的 M.一些 N.三十
O.十二 P.雙親之一 Q.女兒 R.結婚 S.第十四 T.一百

Preface

|||||||||||||||||||||||||||||||||||||||||||||||||||||||||||||||||||||||

　　我們的教育讓大多數人從小開始接觸英文，或許因為學習效果不佳，或是不得法，讓不少人視英文學習為畏途。但既然英文已是全球共通語言，考試躲不掉，求職是門檻，旅遊要會說，社交平台和資訊取得更是重要工具，與其逃避、放棄，不如狠下心、正面對決，好好學一次。從最重要的基礎，也就是「單字」，好好開始吧；尤其對學生來說，「單字」更是至關重要！

　　誠如上面說的，世界大門已大開，不論是學生應付考試或是成人為了生存與發展，基本的英語能力已是必備。聽到這裡，我想已經有不少人擔心起來：

　　「哇，怎麼辦？學了這麼多年，英文還是很爛？」

　　「我連單字都記不住，考試成績都無法提升？」

　　「到底要怎麼開始打好基礎？」……

　　先別恐懼！根據研究報告指出：「**八成以上的口語英文所需要的字彙量，只需要約莫兩千字！同時，也足夠應付許多的重要考試。**」**尤其對國小、國高中生來說**，與其死背一大堆單字，倒不如先好好學會這重要的2000字彙，不僅能扎穩基礎，同時也是會考、英檢考試的必須學習內容。另外，也要提醒讀者們，一開始的學習，千萬別讓坊間壓縮時間的快速學習法徒增自己的壓力與恐懼，只要抱著徹底學好這兩千字的決心，狠狠學一次，不論學生們，或是想從頭來把英文學好的人，一定能感受到英文加速往上攀升的成就感與考試分數跳躍式的進步。

　　準備好了嗎？祝福你往成功的方向前進！

Contents 目錄
|||||||||||||||||||||||||||||||||||||||||||||||||||||||||||||||||||||

◑ Part 2 依詞性分類的生活單字

全書音檔雲端連結
因各家手機系統不同， 若無法直接掃描，仍可以至以下電腦雲端連結下載
收聽。（https://tinyurl.com/yjsp446x）

Part

1

生活情境單字

Part 1 音檔雲端連結

因各家手機系統不同，若無法直接掃描，
仍可以至以下電腦雲端連結下載收聽。
（https://tinyurl.com/27zab2pm）

Chapter 1 人、個人特質

Track 001

adult [ə'dʌlt]
名 成年人

名詞複數 adults　　反義字 child 小孩
延伸片語 adult movie 成人電影
adult education 成人教育

實境對話
A: I don't want to do this. It's so stupid.　我不想這樣做，太愚蠢了。
B: You are an **adult** now. You are not a child any longer.
你現在是一個**成年人**，不再是一個孩子了了。

baby ['bebɪ]
名 嬰兒

名詞複數 babies　　同義字 infant 嬰兒
延伸片語 baby blue 淡藍色
baby break 育嬰假

實境對話
A: Look at that **baby**.　快看那個嬰兒！
B: She's so cute.　她太可愛了。

boy [bɔɪ]
名 男孩

名詞複數 boys　　反義字 girl 女孩
延伸片語 boy friend 男朋友
boy wonder 神童

實境對話
A: What happened?　發生什麼事情了？
B: That **boy** broke the window.　那個**男孩**子把玻璃打破了。

child [tʃaɪld]
名 小孩

名詞複數 children　　同義字 kid 小孩
延伸片語 only child 獨生子
from a child 自幼、從小

實境對話
A: Do you know the **child** in white?　你認識那個穿白衣服的小孩子嗎？
B: He's the son of my colleague.　他是我同事的兒子。

couple ['kʌpl̩]
名 一對

名詞複數 couples
延伸片語 a couple of 幾個
newly wed couple 新婚夫婦

實境對話
A: How do you know the **couple**.　你們是怎樣認識這**一對**夫婦的？
B: They helped us repair the car.　他們曾經幫助我們修理過汽車。

customer
['kʌstəmɚ]
名 顧客

名詞複數 customers　　同義字 client 客戶
延伸片語 customer value 顧客價值
regular customer 老主顧

實境對話
A: Don't you think that **customer** is a little strange?　你不覺得那位顧客有點奇怪嗎？
B: Yes, you are right.　嗯，你說得對。

Part 1 生活情境單字

fool [ful]
動 愚弄 **名** 呆子

| 名詞複數 | fools | 同義字 | trick 戲弄 |

動詞變化 fooled, fooled, fooling, fools

延伸片語 fool away 浪費（時間、金錢等）
fool around 游手好閒、胡搞、婚外情

實境對話
A: How embarrassed I was. I looked like a **fool**. 真是太尷尬了，我就像一個呆子。
B: It couldn't be so terrible. 情況不會那樣糟糕的。

genius [ˈdʒinjəs]
名 天才

名詞複數 geniuses, genii 同義字 prodigy 天才、神童
延伸片語 genius in... 某方面的天才
sb.'s evil genius 對某人有壞影響者

實境對話
A: You are totally a **genius**. 你真是一個天才！
B: It's very kind of you to say so. 您這樣說真好。

gentleman [ˈdʒɛntḷmən]
名 紳士

名詞複數 gentlemen 同義字 gent 紳士、男子（口語用法）
延伸片語 gentleman farmer 鄉紳
gentleman's agreement 君子協定

實境對話
A: Do you think that he is a **gentleman**? 你認為他是一位紳士嗎？
B: Obviously not. 很明顯不是。

giant [ˈdʒaɪənt]
名 巨人 **形** 巨大的

名詞複數 giants 同義字 huge 巨大的
延伸片語 giant-sized 特大號的
giant killer 打敗強大對手的人或球隊等

實境對話
A: Do you know the end of the story? 你知道小說結局是什麼嗎？
B: The hero killed the evil **giant** finally. 英雄最後殺死了邪惡的巨人。

girl [gɝl]
名 女孩

名詞複數 girls 反義字 boy 男孩
延伸片語 material girl 拜金女
girl friend 女朋友

實境對話
A: Today I saw a **girl** who's wearing a skirt. 今天我看見了一個穿裙子的女孩。
B: Really? She must be crazy. It's too cold outside. 真的嗎？她一定瘋了，外面那麼冷。

guest [gɛst]
名 客人

名詞複數 guests 反義字 host 主人、東道主
延伸片語 guest of honor 主客、貴賓
guest room 客房

實境對話
A: How many **guest**s came to the party? 有多少客人參加了聚會？
B: About thirty people. 大概三十人吧。

guy [gaɪ]
名 傢伙、人

名詞複數 guys 同義字 fellow 男人、傢伙、人
延伸片語 fall guy 代罪羔羊
tough guy 硬漢

實境對話
A: He is the **guy** who always has good ideas in mind. 他是一個總能想出好點子的人。
B: He must be very popular. 那他一定相當受歡迎。

hero [ˈhɪro]
名 英雄

名詞複數 heroes　　同義字 brave 勇士
延伸片語
hero worship 英雄崇拜
make a hero of 極力讚揚、推崇

實境
對話
A: When I was a child I wanted to be a **hero**.　小的時候，我想當一個英雄。
B: That could be everyone's dream.　那幾乎是所有人夢想。

host [host]
名 主人、東道主
動 主辦、作……主人

名詞複數 hosts　　反義字 guest 客人
動詞變化 hosted, hosted, hosting, hosts
延伸片語 a host of 許多、一大群

實境
對話
A: Who's the **host** of the party?　誰是聚會的主人啊？
B: Mr. Black.　布萊克先生。

kid [kɪd]
名 小孩

名詞複數 kids　　同義字 child 小孩
延伸片語 kids' stuff 簡單容易的事
　　　　 whizz kid 天才兒童、神童

實境
對話
A: Are you free this weekend?　這週末有空嗎？
B: I'm afraid not. I have to look after my **kid**.　恐怕沒有，我得照顧小孩。

king [kɪŋ]
名 國王

名詞複數 kings　　同義字 ruler 統治者
延伸片語 the king of... ……之王

實境
對話
A: The **king** was murdered at night.　國王在夜裡被人暗殺了。
B: That's horrible.　真是太恐怖了。

lady [ˈledɪ]
名 淑女

名詞複數 ladies　　反義字 gentleman 紳士
延伸片語 fair lady 窈窕淑女
　　　　 young lady 年輕的小姐

實境
對話
A: Who's that **lady**?　那位淑女是誰？
B: She is my English teacher.　她是我的英語老師。

male [mel]
名 男性

名詞複數 males　　反義字 female 女性的
延伸片語 male chauvinist 大男人主義者
　　　　 a male choir 男聲合唱團

實境
對話
A: Who is your father talking to?　你父親在跟誰説話？
B: I don't know. It's a strange **male** voice.　我不知道。那是一個陌生男人的聲音。

man [mæn]
名 男人、人類

名詞複數 men　　反義字 woman 女人
延伸片語 be one's own man 獨立自主
　　　　 a man of honor 講信用的人

實境
對話
A: Do you notice the **man** behind your brother in the picture?
你注意到照片上你哥哥背後的那個人了嗎？
B: He's just a passerby.
他只是個路人。

Part **1** 生活情境單字

master [ˈmæstɚ]
名 主人 動 精通

名詞複數	masters
動詞變化	mastered, mastered, mastering, masters
延伸片語	be master of 控制、掌握
	be one's own master 不受他人控制

實境對話
A: Who's the **master** of this dog? 這隻狗的主人是誰?
B: I am. 是我。

neighbor [ˈnebɚ]
名 鄰居 動 與……為鄰

名詞複數	neighbors
動詞變化	neighbored, neighbored, neighboring, neighbors
延伸片語	in the neighbor of... 在……的附近
	neighbor with 與……毗鄰

實境對話
A: Have you seen your **neighbor** yet? 你見過你的鄰居了嗎?
B: Not yet. There is nobody living next door. 還沒有,隔壁還沒有人。

partner [ˈpɑrtnɚ]
名 夥伴

名詞複數	partners	同義字	mate 同伴、夥伴
延伸片語	to join as partner 做……的夥伴		
	silent partner 不過問業務的合夥人		

實境對話
A: What should I do? 我應該做些什麼?
B: Find a **partner** first. 首先,要找到一個夥伴。

people [ˈpipl]
名 人們

同義字	persons 人們
延伸片語	common people 普通人
	people say that... 據說……

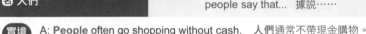
實境對話
A: **People** often go shopping without cash. 人們通常不帶現金購物。
B: It's quite convenient to use credit card. 用信用卡很方便啊。

person [ˈpɝsṇ]
名 人

名詞複數	persons
延伸片語	first person (文法)第一人稱
	missing person 失蹤人口

實境對話
A: What kind of **person** is he? 他是一個什麼樣的人?
B: He's very kindhearted. 他非常的善良。

prince [prɪns]
名 王子

名詞複數	princes	反義字	princess 公主
延伸片語	a merchant prince 商界鉅子		
	Prince Charming 白馬王子		

實境對話
A: Have you seen the wedding of **Prince** William? 你看威廉王子的婚禮了嗎?
B: Of course. It was a wedding that every girl might hope for.
當然了,那真是所有女孩夢想的婚禮。

princess [ˈprɪnsɪs]
名 公主

名詞複數	princesses	反義字	prince 王子
延伸片語	crown princess 王妃、女王儲		
	princess dress 公主風女裝		

實境對話
A: I can do everything for you, my **princess**. 我能為您做任何事,我的公主。
B: Oh! You are so sweet. 噢!你真貼心。

queen [kwin]
名 女王

名詞複數 queens　反義字 king 國王
延伸片語 a social queen 交際花
beautiful queen 選美皇后

A: I'm reading a book about **Queen** Elizabeth.　我在讀一本關於伊麗莎白女王的書。
B: Can you borrow it after you finish reading it?　你讀完後，我能向你借來看嗎？

stranger [ˈstrendʒɚ]
名 陌生人

名詞複數 strangers　反義字 acquaintance 熟人
延伸片語 the little stranger 快出生的嬰孩
make no stranger of 熱情地對待

A: Don't talk to **strangers**.　不要和陌生人說話。
B: I'll keep that in mind.　我會記住的。

teenager [ˈtinˌedʒɚ]
名 十幾歲的孩子

名詞複數 teenagers　同義字 youth 青少年
延伸片語 teenager problem 青少年問題

A: He is just a **teenager**. You can't shout at him like that.　他只是個十幾歲的孩子，你不能那樣吼他。
B: Sorry, I was too angry.　對不起，我太生氣了。

visitor [ˈvɪzɪtɚ]
名 訪客、旅客

名詞複數 visitors　同義字 tourist 觀光客
延伸片語 **visitor center** 遊客中心

A: This town is quite beautiful.　這個小鎮真是太美了！
B: That's why there are so many **visitors** every year.
　這就是為什麼每年都會有這麼多遊客的原因。

woman [ˈwʊmən]
名 女人

名詞複數 women　反義字 man 成年男人
延伸片語 woman of the street 精通世故的女人
woman's rights 女權

A: Look at that **woman**. She's so graceful.　你看那個女人，她舉止很優雅。
B: She must have good family education.　她一定有很好的家教。

youth [juθ]
名 青少年、青少年時代

名詞複數 youths　同義字 teenage 青少年
延伸片語 in the youth 在年輕時
youth culture 青少年的喜好或價值觀

A: Where did you spend your **youth**?　你在哪裡度過你的青少年時代？
B: Taipei.　臺北。

beautiful [ˈbjutəfəl]
形 漂亮的

形容詞變化 more beautiful, the most beautiful
反義字 ugly 醜陋的
延伸片語 beautiful weather 晴朗宜人的天氣
beautiful people 名流、風雲人物

A: I bought this new dress yesterday.　昨天我買了這件新的洋裝。
B: It's so **beautiful**.　好漂亮啊。

blind [blaɪnd]
形 瞎的、盲目的

同義字 sightless 看不見的、盲目的
延伸片語 the blind 盲人
blind alley 死巷子、沒有前途的職業

實境對話
A: Is she **blind**? 她是盲人嗎？
B: No, she just has poor eyesight. 不是，她只是視力不好。

chubby [ˈtʃʌbɪ]
形 豐滿的、圓胖的

形容詞變化 chubbier, the chubbiest
同義字 plump 胖嘟嘟的、豐滿的
延伸片語 a chubby baby 圓滾滾的嬰兒
a chubby face 圓胖的臉

實境對話
A: How's your new girl friend like? 你的新女友看起來怎麼樣？
B: She's a little **chubby**. 她有點豐滿。

cute [kjut]
形 可愛的

形容詞變化 cuter, the cutest 同義字 pretty 可愛的
延伸片語 a cute trick 詭計
meet cute 美麗的邂逅

實境對話
A: How **cute** your little cat is! 你的小貓真可愛！
B: Yes, I like it very much. 是啊，我非常喜歡牠。

deaf [dɛf]
形 聾的、不願聽的

形容詞變化 deafer, the deafest
延伸片語 turn a deaf ear to... 對……充耳不聞
deaf-and-dumb 聾啞的

實境對話
A: There must be something wrong with my uncle's ears.
He always can't listen to me clearly.
我叔叔的耳朵一定出了問題，他總聽不清我說什麼。
B: One of his ear is **deaf**. 他的一隻耳朵聾了。

dumb [dʌm]
形 愚笨的、啞的

形容詞變化 dumber, the dumbest 同義字 mute 啞的
延伸片語 dumb show 默劇
dumb dog 沉默寡言的人

實境對話
A: Why doesn't he speak to me? 他為什麼不和我說話？
B: He is **dumb**. 他是啞巴。

fat [fæt]
形 胖的

形容詞變化 fatter, the fattest 反義字 thin 瘦的
延伸片語 get / grow fat 發胖
a fat chance 微小的希望

實境對話
A: That dog is too **fat** to jump the barrier. 那隻狗太胖而跨不過障礙。
B: But it looks so cute. 但牠看起來很可愛。

handsome [ˈhænsəm]
形 英俊的

形容詞變化 handsomer, the handsomest
同義字 attractive 吸引人的
延伸片語 come down handsome 揮金如土

實境對話
A: Do you know our monitor? 你認識我們班長嗎？
B: You mean that **handsome** boy? 你指那個英俊的男孩嗎？

heavy [ˈhɛvɪ]
形 重的

形容詞變化 heavier, the heaviest　　反義字 light 輕的
延伸片語　heavy work　繁重的工作
　　　　　heavy traffic　交通壅塞

實境對話
A: Can I help you?　需要幫助嗎？
B: Yes, thanks. It's really too **heavy** for me.　是的，謝謝，它真是太重了。

nice-looking [ˈnaɪsˈlʊkɪŋ]
形 好看的

同義字 good-looking 好看的
反義字 ugly 醜的

實境對話
A: What do you think of Amy's boyfriend?　你覺得艾咪的男友怎麼樣？
B: He's just a man **nice-looking**.　不過是個帥哥罷了。

old [old]
形 年老的

形容詞變化 older, the oldest　　反義字 young 年輕的
延伸片語　as of old　一如既往
　　　　　never too old to learn　學無止境

實境對話
A: That **old** lady may need help.　那位老婦人可能需要幫助。
B: Let's go and ask.　我們去問一下。

overweight [ˈovɚˌwet]
形 超重的

同義字 obese 過胖的
反義字 underweight 重量不足

實境對話
A: I'm afraid that you need to pay more for your **overweight** luggage.
　恐怕你得為你的行李多付些錢，它超重了。
B: All right.　好吧。

pretty [ˈprɪtɪ]
形 漂亮的

形容詞變化 prettier, the prettiest　　同義字 lovely 可愛的
延伸片語　pretty as a picture　非常漂亮
　　　　　pretty penny　一大筆錢

實境對話
A: Do you like my new hairstyle?　你喜歡我的新髮型嗎？
B: Yes, It's **pretty**.　嗯，很漂亮。

short [ʃɔrt]
形 矮的、短的

形容詞變化 shorter, the shortest　　反義字 long 長的、遠的
延伸片語　be short of sth.　某物短缺
　　　　　a short memory　記憶力不好

實境對話
A: Would you please change one for me? It's a little **short**.　能幫我換一件嗎？這個有點短。
B: Of course, please wait a minute.
　當然可以，請稍等。

skinny [ˈskɪnɪ]
形 很瘦的

形容詞變化 skinnier, the skinniest
同義字 lean 瘦的
反義字 chubby 豐滿的

實境對話
A: You should eat more meat. You are too **skinny**.　你得多吃些肉，太瘦了。
B: All right.　好吧

Part 1 生活情境單字

slender [ˈslɛndɚ]
形 纖細的

形容詞變化 slenderer, the slenderest　　同義字 slim 苗條的
延伸片語　slender hope　微薄的希望
　　　　　slender meals　便餐

實境對話
A: I want to be a fashion model.　我想當時裝模特兒。
B: Then you must be **slender** enough.　那你得夠苗條才行。

slim [slɪm]
形 細長的、微小的

形容詞變化 slimmer, the slimmest　　同義字 thin 瘦的
反義字 fat 胖的
延伸片語　slim down　消瘦

實境對話
A: She is tall and **slim**.　她又高又苗條。
B: But I think she's skinny.　但我覺得她太瘦了。

tall [tɔl]
形 高的

形容詞變化 taller, the tallest　　反義字 short 矮的
延伸片語　a tall tree　高大的樹
　　　　　a tall order　困難的任務

實境對話
A: Where do you live?　你住在哪裡？
B: The **tall** building over there.　那邊的高樓裡。

thin [θɪn]
形 瘦的、薄的

形容詞變化 thinner, the thinnest　　同義字 slender 薄的
延伸片語　wear thin　穿薄、逐漸消失
　　　　　out of thin air　無中生有、憑空捏造

實境對話
A: I have to lose weight to be **thin**.　我得減肥才能瘦一些。
B: Health is the most important.　健康才是最重要的。

under-weight
[ˌʌndɚˈwet]
名 未到達重量的

反義字 overweight 重量過重
同義字 short weight, deficiency in weight 重量不足

實境對話
A: You don't need to pay for your luggage because it's **under-weight**.
　你不需要為你的行李再買票了，因為它還沒達到重量。
B: OK. Thank you.　好的，謝謝。

ugly [ˈʌglɪ]
形 醜的

形容詞變化 uglier, the ugliest　　反義字 beautiful 美麗的
延伸片語　ugly duckling　醜小鴨
　　　　　an ugly laugh　奸險的笑聲

實境對話
A: Why did you buy so many clothes?　你怎麼買了這麼多衣服啊？
B: The old ones are **ugly**.　那些舊的穿起來都很醜。

young [jʌŋ]
形 年輕的

形容詞變化 younger, the youngest　　反義字 old 年老的
延伸片語　young man　年輕人
　　　　　young and old　老老少少

實境對話
A: Why do you keep silent?　你為什麼要保持沉默？
B: You are too **young** to understand.　你還太年輕，不會理解的。

Chapter 1 人、個人特質 People & Personal Characteristics

---

active [ˈæktɪv]

形 活躍的

形容詞變化 more active, the most active
同義字 energetic 精力充沛的
延伸片語 be active in... 在……方面積極、活躍
active part 積極作用

實境對話
A: Jim is an **active** speaker. 吉姆是一個很**活躍的**演說者。
B: He always makes everybody laugh. 他總能把大家逗笑。

---

angry [ˈæŋgrɪ]

形 生氣的

形容詞變化 angrier, the angriest
同義字 furious 狂怒的
延伸片語 be angry with sb. 生某人的氣
be angry at / about sth. 因某事而生氣

實境對話
A: How could he do that to me? 他怎麼能那樣對我？
B: Please don't be **angry**. You misunderstood him. 別**生氣**，你誤會他了。

---

bad [bæd]

形 壞的

形容詞變化 worse, the worst　反義字 good 好的
延伸片語 bad news 壞消息　in bad 倒楣，失寵

實境對話
A: It's raining outside. 外面下雨啦。
B: That's too **bad**. 真糟糕。

---

bored [bord]

形 無聊的

形容詞變化 more bored, the most bored
反義字 interesting 有趣的
延伸片語 be bored with 對……厭倦　get bored 感到厭煩

實境對話
A: How was the movie tonight? 今晚的電影怎麼樣？
B: I was **bored** with it. 我覺得很無聊。

---

boring [ˈborɪŋ]

形 令人厭煩的

形容詞變化 more boring, the most boring
同義字 dull 無聊的
延伸片語 a boring job 令人厭倦的工作
a boring novel 一本無趣的小說

實境對話
A: Is the lecture interesting? 講座有趣嗎？
B: I think it's so **boring**. 我覺得很無聊。

---

brave [brev]

形 勇敢的

形容詞變化 braver, the bravest　同義字 valiant 勇敢的
延伸片語 brave difficulties 敢於面對困難
a brave new world 美好的新世界

實境對話
A: Today I saw a man catching a thief. 今天我看見一個人抓小偷。
B: He was so **brave**. 他真勇敢。

---

busy [ˈbɪzɪ]

形 忙碌的

形容詞變化 busier, the busiest　反義字 free 空閒的
延伸片語 be busy with sth. 忙於某事
busy as a bee 忙得不可開交

實境對話
A: Are you **busy** this afternoon? 今天下午忙嗎？
B: Not really. 不會很忙。

Part **1** 生活情境單字

careful [ˈkɛrfəl]
形 小心的

形容詞變化 more careful, the most careful
同義字 cautious 十分小心的
延伸片語 be careful about 注意、關切、講究
be careful of 當心

實境對話
A: Be **careful**. It's raining outside. 小心點，外面下雨了。
B: Thank you. I will. 謝謝你，我會的。

careless [ˈkɛrlɪs]
形 粗心的

形容詞變化 more careless, the most careless
同義字 slapdash 粗心的
延伸片語 be careless about 不小心的 be carelessl of 不注意的

實境對話
A: I lost my wallet. 我弄丟錢包了。
B: You shouldn't be so **careless**. 你不應該這麼粗心。

childish [ˈtʃaɪdɪʃ]
形 幼稚的

同義字 naive 天真的
延伸片語 Don't be childish! 別孩子氣！
tired of your childish 厭煩你的幼稚

實境對話
A: Don't be so **childish**. 別這麼幼稚。
B: Sorry. 抱歉。

childlike
[ˈtʃaɪdˌlaɪk]
形 天真的

反義字 mature 成熟的
延伸片語 childlike eyes 天真的眼睛

實境對話
A: I like her **childlike** smile. 我喜歡她那天真的笑容。
B: She looks like an angel. 她看起來就像個天使一樣。

clever [ˈklɛvɚ]
形 聰明的

形容詞變化 cleverer, the cleverest 反義字 stupid 愚蠢的
延伸片語 clever-clever 賣弄小聰明的
clever at doing sth. 擅長做某事

實境對話
A: Which animal do you like? 你喜歡什麼動物？
B: I like dogs. They're so **clever**. 我喜歡狗，牠們很聰明。

confident
[ˈkɑnfədənt]
形 有信心的

形容詞變化 more confident, the most confident
同義字 certain 有把握的
延伸片語 be confident of / that 對……有自信、有信心
confident about 對……有信心

實境對話
A: It's difficult for me. 這件事對我來說太難了。
B: You should be **confident**. 你應該自信些。

considerate
[kənˈsɪdərɪt]
形 體諒的、體貼的

形容詞變化 more considerate, the most considerate
同義字 thoughtful 深思的
延伸片語 a considerate plan 周詳的計畫
be considerate of 對……考慮周到

實境對話
A: How do you think of John? 你們覺得約翰怎麼樣？
B: He's a **considerate** man. 他是個體貼的人。

cool [kul]
形 涼快的、冷靜的、酷的

形容詞變化 cooler, the coolest　　反義字 hot 熱的
延伸片語 as cool as a cucumber　不慌不忙
play it cool　泰然處之

實境對話
A: I just can't stand her attitude.　我受不了她的態度。
B: Hey! Stay **cool**.　嘿！保持冷靜。

crazy [ˈkrezɪ]
形 古怪的、著迷的

形容詞變化 crazier, the craziest　　同義字 mad 發狂的
延伸片語 go crazy　變得瘋狂
crazy about　熱衷

實境對話
A: She's **crazy** about the Michael Jackson.　她對麥克傑克森非常著迷。
B: Oh, me too.　我也是。

cruel [ˈkruəl]
形 殘酷的

形容詞變化 crueler, the cruelest　　同義字 mean 殘忍的
延伸片語 be cruel to sb.　對某人殘忍
cruel blow　殘酷的打擊

實境對話
A: Why do they treat me like that?　為什麼他們那樣對我？
B: Take it easy. It's a **cruel** world.　放輕鬆，這是一個殘酷的世界。

curious [ˈkjurɪəs]
形 好奇的

形容詞變化 more curious, the most curious
同義字 inquisitive 好奇的
延伸片語 be curious of...　對……感到好奇
be curious about sth.　對……很好奇

實境對話
A: When did you break up with John?　你和約翰何時分手的？
B: Why are you so **curious** about me?　為什麼你對我這麼好奇呢？

diligent [ˈdɪlədʒənt]
形 勤勉的

形容詞變化 more diligent, the most diligent
同義字 busy 忙碌的
延伸片語 be diligent in　認真刻苦的做某事
be diligent about　認真做某事

實境對話
A: I failed the exam.　我考試不及格。
B: You should be **diligent** as your classmates.　你要像你同學一樣勤勉才行。

dishonest [dɪsˈɑnɪst]
形 不誠實的

形容詞變化 more dishonest, the most dishonest
反義字 honest 誠實的
延伸片語 be dishonest to　……是不誠實的
be dishonest in　在……不誠實

實境對話
A: I heard that he is **dishonest** to his friends.　聽說他對朋友不誠實。
B: I don't know about this.　這個我不知情。

evil [ˈivl̩]
形 邪惡的 名 邪惡

形容詞變化 eviler, the evilest　　同義字 wicked 邪惡的
名詞複數 evils
延伸片語 evil-minded　心地邪惡的、惡毒的

實境對話
A: I hate the **evil** lady in the movie.　我討厭電影裡那個邪惡的老太婆。
B: Me, too.　我也是。

energetic
[ˌɛnɚˋdʒɛtɪk]
形 精力充沛的

形容詞變化 more energetic, the most energetic
同義字 vigrous 精力旺盛的
延伸片語 boundlessly energetic 氣勢磅礡

 實境對話
A: He looks so lazy. 他看起來好懶散。
B: When he plays computer, he'll be **energetic**. 當他玩電腦時整個人就**精力充沛的**。

excited [ɪkˋsaɪtɪd]
形 感到興奮的

形容詞變化 more excited; the most excited
反義字 unexcited 不激動的
延伸片語 be excited about 對某事感到興奮

 實境對話
A: What are you going to do tomorrow? 你們明天要做什麼？
B: We are going mountain climbing. I'm so **excited**. 要去爬山，我好**興奮**。

exciting [ɪkˋsaɪtɪŋ]
形 令人興奮的

形容詞變化 more exciting, the most exciting
同義字 thrilling 令人興奮的
延伸片語 an exciting film 一場令人激動的電影

 實境對話
A: Do you like bungee-jumping? 你喜歡高空彈跳嗎？
B: Yes, It's quite an **exciting** sport. 是啊，真是**令人興奮的**運動。

famous [ˋfeməs]
形 著名的

形容詞變化 more famous, the most famous
同義字 noted 著名的
延伸片語 be famous for... 因……而出名

 實境對話
A: Lady Gaga **is famous for** her distinct style. Lady Gaga 以有特色著名。
B: Indeed. She's a very special singer. 的確，她是位很特別的歌手。

foolish [ˋfulɪʃ]
形 愚蠢的

形容詞變化 more foolish, the most foolish
同義字 silly 愚蠢的
反義字 wise 聰明的
延伸片語 a foolish idea 一個愚蠢的主意

 實境對話
A: How **foolish** I was to buy so many useless things. 買了這麼多沒用的東西，我真是太**愚蠢**了。
B: You can use them anyway. 無論如何都是會派上用場的。

frank [fræŋk]
形 坦白的

形容詞變化 franker, the frankest
同義字 sincere 真誠的
延伸片語 to be frank 坦白說

 實境對話
A: To be **frank**, I don't want to go to the party. **坦白說**，我不想去參加聚會。
B: OK. It's up to you. 好的，這取決於你。

friendly [ˋfrɛndlɪ]
形 友善的

形容詞變化 more friendly, the most friendly
延伸片語 be friendly to... 對……友好

 實境對話
A: Mary is always **friendly** to strangers. 瑪麗通常對陌生人都是很**友善**的。
B: Yeah, she's a good girl. 是啊，她是一個好女孩。

funny [ˈfʌnɪ]
形 可笑的、滑稽的

形容詞變化 funnier, the funniest　　同義字 humourous 滑稽的

延伸片語 feel funny 感覺不舒服
a funny thing 一件古怪的事

實境對話
A: You can never imagine how **funny** the situation was.　你永遠也想像不到那場景有多**有趣**。
B: Too bad that I missed it.　錯過它真是太遺憾了。

gentle [ˈdʒɛntl̩]
形 溫柔的

形容詞變化 gentler, the gentlest　　同義字 soft 柔和的

延伸片語 gentle breeze 微風
gentle with 對某人溫柔

實境對話
A: Do you know about Jenny?　你認識珍妮嗎？
B: Yes, she is my friend, a **gentle** girl.　她是我朋友，一個很**溫柔的**女孩。

generous [ˈdʒɛnərəs]
形 慷慨的

形容詞變化 more generous, the most generous

反義字 harsh 嚴厲的

延伸片語 be generous to... 對……寬容的
generous offer 慷慨的說明

實境對話
A: He is **generous** to his friends.　他對朋友很**慷慨**。
B: I see it.　看得出來。

good [gʊd]
形 好的

形容詞變化 better, the best　　同義字 fine 好的

延伸片語 as good as one's word 説到做到
be good at... 擅長做某事

實境對話
A: Don't you think it's a **good** idea?　難道你不認為這是一個**好**主意嗎？
B: No, I don't.　不，我不覺得。

greedy [ˈgridɪ]
形 貪婪的

形容詞變化 greedier, the greediest

延伸片語 be greedy for 貪求……
be greedy of 貪圖……

實境對話
A: People feel unhappy because they are too **greedy**.
人們總是覺得不開心是因為太**貪婪**的緣故。
B: I agree with you.　我贊同你的觀點。

happy [ˈhæpɪ]
形 高興的

形容詞變化 happier, the happiest　　反義字 sad 悲傷的

延伸片語 be happy about / at 因……感到開心
be happy to do sth. 喜歡做某事

實境對話
A: Any **happy** news?　有什麼**高興的**事情嗎？
B: My sister is getting married.　我姐姐要結婚啦。

hard-working [ˌhɑrdˈwɝkɪŋ]
形 勤勉的

形容詞變化 more hard-working, the most hard-working
同義字 laborious 費力的、勤勉的
反義字 lazy 懶惰的

延伸片語 a hard-working teacher 努力工作的教師
a hard-working student 一個勤勉的學生

實境對話
A: I need to be more **hard-working**.　我得更加勤勉才行。
B: It's good for you to think so.　你這樣想很好。

honest [ˈɑnɪst]
形 誠實的

形容詞變化 more honest, the most honest
同義字 frank 坦白的
延伸片語 to be honest 老實說

實境對話
A: Sometimes being **honest** is hard. 有時候誠實很難。
B: I totally agree with you. 我完全贊同你的說法。

humble [ˈhʌmbḷ]
形 謙恭的

形容詞變化 humbler, the humblest 同義字 modest 謙虛的
延伸片語 eat humble pie 低聲下氣地道歉

實境對話
A: What's the name of that **humble** servant in the novel?
小說裡那個謙恭的僕人叫什麼名字來著？
B: Haley. 哈利。

humorous
[ˈhjumərəs] 形 幽默的

形容詞變化 more humorous, the most humorous
同義字 funny 好笑的
延伸片語 a humorous story 詼諧的故事
a humorous movie 一個幽默的電影

實境對話
A: My teacher told us a **humorous** story today. 老師今天講了一個幽默的故事給我們聽。
B: What was it about? 是什麼？

impolite
[ˌɪmpəˈlaɪt]

形 沒禮貌的

形容詞變化 more impolite, the most impolite
同義字 rude 粗魯的
延伸片語 an impolite behavior 不禮貌的行為

實境對話
A: That man cut in the line in front of me. 那個人在我面前插隊。
B: He was so **impolite**. 他很沒有禮貌。

intelligent
[ɪnˈtɛlədʒənt] 形 有才智的

形容詞變化 more intelligent, the most intelligent
同義字 clever 聰明的
延伸片語 artificial intelligent 人工智慧的
intelligent beings 智慧生物

實境對話
A: Who's Helen? 海倫是誰？
B: She's the most **intelligent** student in my class. 她是我們班上最有才智的學生。

interested
[ˈɪntərɪstɪd] 形 感興趣的

形容詞變化 more interested, the most interested
反義字 uninterested 不感興趣的
延伸片語 be interested in 對……感興趣
interested listener 津津有味的聽眾

實境對話
A: Are you **interested** in playing table tennis? 你對打乒乓球感興趣嗎？
B: Yes, very much. 是的，非常喜歡。

jealous [ˈdʒɛləs]
形 嫉妒的

形容詞變化 more jealous, the most jealous
同義字 envious 嫉妒的、羨慕的

實境對話
A: Lily is showing off her new clothes again. 莉莉又在炫耀她的新衣服了。
B: Come on. You're just **jealous**. 少來了，你只是在嫉妒而已。

kind [kaɪnd]
形 仁慈的 名 種類

名詞複數 kinds
形容詞變化 kinder, the kindest　　反義字 cruel 殘酷的
延伸片語 a kind of 一種
it's very kind of sb. to do sth. 某人如此之好，做了某事

 實境對話
A: I''ll never forget Leo. 我永遠也忘不了利奧。
B: He's really a **kind** man. 他確實是一個仁慈的人。

lazy [ˈlezɪ]
形 懶惰的

形容詞變化 lazier, the laziest
反義字 diligent 勤勉的、勤奮的
延伸片語 be too lazy to do sth. 太懶了以致不願做某事
lazy eye 弱視

 實境對話
A: You are too **lazy**. 你也太懶了吧。
B: Hey, it's none of your business. 嘿，這和你無關。

lonely [ˈlonlɪ]
形 寂寞的

形容詞變化 lonelier, the loneliest　　同義字 solitary 單獨的
延伸片語 lonely life 孤獨的生活
the lonely 孤獨的人

 實境對話
A: I've been very **lonely** since I left home. 離開家之後，我覺得好寂寞。
B: You have to be independent as soon as possible. 你得儘快獨立起來。

lovely [ˈlʌvlɪ]
形 動人的

形容詞變化 lovelier, the loveliest　　同義字 charming 迷人的
延伸片語 lovely hair 秀髮
a lovely time 過得愉快

 實境對話
A: You look so **lovely** today. 你今天看起來很動人。
B: Thank you. 謝謝。

mad [mæd]
形 發火、發瘋、發狂的

形容詞變化 madder, the maddest　　同義字 crazy 瘋狂的
延伸片語 go mad 發瘋了
be mad at... 對……發怒

 實境對話
A: My cat almost makes me **mad**. 我家的貓快讓我**發瘋**了。
B: The cat likes scratching everywhere. 貓就是喜歡到處抓東西。

naughty [ˈnɔtɪ]
形 頑皮的

形容詞變化 naughtier, the naughtiest
同義字 disobedient 不守規矩的
延伸片語 a naughty boy 淘氣的男孩子
naughty words 下流話

 實境對話
A: Don't throw food on the floor! 不要把食物丟在地上！
B: He's very **naughty**. 他很頑皮。

nervous [ˈnɝvəs]
形 緊張的

形容詞變化 more nervous, the most nervous
同義字 upset 不安的
延伸片語 be nervous about sth. 因某事忐忑不安
get nervous 感到緊張

 實境對話
A: I can't help sweating. 我流汗了。
B: Don't be **nervous**. 別緊張。

Part **1** 生活情境單字

nice [naɪs]
形 好的

形容詞變化 nicer, the nicest　　反義字 fine 好的
延伸片語 more nice than wise 因愛面子而損害自己的利益
be nice to sb. 對某人很親切

實境對話
A: What a **nice** day.　多美好的一天啊!
B: I hope it would have never passed.　我希望今天永遠不要結束。

patient [ˈpeʃənt]
形 有耐心的 名 病人

名詞複數 patients
形容詞變化 more patient, the most patient
反義字 impatient 沒有耐心的
延伸片語 be patient with... 對……有耐心

實境對話
A: I want to be a teacher.　我想成為一名老師。
B: You should be **patient** with the students.　你必須對學生有耐心。

polite [pəˈlaɪt]
形 禮貌的

形容詞變化 more polite, the most polite
反義字 impolite 不禮貌的
延伸片語 be polite to sb. 對某人禮貌
a polite child 一個懂禮貌的孩子

實境對話
A: Be **polite** to your teachers.　你對老師要有禮貌。
B: I will, Mom.　知道啦，老媽。

poor [pʊr]
形 貧窮的

形容詞變化 poorer, the poorest　　同義字 needy 貧窮的
延伸片語 be poor in sth. 缺乏某物
be in poor health 健康欠佳

實境對話
A: She is **poor**, but she's happy.　她雖貧窮，卻很快樂。
B: She always wears a smile on her face.　她臉上總是帶著微笑。

proud [praʊd]
形 驕傲的

形容詞變化 prouder, the proudest
同義字 arrogant 傲慢的
延伸片語 be proud of... 以……為傲
do sb. proud 使某人受到隆重待遇

實境對話
A: I'm so **proud** of you, my son.　我真為你驕傲，我的孩子。
B: Thank you, Mom.　謝謝您，媽媽。

rich [rɪtʃ]
形 富有的

形容詞變化 richer, the richest　　同義字 wealthy 富裕的
延伸片語 be rich in... 在……很充裕
the rich 富人

實境對話
A: I guess he's **rich**.　我猜他很富有。
B: Maybe.　可能吧。

rude [rud]
形 粗魯的

形容詞變化 ruder, the rudest　　同義字 rough 粗野的
延伸片語 be rude to... 對……粗魯
in rude health 十分健壯

實境對話
A: It was **rude** of him to say that.　他那樣說太粗魯了。
B: He hurts me.　他傷到我了。

Chapter

1

人、個人特質 People & Personal Characteristics

| 027 |

sad [sæd]
形 悲傷的

形容詞變化 sader, the sadest
同義字 sorrowful 悲哀的
延伸片語 be sad at... 對……感到傷心
sad to say 不幸的是

實境對話
A: Are you crying? 你在哭嗎？
B: I can't help. It is such a **sad** movie. 我忍不住啊，這真是一部悲傷的電影。

selfish [ˈsɛlfɪʃ]
形 自私的

形容詞變化 more selfish, the most selfish
同義字 self-serving 自私自利的
延伸片語 a selfish person 自私的人
a selfish refusal 出於自私動機的拒絕

實境對話
A: I can't believe that he is so **selfish**. 我真不敢相信他竟然這麼自私。
B: Maybe you misunderstand him. 你可能誤會他了。

shy [ʃaɪ]
形 害羞的

形容詞變化 shier, the shiest 反義字 bold 大膽的
延伸片語 shy at sth. （指馬）受驚

實境對話
A: I don't know what to say. 我不知道該說些什麼。
B: Don't be **shy**. Just say hello to everybody. 別害羞，和大家打個招呼就好。

silly [ˈsɪlɪ]
形 傻的、無聊的

形容詞變化 sillier, the silliest 同義字 foolish 愚蠢的
延伸片語 be silly 傻的
the silly season 新聞淡季

實境對話
A: I saw a person standing in the sun for the whole noon.
我看見一個人整個中午都站在太陽下。
B: He was too **silly**. 他也太傻了吧。

sincere [sɪnˈsɪr]
形 誠懇的

形容詞變化 more sincere, the most sincere
同義字 genuine 真誠的
延伸片語 sincere thanks 真誠的感謝
sincere apologies 誠懇的歉意

實境對話
A: What do you think of Bob? 你認為鮑伯怎麼樣？
B: He's **sincere**. You can trust him. 他是一個真誠的人，你可以信任他。

smart [smɑrt]
形 聰明的

形容詞變化 smarter, the smartest 同義字 intelligent 聰明的
延伸片語 get smart with 對……無禮

實境對話
A: What about this idea? 這個主意怎麼樣？
B: Excellent. You are so **smart**. 太棒了，你真聰明。

sneaky [ˈsnikɪ]
形 鬼鬼祟祟的

形容詞變化 sneakier, the sneakiest
反義字 aboveboard 光明正大的
延伸片語 a sneaky man 一個鬼鬼祟祟的人
a sneaky plan 一個陰謀

實境對話
A: Don't be so **sneaky**. You are just like a thief. 別這麼鬼鬼祟祟的，你就像個小偷一樣。
B: We must be quiet so we can slip into the hall being noticed.
我們必須得安靜些才能溜進大廳，不被人發現。

Part 1 生活情境單字

stingy [ˈstɪndʒɪ]
形 小氣的

形容詞變化 stingier, the stingiest
反義字 generous 慷慨的
延伸片語 be stingy with 吝嗇某物
a stingy portion of food 份量很少的食物

實境對話
A: She is the **stingiest** woman I have met. 她是我見過最小氣的人了。
B: That's why she can hardly make friends with others. 所以她幾乎交不到朋友。

stupid [ˈstjupɪd]
形 愚蠢的

形容詞變化 stupider, the stupidest　反義字 wise 聰明的
延伸片語 a stupid question 愚蠢的問題
a stupid idea 一個蠢主意

實境對話
A: I can't understand why you did that **stupid** thing.
我不能理解你為什麼會做那麼愚蠢的事情。
B: I'll tell you the whole story later. 我之後會告訴你整個事情的經過。

successful [səkˈsɛsfəl]
形 成功的

形容詞變化 more successful, the most successful
反義字 unsuccessful 失敗的
延伸片語 successful in doing sth. 成功做某事
highly successful 圓滿成功

實境對話
A: I hope we'll be **successful**. 我希望我們會成功。
B: I believe we will. 我相信我們可以。

talkative [ˈtɔkətɪv]
形 好說話的、健談的

形容詞變化 more talkative, the most talkative
反義字 mute 沉默的
同義字 conversable 健談的
延伸片語 a talkative person 一個夸夸其談的人
a talkative neighbour 一個健談的鄰居

實境對話
A: He's a **talkative** man. 他是一個健談的人。
B: Really? Why does he keep silent with me? 真的嗎，為什麼他和我在一起總是保持沉默？

unhappy [ʌnˈhæpɪ]
形 不高興的

形容詞變化 unhappier, the unhappiest
反義字 happy 高興的
延伸片語 an unhappy childhood 一個不幸的童年
an unhappy coincidence 不幸的巧合

實境對話
A: What's wrong? You look **unhappy**. 出什麼事了？你看起來很不開心。
B: I lost my bicycle. 我的自行車不見了。

wise [waɪz]
形 有智慧的

形容詞變化 wiser, the wisest　同義字 smart 聰明的
延伸片語 in any wise 無論如何
be wise to sth. / sb. 瞭解某事或某人的品行

實境對話
A: I decided to tell them the truth. 我決定告訴他們真相。
B: That's a very **wise** decision. 那是非常明智的決定。

用簡單的小測驗，驗收一下，單字記住了嗎？

( )1 talkative

( ) 2 adult

( ) 3 customer

( ) 4 interested

( ) 5 genius

( ) 6 host

( ) 7 king

( ) 8 lady

( ) 9 neighbor

( ) 10 people

( ) 11 stranger

( ) 12 prince

( ) 13 jealous

( ) 14 handsome

( ) 15 blind

( ) 16 overweight

( ) 17 thin

( ) 18 ugly

( ) 19 chubby

( ) 20 angry

A 國王   B 鄰居   C 嫉妒的 D 生氣的 E 成年人 F 感興趣的
G 醜的   H 主人   I 豐滿的 J 健談的 K 瘦的   L 陌生人 M 瞎的
N 英俊的 O 人們   P 顧客   Q 淑女   R 王子   S 天才   T 超重的

答案
1(J) 2(E) 3(P) 4(F) 5(S) 6(H) 7(A) 8(Q) 9(B) 10(O) 11(L) 12(R) 13(C) 14(N)
15(M) 16(T) 17(K) 18(G) 19(I) 20(D)

beard [bɪrd]
名 鬍子

名詞複數 beards	同義字 mustache 鬍子
延伸片語	speak in one's beard 喃喃自語
	to sb.'s beard 當面、公然地

實境對話
A: Who's that man with **beard**? 那個留著鬍子的男人是誰？
B: It's David's father. 那是大衛的父親。

chin [tʃɪn]
名 下巴

名詞複數 chins	同義字 jaw 下巴
延伸片語	jaws of death 鬼門關
	hold your jaw 表示下決心

實境對話
A: There's something on your **chin**. 下巴上黏到東西了。
B: Oh, thanks. 哦，謝謝。

ear [ɪr]
名 耳朵

名詞複數 ears	
延伸片語	be all ears 專心聆聽、迫不及待地想聽
	bend sb's ear 喋喋不休地煩擾人

實境對話
A: What's wrong with your right **ear**? 你的右耳朵怎麼了？
B: It was hurt when I fell down on the ground. 我摔倒的時候被弄傷了。

eye [aɪ]
名 眼睛

名詞複數 eyes	
延伸片語	all eyes 聚精會神地看
	an eye for an eye 以眼還眼

實境對話
A: I don't know you have brown **eyes**. 我都沒發現原來你的眼睛是棕色的。
B: They're not obvious. 很不明顯啊。

face [fes]
名 臉

名詞複數 faces	
延伸片語	on the face of it 從表面看來
	face the music 勇敢地面對困難

實境對話
A: Can you point out his **face** in the picture? 你能在照片上指出他的臉來嗎？
B: Sure, I can. 當然，我可以。

hair [hɛr]
名 頭髮

延伸片語	bad hair day 不如意的一天
	not turn a hair 不動聲色

實境對話
A: What can I do for you? 需要什麼服務嗎？
B: I want to cut my **hair** short. 我想剪短頭髮。

lip [lɪp]
名 嘴唇

名詞複數 lips

延伸片語 on everyone's lips 大家都在談論的
a stiff upper lip 不漏聲色、泰然自若

實境對話
A: If you want to pronounce this word, you have to round your **lips**.
如果你想發這個音，得收圓嘴唇。
B: I'll try it again. 我再試一遍。

mouth [maʊθ]
名 嘴巴

名詞複數 mouths

延伸片語 mouth off 粗暴地講話
to make a mouth 做鬼臉

實境對話
A: It's impolite to speak with your **mouth** full. 嘴裡吃東西的時候和人說話是不禮貌的。
B: I'm so sorry. 不好意思啦。

nose [noz]
名 鼻子

名詞複數 noses

延伸片語 nose out 比……略勝一籌
on the nose 正好、恰恰

實境對話
A: What happened? 發生什麼事情了？
B: I bumped my **nose** when I walked in. 進門的時候撞到鼻子了。

tongue [tʌŋ]
名 舌頭

名詞複數 tongues

延伸片語 hold one's tongue 保持沉默
lose one's tongue 失聲

實境對話
A: Why do you look so painful? 你為什麼看起來這麼痛苦？
B: I bit my **tongue** carelessly just now. 我剛剛不小心咬了自己的舌頭。

tooth [tuθ]
名 牙齒

名詞複數 teeth

延伸片語 to the teeth 公然、當面
armed to the teeth 全副武裝的

實境對話
A: Do not forget to brush your **teeth** before you sleep. 睡覺前別忘了刷牙。
B: I won't. 不會忘的。

ankle [ˈæŋkl̩]
名 腳踝

延伸片語 ankle socks 短襪
sprain the ankle 扭傷腳踝

實境對話
A: Are you OK? 你還好吧？
B: I'm afraid not. I wrenched my **ankle**. 恐怕不好，我扭傷了腳踝。

arm [ɑrm]
名 胳膊

名詞複數 arms

延伸片語 an arm and a leg 非常昂貴的代價
arm in arm 臂挽臂

實境對話
A: How did your **arm** get hurt? 你的胳膊怎麼受傷的？
B: Well, a car accident. 車禍弄傷的。

Part **1** 生活情境單字

back [bæk]
名 後背 副 回原處

名詞複數 backs
延伸片語 back to back 背靠背
back and fill 出爾反爾

 A: What's the matter with you? 你有什麼問題？
B: My **back** really hurts. 我的後背很疼。

body [`bɑdɪ]
名 身體

名詞複數 bodies
延伸片語 body and soul 完全
over my dead body 絕不要想……

 A: What should I do? 我該怎麼做？
B: Stretch your **body** and relax. 伸展你的身體然後放鬆。

bone [bon]
名 骨頭

名詞複數 bones
延伸片語 bone of contention 爭論的焦點
all skin and bone 皮包骨、非常瘦

 A: Are the **bones** injured? 傷到骨頭了嗎？
B: Not clear. 還不清楚。

finger [`fɪŋgɚ]
名 手指

名詞複數 fingers
延伸片語 be all fingers and thumbs 笨手笨腳的
burn one's fingers （因為大意或者愛管閒事而）招惹麻煩

 A: Peter, don't put your **finger** in your mouth. 彼得，別把手指放在嘴裡。
B: Oh, Mom. Please don't make me embarrassed. 哦，媽媽，別讓我這麼難堪好嗎？

foot [fʊt]
名 腳

名詞複數 feet
延伸片語 at a foot's pace 一步之遙
at one's feet 拜倒在某人腳下

 A: Jim always kicks the door with his **foot**. 吉姆總是用腳踢門。
B: That's so rude. 太無禮了。

hand [hænd]
名 手 動 面交、給、傳遞

名詞複數 hands
延伸片語 at hand 近處
bear a hand in 參與

 A: Take care of your **hand**. 小心你的手。
B: Oh, thank you. 哦，謝謝。

head [hɛd]
名 頭

名詞複數 heads
延伸片語 give one his head 隨心所欲
get it into one's head 懷有偏見

 A: Please don't put your **head** out. It's too dangerous. 請不要將頭伸出窗外，太危險了。
B: OK. Thank you for your reminding. 好的，多謝您的提醒。

hip [hɪp]
名 臀部

名詞複數 heads
延伸片語 get hip to sth. 通曉、熟悉
hip bath 坐浴

實境對話
A: How did the man harass you? 那個男人如何騷擾你？
B: He put his hands on my **hip**. 他把手放在我的屁股上。

knee [ni]
名 膝蓋

名詞複數 knees
延伸片語 give a knee to 給予援手
on one's knees 謙遜的、卑屈的

實境對話
A: There's something wrong with my **knee**. 我的膝蓋有問題。
B: You'd better see a doctor. 你最好看一下醫生。

leg [lɛg]
名 腿

名詞複數 legs
延伸片語 take to one's legs 逃走
leg work 跑腿活

實境對話
A: The dog's **leg** is badly hurt. 那隻狗的腿受了很嚴重的傷。
B: How poor it is. 牠好可憐啊。

nail [nel]
名 釘子、指甲

名詞複數 nails
延伸片語 fight tooth and nail 盡全力以攻擊
on the nail 立刻

實境對話
A: I want to varnish my **nail**. 我想上點指甲油。
B: Which color would you like? 你喜歡什麼顏色？

neck [nɛk]
名 脖子

名詞複數 necks
延伸片語 neck and neck 並駕齊驅
a pain in the neck 討厭的人或物

實境對話
A: How do you feel now? 你現在感覺怎樣？
B: My **neck** still hurts. 脖子還是疼。

shoulder [ˈʃoldɚ]
名 肩膀

名詞複數 shoulders
延伸片語 shoulder to shoulder 齊心協力的
straight from the shoulder 一針見血地

實境對話
A: What's on your **shoulder**? 你肩膀上是什麼？
B: It's a butterfly. 是隻蝴蝶。

skin [skɪn]
名 皮膚

名詞複數 skins
延伸片語 skin and bones 骨瘦如柴的人
change one's skin 改變本性

實境對話
A: What's wrong with your **skin**? 你的皮膚怎麼了？
B: I got a sunburn. 我曬傷了。

Part **1** 生活情境單字

throat [θrot]
名 喉嚨

名詞複數 throats
延伸片語 a lump in one's throat 如鯁在喉
at the top of one's throat 用最大的嗓門

 實境對話
A: I get some tickle in my **throat**. 我喉嚨有點癢。
B: Drink some water and you'll feel better. 喝點水你就會感覺好些。

thumb [θʌm]
名 拇指

名詞複數 thumbs
延伸片語 all thumbs 笨手笨腳
thumbs up 表示贊許

 實境對話
A: Be careful. The door will crush your **thumb**. 小心點，門會夾傷你的拇指的。
B: Thank you for reminding me. 謝謝提醒。

toe [to]
名 腳趾

名詞複數 toes
延伸片語 toe to toe 相對
turn up one's toes 死亡

 實境對話
A: Hey. You are stepping on my **toe**. 嘿，你踩到我的腳趾了。
B: I'm sorry about that. 非常抱歉。

waist [west]
名 腰

名詞複數 waists
延伸片語 waist deep 齊腰深的
stripped to the waist 打赤膊

 實境對話
A: I feel painful on my **waist**. 我感覺腰疼。
B: Have a seat, please. 請坐下來。

wrist [rɪst]
名 手腕

名詞複數 wrists
延伸片語 a slap on the wrist 小處罰
wrist watch 手錶

 實境對話
A: Can you move your **wrist** a little? 你能動一下你的手腕嗎？
B: It's too hard for me. 這對我來說有些困難。

heart [hɑrt]
名 心臟

名詞複數 hearts
延伸片語 by heart 記牢
at heart 本質上

 實境對話
A: His words broke my **heart**. 他的話讓我心碎了。
B: How could he do that to you. 他怎麼能這樣對你！

stomach [ˈstʌmək]
名 胃

延伸片語 have butterflies in one's stomach 緊張兮兮
have no stomach for 沒心情做某事

 實境對話
A: My **stomach** doesn't feel good. 我的胃很不舒服。
B: Get some pills. 吃點藥吧。

comfortable
[ˈkʌmfətəbl]
形 舒適的

形容詞變化 more comfortable, the most comfortable
同義字 restful
延伸片語 a comfortable chair 舒服的椅子
comfortable as on old shoe 輕鬆愉快的

實境對話
A: I like staying at home. It makes me **comfortable**. 我喜歡宅在家裡，那讓我感覺很**舒服**。
B: Me too. 我也是。

dizzy [ˈdɪzɪ]
形 暈眩的

形容詞變化 dizzier, the dizziest 同義字 confused
延伸片語 to make dizzy 使頭昏眼花
feel dizzy 感到眩暈

實境對話
A: The light changes too fast. I feel **dizzy**. 燈光變換地太快了，我有點暈眩。
B: You'd better go outside. 你最好到外面去。

healthy [ˈhɛlθɪ]
形 健康的

形容詞變化 healthier, the healthiest 反義字 unhealthy
延伸片語 healthy food 有益健康的食物
a healthy person 一位健康的人

實境對話
A: You can be **healthy** only if you have the enough vegetables everyday.
只有每天食用足夠的蔬菜你才能健康。
B: But I hate vegetables. 但是我討厭蔬菜。

ill [ɪl]
形 生病的 名 不幸、禍害

形容詞變化 worse, the worst 同義字 sick
延伸片語 ill at ease 感到拘束
for good or ill 好歹

實境對話
A: I heard that you are **ill**. 聽說你生病了。
B: It's just a cold. 只是感冒而已。

painful [ˈpenfəl]
形 痛的

形容詞變化 more painful, the most painful
同義字 distressed 痛苦的
延伸片語 painful memories 痛苦的記憶
painful experience 痛苦的經歷

實境對話
A: It's **painful** to face the truth for him. 要他面對真相會很痛苦。
B: But there's no way to avoid it. 但是這無法逃避。

pale [pel]
形 蒼白的、暗淡的

形容詞變化 paler, the palest 同義字 wan 蒼白的
延伸片語 beyond the pale 在範圍之外
become pale 變得蒼白

實境對話
A: Are you OK? You look **pale**. 你沒事吧，你看起來臉色蒼白。
B: I stayed up the whole night. 我整晚都在熬夜。

sick [sɪk]
形 生病的

形容詞變化 sicker, the sickest 同義字 ill 生病的
延伸片語 sick and tired 筋疲力盡的
sick at heart 深為悲傷

實境對話
A: Where's Oliver? 奧利佛在哪裡？
B: He's **sick**. He can't come today. 他生病了，他今天來不了了。

Part 1 生活情境單字

strong [strɔŋ]
形 強壯的

形容詞變化 stronger, the strongest
延伸片語 strong man （政治）強人
strong room 保險庫

 實境對話
A: You'd better take some exercises. It'll make you **strong**.
你最好多做些運動,那會讓你**強壯**起來。
B: But you know I'm lazy. 但是你知道我很懶的。

tired [taɪrd]
形 疲倦的

形容詞變化 more tired, the most tired 　同義字 ill 生病的
延伸片語 be tired of 對……厭倦的
get tired of 對（人、事物）厭倦了

 實境對話
A: It's time to get up. 該起床了。
B: But I am still so **tired**. 但是我還是感覺很累啊。

weak [wik]
形 虛弱的

形容詞變化 weaker, the weakest 　同義字 feeble 虛弱的
延伸片語 weak at （做事）拙於
weak as a kitten 非常虛弱

 實境對話
A: He looks **weak**. 他看起來很虛弱。
B: He just recovered from his illness. 他病才剛好。

well [wɛl]
形 健康的 副 很好地、充分地
感 啊、那麼

形容詞變化 better, the best 　同義字 fine 好的
延伸片語 well away 順利進行中
wish sb. well 祝福某人

 實境對話
A: I feel not **well** today. 我今天感覺不舒服。
B: You can ask for leave. 你可以請個假。

wound [waʊnd]
名 傷口 動 傷害

名詞複數 wounds 　同義字 hurt 傷害
動詞變化 wounded, wounded, wounding, wounds
延伸片語 suffer a wound 受傷
gunshot wound 槍傷

 實境對話
A: Do you notice the **wound** on his arm? 你注意到他胳膊上的傷口了嗎？
B: Yes. It looks so horrible. 有啊。看起來真嚇人啊。

cancer [ˈkænsɚ]
名 癌症

延伸片語 cancer stick 香菸
died of cancer 死於癌症

 實境對話
A: There are so many people died of **cancer**. 有很多人死於癌症。
B: It's too terrible. 太糟糕了。

cold [kold]
形 寒冷的

形容詞變化 colder, the coldest 　同義字 chilly 寒冷的
延伸片語 catch a cold 感冒
a cold fish 冷漠的人

 實境對話
A: It's **cold** outside. 今天外面很冷。
B: We'd better put on more clothes. 我們最好多穿些衣服。

flu [flu]
名 流行性感冒

延伸片語 get the flu 患上了流感
a flu virus 流感病毒

實境對話
A: Bird **flu** has broken out in many places. 禽流感已經在很多地區爆發了。
B: What shall we do to prevent it? 我們該如何預防呢？

headache ['hɛd,ek]
名 頭痛

延伸片語 have a headache 頭痛

實境對話
A: What's wrong with you? 你怎麼了？
B: I have a bad **headache**. 我頭痛得厲害。

stomachache ['stʌmək,ek]
名 胃痛

延伸片語 get a stomachache 胃疼

實境對話
A: I have a **stomachache**. 我胃痛。
B: You ate too much. 你吃太多了啦。

toothache ['tuθ,ek]
名 牙痛

延伸片語 terrible toothache 可怕的牙痛

實境對話
A: I have a **toothache**. 我牙痛。
B: You'd better see the dentist. 你最好去看牙醫。

cough [kɔf]
名 咳嗽

延伸片語 cough up 勉強説出
cough out 咳出（痰等）

實境對話
A: You have a bad **cough**. 你咳嗽得很厲害，可能是感冒了。
B: Yeah, I need to see a doctor. 是啊，我得去看醫生了。

fever ['fivɚ]
名 發燒

延伸片語 in a fever 極為興奮地
put into a fever 使發燒

實境對話
A: I may have a light **fever**. 我可能有點發燒。
B: You should have some pills. 你應該吃點藥。

pain [pen]
名 疼痛、痛苦

名詞複數 pains 同義字 ache 疼痛
延伸片語 at pain 辛勤地
for one's pains 白費心力

實境對話
A: I have a headache. 我有些頭痛。
B: Do you need a **pain** killer? 要不要來點止痛藥？

Part **1** 生活情境單字

sore [sor]
名 痛苦 形 疼痛的

形容詞變化 sorer, the sorest　同義字 ache 疼痛
延伸片語 sight for sore eyes 悦目的情景
get sore 發怒

實境對話
A: I have a **sore** throat.　我喉嚨痛。
B: Drink some warm water.　喝些溫開水吧。

cure [kjur]
動 治癒、治療

動詞變化 cured, cured, curing, cures　同義字 heal 治癒
延伸片語 cure sb.(of sth.) 治癒某人
kill or cure 好歹

實境對話
A: How is this doctor?　這位醫生怎麼樣？
B: You can trust him. He has **cured** so many patients.　你可以相信他，他治癒了很多患者。

recover [rɪˈkʌvɚ]
動 恢復

動詞變化 recovered, recovered, recovering, recovers
同義字 regain 恢復
延伸片語 recover oneself 恢復
to recover damages 取得損害賠償

實境對話
A: I hope you will **recover** soon.　希望你能早日康復。
B: Thanks.　謝謝。

death [dɛθ]
名 死亡

延伸片語 at death's door 生命危在旦夕
be the death of 把人笑死（常指笑話）

實境對話
A: Everyone is afraid of **death**.　所有人都害怕死亡。
B: That's the instinct of life.　那是生命的本能。

health [hɛlθ]
名 健康

延伸片語 health food 保健食品
health service 公共衛生服務

實境對話
A: You should pay more attention to your **health**.　你應該多關注自身的健康。
B: Yes, you are right.　是的，你說得對。

life [laɪf]
名 生命

名詞複數 lives
延伸片語 life an limb 活生生的
for life 終身

實境對話
A: Nobody has the right to deprive of other's **life**.　沒有人有權利剝奪別人的生命。
B: Exactly.　沒錯。

medicine [ˈmɛdəsn̩]
名 藥

名詞複數 medicines　同義字 pill 藥
延伸片語 take one's medicine 受罰

實境對話
A: Do you need to take some **medicine**?　需要吃些藥嗎？
B: No, I just need to have a rest.　不，我休息一下就好。

用簡單的小測驗，驗收一下，單字記住了嗎？

( ) 1 pale

( ) 2 mouth

( ) 3 sad

( ) 4 successful

( ) 5 finger

( ) 6 death

( ) 7 cure

( ) 8 hand

( ) 9 shoulder

( ) 10 thumb

( )11 chin

( ) 12 toothache

( ) 13 wound

( ) 14 toe

( ) 15 heart

( ) 16 healthy

( ) 17 unhappy

( ) 18 weak

( ) 19 ankle

( ) 20 pain

A 牙痛　　B 悲傷　　C 健康的　D 不高興的　　　　E 肩膀　　F 疼痛
G 心臟　　H 治療　　I 手　　　J 手指　　K 死亡　　L 傷口　　M 成功的
N 腳趾　　O 虛弱的　P 腳踝　　Q 蒼白的　R 下巴　　S 嘴巴　　T 拇指

答案
1(Q)　2(S)　3(B)　4(M)　5(J)　6(K)　7(H)　8(I)　9(E)　10(T)　11(R)　12(A)　13(L)　14(N)
15(G)　16(C)　17(D)　18(O)　19(P)　20(F)

Chapter 3 家族成員、稱謂

aunt [ænt]
名 姨媽

名詞複數 aunts
延伸片語 be an Aunt Sally 成為被戲弄的對象
Aunt Flo 【俚】女人的月經期

實境對話
A: What does your **aunt** do? 你的姨媽是做什麼的？
B: She's a Chinese teacher. 她是一名中文老師。

brother [ˈbrʌðɚ]
名 兄弟

名詞複數 brothers
延伸片語 half-brother 同父異母（或同母異父）兄弟
brother-in-law 大伯、小叔、姊夫、妹夫

實境對話
A: When did you leave your elder **brother**? 你什麼時候離開了你哥哥？
B: About three years ago. 大概三年前吧。

cousin [ˈkʌzn̩]
名 表（堂）兄弟姐妹

名詞複數 cousins
延伸片語 kissing cousin 【美】關係密切的人
country cousin 鄉巴佬

實境對話
A: Who's that man? 那個男人是誰？
B: He's my **cousin**. 他是我堂兄。

daughter [ˈdɔtɚ]
名 女兒

名詞複數 daughters
延伸片語 mother daughter outfits 母女裝
daughter-in-law 兒媳婦

實境對話
A: Is this pretty girl your **daughter**? 這個漂亮的小女孩是您**女兒**嗎？
B: Yes, she is. 是的，她是我女兒。

elder [ˈɛldɚ]
名 長輩 形 年紀較長的

名詞複數 elders

實境對話
A: You'd better listen to your **elder**. 你最好聽從長輩的話。
B: I will if they are right. 如果他們是對的，我就會聽。

family [ˈfæməlɪ]
名 家庭

名詞複數 families

實境對話
A: How many people are there in your **family**? 你家裡有多少人？
B: There are four. 四個人。

father (dad, daddy) [ˈfɑðɚ]
名 父親

名詞複數 fathers

實境對話
A: What's your **father**? 你父親是做什麼的？
B: He's a worker. 他是一個工人。

granddaughter
[ˋgrænd͵dɔtɚ]

名詞複數 granddaughters

名 孫女、外孫女

 實境對話
A: Do you know Mrs. Tang?　您認識唐女士嗎？
B: Of course, I'm her **granddaughter**.　當然，我是她的**外孫女**。

grandfather
[ˋgrænd͵fɑðɚ]

名詞複數 grandfathers
同義字 grandpa 祖父、外祖父

名 祖父、外祖父

 實境對話
A: It's a picture of my **grandfather**.　這是我**祖父**的照片。
B: He was handsome.　他很帥呢。

grandmother
[ˋgrænd͵mʌðɚ]

名詞複數 grandmothers
同義字 grandma 祖母、外祖母

名 祖母、外祖母

 實境對話
A: My **grandmother** gave me a ring before she died.　我**祖母**在去世前給了我一枚戒指。
B: It must be very precious.　那一定非常珍貴。

grandson
[ˋgrænd͵sʌn]

名詞複數 grandsons

名 孫子、外孫

 實境對話
A: Yesterday I saw you walking with your **grandson**.　昨天我看見你和**孫子**一起散步。
B: Yeah, we always take a walk together after dinner.　是啊，我們總在晚餐後一起散步。

husband
[ˋhʌzbənd]

名詞複數 husbands

名 丈夫

 實境對話
A: Where's your **husband** going?　你**丈夫**要去哪裡啊？
B: He's going to Europe for business.　他要去歐洲出公差。

mother [ˋmʌðɚ]

名詞複數 mothers
同義字 mom / mommy 母親

名 母親

 實境對話
A: What food does your **mother** like best?　你**母親**最喜歡吃什麼食物？
B: She likes dumplings best.　她最喜歡吃餃子了。

Part 1 生活情境單字

nephew [ˈnɛfju]
名 侄子、外甥

名詞複數 nephews
反義字 niece 侄女、外甥女

A: Last week I went fishing with my **nephew**.　上周我和我小侄子去釣魚了。
B: Cool!　真好！

niece [nis]
名 侄女、外甥女

名詞複數 nieces
反義字 nephew 侄子、外甥

A: What's wrong?　有什麼事嗎？
B: My **niece** wants me to teach her math.　我小侄女想讓我教她數學。

parent [ˈpɛrənt]
名 雙親之一

名詞複數 parents

A: Before you do it you'd better ask your **parents**.　在做事之前你最好問一下父母。
B: I'm sure they will support me.　我肯定他們一定會支持我。

relative [ˈrɛlətɪv]
名 親戚

名詞複數 relatives

A: What about your baby when you go travel?　去旅行時，你的孩子怎麼辦？
B: My **relative** will help take care of him.　我的親戚會幫我照顧。

sister [ˈsɪstɚ]
名 姐妹

名詞複數 sisters

A: Do you have any **sisters**?　你有姐妹嗎？
B: Yeah, I have an elder sister.　是的，我有一個姐姐。

son [sʌn]
名 兒子

名詞複數 sons

A: Mr. Liu, your **son** had broken my door.　劉先生，您的兒子弄壞了我的門。
B: I feel so sorry about that. I'll pay for it.　真是非常抱歉，我會賠償您的。

uncle [ˈʌŋkl̩]
名 叔叔

名詞複數 uncles

A: My **uncle** gave me two tickets for the movie tonight. Would you like go with me?
　我叔叔給我了兩張今晚的電影票，你願意一起去看嗎？
B: I'd love to.
　我非常願意。

wife [waɪf]
名 妻子

名詞複數 wives

實境對話
A: Is your **wife** a doctor? 您妻子是醫生嗎？
B: Yes, she is. 是的。

born [bɔrn]
形 出生的

延伸片語 be born to 命中註定的
be born yesterday 容易上當

實境對話
A: Where were you **born**? 你出生在哪裡？
B: I was **born** in the Hong Kong. 我在香港出生。

grow [gro]
動 成長

動詞變化 grew, grown, growing, grows
同義字 cultivate 培養
延伸片語 grow away from 疏遠
grow into 變成

實境對話
A: When you **grow** up, you'll understand this. 當你長大了你就會理解這件事了。
B: Really? I doubt it. 真的嗎？我保持懷疑。

live [lɪv]
動 生活

動詞變化 lived, lived, living, lives
同義字 dwell 居住
延伸片語 live by 以……維生
live in 住在

實境對話
A: Where do you **live**? 你住在哪裡？
B: I **live** in the center of city. 我住在城市中心。

marry [ˈmærɪ]
動 結婚

動詞變化 married, married, marrying, marries
同義字 dwell 居住
延伸片語 marry with 和（某人）結婚
get married 結婚

實境對話
A: Will you **marry** Jessica? 你會和潔西卡結婚嗎？
B: I'm not sure. 我還不確定。

married [ˈmærɪd]
形 已婚的 名 已婚者

實境對話
A: Is she **married**? 她結婚了嗎？
B: I guess she is. 我猜是這樣吧。

Dr. [ˈdɑktə]
名 博士、醫生

實境對話
A: Are you **Dr.** Green, please? 請問您是格林醫生嗎？
B: Yes, I am. 是的，我是。

Part 1 生活情境單字

Mr. [ˋmɪstɚ]
名 先生

 實境對話
A: Do you have a reservation, **Mr.** Wang?
您有預約嗎，王先生？
B: Yes, I have.
有的。

Mrs. [ˋmɪsɪz]
名 女士

 實境對話
A: Sorry, we have no information about **Mrs.** Zhou.
抱歉，我們沒有關於周女士的資料。
B: OK, thank you all the same.
好，仍然很感謝您。

Miss [mɪs]
名 小姐

 實境對話
A: **Miss** Gao will be our English teacher next term.
高小姐下學期教我們英語。
B: Really? I like her very much.
真的嗎？ 我非常喜歡她呢。

Ms. [mɪs]
名 女士、小姐

 實境對話
A: What can I do for you, **Ms.**Chen？
請問陳女士，我能為您做些什麼嗎？
B: No, thanks.
不勞煩，謝謝您。

sir [sɝ]
名 先生

 實境對話
A: Do you have you the invitation, **sir**?
先生，請問您有請柬嗎？
B: Yes, here you are.
是的，在這裡。

ma'am [mæm]
名 夫人、女士

 實境對話
A: Can I help you, **ma'am**?
需要幫忙嗎，夫人？
B: Yes, please carry this for me. Thank you very much.
是的，請幫我扛這個東西，非常感謝。

name [nem]
名 名字

名詞複數 names　　**同義字** title 標題
延伸片語 call sb. names　謾罵
in the name of　看在……的名分上

實境對話
A: May I have your **name**? 您叫什麼名字？
B: Peter. 彼得。

Track 033 🎧

zero [ˋzɪro]
形 零的 名 零

延伸片語　zero in on　集中注意力
zero hour　零時

 實境對話
A: What's the temperature outside?　外面氣溫多少？
B: It's ten below **zero**.　零下十度。

one [wʌn]
形 一的 名 一

延伸片語　in one　集於一身
one and only　絕無僅有的

 實境對話
A: I only see **one** person in the hall.　我只在大廳裡看見一個人。
B: Where are the others?　其他的人去哪兒了？

two [tu]
形 二的 名 二

延伸片語　in two　一分為二
fall between two stools　兩頭落空

 實境對話
A: Did you see **two** books in the desk?　你看見書桌裡的**兩本書**了嗎？
B: No, I didn't.　沒有啊。

three [θri]
形 三的 名 三

延伸片語　in twos and threes　三三兩兩
three quarters　四分之三

 實境對話
A: Do you like this movie?　你喜歡這部電影嗎？
B: I like it very much. I have seen it **three** times.　我非常喜歡，我都看了三遍了。

four [for]
形 四的 名 四

延伸片語　on all fours　匍匐著
these four falls　（用於叮囑保守秘密）到此為止

 實境對話
A: What can you see in the picture?　你在圖片上看到了什麼？
B: I can see **four** birds.　我能看見四隻鳥。

five [faɪv]
形 五的 名 五

延伸片語　give somebody five　與某人擊掌問候（或者慶祝勝利）
five-star　五星級的

 實境對話
A: Could you please bring me **five** plates?　你能拿給我五個盤子嗎？
B: Sure.　當然可以。

six [sɪks]
形 六的 名 六

延伸片語 hit somebody for six 影響某人極大
it's six of one and half a dozen of the other
半斤八兩、不相上下

實境對話
A: How many pens do you have? 你有幾支鋼筆？
B: I have **six**. 有六支。

seven [ˈsɛvn̩]
形 七的 名 七

延伸片語 at sixes and sevens 亂七八糟
seven seas 世界七大洋

實境對話
A: Have you heard of the story about Snow White and **seven** dwarfs?
你聽說過白雪公主和七個小矮人的故事嗎？
B: Of course I have.
當然聽過啦。

eight [et]
形 八的 名 八

延伸片語 have one over the eight 大醉
behind the eight ball 處於不利的地位

實境對話
A: What's the time now? 現在幾點了？
B: It's **eight** o'clock. 八點了。

nine [naɪn]
形 九的 名 九

延伸片語 have nine lives 命大
a nine day's wonder 曇花一現的人或事物

實境對話
A: It's five past **nine**. We'll be late. 九點五分了，我們要遲到了。
B: Don't worry. We can get there in time . 別擔心，我們會及時到達的。

ten [tɛn]
形 十的 名 十

延伸片語 ten out of ten 完全正確
ten to one 十之八九

實境對話
A: Here are **ten** pounds. 這是十英鎊。
B: Thank you. 謝謝。

eleven [ɪˈlɛvn̩]
形 十一的 名 十一

實境對話
A: They have **eleven** children. 他們有十一個孩子。
B: Wow! That's amazing. 哇！真不得了啊。

twelve [twɛlv]
形 十二的 名 十二

同義字 dozen 十二個、一打
延伸片語 twelve-tone 十二音的

實境對話
A: How old are you? 你幾歲了？
B: I'm **twelve** years old. 我十二歲了。

thirteen [ˈθɝˈtin]
形 十三的 名 十三

實境對話
A: How far is the destination? 目的地有多遠？
B: About **thirteen** kilometers away. 大概十三公里遠吧。

---

fourteen [ˈforˈtin]
形 十四的 名 十四

實境對話
A: How many floors are there in your building?
你住的大樓有幾層？
B: There are **fourteen** floors.
有十四層。

---

fifteen [ˈfɪfˈtin]
形 十五的 名 十五

延伸片語 fifteen minutes of fame
（因新聞媒體的報導）短暫出名、大出風頭

實境對話
A: How many guests are there in the party? 聚會上有多少人？
B: There are **fifteen**. 有十五個。

---

sixteen [ˈsɪksˈtin]
形 十六的 名 十六

實境對話
A: Can you find out **sixteen** animals in the picture?
你能在圖片上找出十六隻動物嗎？
B: It's a little difficult for me.
這對我來説有點難。

---

seventeen
[ˌsɛvnˈtin]
形 十七的 名 十七

實境對話
A: There are **seventeen** stories in this book.
這本書裡有十七個小故事。
B: What are they about?
是關於什麼的故事呢？

---

eighteen [ˈeˈtin]
形 十八的 名 十八

實境對話
A: We can't sell alcohol to the juveniles.
我們不向未成年人售酒。
B: Don't worry. I'm **eighteen** years old.
別擔心，我十八歲了。

---

nineteen
[ˈnaɪnˈtin]
形 十九的 名 十九

延伸片語 talk, etc. nineteen to the dozen 喋喋不休

實境對話
A: We've known each other since we were **nineteen**. 我們從十九歲時就認識對方了。
B: Wow! You have known each other for twenty years. 哇！你們已經認識廿年了耶。

twenty [ˈtwɛntɪ]
形 二十的 名 二十

延伸片語 in your twenties　20多歲

實境對話
A: There are almost **twenty** cats in her home.　她家有差不多二十隻貓！
B: I can't believe that.　真不敢相信。

thirty [ˈθɝtɪ]
形 三十的 名 三十

實境對話
A: She is **thirty** years old.　她有三十歲了。
B: She looks younger than her real age.
她看起來比她實際年齡年輕。

forty [ˈfortɪ]
形 四十的 名 四十

延伸片語 forty winks　（尤指白天）打盹

實境對話
A: How many students are there in your class?　你班上有多少名學生？
B: There are **forty**.　四十名。

fifty [ˈfɪftɪ]
形 五十的 名 五十

延伸片語 fifty-fifty　對半的

實境對話
A: Please turn to page **fifty**.　請翻到第五十頁。
B: Yes, ma'am.　是的，老師。

sixty [ˈsɪkstɪ]
形 六十的 名 六十

延伸片語 sixty-four dollar question　最重要之問題

實境對話
A: We have only **sixty** books for the students.　我們只為學生們準備了六十本書。
B: That's not enough at all.　那根本不夠啊。

seventy [ˈsɛvn̩tɪ]
形 七十的 名 七十

實境對話
A: This classroom has a capacity of **seventy** students.
這間教室能容納七十個學生。
B: OK, that's enough.
好的，足夠了。

eighty [ˈetɪ]
形 八十的 名 八十

延伸片語 ten-eighty　殺鼠藥

實境對話
A: How big is your office?　你的辦公室有多大？
B: It's at least **eighty** square meters.　至少有八十平米吧。

ninety [`naɪntɪ]
形 九十的 名 九十

延伸片語 ninety-nine times out of a hundred
幾乎沒有例外
nine times out of ten 十有八九

 實境對話
A: Now we have **ninety** fans. 現在我們有九十名粉絲了。
B: I feel quite excited. 我感到很興奮。

hundred
[`hʌndrəd]
形 一百的 名 一百

名詞複數 hundreds
延伸片語 hundred of 數百的、很多的
the hundred percent 百分之百地

 實境對話
A: How much is it? 這個多少錢啊？
B: It cost me one **hundred** dollars. 花了我一百美元呢。

thousand
[`θaʊznd]
形 千的 名 一千

名詞複數 thousands
延伸片語 a thousand to one 千對一、幾乎絕對的
by the thousand(s) 數以千計、無數地

 實境對話
A: How long is the river? 這條河有多長啊？
B: About two **thousand** meters long. 大概兩千米長。

million [`mɪljən]
名 百萬

名詞複數 millions
延伸片語 feel like a million dollars 感覺好極了
one in a million 萬裡挑一的人或物

 實境對話
A: How many people are there in this city? 這個城市裡有多少人？
B: About one **million**. 大概有一百萬人。

first [fɜst]
形 第一

延伸片語 at first 起初
first and last 從各方面看

 實境對話
A: Who was the **first** one to arrive? 誰是第一個到達的？
B: It was me. 是我。

second [`sɛkənd]
形 第二

延伸片語 second name 姓
second-hand 二手的

 實境對話
A: Where does she live? 她住在哪裡？
B: She lives on the **second** floor in this building. 她住在這棟樓的第二層。

third [θɝd]
● 第三

延伸片語 third party 第三方
third-rate 劣質的

 實境對話
A: Who was the **third** president of the United States? 誰是美國第三任總統？
B: It was Thomas Jefferson. 是湯瑪斯·傑弗遜。

fourth [forθ]
形 第四

同義字	quarter 四分之一的
延伸片語	Fourth of July 美國獨立紀念日
	fourth-class 【美】小包郵件的;以四等郵品郵寄的

實境對話
A: Which is the **fourth** long river in the world? 世界上第四長河是哪一個？
B: It's the Mississippi River. 密西西比河。

fifth [fɪfθ]
形 第五

實境對話
A: Have you been to the **Fifth** Avenue in New York?
去過紐約的第五大道嗎？
B: No, I haven't. 沒有。

sixth [sɪksθ]
形 第六

延伸片語
sixth sense 第六感
sixth form college 【英】(供16歲以上學生就讀的)高級中學

實境對話
A: What grade are you in? 你幾年級了？
B: I'm in the **sixth** grade. 我六年級了。

seventh [ˋsɛvnθ]
形 第七

延伸片語 in seventh heaven 極樂

實境對話
A: Where is the fitness center? 健身中心在哪裡？
B: It's on the **seventh** floor of this building. 在這棟大樓的七樓。

eighth [etθ]
形 第八

實境對話
A: Who's that boy? 那男孩是誰？
B: He is the **eighth** child of Mr. Jonathen.
他是強納森先生的第八個孩子。

ninth [naɪnθ]
形 第九

延伸片語 ninth chord 九音和鉉

實境對話
A: How many times have you been here? 你來這幾次了？
B: This is the **ninth** time. 這是第九次。

tenth [tɛnθ]
形 第十

實境對話
A: What's the date today? 今天幾號啊？
B: It's July the **tenth**. 七月十號。

eleventh [ɪˋlɛvn̩θ]
形 第十一

延伸片語 eleventh hour　在最後時刻

實境對話
A: Today is our **eleventh** anniversary.　今天是我們的十一週年結婚紀念日。
B: Congratulations!　恭喜啊！

twelfth [twɛlvθ]
形 第十二

延伸片語 Twelfthe Night　主顯節前夕

實境對話
A: Have you seen **Twelfth** Night of Shakespeare?　你看過莎士比亞的「第十二夜」嗎？
B: Yes, I like it very much.　看過，我非常喜歡。

thirteenth [ˋθɝˋtinθ]
形 第十三

實境對話
A: Tomorrow will be my **thirteenth** birthday.
明天將是我十三歲生日。
B: Are you going to give a party?
你會辦派對嗎？

fourteenth [ˋforˋtinθ]
形 第十四

實境對話
A: Where did you find this sentence in the book?
你在書上哪裡找到這句話的？
B: It's on the **fourteenth** page .
在第十四頁。

fifteenth [fɪfˋtinθ]
形 第十五

實境對話
A: What did the teacher want us to read-before class?
老師要我們在課前讀什麼？
B: The **fifteenth** chapter of the book.
這本書的第十五章節。

sixteenth [ˋsɪksˋtinθ]
形 第十六

實境對話
A: How are you going to celebrate your **sixteenth** birthday?
你要怎麼慶祝十六歲生日？
B: I'll go bungee jumping.
我要去高空彈跳。

seventeenth [͵sɛvn̩ˋtinθ]
形 第十七

實境對話
A: Where is the mall?　購物中心在哪裡？
B: It's on the **Seventeenth** Street.　在第十七街上。

Part 1 生活情境單字

eighteenth
[ˋeˋtinθ]
形 第十八

實境對話
A: Which floor are we on? 我們現在在幾樓啊？
B: The **eighteen** floor. 十八樓。

nineteenth
[ˋnaɪnˋtinθ]
形 第十九

實境對話
A: What are you watching?
你在看什麼節目呢？
B: The **nineteenth** witness. It's a little horrible.
「第十九個目擊者」，有點小恐怖哦。

twentieth
[ˋtwɛntɪθ]
形 第二十

實境對話
A: How many people are on the list?
名單上有多少人？
B: There are twenty. You are the **twentieth**.
一共有二十人，你是第二十個。

thirtieth [ˋθɝtɪθ]
形 第三十

實境對話
A: Why are you so busy?
你怎麼這麼忙啊？
B: I have to finish the whole project by the **thirtieth** day.
我必須得在第三十天前完成全部的工程。

all [ɔl]
形 全部的 代 一切

延伸片語 all day long 一整天
all ears 傾聽

實境對話
A: **All** apples are sold out. 所有的蘋果都賣完了。
B: We are late. 我們還是晚了。

a few [ə fju]
片 一些

實境對話
A: There are **a few** eggs in the refrigerator.
冰箱裡有一些雞蛋。
B: OK, I'll make some fried rice with eggs for dinner.
好的，我來做個蛋炒飯當晚餐。

Chapter **4** 數字、數量 Numbers

a little [ə ˋlɪtl̩]
● 一點點

實境對話 A: What's the weather like today? 今天天氣怎麼樣？
B: It's **a little** cold. 有點冷。

a lot [ə lɑt]
片 很多

實境對話 A: What did you do last Sunday?
上周日你都做什麼了？
B: I spent **a lot** of time doing my homework.
我花了**好多**時間做作業。

any [ˋɛnɪ]
形 任何的 代 任何一個

延伸片語 any more 另外
any more than 較……更多

 實境對話 A: Do you have **any** questions? 大家有任何問題嗎？
B: Yes, I have one. 是的，我想請教一個問題。

both [boθ]
形 兩個的

延伸片語 have it both ways 使用兩種論法
the best of both worlds 兩頭獲利

實境對話 A: Which do you like better, apples or pears? 蘋果和梨，你更喜歡哪一個？
B: I love **both**. 我**兩個**都喜歡。

few [fju]
形 少數的、一些
代 （與 a 和 the 連用）一些

形容詞變化 fewer, the fewest
延伸片語 no fewer than 不下於
at the fewest 至少

 實境對話 A: We have **few** friends here. 我們在這裡**沒有多少**朋友。
B: That's because you just moved here. 那是因為你們才剛搬來這裡呀。

less [lɛs]
形 較少的

延伸片語 more or less 大約
less and less 越來越少

實境對話 A: How many cups do we have? 我們還有多少茶杯了？
B: There're **less** than five. 少於五個。

little [ˋlɪtl̩]
形 很少的 副 一點點

形容詞變化 less, the least
延伸片語 no little 不少的
the little 不重要的人

實境對話 A: You can drink some water in that bottle. 你可以喝點壺裡的水。
B: There's **little** left. 少得幾乎不剩了。

Part 1 生活情境單字

many [ˋmɛnɪ]
形 很多的 代 許多

形容詞變化 more, the most
延伸片語 a great many 非常多
in so many words 明白地

 實境 對話
A: Why are there so **many** people there? 為什麼那裡有那麼多人？
B: There's an accident. 那裡有發生事故。

more [mor]
名 更多的數量 形 更多的

延伸片語 more and more 越來越多
more or less 幾乎

 實境 對話
A: Do we have enough vegetables? 我們有足夠多的蔬菜嗎？
B: No. We need **more**. 不夠，我們需要更多蔬菜。

much [mʌtʃ]
形 很多的

形容詞變化 more, the most
延伸片語 as much 一樣
not much of a 不是很好

 實境 對話
A: I don't have **much** time. 我沒有很多時間唷。
B: OK, I'll make it short. 好，我會說簡單點。

number [ˋnʌmbɚ]
名 號碼、數字

名詞複數 numbers
延伸片語 numbers of 許多
beyond number 無數的

 實境 對話
A: What's your phone **number**? 你的電話號碼幾號？
B: It's 0985388138. 0985388138。

several [ˋsɛvərəl]
形 幾個的

同義字 some 幾個的

 實境 對話
A: Remember to bring **several** eggs when you come back. 回來時別忘了帶幾個雞蛋。
B: OK. I get it. 好的，我記住了。

some [ˋsʌm]
形 幾個的

延伸片語 some day 來日
some day or other 遲早

 實境 對話
A: I saw **some** boys swimming in the river. 我看見幾個男孩在河裡游泳。
B: It might be dangerous. The river is deep. 可能會很危險啊，那條河很深。

total [ˋtotḷ]
形 全部的 名 總共

同義字 total 總共的
延伸片語 total darkness 完全黑暗
the total amount 總數

 實境 對話
A: What's the **total** population in this city? 這個城市總的人口數是多少？
B: About one million people. 大概一百萬人。

用簡單的小測驗，驗收一下，單字記住了嗎？

(   ) 1 mother   (   ) 11 daughter

(   ) 2 twelve   (   ) 12 both

(   ) 3 parent   (   ) 13 many

(   ) 4 marry   (   ) 14 fifteen

(   ) 5 Mr.s   (   ) 15 thirty

(   ) 6 Miss   (   ) 16 several

(   ) 7 hundred   (   ) 17 son

(   ) 8 fourteenth   (   ) 18 million

(   ) 9 name   (   ) 19 eighth

(   ) 10 seven   (   ) 20 a few

A. 小姐   B 十五   C 兩個的   D 百萬   E 母親   F 女士   G 很多的
H 七   I 兒子   J 第八   K 名字   L 幾個的   M 一些   N 三十
O 十二   P 雙親之一   Q 女兒   R 結婚   S 第十四   T 一百

答案

1(E)   2(O)   3(P)   4(R)   5(F)   6(A)   7(T)   8(S)   9(K)   10(H)   11(Q)   12(C)   13(G)   14(B)
15(N)   16(L)   17(I)   18(D)   19(J)   20(M)

Track 043

dawn [dɔn]
名 黎明 動 破曉

動詞變化 dawned, dawned, dawning, dawns

延伸片語 the crack of dawn 破曉
at down 拂曉

實境對話
A: When shall we get up tomorrow? 我們明天幾點起床？
B: We have to get up at **dawn**. 我們天一亮就得起床。

morning [`mɔrnɪŋ]
名 早晨

名詞複數 mornings

延伸片語 the morning of the life 人生之初期
in the morning 早晨

實境對話
A: Do you take exercises in the **morning**? 你早上鍛鍊身體嗎？
B: Yes, I do it everyday. 是的，每天都會。

noon [nun]
名 中午

延伸片語 the noon of life 壯年
at noon 在中午

實境對話
A: Can you come back at **noon**? 你中午能回來嗎？
B: I'm afraid not. 恐怕不能。

afternoon
[ˌæftə`nun] 名 下午

延伸片語 the afternoon tea 下午茶
in the afternoon 在下午

實境對話
A: What will you do in the **afternoon**? 下午你打算做什麼？
B: I'm planning to play tennis. 我想去打網球。

evening [`ivnɪŋ]
名 傍晚

延伸片語 evening meal 晚飯
in the evening 夜晚

實境對話
A: What do you do in the **evening**? 你晚上做什麼？
B: I often watch TV. 我經常看電視。

night [naɪt]
名 夜晚

延伸片語 night after night 每晚
all night 徹夜

實境對話
A: Did you hear anything last **night**? 你昨天晚上聽到什麼了嗎？
B: No, totally not. 沒，一點都沒有。

midnight
[`mɪdˌnaɪt] 名 午夜

延伸片語 burn the midnight oil 用功到深夜
at midnight 在午夜

實境對話
A: You look so tired. 你看起來很疲倦。
B: I kept writing until **midnight**. 我一直寫作到午夜。

Monday [ˈmʌnde]
名 星期一

延伸片語 Easter Monday　復活節後的星期一
Black Monday　黑色星期一
（一九八七年十月十九日紐約股市大崩盤）

實境對話 A: What's the day today?　今天星期幾啊？
B: It's **Monday**.　今天星期一。

Tuesday [ˈtjuzde]
名 星期二

延伸片語 Shrove Tuesday　懺悔日（基督教大齋期的前一天）
super Tuseday
超級星期二（美國總統大選年若干州初選的星期二）

實境對話 A: Would you like to go shopping with me on **Tuesday** evening?
你願意週二晚上和我去逛街嗎？
B: I'd love to.　當然願意啦。

Wednesday [ˈwɛnzde]
名 星期三

延伸片語 Ash Wednesday　聖灰星期三（基督教四旬期首日）

實境對話 A: Are you free on **Wednesday**?　你週三有時間嗎？
B: I'm afraid not.　恐怕沒有。

Thursday [ˈθɝzde]
名 星期四

延伸片語 Holy Thursday　（天主教）聖星期四（復活節前之星期四）
Maundy Thursday　（基督教）聖週四，建立聖餐日

實境對話 A: When shall we hand in our homework?　我們什麼時候交作業？
B: By **Thursday**.　週四前要交。

Friday [ˈfraɪde]
名 星期五

延伸片語 Good Friday　耶穌受難日（復活節前的星期五）
girl Friday　女助手

實境對話 A: We'll hold a party on **Friday** night.　我們週五晚上要舉行一個聚會。
B: Great. May I join you?　太棒了，我能參加嗎？

Saturday [ˈsætəde]
名 星期六

實境對話 A: Do you have time on **Saturday**?　你星期六有時間嗎？
B: I'm afraid not. I have a date.　恐怕沒有，我有個約會。

Sunday [ˈsʌnde]
名 星期日

延伸片語 Sunday-school　主日學校
Easter Sunday　復活節日

實境對話 A: Will you go to the concert on **Sunday** evening?　你周日晚上會去看音樂會嗎？
B: Yeah, I will.　是啊，我會去的。

week [wik]
名 周、星期

名詞複數 weeks
延伸片語 week in, week out 一周又一周
knock into the middle of next week 將……揍扁

 實境對話
A: I go to the gym twice a **week**. 我每週會去健身房兩次。
B: That's good for your health. 那對你的健康會很有好處。

weekday
['wik/de]
名 工作日

名詞複數 weekdays

 實境對話
A: I'm so busy on **weekdays**. 我工作日都會很忙。
B: You should pay more attention to your health. 你應該多關注一下你的健康狀況。

weekend
['wik`ɛnd]
名 週末

名詞複數 weekends

 實境對話
A: Where will you go this **weekend**? 這週末你要去哪裡呢？
B: I'll go home. 我會回家。

month [mʌnθ]
名 月

名詞複數 months
延伸片語 month by month 每個月
a month of Sundays 長時間

 實境對話
A: We have to finish the work in one **month**. 我們得在一個月內完成任務。
B: That's impossible! 那是不可能的！

January
['dʒænju/ɛrɪ]
名 一月

 實境對話
A: What's the weather like in **January**? 一月份的天氣如何？
B: It's quite cold. 非常冷。

February
['fɛbru/ɛrɪ]
名 二月

 實境對話
A: Which month were you born? 你出生在哪個月份？
B: I was born in **February**. 我生在二月份。

March [martʃ]
名 三月

 實境對話
A: When will you go to Europe? 你什麼時候去歐洲？
B: I make it in **March**. 我將行程定在三月。

April [ˋeprəl]
名 四月

延伸片語 April fool 愚人節中受愚弄者
April Fool's Day 愚人節

實境對話
A: Have you been fooled on **April** the first? 你四月一日被捉弄過嗎？
B: Definitely yes. 當然啦。

May [me]
名 五月

延伸片語 May Day 五一勞動節

實境對話
A: It's still cold in **May**. 五月還是很冷啊。
B: It's quite different from my hometown. 這和我的家鄉還真不一樣。

June [dʒun]
名 六月

實境對話
A: We're going to have a picnic in **June**.
我們打算六月份去野餐。
B: That's a good idea.
真是一個不錯的主意。

July [dʒuˋlaɪ]
名 七月

實境對話
A: I hate **July**. It's too hot outside.
我討厭七月，外面太熱了。
B: It's not only hot but also humid.
不只熱還很潮濕。

August [ˋɔgəst]
名 八月

實境對話
A: Is it cool in **August**?
八月天氣涼爽些了嗎？
B: No, it's still quite hot.
沒有，始終很炎熱。

September
[sɛpˋtɛmbə]
名 九月

延伸片語 September people "九月天"；不惑之年的人
（指中年晚期或接近老年的人們）

實境對話
A: When will the school begin? 你們什麼時候開學？
B: In **September**. 九月份。

October [ɑkˋtobə]
名 十月

實境對話
A: You can receive the parcel on **October** the fifth.
您會在十月五日收到包裹。
B: OK, thanks very much.
好的，非常感謝。

November
[noˋvɛmbɚ]
名 十一月

實境對話
A: In **November,** there will be some good movies on.
十一月會有一些不錯的電影上映。
B: That's cool.
太好啦。

December
[dɪˋsɛmbɚ]
名 十二月

實境對話
A: Does it snow in **December** in your country?
你的國家十二月份會下雪嗎？
B: Yes, but not too much.
是的，但不經常。

season [ˋsizn̩]
名 季節

名詞複數 seasons   同義字 period 時期
延伸片語 high season 旺季
off season 淡季

實境對話
A: Which **season** do you like best?　你最喜歡哪個季節？
B: I like autumn best.　我最喜歡秋天。

spring [sprɪŋ]
名 春天

名詞複數 springs
延伸片語 spring chicken 年輕人
spring fever 浮躁心情

實境對話
A: Which sport do you do in **spring**?　春天你會做什麼運動？
B: I always fly kites.　我經常放風箏。

summer [ˋsʌmɚ]
名 夏天

名詞複數 summers
延伸片語 summer camp 夏令營
high summer 盛夏

實境對話
A: Is the **summer** hot in your hometown?　在你家鄉夏天會很熱嗎？
B: No, it's quite cool.　不，會很涼爽。

autumn (fall)
[ˋɔtəm]
名 秋天

名詞複數 autumns
延伸片語 Mid-autumn Festival 中秋節

實境對話
A: The weather in **autumn** is very cool.　秋天的天氣很涼爽啊。
B: That's the reason why I like it best.　這就是我最愛秋天的原因。

winter [ˋwɪntɚ]
● 冬天

名詞複數 winters
延伸片語 in the dead of winter 在隆冬
winter sports 冬季運動

實境對話
A: I can't adapt to the cold days in **winter** in the north.　我無法適應北方冬天寒冷的日子。
B: Me, either.　我也是。

alarm [ə'lɑrm]
名 鬧鐘

名詞複數 alarms
延伸片語 alarm clock 鬧鐘
a warning of danger 警報

實境對話
A: Did you see my **alarm** on the table? 你看到我桌子上的鬧鐘了嗎？
B: No, I didn't. 沒有看到啊。

clock [klɑk]
名 時鐘

名詞複數 clocks
延伸片語 around the clock 通宵達旦的人
put the clock back 開倒車

實境對話
A: What's the time now? 現在幾點了？
B: I can't see the **clock**. 我看不見時鐘。

calendar ['kæləndɚ]
名 日曆、月曆、行事曆

名詞複數 calendars
延伸片語 on the calendar 日程表上
calendar clock 日曆鐘

實境對話
A: What's the date of your birthday? 你的生日是幾號呢？
B: July the sixth according to the solar **calendar**. 按照陽曆，是七月六號。

watch [wɑtʃ]
名 手錶

名詞複數 watches
延伸片語 keep watch 看守
on the watch 看守著

實境對話
A: Is this your new **watch**? 這是你的新手錶嗎？
B: Yes, it is. 是的。

stop [stɑp]
動 暫停

動詞變化 stopped, stopped, stopping, stops
同義字 pause 暫停
延伸片語 stop breath 屏息
stop by 順道拜訪

實境對話
A: Would you please **stop** singing? 你能停止唱歌嗎？
B: Sorry. I didn't mean to disturb you. 抱歉，我不是故意要打擾你。

a.m. [e ɛm]
名 上午

實境對話
A: When will the flight leave for Beijing?
飛機什麼時候去北京？
B: At 9 **a.m.** tomorrow.
明天上午九點。

p.m. [pɪ ɛm]
名 下午

實境對話
A: When is the last train? 最後一趟火車是幾點？
B: At 5 **p.m.** 下午五點。

Part **1** 生活情境單字

half [hæf]
名 一半

名詞複數 halves
延伸片語 by half 非常
at half cock 準備不充分即行動

實境對話
A: What time is it? 現在幾點？
B: It's **half** past three. 三點半。

hour [aʊr]
名 小時

名詞複數 hours
延伸片語 at all hours 隨時
in an evil hour 不巧

實境對話
A: It took me **hours** to finish my homework. 我花了幾個小時做作業。
B: Why did you spend so much time? 你怎麼花了這麼長時間？

minute [`mɪnɪt]
名 分鐘

名詞複數 minutes
延伸片語 in a minute 立刻
the minute(that) 一……就……

實境對話
A: How soon can you get here? 你還有多長時間趕到這裡？
B: In ten **minutes**. 十分鐘之後吧。

moment
[`momənt]
名 瞬間

名詞複數 moments
延伸片語 at any moment 隨時
for the moment 目前

實境對話
A: May I speak to Jack? 我要找傑克。
B: A **moment**, please. 請稍等片刻。

o'clock [ə`klɑk]
名 幾點鐘

實境對話
A: What time is it? 現在幾點了？
B: It's two **o'clock**. 兩點了。

past [pæst]
介 越過

實境對話
A: What time is it now? 現在幾點了？
B: Half **past** five. 五點過半了。

quarter [`kwɔrtɚ]
名 四分之一

名詞複數 quarters
延伸片語 at close quarters 非常接近地
beat up the quarters of 拜訪

實境對話
A: Do you have the time? 你知道時間嗎？
B: It's a **quarter** past ten. 十點十五了。

second [`sɛkənd]
名 秒

名詞複數 seconds
延伸片語 second hand 秒針
at second hand 間接的

實境對話
A: I'm here for my bag. 我來拿我的背包。
B: OK. Please wait for a **second**. 好的，請等我片刻。

time [taɪm]
名 時間

延伸片語 time after time 屢次、多次
time of day 時辰

實境對話
A: It's **time** to get up. 該到起床的時間了。
B: I feel too sleepy. 我實在是太睏了。

ago [ə'go]
副 以前

同義字 before 之前
延伸片語 long ago 許久以前
a hundred years ago 一百年前

實境對話
A: When did you buy this watch? 你什麼時候買這支手錶？
B: Two years **ago**. 兩年前。

already [ɔl'rɛdɪ]
副 已經

實境對話
A: Have you seen this movie? 你看過這部電影嗎？
B: Yes, I have seen it **already**. 是的，我已經看過了。

current [`kɜ˞ənt]
形 現行的 名 水流、電流

同義字 existing 目前的
延伸片語 the current of the times 時代潮流
swim with the current 順應潮流

實境對話
A: Who's your **current** president? 你們現任總統是誰？
B: It's Barrack Obama. 是歐巴馬。

early [`ɜ˞lɪ]
形 早的 副 早、提早

形容詞變化 earlier, the earliest
反義字 late 晚的
延伸片語 early on 初期
early bird 早起者、搶先者

實境對話
A: You'd better get up **early** tomorrow. 你明天最好早起。
B: I know. But it's really hard for me. 我知道，但是對我來說太難了。

last [læst]
形 最後的 動 持續 副 最後地

動詞變化 lasted, lasted, lasting, lasts
延伸片語 at last 最後
to the last 直到最後

實境對話
A: Am I late? 我遲到了嗎？
B: No, but you are the **last** one to arrive. 沒有，但你是最後一個到的。

late [let]
形 晚的

形容詞變化 later, the latest
反義字 early 早的
延伸片語 a late hour of the day 日暮
a late spring 晚到的春天

實境對話
A: It's too **late** to get on the bus. 太晚了搭不上車了。
B: We can take a taxi. 我們可以搭計程車。

later [ˈletə]
副 稍後

> 延伸片語 later on 後來
> sooner or later 遲早

> 實境對話
> A: You can give the picture to me **later**. 你可以稍後將圖片給我。
> B: OK. 好的。

next [nɛkst]
形 下一個的

> 延伸片語 next before 前一個的
> next time 下一次

> 實境對話
> A: Who's the **next**? 誰是下一位？
> B: I am. 是我。

now [naʊ]
副 現在

> 延伸片語 just now 剛才
> now that 既然

> 實境對話
> A: When will you prepare the dinner? 你什麼時候準備晚飯？
> B: I'll do it **now**. 現在就做。

once [wʌns]
副 一次、曾經

> 延伸片語 at once 立刻
> once and all 每個人、全體一致

> 實境對話
> A: Have you been to Japan? 你去過日本嗎？
> B: Yes, I've been there **once**. 是，去過一次。

future [ˈfjutʃə]
名 未來

> 延伸片語 in future 今後
> in the future 在將來

> 實境對話
> A: What do you want to do in the **future**? 未來你想要做什麼？
> B: I want to be a doctor. 我想成為一名醫生。

soon [sun]
副 一會兒

> 副詞變化 sooner, the soonest
> 同義字 immediately 立刻
> 延伸片語 no sooner than 一……就……
> sooner or later 遲早

> 實境對話
> A: Hurry up! 快點！
> B: I'll be ready **soon**. 我馬上就好。

today [təˈde]
名 今天

> 實境對話
> A: What are you going to do **today**? 你今天打算幹什麼？
> B: I want to go swimming. 我想去游泳。

tonight [təˋnaɪt]
名 今晚

實境對話
A: How about having a meal together **tonight**?
今晚一起吃個飯怎麼樣？
B: OK. I'd love to.
好的，我很樂意去。

tomorrow
[təˋmɔro]
名 明天

延伸片語 the day after tomorrow 後天
the day before yesterday 前天

實境對話
A: It will be rainy **tomorrow**. 明天會下雨。
B: That's terrible. I can't go out for picnic. 那太糟糕了，我不能去野餐了。

weekend
[ˋwikˏɛnd]
名 週末

名詞複數 weekends
延伸片語 to spend the weekend 度過週末
at the weekend 在週末

實境對話
A: If you are free on the **weekend**, we can go fishing together.
如果你週末有時間，我們可以一起去釣魚。
B: OK.
好的。

year [jir]
名 年

名詞複數 years
延伸片語 year in year 年復一年
all the year round 整年

實境對話
A: Which **year** did you get the prize? 你哪一年獲獎的？
B: In 2009. 2009年。

yesterday
[ˋjɛstəde]
名 昨天

延伸片語 not be born yesterday
（表示自己並不傻，不會輕信別人的話）
yesterday's men 過期的政客

實境對話
A: What did you do **yesterday**? 你昨天做了什麼？
B: I finished reading this book. 我讀完了這本書。

day [de]
名 白天、日

名詞複數 days
延伸片語 day and night 夜以繼日
day after day 日復一日

實境對話
A: He wasn't at home during the **day**. 他白天不在家。
B: No wonder no one answered the phone. 難怪沒人接電話。

Part 1 生活情境單字

練習試試看 📖

( ) 1 dawn

( ) 2 evening

( ) 3 Thursday

( ) 4 Sunday

( ) 5 week

( ) 6 January

( ) 7 September

( ) 8 clock

( ) 9 calendar

( ) 10 watch

( ) 11 hour

( ) 12 past

( ) 13 already

( ) 14 future

( ) 15 yesterday

( ) 16 cash

( ) 17 borrow

( ) 18 cost

( ) 19 cheap

( ) 20 last

A. 周	B 時鐘	C 最後的	D 黎明	E 小時	F 星期四	G 一月
H 日曆	I 已經	J 昨天	K 借	L 花費	M 便宜的	N 九月
O 傍晚	P 手錶	Q 星期日	R 越過	S 現款	T 未來	

答案

1(D) 2(O) 3(F) 4(Q) 5(A) 6(G) 7(N) 8(B) 9(H) 10(P) 11(E) 12(R) 13(I) 14(T)
15(J) 16(S) 17(K) 18(L) 19(M) 20(C)

Chapter 6 金錢

---

bill [bɪl]
名 帳單、鈔票 動 記入帳

名詞複數 bills
同義字 check 支票
延伸片語 foot the bill 負擔費用
bill and coo 卿卿我我、情話綿綿

 實境對話
A: Here is your **bill**. 這是您的帳單。
B: OK, thank you. 好的，謝謝。

---

cash [kæʃ]
動 兌現 名 現金

動詞變化 cashed, cashed,cashing, cashes
名詞複數 cashes 同義字 money 金錢
延伸片語 cash down 即付現款

實境對話
A: Do you accept credit cards? 可以刷卡嗎？
B: Sorry, only **cash**. 抱歉，只收現金。

---

cent [sɛnt]
名 分

名詞複數 cents
延伸片語 red cent 很少的錢
five-and-ten-cent store 廉價商店

實境對話
A: Do you have five **cents**? 您有五分嗎？
B: Yes, here you are. 有，給您。

---

change [tʃendʒ]
動 改變 名 零錢

動詞變化 changed, changed, changing, changes
名詞複數 changes 同義字 transform 轉變
延伸片語 change hands 轉手

 實境對話
A: $48 in all, please. 總共是四十八美元。
B: Here's a 50-dollar bill. Keep the **change**. 這是五十美元，不用找零錢了。

---

coin [kɔɪn]
名 硬幣

名詞複數 coins
延伸片語 coin money 暴富

實境對話
A: Do you have any **coins**? 你有硬幣嗎？
B: Nope. 沒有。

---

credit [ˈkrɛdɪt]
名 信用

延伸片語 credit card 信用卡
do somebody credit 使值得讚揚

 實境對話
A: Can I pay by **credit** card? 我能用信用卡結帳嗎？
B: Yes, please. 可以，請吧。

---

card [kɑrd]
名 卡、紙牌

名詞複數 cards
延伸片語 have a card up your sleeve 有錦囊妙計
get your cards 被解雇

實境對話
A: Would you like to play **cards** with us? 你願意和我們一起來玩牌嗎？
B: Yes, of course. 當然願意啦。

dollar [ˈdɑlɚ]
名 美元

名詞複數	dollars
延伸片語	you can bet your bottom dollar 毫無疑問 sixty-four dollar question 【美】最重要的問題

 實境對話
A: How much does it cost? 它花了你多少錢？
B: 20 **dollars**. 20美元。

money [ˈmʌnɪ]
名 錢

同義字	fund 資金
延伸片語	on the money 正確的 money talks 財大氣粗

 實境對話
A: Can you lend me some **money**? 你能借我點錢嗎？
B: Yes. ow much do you need? 好的，你需要多少錢？

price [praɪs]
名 價錢

同義字	value 價值
延伸片語	at any price 無論如何 at a price 花大錢

 實境對話
A: The bag cost me $100. 那個包包花了我一百美元。
B: The **price** is a little high. 價格有點高啊。

borrow [ˈbɑro]
動 借

動詞變化	borrowed, borrowed, borrowing, borrows
同義字	lend 借出
延伸片語	borrow trouble 杞人憂天 be on borrowed time 大限將至

 實境對話
A: Can I **borrow** your book? 我能借你的書看一下嗎？
B: Sure. 當然可以。

buy [baɪ]
動 買

動詞變化	bought, bought, buying, buys
同義字	purchase 購買
延伸片語	buy in 大宗買進 buy back 產品返銷

 實境對話
A: What are you going to **buy**? 你要買什麼？
B: I'm going to **buy** some clothes. 我買一些衣服。

charge [tʃɑrdʒ]
動 索價 名 費用

動詞變化	charged, charged, charging, charges
同義字	fee 費用
延伸片語	in charge 負責 free of charge 免費

實境對話
A: These eggs **charge** 70 US cents. 這些雞蛋要七十美分。
B: They're cheap. 挺便宜的。

cost [kɔst]
動 花費 名 費用

動詞變化	cost, cost, costing, costs
同義字	spend 花費
延伸片語	at the cost of 以……為代價 low cost 低成本

實境對話
A: It **cost** me $50 in all. 它一共花了我五十美元。
B: That was quite expensive. 太貴了吧。

Chapter **6** 金錢 Money

earn [ɜn]
動 賺到

動詞變化 earned, earned, earning, earns
同義字 acquire 獲得
延伸片語 earn a living 謀生
earn interest 賺取利息

實境對話
A: What's your dream? 你的夢想是什麼？
B: I want to **earn** enough money to run a shop of my own.
我想要賺到足夠的錢來開一家自己的店。

lend [lɛnd]
動 出借

動詞變化 lent, lent, lending, lends
同義字 borrow 借
延伸片語 lend itself to 適用於
lend an ear 傾聽

實境對話
A: How can you get enough money? 你怎樣才能得到足夠的錢？
B: My brother said he could **lend** me some. 我哥哥說他可以借給我一些錢。

pay [pe]
動 付錢

動詞變化 paid, paid, paying, pays
同義字 spend 花費
延伸片語 pay off 成功
pay up 付清所有欠款

實境對話
A: $68, please. 一共是六十八美元。
B: Can I **pay** by credit card? 我能用信用卡付款嗎？

spend [spɛnd]
動 花費

動詞變化 spent, spent, spending, spends
同義字 cost 花費
延伸片語 spend a penny 解手、方便
spend money like water 揮金如土

實境對話
A: How much time will you **spend** in cooking? 你做飯會花費多少時間？
B: About half an hour. 大概半個小時。

cheap [tʃip]
形 便宜的

形容詞變化 cheaper, the cheapest
同義字 inexpensive 便宜的
延伸片語 dirt cheap 非常便宜的
cheap shot 惡意中傷

實境對話
A: Vegetables are very **cheap** now. 現在蔬菜很便宜。
B: Good for health. 有益健康。

expensive [ɪkˋspɛnsɪv]
形 貴的

形容詞變化 more expensive, the most expensive
同義字 dear 昂貴的
延伸片語 a bit expensive 有點貴
less expensive 有點便宜的

實境對話
A: The iPad is too **expensive**. I don't think I can afford it. iPad太貴了，我買不起。
B: Maybe you can borrow some money. 也許你能借到一些錢。

Part **1** 生活情境單字

Track 056 🎧

---

fruit [frut]
名 水果

名詞複數 fruits
延伸片語 first fruit 初步成果
fruit juice 果汁

實境對話
A: Could you buy some **fruit** on the way home? 你能在回家路上買些水果嗎？
B: No problem. 沒問題。

---

apple [ˋæpḷ]
名 蘋果

名詞複數 apples
延伸片語 Big apple 紐約市
Adam's Apple 喉結

實境對話
A: Which do you prefer, **apples** or pears? 蘋果和梨，你比較喜歡哪一個？
B: I prefer **apples**. 我比較喜歡蘋果。

---

banana [bəˋnænə]
名 香蕉

名詞複數 bananas
延伸片語 banana skin
造成麻煩（或使人當眾出醜）的事物
banana republic
香蕉共和國（政府無能、依靠外資的貧窮小國）

實境對話
A: What do monkeys like to eat? 猴子喜歡吃什麼？
B: I think they like **bananas** best. 我想牠們最愛吃香蕉吧。

---

grape [grep]
名 葡萄

名詞複數 grapes
延伸片語 grape sugar 葡萄糖
sour grapes 酸葡萄心理

實境對話
A: Which fruit do you like in autumn? 你秋天喜歡吃什麼水果？
B: **Grapes** are my favorite. 葡萄是我的最愛。

---

guava [ˋgwɑvə]
名 芭樂

實境對話
A: Do you like **guavas**? 你喜歡芭樂嗎？
B: No, I don't. 我不喜歡。

---

lemon [ˋlɛmən]
名 檸檬

延伸片語 lemon law 不良品賠償法
lemon juice 檸檬汁

實境對話
A: Where can I buy some **lemons**? 我到哪裡能買到檸檬？
B: Try the shop near the corner. 到街角附近那家店試試。

mango [ˋmæŋgo]
名 芒果

名詞複數 mangoes

 實境對話
A: Is there anything to eat in the refrigerator? 冰箱裡有什麼吃的嗎？
B: There's only a **mango**. 只有一個芒果。

orange [ˋɔrɪndʒ]
名 柳橙

名詞複數 oranges

 實境對話
A: I find the **oranges** bad. 我發現柳橙壞掉了。
B: Throw them away. 扔掉吧。

papaya [pəˋpaɪə]
名 木瓜

實境對話
A: Do you have **papayas**? 有木瓜嗎？
B: They are sold out. 都賣光了。

peach [pitʃ]
名 桃子

名詞複數 peaches
同義字 nectarine 油桃

實境對話
A: You can take some **peaches** for food. 你可以帶些桃子作為食物。
B: No, thanks. 不用了，謝謝。

pear [pɛr]
名 梨

名詞複數 pears
同義字 avocado 酪梨

實境對話
A: The **pears** are so fresh. 這些梨真新鮮。
B: We can buy some. 我們可以買一些。

pineapple [ˋpaɪnˌæpḷ]
名 鳳梨

名詞複數 pineapples
同義字 ananas 鳳梨

 實境對話
A: Are there **pineapples** in this season? 這個季節有鳳梨嗎？
B: Maybe not. 可能沒有了。

strawberry [ˋstrɔˌbɛrɪ]
名 草莓

名詞複數 strawberries

 實境對話
A: When did you buy these **strawberries**? 你什麼時候買的這些草莓啊？
B: Yesterday. 昨天。

tangerine
[ˈtændʒəˌrin]
 名 橘子

名詞複數	tangerines

 實境對話
A: Are these **tangerines** ripe?　這些橘子都熟了嗎？
B: Yes, they are.　是的。

tomato [təˈmeto]
名 番茄

名詞複數	tomatoes

實境對話
A: Are **tomatoes** vegetables or fruit?　番茄是屬於蔬菜還是水果呢？
B: They are vegetables, I think.　我認為是蔬菜吧。

watermelon
[ˈwɔtəˌmɛlən]
名 西瓜

延伸片語	Chinese watermelon 冬瓜

實境對話
A: It will cool you down to eat some **watermelon** in summer.　夏天吃些西瓜感覺會很清爽。
B: Yeah, I like **watermelon**.　是的，我喜歡吃西瓜。

vegetable
[ˈvɛdʒətəbl]
名 蔬菜

名詞複數	vegetables
延伸片語	root vegetable （馬鈴薯、胡蘿蔔等的）根用蔬菜

實境對話
A: Did you buy the **vegetables** this morning?　早上買蔬菜了嗎？
B: Sorry, I forgot it.　對不起，我忘記了。

bean [bin]
名 豆子

名詞複數	beans
延伸片語	full of beans　精力充沛 not have a bean　沒錢

實境對話
A: We need some **beans**.　我們需要些豆子。
B: I'll buy it.　我會去買。

cabbage
[ˈkæbɪdʒ]
名 甘藍菜、高麗菜

名詞複數	cabbages
延伸片語	Chinese cabbage　大白菜

實境對話
A: The **cabbage** in the market is quite cheap today.　今天市場裡的甘藍菜非常便宜。
B: Really? I'll go buy some.　真的嗎？我要去買一些回來。

carrot [ˈkærət]
名 胡蘿蔔

名詞複數	carrots
延伸片語	the carrot and stick　威逼利誘

 實境對話
A: My dog likes to eat **carrots**.　我的狗喜歡吃胡蘿蔔。
B: That's a little strange.　那可是有點奇怪。

corn [kɔrn]
 名 玉米

名詞複數 corns
同義字 cereal 穀物

實境對話
A: I bought some **corns** for dinner. 我買了一些玉米做晚飯。
B: Oh, I hate **corns**. 哦，我討厭玉米。

lettuce [ˈlɛtɪs]
名 生菜、萵苣

A: I'll buy some **lettuce** to make salad.
我來買些萵苣做沙拉。
B: I don't like **lettuce**.
我不喜歡吃萵苣。

nut [nʌt]
名 核果

名詞複數 nuts
延伸片語 do your nut 暴跳如雷
a hard nut 難對付的人

實境對話
A: It's inconvenient to eat **nuts**. 吃堅果太麻煩了。
B: You can use the nutcracker. 你可以用堅果鉗。

onion [ˈʌnjən]
名 洋蔥

名詞複數 onions

實境對話
A: You put the **onion** in the dish. 你菜裡放洋蔥了。
B: You didn't tell me that you don't like **onion**. 你沒告訴我你不喜歡吃洋蔥啊。

potato [pəˈteto]
名 馬鈴薯

名詞複數 potatoes
同義字 spud 馬鈴薯
延伸片語 couch potato 老泡在電視機前的人

實境對話
A: I plant **potatoes** in the backyard. 我在後院種了些馬鈴薯。
B: What else do you plant? 你還種了些什麼？

pumpkin
[ˈpʌmpkɪn]
名 南瓜

名詞複數 pumpkins

實境對話
A: What do you want to eat? 你想吃什麼？
B: I love the **pumpkin** pie you make. 我喜歡吃你做的南瓜派。

meat [mit]
名 肉

延伸片語 meat and drink to somebody
讓某人非常開心的事
meat and potatoes 根本的

實境對話
A: Where are you going? 你要去哪裡？
B: I'm going to buy some **meat**. 我要去買肉。

Part **1** 生活情境單字

beef [bif]
名 牛肉

延伸片語 ▶ beef sth. up 使更大（更好、更多意思等）

 A: I love **beef** steak very much. 我非常喜歡牛排。
B: I know. I'll cook it for you tonight. 我知道，今晚就做給你吃。

bread [brɛd]
名 麵包

延伸片語 ▶ take the bread out of somebody's mouth
剝奪某人的生計
bread-and-butter 基本的、很重要的

 A: What do you eat for breakfast? 你早飯都吃些什麼？
B: I eat **bread** and milk. 牛奶和麵包。

bun [bʌn]
名 小圓麵包

名詞複數 buns
延伸片語 ▶ steamed bun 饅頭
steamed stuffed bun 包子

 A: Would you like some more **buns**? 要不要再來點小圓麵包？
B: Sure. 當然。

burger [ˈbɝgɚ]
名 漢堡

名詞複數 burgers

 A: I'm hungry. I want to have a **burger**. 我餓了，我想吃一個漢堡。
B: There's one in the refrigerator. 冰箱裡有一個。

cereal [ˈsɪrɪəl]
名 穀類、玉米穀片

同義字 corn 穀物

 A: Eating **cereal** is good for your health. 吃穀類食物對健康會有好處。
B: I agree with you . 我贊同。

chicken [ˈtʃɪkɪn]
名 雞肉

延伸片語 ▶ chicken feed 一筆微不足道的錢
chicken run 養雞場

 A: What do you prepare for supper? 你晚飯準備什麼了？
B: **Chicken**. 雞肉。

dumpling
[ˈdʌmplɪŋ]
名 餃子

名詞複數 dumplings
延伸片語 ▶ boile d dumpling 水餃
steamed dumpling 蒸餃

A: What do you eat on Spring Festival? 你們春節吃什麼？
B: We eat **dumplings**. 我們吃餃子。

右側直排：
Chapter **7** 飲食、餐具 Food & Drink & Tableware

egg [ɛg]
名 雞蛋

名詞複數 eggs
延伸片語 have egg on over your face　出醜
egg somebody on　鼓動

實境
對話
A: Do you often eat **eggs**?　你經常吃雞蛋嗎？
B: Yes, I eat two **eggs** every day.　是的，我一天吃兩個雞蛋。

fast food [fæst fud]
名 速食

實境
對話
A: I feel too tired to cook.
我太累了，做不了飯了。
B: We can eat some **fast food** outside.
我們可以到外面吃些**速食**。

fish [fɪʃ]
名 魚肉

延伸片語 go fishing　釣魚
fish for something　旁敲側擊地打聽

實境
對話
A: Do you like to eat **fish**?　你喜歡吃魚嗎？
B: Yes, I love **fish**.　我很愛吃魚。

flour [flaʊr]
名 麵粉

實境
對話
A: What should I do now?　我現在應該怎麼做？
B: Put the milk and **flour** in.　將牛奶和麵粉放進去。

food [fud]
名 食物

延伸片語 food chain　食物鏈
food for thought　引人深思的想法

實境
對話
A: French fries is not healthy **food**.　薯條不是健康的食物。
B: But it's my favorite.　但是那是我最愛吃的。

French fries [frɛntʃ fraɪz]
名 薯條

實境
對話
A: Have you had **French fries**?　你吃過薯條嗎？
B: Not yet.　還沒吃過。

ham [hæm]
名 火腿

名詞複數 hams
延伸片語 ham it up
尤指演員有意誇張表情（或動作）；表演過火

實境
對話
A: Did you have the breakfast?　你吃早餐了嗎？
B: Yes, I had **ham** and milk.　嗯，我吃了**火腿**和牛奶。

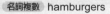

hamburger
[ˈhæmbɝɡɚ]
名 漢堡

名詞複數　hamburgers

實境
對話
A: I had nothing in the morning.　我早上什麼都沒有吃。
B: Here's a **hamburger** for you.　這是給你的漢堡。

hot dog [hɑt dɔg]
名 熱狗

實境
對話
A: How much is the **hot dog**?　熱狗多少錢？
B: Two dallors.　兩美元。

instant noodle
[ˈɪnstənt ˈnudl]
名 泡麵

實境
對話
A: Let's have some **instant noodles** for lunch.
　我們午餐吃泡麵吧。
B: OK.
　好的。

noodle [ˈnudl]
名 麵條

名詞複數　noodles
延伸片語　sliced noodle　刀削麵

實境
對話
A: If you have time, you can make some **noodles** for dinner.
　如果你有時間可以晚飯做些麵條吃。
B: But I don't like **noodles**.　但是我不喜歡吃麵條。

pizza [ˈpitsə]
名 披薩

名詞複數　pizzas

實境
對話
A: I'd like to have some **pizza** tonight.　我今晚想吃披薩。
B: OK.　好。

pork [pork]
名 豬肉

延伸片語　pork barrel　分肥專案，分肥撥款
　（議員等為爭取選票而促使政府撥款給所屬地區的發展專
　案）

實境
對話
A: Is there any **pork** in the kitchen?　廚房裡有豬肉嗎？
B: Yes, but there's only a little.　有，但是只有一點。

rice [raɪs]
名 米飯

延伸片語　brown rice　糙米
　　　　　rice wine　米酒

實境
對話
A: Do you want some **rice**?　要來些米飯嗎？
B: Yes, thank you.　好的，謝謝。

salad [`sæləd]
名 沙拉

延伸片語 your salad days 年少不諳世事的歲月

實境對話
A: Are you fond of **salad**? 你喜歡沙拉嗎？
B: Very much. 非常喜歡。

sandwich [`sændwɪtʃ]
名 三明治

名詞複數 sandwiches
延伸片語 sandwich A and B together 用……結合、粘合

實境對話
A: I made some **sandwiches** for you. 我做了些三明治給你。
B: Thank you very much. 非常感謝。

seafood [`si,fud]
名 海鮮

實境對話
A: Do you like **seafood**? 你喜歡吃海鮮嗎？
B: No, I'm allergic to **seafood**. 不，我對海鮮過敏。

shrimp [ʃrɪmp]
名 蝦

實境對話
A: Shall we buy some **shrimps**? 我們要買些蝦嗎？
B: No, they're quite expensive here. 不，這裡的蝦太貴了。

soup [sup]
名 湯

延伸片語 in the soup 在困境中
alphabet soup 代號語言

實境對話
A: I feel better now. 我現在感覺好多了。
B: You'd better have a bowl of chicken **soup**. 你最好喝一碗雞湯。

spaghetti [spəˋgɛtɪ]
名 義大利式細麵條

延伸片語 spaghetti junction 混亂的公路交叉口
spaghetti strap 女裝上的細肩帶

實境對話
A: How about **spaghetti**? 義大利式細麵條怎麼樣？
B: It's my favorite food. 它是我最愛吃的食物。

steak [stek]
名 牛排

延伸片語 beef steak 牛排

實境對話
A: What do we eat for dinner? 我們晚飯吃什麼？
B: We'll have beef **steak** for dinner. 我們晚飯吃牛排。

Part 1 生活情境單字

tofu [ˈtofu]
名 豆腐

實境對話
A: I like eating **tofu**. 我喜歡吃豆腐。
B: I can cook it for you some day. 哪天我做給你吃。

---

breakfast [ˈbrɛkfəst]
名 早餐

延伸片語
a dog's breakfast 亂七八糟
bed and breakfast 住宿加次日早餐

實境對話
A: Shall we buy something for **breakfast** tomorrow? 我們要為明天的早飯買些什麼嗎？
B: No, we have enough food. 不用，我們有足夠的食物。

---

brunch [brʌntʃ]
名 早午餐

實境對話
A: What do you want to eat for **brunch**? 你早午餐想吃什麼？
B: Bread and milk. 麵包和牛奶。

---

dinner [ˈdɪnɚ]
名 晚餐

名詞複數 dinners　同義字 meal 一餐
延伸片語
at dinner 用餐
dinner table 餐桌

實境對話
A: Shall we have **dinner** in or out? 我們是在家吃還是出去吃晚飯？
B: It's up to you. 你決定就好。

---

lunch [lʌntʃ]
名 午餐

延伸片語
there's no such thing as a free lunch 沒有免費的午餐
lunch hour 午餐時間

實境對話
A: Did you have anything for **lunch**? 吃過午餐了嗎？
B: Nothing. 什麼都沒吃呢。

---

meal [mil]
名 一頓飯

名詞複數 meals
延伸片語
make a meal of something 小題大作
No mill, no meal. 不播種，沒收穫。

實境對話
A: Don't you have the **meal** before leaving? 走之前不吃飯了嗎？
B: Sorry, I have no time. 對不起，沒有時間了。

---

snack [snæk]
名 小吃、點心

延伸片語
snack bar 小吃店
snack street 小吃街

實境對話
A: I feel a little hungry. 我有點餓了。
B: You can have some **snacks** first. 你可以先吃點點心。

Chapter **7** 飲食、餐具 Food & Drink & Tableware

supper [`sʌpɚ]

名 晚餐

延伸片語 Last Supper
（耶穌受難前夕與十二使徒共進的）最後晚餐

實境對話
A: I'll have **supper** at my friend's home.　我要去朋友家吃**晚飯**。
B: Have a good time.　玩得開心啊。

beer [bɪr]

名 啤酒

延伸片語 beer money　零花錢
small beer　無足輕重的人

實境對話
A: Would you like another glass of **beer**?　要再來一杯**啤酒**嗎？
B: No, thanks.　不了，謝謝。

coffee [`kɔfɪ]

名 咖啡

延伸片語 coffee break　工作喝咖啡休息時間
coffee house　咖啡館

實境對話
A: Which do you prefer, **coffee** or tea?　你更喜歡哪一個，**咖啡**還是茶？
B: **Coffee**.　咖啡。

Coke [kok]
名 可口可樂

實境對話
A: Please bring me a large **Coke**.　請給我一大杯可樂。
B: OK, just a minute.　好，馬上來。

drink [drɪŋk]

動 喝 名 酒、飲料

動詞變化 drank, drunk, drinking. **名詞複數** drinks
延伸片語 drink sth. in　盡情地欣賞、陶醉於
drink to sb./sth.　為……乾杯

實境對話
A: Would you like something to **drink**?　想喝些什麼嗎？
B: I'll have some tea, please.　我想喝茶。

ice [aɪs]

名 冰

延伸片語 break the ice　打破隔閡
cut no ice　對某人無影響、不起作用

實境對話
A: Want some **ice**?　加冰嗎？
B: No, thanks.　不了，謝謝。

juice [dʒus]

名 果汁

延伸片語 juice up　使生氣、使更動人
let sb. stew in their own juice　讓某人自作自受

實境對話
A: Here's your **juice**.　這是您的果汁。
B: Thank you.　謝謝。

liquid [`lɪkwɪd]

名 液體

延伸片語 liquid assets　流動資產

實境對話
A: He can only have **liquid** diet right now.　他現在只能吃流質食物。
B: I see.　原來如此。

milk [mɪlk]
名 牛奶

延伸片語 cry over spilt milk
枉為無可挽回的事憂傷

實境對話
A: I drink **milk** every morning. 我每天早上都會喝牛奶。
B: It's very healthy. 那樣非常健康哦。

milk shake
[mɪlk ʃek]
名 奶昔

實境對話
A: I can make **milk shake**. 我會做奶昔。
B: I want to have a taste. 我好想嚐一嚐啊。

soda [ˈsodə]
名 蘇打

實境對話
A: I want some **soda**, please. 我想要些蘇打水。
B: I'll get it. 我這就去拿。

soft drink
[sɔft drɪŋk]
名 軟飲料、不含酒精的飲料

實境對話
A: Do you have any **soft drinks**? 你這有不含酒精的飲料嗎？
B: Yes, which one? 有，您要哪一種？

tea [ti]
名 茶

延伸片語 black tea 紅茶
cup of tea 命運、心愛之人或物

實境對話
A: My mother drinks **tea** every day. 我媽媽每天都喝茶。
B: **Tea** is good for health. 喝茶有益健康。

water [ˈwɔtɚ]
名 水

延伸片語 by water 乘船
it's water under the bridge 往事如煙

實境對話
A: Would you like something to drink? 你想喝些什麼嗎？
B: Just give me **water**, please. 給我水就好。

cake [kek]
名 蛋糕

名詞複數 cakes
延伸片語 have your cake and eat it 得其利而無其弊

實境對話
A: He bought me a big **cake** on my birthday. 我生日那天他為我買了一個大蛋糕。
B: He was so nice. 他人真好。

candy [ˈkændɪ]
名 糖果

同義字 sugar 糖
延伸片語 eye candy 中看不中用的東西

實境對話
A: Eating too many **candies** is bad for your teeth. 吃太多糖對牙齒不好。
B: This is the last one. 這是最後一塊了。

cheese [tʃiz]
名 乳酪

實境對話
A: Are you fond of **cheese**?　你喜歡吃**乳酪**嗎？
B: Not much.　不是很喜歡。

chocolate [`tʃɔkəlɪt]
名 巧克力

延伸片語　plain chocolate　純巧克力
　　　　　 hot chocolate　巧克力熱飲

實境對話
A: I made a **chocolate** cake for dessert tonight.　我做了一個**巧克力**蛋糕當晚上的點心。
B: Great!　太棒了。

cookie [`kʊkɪ]
名 餅乾

名詞複數　cookies
延伸片語　tough cookie　非常堅強的人
　　　　　 that's the way the cookie crumbles　情況就是這樣

實境對話
A: What can I do for you?　您需要什麼服務嗎？
B: Please give me some **cookies** and a cup of coffee.　請給我一些**餅乾**和一杯咖啡。

dessert [dɪ`zɝt]
名 餐後甜點

實境對話
A: Would you like some **dessert**?　您需要**餐後甜點**嗎？
B: Yes, please.　好的。

doughnut [`do‚nʌt]
名 甜甜圈、油炸圈餅

實境對話
A: There are no **doughnuts**.　沒有**甜甜圈**了。
B: That's OK.　那好吧。

ice cream [aɪs krim]
名 冰淇淋

實境對話
A: Here's your **ice cream** for you.　這是你的**冰淇淋**。
B: Thanks a lot.　多謝啦。

moon cake [mun kek]
名 月餅

名詞複數　moon cakes

實境對話
A: What do you eat on Moon Festival?　你們中秋節會吃什麼？
B: We eat **moon cakes**.　我們吃**月餅**。

pie [paɪ]
名 派

同義字 pastie 餡餅

延伸片語 pie in the sky 難以實現的事
a piece of the pie 金錢、利潤等的一份

實境對話
A: I'll go to the market. Do you want anything? 我要去超市，你要些什麼嗎？
B: Bring me some apple **pies**, please. 幫我帶些蘋果派吧。

popcorn [ˈpɑpˌkɔrn]
名 爆米花

同義字 puffed rice 爆米花

實境對話
A: The movie will start in ten minutes. 電影十分鐘之後開演。
B: I'll go buy some **popcorns**. 我去買些爆米花。

toast [tost]
名 烤麵包、吐司

延伸片語 milk-toast 軟弱的
propose a toast to sb. 為某人祝酒

實境對話
A: Could you bring me some **toast**? 能拿給我一些烤麵包嗎？
B: OK. 好的。

butter [ˈbʌtɚ]
名 奶油

延伸片語 bread-and-butter 基本的、很重要的

實境對話
A: Would you please pass the **butter**? 可以把奶油遞給我嗎？
B: Sure. 當然可以。

ketchup [ˈkɛtʃəp]
名 番茄醬

實境對話
A: There's no **ketchup** in the supermarket.
超市裡沒有番茄醬了。
B: Are you kidding? It's impossible.
你在開玩笑嗎？ 不可能。

cream [krim]
名 奶油

延伸片語 cream tea 奶油茶點
face cream 面霜

實境對話
A: I don't like the **cream** at all. 我一點都不喜歡奶油。
B: It's a pity. 那真可惜。

jam [dʒæm]
名 果醬

延伸片語 traffic jam 塞車
be in a jam 陷入困境

實境對話
A: There's some **jam** on your shirt. 你的襯衫上有果醬。
B: Oh, it's terrible. 哦，真糟糕。

Chapter 7 飲食、餐具 Food & Drink & Tableware

oil [ɔɪl]
名 沙拉油、石油

延伸片語 oil painting 油畫
corn oil 玉米油

實境對話
A: Any good news? 有什麼好消息嗎？
B: No, the price of **oil** is increasing. 沒有，石油漲價了。

pepper [ˋpɛpɚ]
名 胡椒

延伸片語 pepper sth. with sth. 大量加入
pepper sb./sth. with sth. 頻繁擊打

實境對話
A: I'd like to add some **pepper** in the dish. 我想在這道菜裡加點**胡椒**。
B: I'll get the **pepper** for you. 我去幫你拿**胡椒**來。

soy-sauce
[sɔɪ sɔs]
名 醬油

實境對話
A: We have no **soy-sauce**. Can you go buy some?
我們沒有**醬油**了，你能去買些回來嗎？
B: But I'm busy writing.
但是我在忙著寫東西啊。

salt [sɔlt]
名 鹽

延伸片語 salt sth. away （通常指以欺瞞手段）祕密貯存
the salt of the earth 指善良而信實的人

實境對話
A: You must forget to add **salt**. 你一定忘了加**鹽**了。
B: I'm sorry. 太抱歉了。

sugar [ˋʃʊgɚ]
名 糖

同義字 candy 糖果

實境對話
A: Do you want some **sugar**? 要加點**糖**嗎？
B: A little, please. 一點就好。

vinegar [ˋvɪnɪgɚ]
名 醋

實境對話
A: I'd like to add some **vinegar** in the noodles.
我喜歡吃麵條時加些**醋**在裡面。
B: Me, too.
我也是啊。

hungry [ˋhʌŋgrɪ]
形 饑餓的

形容詞變化 hungrier, the hungriest
延伸片語 hungry for 渴望
go hungry 挨餓

實境對話
A: Are you **hungry** now? 你現在**餓**嗎？
B: Yes, very much. 嗯，非常餓。

full [fʊl]
形 飽的

形容詞變化 fuller, the fullest
反義字 hungry 饑餓的
延伸片語 full of oneself 驕傲
in full 全部

實境對話
A: I'm **full**. 我吃飽了。
B: Would you like to take a walk outside? 要不要去外面散散步呢？

thirsty [ˈθɝstɪ]
形 口渴的

形容詞變化 thirstier, the thirstiest

實境對話
A: Is anything to drink? I'm **thirsty**. 有什麼喝的嗎？我渴了。
B: How about some orange juice? 要不要來點柳橙汁？

bitter [ˈbɪtɚ]
形 苦澀的

延伸片語 a bitter pill 嚴酷的現實
to the bitter end 堅持到底

實境對話
A: Why is it so **bitter**? 怎麼這麼苦啊？
B: Good medicine tastes **bitter**. 良藥苦口啊。

delicious [dɪˈlɪʃəs]
形 美味的

形容詞變化 more delicious, the most delicious
同義字 yummy 美味的

實境對話
A: How was the meal? 這頓飯怎麼樣？
B: It was very **delicious**. 非常好吃啊。

hot [hɑt]
形 酷熱的

形容詞變化 hotter, the hottest
延伸片語 be in hot water 有麻煩
go like hot cakes 暢銷

實境對話
A: You'd better not play outside. It's too **hot**. 你最好不要去外面玩，太熱了。
B: I'll just go out for a while. 我只出去一會兒。

sour [ˈsaʊr]
形 酸的

延伸片語 go sour 變壞
sour grapes
（表示某人表面貶低某事物，實則是嫉妒）酸葡萄

實境對話
A: It tastes a little **sour**. 嚐起來有點酸啊。
B: I might put too much vinegar. 我可能放了太多醋了。

sweet [swit]
形 甜的

形容詞變化 sweeter, the sweetest
延伸片語 be sweet on somebody 熱戀某人
keep somebody sweet 討好某人

實境對話
A: I like **sweet** food. 我喜歡甜品。
B: You must like eating cakes. 那你一定喜歡吃蛋糕了。

Chapter
7
飲食、餐具 Food & Drink & Tableware

yummy [ˈjʌmɪ]
形 美味的

形容詞變化 yummier, the yummiest
同義字 delicious 美味的

實境對話
A: It tastes so **yummy**. 真好吃啊。
B: It's nice of you to say so. 你這樣說真好。

bake [bek]
動 烘烤

動詞變化 baked, baked, baking, bakes
同義字 roast 烘焙

實境對話
A: Let's **bake** some bread and cake. 咱們烤些麵包和糕點吧。
B: That's a good idea. 好主意。

boil [bɔɪl]
動 煮

動詞變化 boiled, boiled, boiling, boils
延伸片語 boil sth. down 概括
boil over 怒火中燒

實境對話
A: When shall we cook? 我們什麼時候做飯？
B: I'll **boil** the water first. 我得先將水煮開。

burn [bɝn]
動 燒

動詞變化 burnt, burnt, burning, burns
延伸片語 burn your bridges 破釜沉舟
burn the candle at both ends 過度勞累

實境對話
A: Keep away form the fire. You may get **burnt**. 離火遠一些，它會燒到你的。
B: I'll be careful. 我會很小心的。

cook [kʊk]
動 下廚、做飯

動詞變化 cooked, cooked, cooking, cooks
延伸片語 cook the books 篡改
cook sb.'s goose 毀掉某人的成功的機會

實境對話
A: I'm too tired to **cook**. 我累得做不了飯了。
B: Let's eat outside. 咱們到外面去吃吧。

eat [it]
動 吃

動詞變化 ate, eaten, eating, eats
延伸片語 eat out of sb's hand 甘願聽命於某人
eat humble pie 認錯

實境對話
A: What do you want to **eat**? 你想吃什麼？
B: I want to eat dumplings. 我想吃餃子。

order [ˈɔrdɚ]
動 點餐

動詞變化 ordered, ordered, ordering, orders
延伸片語 out of order 出故障
the order of the day 常見的

實境對話
A: May I **order** now? 我現在可以點餐嗎？
B: Yes, please. 是的，可以。

Part 1 生活情境單字

menu [ˈmɛnju]
名 菜單

名詞複數 menus

 A: May I have the **menu**? 可以看一下菜單嗎？
B: Sure. 當然可以。

diet [ˈdaɪət]
名 飲食 動 節食

名詞複數 diets
延伸片語 be on a diet 節食
go on a diet 節食

 A: What did the doctor say? 醫生怎麼說？
B: I need to have liquid **diet** for a while. 我需要吃一陣子流質飲食。

bowl [bol]
名 碗

名詞複數 bowls
延伸片語 bowl somebody over 把某人撞倒
dust bowl 乾旱塵暴區

 A: How many **bowls** do you need? 你需要幾個碗？
B: Five. 五個。

chopsticks
[ˈtʃɑpˌstɪks]
名 筷子

 A: I'm sorry that I dropped my **chopsticks**.
不好意思，我把筷子掉到地上了。
B: It doesn't matter.
沒關係。

cup [kʌp]
名 杯子

名詞複數 cups 同義字 glass 玻璃杯
延伸片語 not sb.'s cup of tea 非某人所好
cup final 尤指足球優勝杯決賽

 A: Where is the **cup**? 杯子在哪裡？
B: Maybe it's in the cupboard. 可能放在碗櫃裡了。

dish [dɪʃ]
名 盤子

名詞複數 dishes 同義字 plate 盤子
延伸片語 dish it out 數落
dish the dirt on sb. 說某人閒話

 A: I'm so sorry to break your **dish**. 很抱歉把你的盤子打碎了。
B: That's OK. 沒關係。

fork [fɔrk]
名 叉子

延伸片語 fork out/over 不情願付出

 A: The westerners use knife and **fork** when having meals. 西方人吃飯的時候用刀和叉。
B: That's quite different form our eating habits. 和我們的飲食習慣還真是有很大差別呢。

glass [glæs]

名 玻璃杯

名詞複數	glasses
同義字	cup 杯子

延伸片語 ▸ raise you're your glass 舉杯祝酒
glass sth. in 給……裝玻璃

實境對話
A: May I have a **glass** of juice? 可以給我一杯果汁嗎？
B: Sure. 當然。

knife [naɪf]

名 刀子

名詞複數	knives

延伸片語 ▸ like a knife through butter 輕而易舉
twist the knife 惡意地說或做

實境對話
A: Don't play with the **knife**. It's too dangerous. 別玩刀，那樣太危險了。
B: OK. 好。

napkin [ˈnæpkɪn]

名 餐巾

名詞複數	napkins

延伸片語 ▸ table napkin 餐巾
sanitary napkin 衛生棉

實境對話
A: I'm nervous. What should I do next? 我好緊張，接下來該怎麼做？
B: Put your **napkin** on your lap first. 先將餐巾放在膝蓋上。

plate [plet]

名 盤

名詞複數	plates
同義字	dish 盤子

延伸片語 ▸ hand sth. to sb. on a plate 把某事物拱手送給某人
have too much on your plate 問題或工作等成堆

實境對話
A: I bought a nice **plate** today. 今天我買了一個漂亮的盤子。
B: It's really pretty. 真的很不錯耶。

saucer [ˈsɔsɚ]

名 淺碟

名詞複數	saucers
同義字	cup 杯子

實境對話
A: I can't find the **saucer**. Did you see it? 我找不到淺碟子了，你有看到嗎？
B: Isn't it on the shelf? 它不在架子上嗎？

spoon [spun]

名 湯匙

名詞複數	spoons
同義字	scooper 勺子

延伸片語 ▸ born with a silver spoon in your mouth 出身富裕
sliver spoon 繼承的財富

實境對話
A: May I have two **spoons**? 我可以拿兩個湯匙嗎？
B: Yes, they are in the kitchen. 可以，在廚房裡。

straw [strɔ]

名 稻草、吸管

延伸片語 ▸ clutch at straws 在危難中抓住救命稻草
the last straw 使人不能忍受的最後一件事

實境對話
A: I forgot to take a **straw**. 我忘記拿吸管了。
B: I'll get it. 我去拿吧。

Part **1** 生活情境單字

✎ 練習試試看 📖

用簡單的小測驗，驗收一下，單字記住了嗎？

( ) 1 fruit

( ) 2 banana

( ) 3 bean

( ) 4 meat

( ) 5 food

( ) 6 noodle

( ) 7 seafood

( ) 8 brunch

( ) 9 juice

( ) 10 water

( ) 11 butter

( ) 12 sugar

r ( ) 13 full

( ) 14 delicious

( ) 15 bake

( ) 16 order

( ) 17 bowl

( ) 18 knife

( ) 19 straw

( ) 20 menu

A. 肉　　B 水　　C 點餐　　D 奶油　　E 碗　　F 海鮮　　G 烘烤
H 吸管　I 香蕉　J 麵條　K 水果　L 食物　M 早午餐 N 刀子
O 果汁　P 豆子　Q 菜單　R 飽的　S 美味的 T 糖

答案
1(K)　2(I)　3(P)　4(A)　5(L)　6(J)　7(F)　8(M)　9(O)　10(B)　11(D)　12(T)　13(R)　14(S)
15(G)　16(C)　17(E)　18(N)　19(H)　20(Q)

Chapter 8 衣服、配件

Track 074 🎧

blouse [blaʊs]
名 女裝短上衣

名詞複數	blouses
延伸片語	sailor blouse 水手服

實境對話
A: I want to buy a **blouse**.   我想買一件女裝短上衣。
B: You can shop around in the mall.   你可以去商場裡轉轉。

coat [kot]
名 外衣

名詞複數 coats	同義字 outerwear 外套
延伸片語	cut your coat according to your cloth 量入為出

實境對話
A: Bring the **coat** with you. It's cold outside.   帶上外套吧，外面很冷。
B: OK, thanks.   好的，謝啦。

dress [drɛs]
名 洋裝 動 穿著

動詞變化	dressed, dressed, dressing, dresses
名詞複數	dresses
延伸片語	dress up 打扮
	dress sb. down 訓斥

實境對話
A: I bought the new **dress**.   我買了新洋裝。
B: You've had so many dresses.   妳都已經買了那麼多洋裝了啊。

jacket [ˋdʒækɪt]
名 夾克

名詞複數	jackets
延伸片語	life jacket 救生衣
	dust jacket 書皮

實境對話
A: How did you make your **jacket** dirty?   你是怎麼把夾克弄髒的？
B: I fell to the ground.   我跌到地上了。

jeans [dʒinz]
名 牛仔褲

延伸片語	jeans wear 牛仔裝

實境對話
A: Don't you like wearing the **jeans**?   你不喜歡穿牛仔褲嗎？
B: It makes me uncomfortable.   感覺不舒服。

pajamas [pəˋdʒæməz]
名 睡衣

延伸片語	cat pajamas 美好的事

實境對話
A: Where can I try on the **pajamas**?   我要去哪裡換睡衣？
B: This way, please.   請這邊來吧。

Part 1 生活情境單字

pants [pænts]
名 褲子

同義字　trousers 褲子
延伸片語　have ants in your pants　焦躁不安
　　　　　catch sb. with their pants down　出其不意

實境對話
A: I'll go buy new **pants**.　我要去買新褲子。
B: I'll go with you.　我和你一起去。

raincoat
[ˈrenˌkot]
名 雨衣

名詞複數　raincoats
同義字　slicker 雨衣

實境對話
A: Do you bring the **raincoat** with you?　你帶雨衣了嗎？
B: Yes, I do 嗯，我帶了。

shirt [ʃɜt]
名 襯衫

名詞複數　shirts
延伸片語　keep your shirt on　別生氣
　　　　　put your shirt on sb./sth.　把所有的錢全押在……上

實境對話
A: What can I do for you?　能幫您做些什麼嗎？
B: I want to shorten my **shirt**.　我想將襯衫截短一點。

shorts [ʃɔrts]
名 短褲

實境對話
A: What did you buy?　你買什麼了？
B: I bought **shorts** and a coat.　我買了短褲和外套。

skirt [skɜt]
名 裙子

名詞複數　skirts

實境對話
A: You look great in this **skirt**.　妳穿這件裙子很好看。
B: Thanks.　謝謝。

suit [sut]
名 一套衣服

延伸片語　suit your book　對某人方便（或有用）
　　　　　suit yourself　隨自己的意願

實境對話
A: What about my new **suit**?　我這身套裝怎麼樣？
B: The style is out of date.　款式過時了。

sweater [ˈswɛtɚ]
名 毛衣

名詞複數　sweaters
延伸片語　green sweater worker　環保分子

實境對話
A: Do you like the red **sweater**?　你喜歡紅毛衣嗎？
B: The color is too bright.　顏色太鮮豔了。

Chapter 8
衣服、配件 Clothing & Accessories

swimsuit
[ˈswɪmˌsut]
名 泳衣

實境對話
A: I bought a new **swimsuit**. Let's go swimming.
我買了一件新泳衣，我們游泳去吧。
B: That's a good idea.
好主意。

trousers
[ˈtrauzəz]
名 褲子

延伸片語 wear the trousers
尤指女人（在婚姻等關係中）處於支配的位置，起指揮的作用

實境對話
A: I was so careless to stain my **trousers**. 我太粗心把褲子弄髒了。
B: It doesn't matter. I can help you clean them. 沒關係，我幫你清洗一下。

uniform
[ˈjunəˌfɔrm]
名 制服

名詞複數 uniforms
延伸片語 dress uniform 軍禮服

實境對話
A: This is my new **uniform**. 這是我的新制服。
B: It's rather pretty. 真漂亮啊。

underwear
[ˈʌndəˌwɛr]
名 內衣

實境對話
A: I don't wear **underwear**. 我不穿內衣的。
B: Me, either. 我也是。

vest [vɛst]
名 背心、汗衫

名詞複數 vests
延伸片語 vest in sb./sth. 權利、財產等屬於
flak vest 防彈背心

實境對話
A: It's so hot that my **vest** are totally wet. 天氣太熱了，我的背心都濕透了。
B: You can have a shower. 你可以去沖個澡。

bag [bæg]
名 背包

名詞複數 bags
延伸片語 bags of bones 瘦骨嶙峋的人或動物
be in the bag 穩操勝券

實境對話
A: What's in your **bag**? It's so heavy. 你包包裡裝了什麼，好重啊。
B: It's full of books. 全都是書。

belt [bɛlt]
名 皮帶

名詞複數 belts
延伸片語 belt and braces 雙管齊下、多重保障
below the belt 說話不公正的、傷人的

實境對話
A: What do you think of this **belt**? 你覺得這條皮帶怎麼樣？
B: I don't think it suits you. 我覺得它並不適合你。

Part 1 生活情境單字

button [ˋbʌtn̩]
名 扣子 動 扣鈕扣

名詞複數 buttons
延伸片語 button it 閉嘴、住口
bright as a button 機靈的、聰穎的

A: I dropped a **button**. 我把一個扣子弄丟了。
B: You were so careless. 你也太粗心了。

cap [kæp]
名 帽子

名詞複數 caps
延伸片語 go cap in hand 謙卑地討要（尤指錢）
if the cap fits 有則改之

A: I'd like this **cap**. 我喜歡這頂**無邊便帽**。
B: The color is a little too dark. 顏色有點太深了。

comb [kom]
名 梳子 動 用梳子梳理

動詞變化 combed, combed, combing, combs
名詞複數 combs
延伸片語 comb out 梳理
go over sth. with a fine-tooth comb 十分認真地檢查

A: Where is my **comb**? 我的梳子在哪裡？
B: You can use mine. 你可以用我的。

contact lens
[ˋkɑntækt lɛns]
名 隱形眼鏡

A: I might throw my **contact lens** with the trash.
我可能把隱形眼鏡和垃圾一起扔掉了。
B: I hope not.
我希望不是。

earrings [ˋɪrˏrɪŋz]
名 耳環

A: These **earrings** are the latest style.
這副**耳環**是最新的款式。
B: They look so beautiful.
真漂亮啊。

glove [glʌv]
名 手套

名詞複數 gloves
延伸片語 fit sb. like a glove 大小、形狀完全合適
hand in glove with sb. 和某人密切合作（尤指勾結）

A: You'd better do the washing with **gloves** on. 你最好戴**手套**做清洗工作。
B: Thanks for reminding me. 謝謝你提醒我。

handkerchief
[ˋhæŋkətʃɪf]
名 手帕

名詞複數 handkerchiefs

A: You are bleeding. Here's the **handkerchief**. 你在流血啊，給你手帕。
B: Thank you. 謝謝你。

Chapter 8 衣服、配件 Clothing & Accessories

hat [hæt]

名 帽子

名詞複數	hats
延伸片語	keep sth. unde your hat　將某事保密
	my hat　（表示驚奇）

實境對話
A: Is the **hat** yours?　那個帽子是你的嗎？
B: Yes, I lost it the day before yesterday.　是我的！我前天把它弄丟了。

mask [mæsk]

名 面具

名詞複數 masks	同義字 face-piece 面具
延伸片語	gas mask　防毒面具
	gauze mask　口罩

實境對話
A: Put on a **mask** if you're coughing.　如果你在咳嗽，請戴口罩。
B: OK.　好的。

necklace [ˈnɛklɪs]
名 項鏈

名詞複數	necklaces

實境對話
A: What are you reading?　你在讀什麼書呢？
B: A short story called **necklace** by Maupassant.　莫泊桑的短篇小說《項鏈》。

pocket [ˈpɑkɪt]

名 口袋

名詞複數	pockets
延伸片語	be in somebody's pocket　受某人的控制
	to have something in your pocket　勝利在握

實境對話
A: Can you lend me some money?　能借我點錢嗎？
B: I don't have a cent in my **pocket**.　我口袋裡一分錢都沒有。

purse [pɝs]
名 錢包

名詞複數	purses
延伸片語	A light purse makes a heavy heart　為人無錢心事重

實境對話
A: Oh, no! I left my **purse** in the office.　天啊，我把錢包忘在辦公室了。
B: Go back and get it.　回去拿吧。

ring [rɪŋ]
名 戒指、鈴聲
動 （種、鈴等）鳴、響

動詞變化 ringed, ringed, ringing, rings
名詞複數 rings
延伸片語　ring a bell　聽起來耳熟
ring in your ears　在耳邊迴響

實境對話
A: I love the moment when the bride and bridegroom exchange the **rings**.
　我特別喜歡新娘和新郎交換戒指的時刻。
B: It's too romantic.
　太浪漫了。

scarf [skɑrf]

名 圍巾

名詞複數	scarves

實境對話
A: What a beautiful **scarf**!　好漂亮的圍巾啊！
B: My girlfriend bought it for me.　我女朋友買給我的。

shoe(s) [ʃu]
名 鞋子

延伸片語 be in somebody's shoes 設身處地
if I were in your shoes 要是我處在你的境地

實境對話
A: What's wrong with your **shoes**? 你的鞋子怎麼了？
B: The bus was too crowed. Many people stepped on my **shoes**.
公車太擠了，很多人踩在我的鞋子上。

slippers [ˈslɪpəz]
名 拖鞋

實境對話
A: Where are my **slippers**? 我的拖鞋在哪裡？
B: Aren't they in the shoe cabinet? 不在鞋櫃裡嗎？

sneakers [ˈsnikəs]
名 球鞋

實境對話
A: Have you washed your **sneakers**? 你洗球鞋了嗎？
B: Not yet. I'm too tired. 還沒有，我太累了。

socks [sɑks]
名 一雙襪子

延伸片語 blow somebody's socks off 使某人萬分驚愕
put a sock in it （讓某人安靜）住嘴、別出聲

實境對話
A: Did you find any gifts in your **socks**? 你在襪子裡找到禮物了嗎？
B: Yes, I got a pretty doll. 是的，我得到了一個漂亮的洋娃娃。

tie [taɪ]
名 領帶、結 動 綁、繫

動詞變化 tied, tied, tying, ties
延伸片語 tie somebody up 把某人捆綁起來
tie in (with something) 與……相配

實境對話
A: I'll buy Tom a **tie**. 我要幫湯姆買一條領帶。
B: What about this blue one? 這條藍的怎麼樣？

umbrella [ʌmˈbrɛlə]
名 雨傘

名詞複數 umbrellas
延伸片語 nuclear umbrella 核保護傘（美國的核武器可用來防衛美國本土及歐洲國家）

實境對話
A: It's raining outside. Take the **umbrella**. 外面下雨了，帶上雨傘吧。
B: Thank you. 謝謝。

wallet [ˈwɑlɪt]
名 錢包、皮夾

名詞複數 wallets
同義字 purse 錢包

實境對話
A: I lost my **wallet** when I got out of the car. 下車時我將錢包給丟了。
B: That's terrible. 太糟糕了。

Chapter **8** 衣服、配件 Clothing & Accessories

| 095 |

clothes [kloz]
名 衣服

延伸片語 plain clothes　員警執行任務時穿的便衣
clothes tree　櫃式衣架

實境對話
A: What will you do next Sunday?　下周日你要做什麼？
B: I have many **clothes** to wash.　我還有很多**衣服**要洗。

cotton [`katṇ]
名 棉花

延伸片語 cotton on　明白、領悟
cotton to somebody/something　向……討好、巴結

實境對話
A: The price of **cotton** is increasing.　棉花價格上漲了。
B: Really? I'm just thinking wheather to buy some.　真的嗎？我剛還在想要不要買一些。

diamond [`daɪmənd]
名 鑽石

名詞複數 diamonds
延伸片語 rough diamond　外粗內秀的人
diamond wedding　鑽石婚（結婚 60 周年紀念）

實境對話
A: I'd like a skirt to match the **diamond**.　我想要買一條裙子來配**鑽石**。
B: You may like this one.　你可能會喜歡這一條。

gold [gold]
名 金 形 金的

形容詞變化 golder, the goldest
延伸片語 a crock of gold　不大可能得到的大筆獎賞
as good as gold　規規矩矩、很乖

實境對話
A: Is it pure **gold**?　是純金嗎？
B: One hundred percent.　百分之一百純金。

silver [`sɪlvɚ]
名 銀 形 銀的

延伸片語 Silver jubilee　25周年紀念

實境對話
A: Why do you often keep silent?　為什麼你常常保持沉默？
B: Speech is **silver**, silence is gold.　雄辯是銀，沉默是金。

iron [`aɪən]
名 鐵、熨斗 動 熨燙

動詞變化 ironed, ironed, ironing, irons
名詞複數 irons
延伸片語 Strike while the iron is hot.　趁熱打鐵

實境對話
A: Keep away from the **iron**. You may get hurt.　離熨斗遠點，會燙到你的。
B: Oh, it's quite dangerous.　哦，太危險了。

wear [wɛr]
動 穿著

動詞變化 wore, worn, wearing, wears
延伸片語 wear out　磨薄、穿破

實境對話
A: Do you know that guy who's **wearing** a white coat?　你認識那邊那個**穿著**白外套的人嗎？
B: He's my classmate, John.　他是我同學，約翰。

Part 1 生活情境單字

用簡單的小測驗，驗收一下，單字記住了嗎？

( ) 1 dress

( ) 2 sweater

( ) 3 uniform

( ) 4 bag

( ) 5 button

( ) 6 pocket

( ) 7 umbrella

( ) 8 wallet

( ) 9 diamond

( ) 10 wear

( ) 11 black

( ) 12 purple

( ) 13 sport

( ) 14 baseball

( ) 15 camp

( ) 16 picnic

( ) 17 ski

( ) 18 band

( ) 19 drama

( ) 20 kite

A. 錢包　　B 扣子　　C 運動　　D 雨傘　　E 樂團　　F 制服　　G 鑽石
H 滑雪　　I 野餐　　J 棒球　　K 戲劇　　L 背包　　M 風箏　　N 口袋
O 穿著　　P 毛衣　　Q 紫色　　R 露營　　S 洋裝　　T 黑色

答案
1(S)　2(P)　3(F)　4(L)　5(B)　6(N)　7(D)　8(A)　9(G)　10(O)B　11(T)　12(Q)　13(C)　14(J)
15(R)　16(I)　17(H)　18(E)　19(K)　20(M)

Chapter 9 顏色

Track 081

---

black [blæk]
形 黑色的 **名** 黑色

形容詞變化 blacker, the blackest
反義字 white 白色的
延伸片語 be in the black 有盈餘
black sheep 害群之馬

 實境對話
A: Give that pen to me, please. 請把那支筆給我。
B: The **black** one? 是那支黑色的嗎？

---

blue [blu]
形 藍色的 **名** 藍色

形容詞變化 bluer, the bluest
延伸片語 out of the blue 出乎意料
somebody's blue-eyed boy 某人的紅人

 實境對話
A: Do you like this **blue** shirt? 你喜歡這件藍色的襯衫嗎？
B: Not very much. 不是很喜歡。

---

brown [braʊn]
形 棕色的 **名** 棕色

形容詞變化 browner, the brownest
延伸片語 in a brown study 沉思、深思
brown sugar 紅糖

 實境對話
A: You have very beautiful **brown** hair. 你有一頭漂亮的棕色長髮。
B: It's very kind of you to say so. 謝謝。

---

color [ˈkʌlə]
名 顏色

名詞複數 colors
延伸片語 a horse of a different color 完全另外一回事
color bar 種族障礙

 實境對話
A: What's your favorite **color**? 你最喜歡的顏色是什麼？
B: Pink. 粉紅色。

---

golden [ˈgoldn̩]
形 金色的 **名** 金色

延伸片語 silence is golden 沉默是金
golden wedding 金婚紀念（結婚 50 周年）

 實境對話
A: The sun is **golden**. 太陽是金色的。
B: What a beautiful sight. 多美的景色啊。

---

gray [gre]
形 灰色的 **名** 灰色

形容詞變化 grayer, the grayest
延伸片語 gray market 水貨市場
gray-headed 白髮的、老年的

 實境對話
A: The sky was **gray** when I got up in the morning. 早上起床時候天空是灰色的。
B: It may rain today. 今天可能會下雨吧。

Chapter **9** 顏色 Colors

---

green [grin]
形 綠色的 名 綠色

形容詞變化 greener, the greenest
延伸片語 green with envy 妒忌的
green fingers 園藝技能

 實境對話
A: I like watching the **green** fields on the side of the road on my way to work.
上班的路上我喜歡看路邊的綠色的大地。
B: The air must be fresh.
空氣一定很清新啊。

---

orange [ˈɔrɪndʒ]
形 橙色的 名 柳橙、橙色

形容詞變化 oranger, the orangest
名詞複數 oranges

 實境對話
A: I like that **orange** sweater. 我喜歡那件橙色的毛衣。
B: It looks warm. 看上去很溫暖。

---

pink [pɪŋk]
形 粉色的 名 粉色

形容詞變化 pinker, the pinkest
延伸片語 pink slip 解雇通知單
in the pink 滿面紅光

 實境對話
A: What can I do for you? 能為您做些什麼嗎？
B: I want that **pink** rabbit. 我想要那隻粉紅色的兔子。

---

purple [ˈpɝpl̩]
形 紫色的 名 紫色

形容詞變化 purpler, the purplest
延伸片語 purple patch 成功的時期
royal purple 深紫紅色

 實境對話
A: Have you read the book **purple**? 你讀過《紫色》這本書嗎？
B: Yes, I have. 是的，我看過。

---

red [rɛd]
形 紅色的 名 紅色

形容詞變化 redder, the reddest
延伸片語 red in tooth and claw 殘酷無情
a red rag to a bull 鬥牛的紅布

 實境對話
A: Which one is your little sister? 哪個是你妹妹？
B: The girl in **red**. 穿紅色衣服的女孩子。

---

white [hwaɪt]
形 白色的 名 白色

形容詞變化 whiter, the whitest
反義字 black 黑色的
延伸片語 white elephant 無價值的東西

實境對話
A: Be careful not to stain your **white** coat. 小心別弄髒了你的白外套。
B: I get it. 我知道了。

---

yellow [ˈjɛlo]
形 黃色的 名 黃色

形容詞變化 yellower, the yellowest
延伸片語 Yellow Pages 黃頁
yellow ribbon
黃絲帶（繫在樹上以期盼遠方的親人能早日返回）

 實境對話
A: There is a **yellow** bird in the tree. 樹上有一隻黃鳥。
B: How cute it is. 好可愛啊。

Track 083

sport [sport]
名 運動

名詞複數 sports
同義字 movement 運動
延伸片語 be a (good) sport （尤指在困境中）開朗大度
make sport of 開……的玩笑

 A: Which **sport** do you like best? 你最喜歡什麼運動？
B: Running is my favorite. 跑步是我的最愛。

badminton [ˋbædmɪntən]
名 羽毛球

名詞複數 badmintons

 A: I heard that you play **badminton** very well. 我聽說你羽毛球打得非常好。
B: Just so so. 一般而已。

baseball [ˋbesˏbɔl]
名 棒球

名詞複數 baseballs

 A: Do you often watch **baseball** games? 你經常看棒球比賽嗎？
B: Yes, I like **baseball** very much. 是啊，我非常喜歡棒球。

basketball [ˋbæskɪtˏbɔl]
名 籃球

名詞複數 basketballs

 A: Next week we'll hold a **basketball** game. 下周我們會舉行一場籃球比賽。
B: May I join your team? 我可以加入你們的隊伍嗎？

dodge ball [dɑdʒ bɔl]
名 躲避球

 A: I quite like playing **dodge ball**. 我特別喜歡玩躲避球。
B: We can play together tomorrow. 明天我們可以一起玩。

football [ˋfʊtˏbɔl]
名 足球

名詞複數 footballs
延伸片語 football pools 足球賽賭博
football boot 足球鞋

 A: We won the **football** match. 我們贏了足球比賽。
B: Congratulations. 恭喜。

frisbee [ˈfrɪzbɪ]
名 飛盤

| 實境對話 | A: Can you play **frisbee**? 你會玩飛盤嗎？
B: Yes, but I'm not good at it. 會，但我不擅長。 |

---

golf [gɔlf]
名 高爾夫

延伸片語 golf course 高爾夫球場
golf links 尤指海邊的高爾夫球場

| 實境對話 | A: How often do you play **golf** in a month? 你一個月會打幾次高爾夫？
B: Three times. 三次吧。 |

---

race [res]
動 與……賽跑
名 競賽、（生物的）種類

動詞變化 raced, raced, racing, races
名詞複數 races
延伸片語 a race against time 爭分奪秒
horse race 賽馬

| 實境對話 | A: Who runs the fastest in the **race**? 誰在賽跑中是最快的？
B: Charles. 查理斯。 |

---

soccer [ˈsɑkɚ]
名 足球

同義字 football 足球

| 實境對話 | A: Do you play **soccer**? 你會踢足球嗎？
B: Not really. 不怎麼會。 |

---

softball [ˈsɔftˌbɔl]
名 壘球

名詞複數 softballs

| 實境對話 | A: Which sport do you like? 你喜歡哪項運動？
B: I'm interested in **softball**. 我對壘球很感興趣。 |

---

table tennis
[ˈtebl ˈtɛnɪs]
名 乒乓球

| 實境對話 | A: What sport is he good at? 他擅長什麼運動？
B: He plays **table tennis** very well. 他乒乓球打得非常好。 |

---

tennis [ˈtɛnɪs]
名 網球

延伸片語 lawn tennis 草地網球
court tennis 室內網球

| 實境對話 | A: What are they doing? 他們做什麼呢？
B: They are playing **tennis**. 他們在打網球。 |

Chapter **10** 運動、興趣、嗜好 Sports,Interests & Hobbies

volleyball
['vɑlɪˌbɔl]
名 排球

實境對話
A: Are you going to play **volleyball**? 你要去打**排球**嗎？
B: Yes. Would you like to go with me? 是啊，你願意一起去嗎？

barbecue
['bɑrbɪkju]
名 烤肉

延伸片語 barbecue sauce 烤肉醬

實境對話
A: We'll have a **barbecue** this Saturday. Would you like to come?
我們週六要去吃**烤肉**，你願意一起來嗎？
B: I'd love to. 我願意。

bowling ['bolɪŋ]
名 保齡球

延伸片語 bowling alley 保齡球場
bowling ball 保齡球

實境對話
A: Are you free tonight? 晚上有時間嗎？
B: I'll go **bowling** with my uncle. 我要和叔叔去打**保齡球**。

camp [kæmp]
動 露營 名 營地

動詞變化 camped, camped, camping, camps
名詞複數 camps
延伸片語 camp out 露宿
camp it up 裝腔作勢

實境對話
A: Let's go **camping**. 我們去露營吧。
B: That's a good idea. 好主意！

climb [klaɪm]
動 爬、攀登

動詞變化 climbed, climbed, climbing, climbs
延伸片語 climb down 從……爬下
climb on the bandwagon 趕時髦

實境對話
A: How can we get to the other side of the wall? 我們怎樣才能到牆的另一邊去？
B: We have to **climb** over the wall. 我們得爬過牆去。

cook [kʊk]
動 烹飪

動詞變化 cooked, cooked, cooking, cooks
延伸片語 be cooking with gas 如火如荼地進行
cook the books 篡改

實境對話
A: When shall we **cook** for dinner? 我們什麼時候煮晚飯？
B: We can start at 5 o'clock. 我們五點開始吧。

dance [dæns]
動 跳舞 名 舞會

動詞變化 danced, danced, dancing, dances
名詞複數 dances
延伸片語 dance the night away 整夜跳舞

實境對話
A: Would you like to **dance** with me? 可以邀請您**跳**一支**舞**嗎？
B: Yes, I'd love to. 我很樂意。

Part 1 生活情境單字

draw [drɔ]
動 繪畫 名 平局、平手

動詞變化 drew, drawn, drawing, draws
同義字 paint 繪畫
延伸片語 draw a blank 無回音
draw a breath 停下來歇口氣

A: What are you **drawing**, baby? 寶貝，你在畫什麼？
B: I'm **drawing** a house. 我在畫一個房子。

exercise
[ˈɛksəˌsaɪz]
名 運動、鍛鍊

名詞複數 exercises
延伸片語 take exercise 做運動
floor exercise 自由體操

A: I don't feel well these days. 這些天我感覺不舒服。
B: You'd better take **exercise** every day. You're a little weak.
你最好每天都鍛鍊身體，你的身體有些虛弱。

fish [fɪʃ]
動 釣魚

動詞變化 fished, fished, fishing, fishes
延伸片語 neither fish nor fowl 非驢非馬、不倫不類
an odd fish 古怪的人

A: Why are you so angry? 你怎麼這麼生氣？
B: They went **fishing** without me. 他們去釣魚卻沒有找我。

hike [haɪk]
動 健行 (hiking) 名 健行

動詞變化 hiked, hiked, hiking, hikes
延伸片語 take a hike 滾開
hitch-hike 免費搭便車

A: Are you fond of **hiking**? 你喜歡健行嗎？
B: Yes, I love it. 是的，我喜歡！

jog [dʒɑg]
動 慢跑

動詞變化 jogged, jogged, jogging, jogs
延伸片語 jog somebody's memory 喚起某人的記憶
jog along 緩慢而平穩地進行

A: Do you take exercise every day? 你每天都會鍛鍊身體嗎？
B: Yes, I go **jogging** in the park every morning. 是的，我每天早上在公園裡慢跑。

picnic [ˈpɪknɪk]
名 野餐

延伸片語 be no picnic 可不容易
have a picnic 舉行野餐

A: What a nice day. 多好的天氣啊！
B: We can go on a **picnic** today. 我們今天可以去野餐。

roller skate
[ˈrolɚ sket]
動 （溜）直排輪

A: Do you do well in **roller-skating**? 你擅長直排輪嗎？
B: No, I'm just a beginner. 不，我只是一個初學者。

run [rʌn]
動 跑步

> **動詞變化** ran, ran, running, runs
> **延伸片語** run for it 逃跑
> run after somebody 追求

實境對話
A: Can you **run** faster? 你能再跑快點嗎？
B: I can't feel up to it. 我跑不動了。

sail [sel]
動 航海

> **動詞變化** sailed, sailed, sailing, sails
> **延伸片語** sail through 順利通過（考試等）
> sail close to the wind 冒大風險

實境對話
A: What's your dream? 你的夢想是什麼？
B: I want a boat and go **sailing**. 我想要擁有一條船然後去**航海**。

sing [sɪŋ]
動 唱歌

> **動詞變化** sang, sung, singing, sings
> **延伸片語** sing a different tune 改變觀點
> sing out 唱出

實境對話
A: Do you hear someone **singing**? 你聽到有人在**唱歌**了嗎？
B: Yes, it may be the little girl living next door. 是的，可能是住在隔壁的那個小女孩。

skate [sket]
動 溜冰 **名** 溜冰鞋

> **動詞變化** skated, skated, skating, skates
> **名詞複數** skates
> **延伸片語** skate over something 回避
> get your skates on 趕緊

實境對話
A: What's wrong with your arm? 你的胳膊怎麼了？
B: I fell down on the ice when I was **skating**. 當我**溜冰**的時候我摔倒了。

ski [ski]
動 滑雪 **名** 滑雪橇

> **動詞變化** skied, skied, skiing, skis
> **名詞複數** skis
> **延伸片語** ski run 滑雪道
> ski boot 滑雪靴

實境對話
A: What are you busy doing these days? 你最近忙什麼呢？
B: I'm busy learning to **ski**. 我忙著學滑雪。

stamp [stæmp]
名 郵票、印章 **動** 蓋印章

> **動詞變化** stamped, stamped, stamping, stamps
> **名詞複數** stamps
> **延伸片語** stamp on something 用力踩
> stamp something on something 在……上打上……印記

實境對話
A: Oh, my. I forgot to **stamp** the letter. 天啊，我忘了在信上貼郵票了。
B: You'd better ask the mail carrier for help. 你最好找郵差幫忙。

surf [sɝf]
動 衝浪 **名** 海浪

> **動詞變化** surfed, surfed, surfing, surfs
> **延伸片語** channel-surf 頻繁地變換頻道
> surf the internet 上網

實境對話
A: How do you think of **surfing**? 你對**衝浪**這個活動怎麼看？
B: It's quite exciting. 很刺激。

Part 1 生活情境單字

| 104 |

Chapter 10 運動、興趣、嗜好 Sports,Interests & Hobbies

swim [swɪm]
動 游泳

動詞變化 swam, swum, swimming, swims
延伸片語 sink or swim 自己努力，以求生存
swim with the tide 隨波逐流

實境對話
A: How long have you learned **swimming**? 你學游泳多長時間了？
B: For three years. 學了三年了。

travel ['trævl̩]
名 旅遊 **動** 旅行

動詞變化 travelled, travelled, travelling, travels
同義字 trip 旅行
延伸片語 travel light 輕裝上路
travel agent 旅行社

實境對話
A: How many countries have you **travelled**? 你旅行過多少國家？
B: Five countries. 五個國家。

trip [trɪp]
名 旅行

名詞複數 trips 同義字 journey 旅行
延伸片語 trip up 犯錯誤
round trip 往返旅程

實境對話
A: Have a good **trip**. 祝你旅行愉快！
B: Thank you. 謝謝。

hobby ['hɑbɪ]
名 興趣

名詞複數 hobbies
延伸片語 hobby horse 熱衷談論的話題

實境對話
A: What's your **hobby**? 你的興趣是什麼？
B: I'm interested in singing. 我很喜歡唱歌。

band [bænd]
名 樂園

名詞複數 bands
延伸片語 big band （演奏爵士樂或舞曲的）大樂隊
brass band 銅管樂隊

實境對話
A: Which **band** do you like? 你喜歡哪個樂隊？
B: I like Backstreet Boys. 新好男孩。

card [kɑrd]
名 卡片

名詞複數 cards
延伸片語 give sb. their cards 解雇、開除
hold all the cards 能控制局勢

實境對話
A: May I send a **card** to her? 我可以寄張卡片給她嗎？
B: Yes, of course. 可以啊。

cartoon [kɑr'tun]
名 卡通動畫

名詞複數 cartoons
延伸片語 cartoon film 卡通片

實境對話
A: Why are you staring at that man? 你為什麼盯著那個男人看呢？
B: He looks like a **cartoon** character. 他看上去像一個卡通人物。

chess [tʃɛs]
名 西洋棋

延伸片語 play chess 下棋
Chinese Chess 中國象棋

實境對話
A: Do you know the rules of **chess**? 你知道**西洋棋**的規則嗎？
B: Yes, I do. 是的，我知道。

comic [ˈkɑmɪk]
名 漫畫 形 滑稽的

同義字 funny 滑稽的
延伸片語 comic opera 喜劇
comic book 漫畫書

實境對話
A: I bought some **comics** yesterday. 我昨天買了幾本**漫畫書**。
B: What kinds of **comics**? 什麼類型的漫畫啊？

computer game
[kəmˈpjutɚ gem]
名 電腦遊戲

實境對話
A: You'd better not be addicted to **computer games**.
你最好不要沉迷於**電腦遊戲**。
B: Don't worry. I won't.
別擔心，我不會的。

doll [dɑl]
名 洋娃娃

名詞複數 dolls
延伸片語 mall doll
花很多時間在「購物中心」裡買東西的年輕女性

實境對話
A: What did you buy for Anne's birthday? 你給安妮買什麼生日禮物了？
B: I bought her a **doll**. 我給她買了一個**洋娃娃**。

drama [ˈdræmə]
名 戲劇

名詞複數 dramas
延伸片語 make a drama out of something 小題大作
costume drama 古裝戲

實境對話
A: What's her major? 她的專業是什麼？
B: Her major is **Drama**. 她的專業是戲劇。

drum [drʌm]
名 鼓

名詞複數 drums
延伸片語 beat the drum 搖旗吶喊
drum something up 竭力爭取

實境對話
A: Who's beating the **drum**? 誰在敲鼓？
B: I think it's Kate. 我想是凱特。

film [fɪlm]
名 電影

名詞複數 films
同義字 movie 電影
延伸片語 film-maker 電影製作人
feature film 劇情片

實境對話
A: I'd like to see a **film** tonight. 我今晚想去看一場**電影**。
B: What about Kung Fu Panda? 功夫熊貓怎麼樣？

Part 1 生活情境單字

flute [flut]
名 橫笛、長笛

名詞複數 flutes
延伸片語 teach a pig to play on a flute 做絕不可能做到的事

實境對話
A: Is it your **flute**? It's so pretty. 這是你的橫笛嗎？好漂亮啊。
B: Yes, I love it very much. 是的，我非常喜歡它。

game [gem]
名 遊戲

名詞複數 games
延伸片語 play the game 辦事公道
the game is up 戲該收場了

實境對話
A: Would you like to join our **game**? 你願意參加我們的遊戲嗎？
B: Sorry, I have a lot of work to do. 抱歉，我有很多事情要做。

guitar [gɪ`tɑr]
名 吉他

名詞複數 guitars

實境對話
A: My father bought me a **guitar** as a gift. 我爸爸給我買了一把吉他作為禮物。
B: It must be really precious to you. 它對你來說一定很珍貴。

instrument
[`ɪnstrəmənt]
名 樂器

實境對話
A: Is it a piano? 那個就是鋼琴嗎？
B: Yes, it's a kind of musical **instrument**.
是的，它是一種樂器。

jazz [dʒæz]
名 爵士

延伸片語 and all that jazz 以及諸如此類的東西
jazz something up 使某事更有趣

實境對話
A: Are you familiar with **jazz**? 你瞭解爵士樂嗎？
B: A little bit. 瞭解一點吧。

kite [kaɪt]
名 風箏

名詞複數 kites
延伸片語 fly a kite 試探輿論
fly your kite 走開、別煩人

實境對話
A: My father often flies a **kite** with me in the spring. 春天我父親經常帶著我放風箏。
B: I haven't flew a **kite** for so many years. 我已經很多年沒放過風箏了。

movie [`muvɪ]
名 電影

名詞複數 movies
同義字 film 電影
延伸片語 action movie 動作影片
event movie 電影大片

實境對話
A: Have you ever seen this **movie** before? 你看過這個電影嗎？
B: No, I haven't. 不，我沒看過。

music [`mjuzɪk]
 名 音樂

延伸片語 music to your ears 好消息
absolute music 純音樂

實境對話 A: What kind of **music** do you like? 你喜歡哪種類型的音樂？
B: I like classical **music**. 我喜歡古典音樂。

novel [`nɑvḷ]
名 小說

名詞複數 novels
同義字 fiction 小說
延伸片語 saga novel 家世小說
dime novel 故事動人但毫無文學價值的小說

實境對話 A: Are you OK? 你沒事吧？
B: I'm fine. The **novel** is so moving that I can't help crying.
我沒事，這本小說太感人了，我禁不住哭了。

paint [pent]
 動 畫圖、油漆

動詞變化 painted, painted, painting, paints
同義字 color 給……塗顏色
延伸片語 paint the town red 花天酒地地玩樂

實境對話 A: Tom, don't forget to **paint** the picture. 湯姆，別忘了畫畫。
B: I got it. 我知道了。

piano [pɪ`æno]
 名 鋼琴

名詞複數 pianos

實境對話 A: Does your son play **piano** well? 您兒子鋼琴彈得好嗎？
B: Just so so. 一般吧。

pop music [pɑp `mjuzɪk]
名 流行音樂

 實境對話 A: Do you care for **pop music**? 你喜歡流行音樂嗎？
B: Yes, I listen to it almost every day. 是，我幾乎天天都聽。

puzzle [`pʌzḷ]
名 謎、拼圖 動 使迷惑

動詞變化 puzzled, puzzled, puzzling, puzzles
同義字 baffle 使迷惑
延伸片語 puzzle over 努力思考
puzzle out 苦苦思索而弄清楚

 實境對話 A: Can you work this **puzzle** out? 你能解開這個謎嗎？
B: Give me some time. It's a little difficult. 給我點時間，有點難。

song [sɔŋ]
 名 歌曲

名詞複數 songs
延伸片語 for a song 非常便宜

實境對話 A: This **song** was very popular in the 1980s. 這首歌在二十世紀八十年代非常流行。
B: That's one of my favorite **songs**. 那是我最愛聽的歌曲之一。

team [tim]

名 小組

名詞複數 teams
同義字 group 小組
延伸片語 team up 合作

實境對話
A: Would you like to join our **team**? 你願意加入我們小組嗎？
B: Of course. It's my honor. 當然，這是我的榮幸。

tent [tɛnt]

名 帳篷

名詞複數 tents
延伸片語 big tent 在一個組織、團體之內，容許不同意見之存在；對不同意見之容許

實境對話
A: I find our **tent** broken. 我發現我們的帳篷壞了。
B: Let me have a look. 我看看。

toy [tɔɪ]

名 玩具

名詞複數 toys
延伸片語 toy with something 不太認真地考慮

實境對話
A: My son wants a **toy** transformer. 我兒子想要一個變形金剛玩具。
B: You can shop around in the mall. 你可以在商場逛逛看。

trumpet [ˈtrʌmpɪt]

名 喇叭 動 吹奏喇叭

名詞複數 trumpets
延伸片語 blow your own trumpet 自吹自擂

實境對話
A: Which instrument do you like? 你喜歡什麼樂器？
B: I like the **trumpet** best. 我最喜歡喇叭。

violin [ˌvaɪəˈlɪn]

名 小提琴

同義字 fiddle 小提琴

實境對話
A: He's the only one who can play the **violin** in my class.
他是我們班級唯一一個會拉小提琴的人。
B: That's so cool. 那太酷了。

lose [luz]

動 浪費

動詞變化 lost, lost, losing, loses
同義字 spend 花費
延伸片語 lose yourself in something 沉迷於
lose your grip 駕馭不住

實境對話
A: You have **lost** so much time on this problem. 你在這個問題上浪費太多時間了。
B: I must work this out. 我必須弄清楚它。

play [ple]

動 玩耍

動詞變化 played, played, playing, plays
延伸片語 play about/around 玩弄
play at something/at doing something 虛與委蛇

實境對話
A: Who will you **play** with? 你要和誰一起玩啊？
B: With Micheal. 和麥克。

loser [ˋluzɚ]
名 失敗者

名詞複數	losers
同義字	underdog 失敗者

實境對話
A: I must win the game. I don't want to be the **loser**.　我要贏得比賽，我不要做失敗者。
B: You should relax yourself.　你需要放鬆一下。

win [wɪn]
動 贏得

動詞變化	won, won, wining, wins
同義字	succeed 成功
延伸片語	win something hands down　輕易取得、唾手可得
	win or lose　不論成敗、無論勝負

實境對話
A: I hope you will **win** the game.　我希望你們能贏得比賽。
B: We will. Thank you.　我們會的，謝謝你。

winner [ˋwɪnɚ]
名 贏家

名詞複數	winners
同義字	victor 勝利者
延伸片語	pick a winner　認定勝利者
	produce an unexpected winner　爆冷門

實境對話
A: Who was the **winner** of the war?　誰是這場戰爭的贏家？
B: No one.　沒有贏家。

fan [fæn]
名 愛好者、迷

名詞複數	fans
延伸片語	fan the flame　火上加油
	fan out　使展開

實境對話
A: I'm a **fan** of Michael Jackson.　我是麥克·傑克森的歌迷。
B: He was an legendary figure.　他是一個傳奇人物。

Part 1 生活情境單字

apartment
[əˈpɑrtmənt]
名 公寓

名詞複數 apartments
同義字 flat 公寓
延伸片語 apartment house 公寓
apartment block 公寓大樓

A: How much rent do you pay for this **apartment**? 你租這棟**公寓**的租金是多少？
B: Twenty thousand dollars. 兩萬元。

building [ˈbɪldɪŋ]
名 建築物

名詞複數 buildings 同義字 construction 建築
延伸片語 body-building 健身
building site 建築工地

A: What does you father do? 令尊從事哪行呢？
B: He works in the **building** trade. 他在建築業工作。

house [haus]
名 房子

名詞複數 houses 同義字 residence 住宅
延伸片語 on the house 免費
big house 監獄

A: The **house** you live is really neat. 你住的**房子**真整齊耶。
B: Actually, I clean it every day. 事實上，我每天打掃房子。

home [hom]
名 家

名詞複數 homes 同義字 residence 住宅
延伸片語 at home 在家
home and abroad 國內外

A: Buy some bread in a bakery on your way **home**. 回家路上到烘焙坊買些麵包。
B: I have no money with me. 我身無分文。

basement
[ˈbesmənt]
名 地下室

名詞複數 basements
同義字 undercroft 地下室

A: How about going to bargain **basement** this evening? 今天晚上到**地下**特價商場好嗎？
B: By all means. 當然好啊。

bathroom
[ˈbæθˌrum]
名 浴室

名詞複數 bathrooms

A: Where is your brother? 你弟弟在哪裡？
B: He is taking a shower in the **bathroom**. 他正在**浴室**洗澡。

bedroom
[ˋbɛdˏrum]
名 臥室

名詞複數	bedrooms
同義字	bedchamber 臥室
延伸片語	master bedroom 主臥室
	single bedroom 單人臥室

 實境對話
A: Neil is doing his homework in his **bedroom**.　奈爾在臥室做功課。
B: It's late now. He should go to bed.　現在很晚了。他應該去睡覺。

dining room
[daɪnɪŋ rum]
名 餐廳

名詞複數	dining rooms
同義字	mess hall 餐廳

實境對話
A: What is Anne doing?　安在做什麼？
B: She is having supper in the **dining room**.　她在餐廳吃晚餐。

fence [fɛns]
名 柵欄

名詞複數	fences
延伸片語	on the fence 保持中立
	fence with 搪塞

實境對話
A: What do you think?　你覺得呢？
B: I think I'll sit **on the fence**.　我想我會持中立態度。

garage [gəˋradʒ]
名 車庫

名詞複數	garages
同義字	carport 車庫

實境對話
A: Where is David?　大衛在哪裡？
B: He is parking his car in the **garage**.　他在車庫停車。

garden [ˋgardn̩]
名 花園

名詞複數	gardens

 實境對話
A: The rose **garden** is so gorgeous.　玫瑰花園是如此美麗。
B: Yes. I agree with you.　是的。我同意。

hall [hɔl]
名 大廳

名詞複數	halls
同義字	passage 門廳

 實境對話
A: What time are we going to meet?　我們什麼時候要見面？
B: Let's meet at 6 pm in the **hall**.　讓我們下午6點在大廳見面吧。

kitchen [ˋkɪtʃɪn]
名 廚房

名詞複數	kitchens
同義字	cook room 廚房

 實境對話
A: Mom is washing the dishes in the **kitchen**.　媽媽正在廚房洗碗。
B: Isn't it your turn?　不是輪到你嗎？

Part **1** 生活情境單字

living room [ˈlɪvɪŋ rum]
名 客廳

名詞複數 living rooms

 實境對話
A: How long has Rita been in the **living room**? 莉塔在客廳裡多久了？
B: For about half an hour. 約半小時。

room [rum]
名 房間

名詞複數 rooms
同義字 apartment [英] 房間

 實境對話
A: Your **room** is messy. 你的房間凌亂。
B: I will clean it on the weekend. 我週末會打掃。

study [ˈstʌdɪ]
名 書房 動 學習

動詞變化 studied, studied, studying, studies
名詞複數 studies

 實境對話
A: Why not go jogging with me later? 何不晚點跟我去跑步？
B: I need to **study** history. 我要讀歷史。

yard [jɑrd]
名 庭院

名詞複數 yards

 實境對話
A: Where did you get the bracelet? 你從哪裡得到手鍊？
B: At a **yard** sale. 在庭院舊貨出售。

balcony [ˈbælkənɪ]
名 陽臺

名詞複數 balconies

 實境對話
A: Ben is taking a rest on the **balcony**. 班在陽臺休息。
B: Really? It is hot. 真的嗎？很熱耶。

ceiling [ˈsilɪŋ]
名 天花板

名詞複數 ceilings
同義字 overhead 天花板

實境對話
A: Why are you staring up at the **ceiling**? 你為什麼盯著天花板？
B: I heard the sound of footsteps. 我聽到腳步聲。

door [dor]
名 門

名詞複數 doors
延伸片語 door to door 挨家挨戶
at the door 在門邊

 實境對話
A: Remember to lock the **door** before leaving. 記得鎖門才離開。
B: Okay. Remind me later. 好。待會兒提醒我。

downstairs
[ˈdaʊnˈstɛrz]
名 樓下 形 樓下的 副 樓下地

實境對話 A: Gary is waiting for you **downstairs.** 蓋瑞在樓下等你。
B: Oh! I have to hurry up. 哦！我要趕快。

floor [flor]
名 地板、（樓房的）層

名詞複數 floors
延伸片語 on the floor 在地板上
ground floor 一樓

實境對話 A: Where does Emma live? 艾瑪住哪裡？
B: She lives on the tenth **floor.** 她住在十樓。

gate [get]
名 大門、登機門

名詞複數 gates
同義字 door

實境對話 A: Flight 100 to London is now boarding at **Gate** 2.
飛往倫敦的100號班機現在請到2號登機門登機。
B: Let's hurry up. 我們快點。

roof [ruf]
名 屋頂、天花板

名詞複數 rooves
同義字 top 屋頂

實境對話 A: Frank is climbing onto the garage **roof.** 法蘭克爬到車庫屋頂。
B: It is dangerous. 很危險耶。

stairs [stɛrz]
名 樓梯

實境對話 A: There are no elevators in the apartment. 公寓沒有電梯。
B: Let's take the **stairs** then. 那我們就走樓梯吧。

upstairs
[ʌpˈstɛrz]
形 樓上的 名 樓上 副 樓上地

實境對話 A: Is the dog yours?
狗是你的嗎？
B: No. It belongs to the girl who lives **upstairs.**
不，牠屬於住在樓上女孩的。

wall [wɔl]
名 牆

名詞複數 walls 同義字 enclosure 圍牆
延伸片語 on the wall 在牆上
Wall Street 華爾街

實境對話 A: What are you going to do this afternoon? 你下午打算做什麼？
B: I am going to paint the **walls.** 我要粉刷牆壁。

Part **1** 生活情境單字

window [ˈwɪndo]
名 窗戶

名詞複數 windows
同義字 out of the window 不再受重視

實境對話
A: It is chilly today. Close the **window**, please. 今天很冷。請關窗。
B: OK. 好。

furniture
[ˈfɜnɪtʃɚ]
名 家具

實境對話
A: Doris is moving into a new apartment.
朵莉絲正搬到新公寓。
B: I think she needs to buy some new **furniture**.
我覺得她需要買一些新家具。

armchair
[ˈɑrmˌtʃɛr]
名 扶手椅子

名詞複數 armchairs

實境對話
A: How much is the **armchair**? 扶手椅多少錢？
B: It is five thousand dollars. 5000元。

bath [bæθ]
名 洗澡 動 洗澡

動詞變化 bathed, bathed, bathing, baths
同義字 shower 淋浴
延伸片語 take a bath 洗澡

實境對話
A: You have to take a **bath** before going to bed. 你睡前要洗澡。
B: But I am too tired to move. 但我太累了動不了。

bed [bɛd]
名 床

名詞複數 beds
延伸片語 in bed 在床上
go to bed 上床睡覺

實境對話
A: It is time to go to **bed**. 上床睡覺時間到了。
B: Come on. The night is still young. 拜託。還早的很。

bench [bɛntʃ]
名 長椅

名詞複數 benches
延伸片語 on the bench 坐板凳

實境對話
A: I am having tired feet. 我腳很痠。
B: You can sit on the **bench**. 你可以坐在長椅上。

bookcase
[ˈbukˌkes]
名 書櫃

名詞複數 bookcases

實境對話
A: There are many books in the **bookcase**. 書櫃有許多書。
B: I really enjoy reading. 我真的很喜歡閱讀。

chair [tʃɛr]
名 椅子

名詞複數 chairs
延伸片語 in the chair 處在主席地位

A: Who is the man sitting on the red **chair**? 坐在紅椅子上的是誰？
B: He is my professor. 他是我教授。

closet [ˈklɑzɪt]
名 壁櫥、衣櫥

名詞複數 closets
延伸片語 water closet 廁所

A: Hang your athletic jacket in the **closet**. 把你的運動夾克掛在衣櫥裡。
B: OK. 好的。

couch [kaʊtʃ]
名 長沙發

名詞複數 couches
延伸片語 on the couch 在沙發上
couch potato 成天躺著或坐在沙發上看電視的人

A: The **couch** is on sale. 長沙發在特價。
B: Wow, it is a good deal. 哇，這是一個很好的交易。

curtain [ˈkɝtn̩]
名 窗簾

名詞複數 curtains
延伸片語 behind the curtain 幕後、祕密

A: It is dark in the room. 房間內很暗。
B: I will pull back the **curtains**. 我將窗簾拉開。

desk [dɛsk]
名 書桌

名詞複數 desks
延伸片語 front desk 前臺
reception desk 接待處

A: I am looking for my dictionary. 我正在找我的字典。
B: It is on your **desk**. 在你的辦公桌上。

drawer [drɔr]
名 抽屜

名詞複數 drawers
延伸片語 top drawer 社會最上層
bottom drawer 嫁衣

A: Mom, where is my bank book? 媽媽，存摺在哪裡？
B: It is in the bottom **drawer** of the desk. 在書桌最底下的抽屜裡。

faucet [ˈfɔsɪt]
名 水龍頭

名詞複數 faucets

A: You forgot to turn the **faucet** off. 你忘了關水龍頭。
B: I am sorry. 我很抱歉。

lamp [læmp]
名 燈

名詞複數 lamps
同義字 light 燈
延伸片語 street lamp 路燈

 實境對話
A: Would you mind turning on the standard **lamp**? 你介意打開落地燈嗎？
B: No, but it is broken. 不介意，但是燈壞了。

light [laɪt]
名 光線、燈　形 輕的

名詞複數 lights　同義字 lamp 燈
延伸片語 in the light of 根據
　　　　 in light of 根據

 實境對話
A: What is your favorite color? 你最喜歡什麼顏色？
B: My favorite is **light** blue. 我最愛的顏色是淺藍。

mirror [ˈmɪrɚ]
名 鏡子

名詞複數 mirrors

實境對話
A: Are you ready to go now? 你準備好出發了嗎？
B: Wait a minute. Let me look at myself in the **mirror**. 等等。讓我照照鏡子。

shelf [ʃɛlf]
名 架子

名詞複數 shelves　同義字 bink 架子
延伸片語 on the shelf 束之高閣
　　　　 off the shelf 現成的

 實境對話
A: What is Kath busy doing? 凱絲在忙什麼？
B: She is busy putting some **shelves** in her study room. 她正忙著在她書房裝上幾個架子。

sink [sɪŋk]
名 水槽　動 沉下、陷於

動詞變化 sank, sank, sinking, sinks
同義字 tank 水槽
延伸片語 sink in 滲入
　　　　 sink into 陷入

 實境對話
A: He left his dirty plates in the **sink**. 他把髒碗盤留在水槽裡。
B: How lazy he was! 他真懶惰！

sofa [ˈsofə]
名 沙發

同義字 lounge 沙發

 實境對話
A: The **sofa** he bought is top-class. 他買的沙發是頂級的。
B: I can tell. 感覺得出來。

table [ˈtebl̩]
名 桌子

名詞複數 tables　同義字 desk 書桌
延伸片語 on the table 公開地
　　　　 at the table 吃飯時

 實境對話
A: How many glasses are there on the **table**? 桌上有多少杯子？
B: There are six glasses on it. 桌上有六個杯子。

tub [tʌb]
名 浴缸

名詞複數 tubs　同義字 bath 浴盆
延伸片語 in the tub 破產

 實境對話
A: Where did you find the cat? 你在哪裡找到貓？
B: It lay in the **tub**. 牠躺在浴缸。

blanket [`blæŋkɪt]
名 毯子

名詞複數 blankets
同義字 soogan 毛毯

 實境對話
A: It is chilly today. 今天真冷。
B: I think you need more **blankets**. 我覺得你需要更多的毯子。

carpet [`kɑrpɪt]
名 地毯

名詞複數 carpets　同義字 footcloth 地毯
延伸片語 on the carpet 再考慮中
red carpet 紅地毯

 實境對話
A: How to make the room look warmer? 要如何讓房間看起來溫暖一些呢？
B: You can fit **carpets**. 你可以鋪上地毯。

hanger [`hæŋɚ]
名 衣架

名詞複數 hangers

 實境對話
A: Can you buy some **hangers** for me? 你能為我買一些衣架嗎？
B: Sure. I need some to hang my shirts, too. 好。我也需要一些衣架掛我的衣服。

pillow [`pɪlo]
名 枕頭

名詞複數 pillows

 實境對話
A: They are a nice couple. 他們都是很棒的情侶。
B: They have **pillow** talk every night. 他們每晚枕邊細語。

sheet [ʃit]
名 床單、一張

同義字 slice 薄片

 實境對話
A: How many sheets of paper does the professor need? 教授需要幾張紙？
B: He needs three **sheets** of paper. 他需要三張紙。

toothbrush [`tuθ,brʌʃ]
名 牙刷

名詞複數 toothbrushes

 實境對話
A: You have to change your **toothbrush** once a month. 你必須每月換一次牙刷。
B: I don't think so. 我不這麼認為。

Part **1** 生活情境單字

soap [sop]
名 肥皂

| 延伸片語 | soap opera 肥皂劇 |
| | soft-soap （為讓某人做某事）説好聽的、奉承 |

 實境對話
A: The bar of **soap** smells great. 這塊肥皂很香。
B: Yes. It scents like jasmine. 是的。聞起來像茉莉花。

towel [taʊl]
名 毛巾

名詞複數 towels
同義字 tissue 毛巾
延伸片語 bath towel 浴巾

 實境對話
A: I am going swimming. 我將去游泳。
B: Bring a **towel** with you. 隨身帶條毛巾。

air conditioner [ɛr kənˈdɪʃənɚ]
名 空調

 實境對話
A: It is hot inside. Why not turn on the **air conditioner**?
室內很熱。為什麼不開空調？
B: Sorry. It's broken.
對不起。它壞了。

camera [ˈkæmərə]
名 相機

名詞複數 cameras
延伸片語 in camera 祕密地
on camera 在電視上播放

實境對話
A: What are your hobbies? 你有什麼嗜好？
B: I like to take a trip and take photos with a **camera**. 我喜歡旅行，並用相機拍照。

cassette [kæˈsɛt]
名 錄音帶

名詞複數 cassettes
延伸片語 audio cassette 錄音帶
radio cassette 卡帶式收錄音機

 實境對話
A: This is the first time that I see a **cassette** recorder.
這是我第一次看到了卡帶式錄音機。
B: Me, too. 我也一樣。

computer [kəmˈpjutɚ]
名 電腦

名詞複數 computers
延伸片語 computer game 電腦遊戲
desktop computer 桌上型電腦

 實境對話
A: How often do you play **computer** games? 你多久玩一次電腦遊戲？
B: Twice a week. 每週兩次。

dresser [ˈdrɛsɚ]
名 衣櫃

名詞複數 dressers

 實境對話
A: The **dresser** is made in France. 衣櫃是法國製的。
B: That's why it is costly. 這就是為什麼它非常昂貴。

dryer [ˈdraɪɚ]
名 烘衣機

名詞複數 dryers

 A: Don't put my dress in the **dryer**. 別把我的洋裝放到**烘衣機**。
B: I won't. 不會啦。

fan [fæn]
名 電風扇、扇子、粉絲

名詞複數 fans

 A: Please switch on the electric **fan**. 請打開電風扇。
B: But I have a cold. 但是我感冒了

flashlight [ˈflæʃˌlaɪt]
名 手電筒

名詞複數 flashlights

 A: You have three **flashlights**. 你有三個手電筒。
B: I think they are useful during blackouts. 我認為它們在停電時會很有用。

freezer [ˈfrizɚ]
名 冷藏室、冷凍庫

名詞複數 freezers
同義字 refrigerator 冰箱

 A: I'd like to have some ice cream. 我想吃冰淇淋耶。
B: You can get some yourself from the **freezer**. 你可以自己從冷凍庫拿一點來吃。

heater [ˈhitɚ]
名 暖氣機

名詞複數 heaters
同義字 warmer 加熱器

 A: What kind of **heater** is it? 這是什麼款式的**暖氣機**？
B: It is a storage **heater**. 那是續熱電暖器。

machine [məˈʃin]
名 機器

名詞複數 machines
同義字 robot 機器

 A: Do you know how to operate the **machine**? 你知道如何操作**機器**嗎？
B: Of course. 當然。

microwave [ˈmaɪkrəˌwev]
名 微波爐

名詞複數 microwaves
延伸片語 microwave oven 微波爐

 A: The coffee is cold. 咖啡冷掉了。
B: You can reheat it in the **microwave**. 你最好在**微波爐**加熱它。

Part **1** 生活情境單字

oven [ˋʌvən]
名 烤箱

名詞複數 ovens

A: Do you smell something strange?　你聞到什麼怪味嗎？
B: I forgot to take the cake out of the **oven**.　我忘了把蛋糕從烤箱拿出來。

radio [ˋredɪo]
名 收音機

名詞複數 radios
延伸片語　on the radio　在廣播中
　　　　　radio station　無線電臺

A: I can't concentrate on my study.　我不能集中精力讀書。
B: Sorry. I will turn off the **radio**.　對不起。我會關掉收音機。

refrigerator
[rɪˋfrɪdʒəˏretə]
名 電冰箱

名詞複數 refrigerators

A: I am so thirsty.　我很渴。
B: There are some coke in the **refrigerator**.　電冰箱裡有一些可樂。

speaker [ˋspikə]
名 喇叭

名詞複數 speakers
延伸片語　public speaker　演講者
　　　　　native speaker　說母語的人

A: What's the difference between these two CD players?　這兩台CD播放機有何區別呢？
B: This one has two **speakers**.　這台有兩個喇叭（揚聲器）。

stove [stov]
名 暖爐、小爐子

名詞複數 stoves

A: Why are you so sweaty?　你為何滿頭大汗？
B: I've been slaving over a hot **stove** all day.　我整天都在灼熱的爐子前忙呀。

tape [tep]
名 錄音帶

名詞複數 tapes

A: My idol is Andy Lau.　我的偶像是劉德華。
B: His new album is available on CD and **tape**.　他的新專輯有CD和錄音帶。

tape recorder
[tep rɪˋkɔrdə]
名 錄音機

名詞複數 tape recorders

A: What are you going to shop?　你打算購物嗎？
B: I am going to buy a **tape recorder** so that I won't miss any call.
　 我準備買一台電話錄音機。我才不會錯過任何來電。

telephone (phone)
[ˈtɛləˌfon] 名 電話

名詞複數 telephones

實境對話
A: You forgot to fill in your **telephone** number. 您忘了填寫您的電話號碼。
B: Can I just fill in my cell phone number? 我可以只填我的手機號碼嗎？

television (TV) [ˈtɛləˌvɪʒən]
名 電視機

名詞複數 televisions
延伸片語 digital television 數位電視
network television 網路電視

實境對話
A: Don usually watches **television** after school. How about you? 丹平時放學後看電視。你呢？
B: I usually do my homework after school. 我平時放學後寫作業。

video [ˈvɪdɪo]
名 錄影機、錄影帶

名詞複數 videos

實境對話
A: I think the wedding is a good subject for **video**. 我認為婚禮是很好的錄影主題。
B: I agree with you. 非常同意。

washing machine
[ˈwɑʃɪŋ məˈʃin] 名 洗衣機

名詞複數 washing machines

實境對話
A: The **washing machine** is broken. 洗衣機壞了。
B: Did you call someone to repair it? 你有叫人來修嗎？

basket [ˈbæskɪt]
名 籃子

名詞複數 baskets

實境對話
A: Where do you put the apples? 蘋果你放在哪裡？
B: I put them in the **basket**. 我把它們放在籃子裡。

brick [brɪk]
名 磚塊

名詞複數 bricks

實境對話
A: Your house is very traditional. 你的房子很傳統。
B: Because it is built of **bricks**. 因為它是用磚塊蓋的。

Part **1** 生活情境單字

bucket [ˋbʌkɪt]
名 水桶

名詞複數 buckets

實境對話
A: Where can I wash my hands? 我要在哪兒洗手？
B: Do you see a **bucket** of water over there? 有沒有看到那兒的一桶水？

candle [ˋkændl̩]
名 蠟燭

名詞複數 candles
延伸片語 burn the candle at both ends 過度勞累
cannot hold a candle to somebody 不如……好

實境對話
A: Make a wish before blowing out the **candle**. 吹蠟燭前先許願。
B: I wish to pass the exam. 我希望考試及格。

hammer [ˋhæmɚ]
名 鐵錘

名詞複數 hammers

實境對話
A: It is noisy. 很吵。
B: Jay is hitting nails with a **hammer**. 傑用鐵錘敲釘子。

housework [ˋhausˏwɝk]
名 家務、家事

延伸片語 do housework 做家務

實境對話
A: Do your **housework** before taking a rest. 家務做完再休息。
B: I am too tired to do anything. 我太累無法做任何事情。

key [ki]
名 鑰匙

名詞複數 keys
延伸片語 key somebody/something to something
使某人（或某事）適合於某事

實境對話
A: Bill left his **key** in the house. 比爾把鑰匙留在屋裡。
B: He was so careless. 他真粗心。

mat [mæt]
名 墊子

名詞複數 mats 同義字 cushion 墊子
延伸片語 on the mat 受責備
floor mat 地毯

實境對話
A: Did you wipe your feet on the **mat**? 你的腳有在墊子上擦乾嗎？
B: I am sorry. I forgot. 抱歉我忘了。

needle [ˋnidl̩]
名 針

名詞複數 needles
延伸片語 pins and needles 如坐針氈
a needle in a haystack 幾乎不可能找到的東西

實境對話
A: Where is the Space **Needle**? 太空針塔在哪裡？
B: It is in Seattle. 西雅圖。

pan [pæn]
名 平底鍋

名詞複數	pans
延伸片語	flash in the pan　曇花一現
	pots and pans　炊事用具

 實境對話
A: It smells good.　聞起來很香。
B: Mom is frying some meat and vegetables in the **pan**.　媽媽在平底鍋裡炒青菜和肉。

pot [pɑt]
名 一罐、一壺

名詞複數	pots
延伸片語	hot pot　火鍋
	keep the pot boiling　謀生

 實境對話
A: I need a **pot** of jam.　我要一罐果醬。
B: Here you are.　給你。

teapot [ˈtiˌpɑt]
名 茶壺

名詞複數	teapots
同義字	teakettle 茶壺
延伸片語	a tempest in a teapot　小題大作

實境對話
A: Sam looks very angry.　山姆看起來很生氣。
B: His anger is just **a tempest in a teapot**.　他在小題大作。

toilet [ˈtɔɪlɪt]
名 廁所

名詞複數	toilets
同義字	bathroom 盥洗室

 實境對話
A: Where is Vic?　維克在哪兒？
B: He went to the **toilet**.　他去了廁所。

wok [wɑk]
名 鍋

名詞複數	woks

 實境對話
A: The **wok** is on sale.　這鍋子在打折。
B: Maybe I can buy it for my mom.　也許我可以買給我的媽媽。

build [bɪld]
動 建築

動詞變化	built, built, building, builts
同義字	establish 建立
延伸片語	build up　增進
	build on　依賴

實境對話
A: The castle is **built** of stone.　城堡用石頭蓋的。
B: I don't think so.　我不這麼認為。

clean [klin]
形 乾淨的 動 清理

動詞變化 cleaned, cleaned, cleaning, cleans
形容詞變化 cleaner, the cleanest　同義字 pure 清潔的
延伸片語 clean up 清理

實境對話
A: How often do you **clean** your study?　你多久清理一次你的書房？
B: Once a week.　每週一次。

decorate ['dɛkəˌret]
動 裝飾

動詞變化 decorated, decorated, decorating, decorates
同義字 paint 裝飾
延伸片語 decorate with 以……來修飾
decorate the house 裝飾房間

實境對話
A: Christmas is coming.　聖誕節即將到來。
B: I will **decorate** my apartment with trees and flowers.　我將用樹木和花朵裝飾我的公寓。

design [dɪ'zaɪn]
動 設計 名 圖案、設計

動詞變化 designed, designed, designing, designs
同義字 project 設計
延伸片語 interior design 室內設計

實境對話
A: I don't like the restaurant.　我不喜歡這間餐廳。
B: It is badly **designed**.　很糟糕的設計。

fix [fɪks]
動 修理

動詞變化 fixed, fixed, fixing, fixes
同義字 mend 修理
延伸片語 fix on 確定

實境對話
A: Do you know how to **fix** the radio?　你知道如何修理收音機嗎？
B: I am not sure.　我不確定。

repair [rɪ'pɛr]
動 修理 名 修理

動詞變化 repaired, repaired, repairing, repairs
同義字 mend 修理

實境對話
A: Why didn't you **repair** the TV?　你為什麼不修電視？
B: Not worth it.　不值得。

sweep [swip]
動 清掃 名 掃除

動詞變化 swept, swept, sweeping, sweeps
同義字 clean 清理
延伸片語 sweep away 清除
clean sweep 全勝

實境對話
A: When will we **sweep** the floor?　我們何時才能掃地？
B: When I am free.　當我有空。

wash [wɑʃ]
動 清洗

動詞變化 washed, washed, washing, washes
同義字 clean 清洗
延伸片語 wash out 淘汰

實境對話
A: Larry helps Mom **wash** the dishes after supper.　賴瑞晚餐後會幫媽媽洗碗。
B: He is nice.　他很乖。

address [əˈdrɛs]
名 地址、演説

| 延伸片語 | home address　家庭住址 |

實境
對話　A: Fill out the form before the interview.　面試前請先填寫表格。
B: Do I need to write my **address**?　我需要寫我的**地址**嗎？

road [rod]
名 道路

| 名詞複數 | roads | 同義字 | street 街道 |

延伸片語　on the road　在旅途中
　　　　　in the road　擋路

實境
對話　A: What are Neil and Ken doing?　奈爾和肯在做什麼？
B: They are taking a walk on the **road.**　他們在路上散步。

street [strit]
名 街道

| 名詞複數 | streets | 同義字 | road 道路 |

延伸片語　down the street　在街邊
　　　　　in the street　在街上

實境
對話　A: I will meet Amy tonight.
　　　我今晚將見艾咪。
B: Don't come home late. It is dangerous to walk alone on the **streets** in the dark.
　　不要太晚回家。黑夜中獨自一人在**街道**上走路是很危險的。

練習試試看

用簡單的小測驗，驗收一下，單字記住了嗎？

( ) 1 basement

( ) 2 garden

( ) 3 kitchen

( ) 4 balcony

( ) 5 stairs

( ) 6 bath

( ) 7 chair

( ) 8 curtain

( ) 9 light

( ) 10 mirror

( ) 11 pillow

( ) 12 camera

( ) 13 freezer

( ) 14 radio

( ) 15 basket

( ) 16 candle

( ) 17 needle

( ) 18 toilet

( ) 19 clean

( ) 20 address

A 枕頭	B 樓梯	C 乾淨的	D 燈	E 花園	F 相機	G 收音機
H 窗簾	I 陽臺	J 冷藏室	K 地下室	L 洗澡	M 鏡子	N 椅子
O 針	P 廁所	Q 地址	R 蠟燭	S 廚房	T 籃子	

答案

1(K) 2(E) 3(S) 4(I) 5(B) 6(L) 7(N) 8(H) 9(D) 10(M) 11(A) 12(F) 13(J) 14(G)
15(T) 16(R) 17(O) 18(P) 19(C) 20(Q)

Track 110

college [ˈkɑlɪdʒ]
名 大學、學院

名詞複數 colleges
同義字 university 大學

 A: When did you graduate from the **college**? 你什麼時候從大學畢業？
B: In 2009. 在2009年。

elementary school
[ˌɛləˈmɛntərɪ skul]
名 小學

 A: Does your daughter go to school yet?
你女兒上學沒？
B: Yes, she goes to an **elementary school** in our neighborhood.
上學了，她在我們家附近一間小學就讀。

junior high school
[ˈdʒunjɚ haɪ skul]
名 國中、初中

 A: Gary is a lazy **junior high school** student.
蓋瑞是懶惰國中學生。
B: He spends too much time playing video games.
他花太多時間玩電玩。

kindergarten
[ˈkɪndɚˌgɑrtn̩] 名 幼稚園

名詞複數 kindergartens

 A: Choosing a good **kindergarten** is important. 選擇一個好的幼稚園是重要的。
B: You are right. 你是對的。

senior high school
[ˈsinjɚ haɪ skul]
名 高中

 A: Ben sleeps five hours a day.
班每天睡五個小時。
B: He is a hard-working **senior high school** student.
他是一個用功的高中學生。

university
[ˌjunəˈvɝsətɪ] 名 大學

名詞複數 universities
同義字 college 大學

 A: What do you major in **university**? 你大學主修什麼？
B: I major in history. 我主修歷史。

campus
['kæmpəs]
名 校園

名詞複數 campuses　同義字 schoolyard 校園
延伸片語 on the campus　校園內
　　　　on campus　在校內

實境對話
A: Do you live in **campus?**　你住在校園？
B: No. I rent an apartment.　不，我租房子。

classroom
['klæs,rum]
名 教室

名詞複數 classrooms　同義字 schoolroom 教室

實境對話
A: The **classroom** is tidy.　教室很整潔。
B: Students clean it every day.　學生每天打掃。

guard [gɑrd]
名 警衛 動 保衛、看守

動詞變化 guarded, guarded, guarding, guards
名詞複數 guards　同義字 alert 警戒
延伸片語 guard against　防止
　　　　on guard　警惕

實境對話
A: How does Fred earn his living?　弗萊德靠什麼維生？
B: He is a **guard.**　他當警衛。

gym [dʒɪm]
名 體育、體育館

名詞複數 gyms

實境對話
A: What are you going to do later?　你待會兒要做什麼？
B: I am going to play basketball in the **gym.**　我會去體育館打籃球。

playground
['ple,graund]　名 操場

名詞複數 playgrounds

實境對話
A: It is cool.　很冷耶。
B: Let's go running on the **playground.**　讓我們去操場跑步。

library ['laɪ,brɛrɪ]
名 圖書館

名詞複數 libraries

實境對話
A: Please be quiet in the **library.**　圖書館內請安靜。
B: Sorry.　抱歉。

class [klæs]
名 教室、上課

名詞複數 classes
延伸片語 in class　上課中
　　　　first class　頭等、最高級

實境對話
A: Was Sally absent from **class?**　莎莉上課缺席嗎？
B: Yes. She caught a cold.　是的。她感冒了。

seesaw [ˈsiˌsɔ]
名 蹺蹺板

同義字 teeterboard 蹺蹺板

實境對話
A: The **seesaw** is very interesting. 蹺蹺板很有趣。
B: Yes, but we are too old to play. 是的，但是我們太老不能玩。

slide [slaɪd]
● 溜滑梯

名詞複數 slides
延伸片語 on the slide 日益惡化
slide down 塌陷、下滑

實境對話
A: Going down the **slide** is exciting. 玩溜滑梯很刺激。
B: Be careful. 小心點。

blackboard
[ˈblækˌbord]
名 黑板

名詞複數 blackboards
同義字 chalkboard 黑板

實境對話
A: Mr. Wang is writing a sentence on the **blackboard**. 王老師在黑板上寫句子。
B: I can't see clearly. 我看不清楚。

book [buk]
名 書

名詞複數 books
延伸片語 book on 有關……的書

實境對話
A: What do you usually do when you are free? 你平時有空時做什麼？
B: I usually read a **book**. 我平時看書。

chalk [tʃɔk]
名 粉筆

名詞複數 chalks
延伸片語 chalk it up 記帳
know chalk from cheese 有判斷力

實境對話
A: Can you lend me a piece of **chalk**? 你能借我粉筆嗎？
B: Here you are. 這裡。

crayon [ˈkreən]
名 蠟筆

名詞複數 crayons
同義字 pastels 蠟筆

實境對話
A: What is Little Johnny doing? 小強尼在做什麼？
B: He is drawing with a **crayon**. 他用蠟筆畫圖。

diary [ˈdaɪərɪ]
名 日記

名詞複數 diaries　同義字 journal 日誌
延伸片語 keep one's dairy 記日記

實境對話
A: Do you keep a **diary**? 你寫日記嗎？
B: No, I don't. 不，我不寫日記。

Chapter **12** 學校及學習活動 School

dictionary
[ˋdɪkʃənˌɛrɪ]
名 字典

名詞複數 dictionaries
同義字 lexicon 字典

實境對話
A: What does the word "encyclopedia" mean? 「百科全書」是什麼意思？
B: I am not sure. Let me look it up in the **dictionary**. 我不知道。讓我查一下**字典**。

envelope
[ˋɛnvəˌlop]
名 信封

名詞複數 envelopes
同義字 cover 信封
延伸片語 red envelope 紅包
push out the envelope 加強操作能力

實境對話
A: You forgot to write the sender on the **envelope**. 你忘了寫信封上的寄件人。
B: Oh, I am such a muddlehead. 噢，我真是個糊塗蟲。

eraser [ɪˋresɚ]
名 橡皮擦

名詞複數 erasers

實境對話
A: There are some errors in your homework. 你作業上有一些錯誤。
B: I need an **eraser** to correct them. 我需要一個**橡皮擦**來訂正。

glasses [ˋglæsɪz]
名 眼鏡

實境對話
A: You look smarter when you wear **glasses**.
當你戴眼鏡時看起來更聰明。
B: That's why I usually wear them.
這就是為什麼我常常戴。

glue [glu]
名 膠水　動 膠合、黏牢

實境對話
A: Can you **glue** the broken mirror together?
你能把破碎的鏡子黏起來嗎？
B: No problem. 沒問題。

ink [ɪŋk]
名 墨水

實境對話
A: The letter looks neat. 信看起來整齊。
B: It is written in **ink**. 這是墨水寫的。

letter [ˋlɛtɚ]
名 信件

名詞複數 letters
延伸片語 by letter 以書信形式
to the letter 嚴格地

實境對話
A: I am going to the post office. 我要去郵局。
B: Please send this **letter** for me. 請幫我寄信。

|131|

magazine
[ˌmæɡəˈzin]
名 雜誌

名詞複數 magazines
延伸片語 weekly magazine 週刊

 A: Do you enjoy reading **magazines**? 你喜歡讀雜誌嗎？
B: Not really. 不盡然。

map [mæp]
名 地圖

名詞複數 maps
延伸片語 off the map 不重要的
map out 在地圖上標出

 A: I will take a trip to Australia. 我要去澳洲旅行。
B: Don't forget to bring a **map** with you. 別忘了隨身帶地圖。

marker [mɑrkɚ]
名 書籤

名詞複數 markers

 A: The **marker** looks very classical. 書籤看起來很古典。
B: Yes. It is from my grandma. 是的。這是我奶奶的。

notebook
[ˈnotˌbʊk] 名 筆記本

名詞複數 notebooks

 A: Eddie took notes of everything in the **notebook**. 艾迪在筆記本寫下每個重點。
B: He is hard-working. 他很勤勞。

page [pedʒ]
名 頁

名詞複數 pages
延伸片語 web page 網頁
page in 置入分頁

 A: Turn to **page** 100. 翻到100頁。
B: It is a blank **page**. 這是一個空白頁。

paper [ˈpepɚ]
名 紙張

延伸片語 on paper 以書面形式

A: I need a piece of **paper**. 我需要一張紙。
B: I only have a piece of brown **paper**. 我只有一張牛皮紙。

pen [pɛn]
名 鋼筆

名詞複數 pens
延伸片語 put pen to paper 開始寫
ball pen 圓珠筆

 A: Leon gave me a **pen** as a birthday present. 李奧給了我一支鋼筆作為生日禮物。
B: It looks expensive. 它看起來昂貴。

pencil [ˈpɛnsḷ]
名 鉛筆

名詞複數 pencils 鉛筆

 A: I need a **pencil**. 我需要一支鉛筆。
B: I will buy one on my way home. 回家時我順便買。

pencil box (pencil case) [ˈpɛnsḷ bɑks]
名 文具盒、鉛筆盒

名詞複數 pencil boxes

 A: I lost my **pencil box**. 我遺失我的鉛筆盒。
B: Don't worry. Check it again. 不用擔心。再檢查看看。

picture [ˈpɪktʃɚ]
名 圖片、畫作

名詞複數 pictures
延伸片語 in the picture 在圖中
the picture of 是……的化身

 A: Let's hang the **picture** of castles on the wall. 我們來把這城堡的畫掛在牆上吧。
B: Great! It is Dave's favorite. 好啊！這是大衛最愛的呢。

postcard [ˈpostˌkɑrd] 名 明信片

名詞複數 postcards

 A: I will send you a **postcard** after I arrive in Seattle. 當我到西雅圖，我會寄給你一張明信片。
B: I look forward to it. 我很期待。

present [ˈprɛznt]
名 禮物

名詞複數 presents

 A: What **presents** do you want for your birthday? 生日想要什麼禮物？
B: A handbag or a bracelet. 手提袋或手鍊。

ruler [rul]
名 尺

名詞複數 rulers

 A: The line is not straight. 線不直。
B: I didn't draw it with a **ruler**. 我沒有用尺畫。

sheet [ʃit]
名 紙片

名詞複數 sheets
同義字 slice 薄片

 A: Write down your information in a **sheet** of paper. 在紙上寫下個人資料。
B: For what? 為什麼？

textbook
[ˈtɛkstˌbʊk] 名 教科書

名詞複數 textbooks
同義字 coursebook 教科書

實境
對話
A: Linda spends two hours on the history **textbook** every day.
琳達每天花兩小時看歷史教科書。
B: She is a good student. 她是一個好學生。

workbook
[ˈwɛkˌbʊk] 名 練習本

名詞複數 workbooks

實境
對話
A: Why is your **workbook** so dirty? 為何你的練習本這麼髒？
B: I carelessly spilt some juice onto it. 杯中的果汁灑出來，濺到練習本上。

course [kors]
名 課程

名詞複數 courses 同義字 process 過程
延伸片語 of course 當然
in the course of 在……過程中

實境
對話
A: What **courses** do you take? 你修什麼課程？
B: Math, History and American Literature. 數學，歷史和美國文學。

art [ɑrt]
名 美術

實境
對話
A: My neighbor, Mark, is an art critic.
我的鄰居，馬克，是藝術評論家。
B: He must be fond of **art**.
他一定是喜歡藝術。

Chinese [tʃaɪˈniz]
名 中文、中國人
形 中國人的、中國的

實境
對話
A: Is Willy **Chinese**? 威利是中國人嗎？
B: Yes. He is from Hong Kong. 是的。他是來自香港。

English [ˈɪŋglɪʃ]
名 英語

實境
對話
A: How long have you studied **English**? 你英語學多久？
B: For three years. 三年。

geography
[dʒɪˈɑgrəfɪ] 名 地理

實境
對話
A: Emma got a degree in **geography**.
艾瑪拿到地理學位。
B: I can't believe it. I thought she was just a senior high school student.
我不相信。我以為她只是一個高中生。

Part 1 生活情境單字

history [ˈhɪstrɪ]
名 歷史

實境對話 A: Vic is bored with **history**. 維克認為歷史很無聊。
B: He is bored with math, too. 他也認為數學很無聊。

biology [baɪˈɑlədʒɪ]
名 生物

實境對話 A: **Biology** is a difficult subject. 生物學是很難的學科。
B: Not me. I think it is pretty fun. 我不認為。我認為非常有趣。

chemistry [ˈkɛmɪstrɪ]
名 化學、化學特性

實境對話 A: What is the **chemistry** of copper? 銅的化學特性是什麼？
B: Actually, I have no idea. 其實，我不知道。

physics [ˈfɪzɪks]
名 物理

實境對話 A: Don't you think the laws of **physics** are complex?
你不認為**物理**定律很複雜嗎？
B: Exactly.
沒錯。

language [ˈlæŋgwɪdʒ] 名 語言

名詞複數 languages

實境對話 A: How many **languages** can you speak? 你會說多少種語言？
B: Two. Mandarin and English. 兩種。中文和英語。

law [lɔ]
名 法律

名詞複數 laws
延伸片語 by law 據法律
civil law 民法

實境對話 A: Is it against the **law** to hit a student in Taiwan? 台灣體罰學生是違法的？
B: Right. It is illegal. 沒錯。是不合法的。

math (mathematics) [mæθ]
數學

實境對話 A: My **math** is better than history. 我的數學比歷史好。
B: I am the complete opposite. 我完全相反。

music [ˈmjuzɪk]
名 音樂

延伸片語 pop music 流行音樂
folk music 民俗音樂

 A: What types of **music** do you like? 你喜歡什麼類型的音樂？
B: I like pop **music** and jazz. 我喜歡流行音樂和爵士樂。

PE (physical education)
[pi i] 名 體育

 A: I am good at sports. 我擅長運動。
B: You must like **PE** class. 你一定很喜歡體育課。

science [ˈsaɪəns]
名 科學

 A: The computer belongs to modern **science**.
電腦屬於現代科學。
B: It is a marvel.
那是一種奇蹟。

social science
[ˈsoʃəl ˈsaɪəns]
名 社會科學

 A: I got an F in **social science**. 我社會科學不及格。
B: Didn't you prepare for it? 你沒準備嗎？

cheer leader
[tʃɪr ˈlidɚ]
名 啦啦隊隊長

名詞複數 cheer leaders

 A: Do you know the **cheer leader**? 你認識啦啦隊隊長嗎？
B: Yes, she is my neighbor. 是的，她是我的鄰居。

class leader
[klæs ˈlidɚ] 名 班長

名詞複數 class leaders

 A: The **class leader** is seldom late for class. 班長上課很少遲到。
B: Only once, I guess. 只有一次，我猜。

classmate
[ˈklæsˌmet] 名 同學

名詞複數 classmates

 A: Who is the tall boy over there? 在那裡的高大的男孩是誰？
B: He is my **classmate**, Johnny. 他是我的同學，強尼。

Part **1** 生活情境單字

friend [frɛnd]

名詞複數 friends

名 朋友

 A: Helen falls in love with a net **friend**. 海倫愛上了一個網友。
B: Are you kidding? 你在開玩笑吧？

principal [ˈprɪnsəpl̩]

名詞複數 principals

名 校長

 A: The **principal** had a car accident this morning. 校長今天上午出車禍。
B: Is he okay? 他還好吧？

student [ˈstjudn̩t]

名詞複數 students

名 學生

 A: How many **students** are there in your class? 你班上有多少學生？
B: Only twenty. 只有二十個。

teacher [ˈtitʃɚ]

名詞複數 teachers

名 教師

A: Mrs. White is very patient and friendly. 白女士是非常有耐心和友善的。
B: She is the most popular **teacher**. 她是最受歡迎的老師。

answer [ˈænsɚ]

動詞變化 answered, answered, answering, answers
同義字 reply 回答
延伸片語 answer for 因……而受罰
in answer to 回答

動 回答

 A: Can you **answer** my question? 你能回答我的問題？
B: Sorry, can you repeat it? 對不起，你能重複一次嗎？

ask [æsk]

動詞變化 asked, asked, asking, asks
同義字 question 詢問
延伸片語 ask for 請求
ask around 四處打聽

動 問

A: Do you have any brothers? 你有沒有兄弟？
B: Don't **ask** me about my family. 不要問我家人的事情。

behave [bɪˈhev]

動詞變化 behaved, behaved, behaving, behaves
延伸片語 behave as if you own the place
喧賓奪主

動 表現

 A: The teacher likes Thomas very much. 老師很喜歡湯瑪士。
B: He **behaves** well. 他表現好。

Chapter 12 學校及學習活動 School

explain [ɪkˋsplen]
動 表達、解釋

動詞變化 explained, explained, explaining, explains
延伸片語 explain away 通過解釋消除

實境對話
A: Can you **explain** the rules of the contest first? 你能先**解釋**比賽規則嗎？
B: OK. Listen carefully. 可以。仔細聽。

fail [fel]
動 失敗、不及格

動詞變化 failed, failed, failing, fails
延伸片語 fail in 失敗
without fail 務必、一定

實境對話
A: Ken looks upset. 肯看起來心煩意亂。
B: He **failed** the test again. 他考試又不及格。

learn [lɝn]
動 學習

動詞變化 learned, learned, learning, learns
同義字 learn 學習
延伸片語 learn from 向……學習

實境對話
A: To **learn** a skill is very important. 學習一技之長是非常重要的。
B: Exactly. I totally agree with you. 沒錯。我完全同意你的看法。

listen [ˋlɪsṇ]
動 聽

動詞變化 listened, listened, listening, listens
同義字 hear 聽見
延伸片語 listen for 傾聽
listen in 收聽

實境對話
A: What are you **listening** to? 你在聽什麼？
B: I am **listening** to the radio. 我在聽收音機。

mark [mɑrk]
動 標誌 **名** 符號

動詞變化 marked, marked, marking, marks
名詞複數 marks
同義字 signal 標記
延伸片語 mark on 標上

實境對話
A: You made a tiny mistake. 你犯了微小的錯誤。
B: You mean the punctuation **marks**? 你指的是標點**符號**？

pass [pæs]
動 及格

動詞變化 passed, passed, passing, passes
延伸片語 pass through 穿過
pass on 傳遞

實境對話
A: You study hard. 你很認真。
B: If I can't **pass** the exam, my parents will be angry. 如果我無法考試**及格**，我父母會生氣。

point to [pɔɪnt tu]
動 指向

動詞變化 pointed, pointed, pointing, points
同義字 direct 指向
延伸片語 point out 指明
at this point 此時此刻

實境對話
A: What is the building that John is **pointing to**? 約翰正**指著**的那幢建築物是什麼？
B: It's the most famous tourist attraction in the city. 那是這城市最有名的觀光景點。

Part 1 生活情境單字

practice
[ˋpræktɪs]
動 練習 名 練習

動詞變化 practiced, practiced, practicing, practices
同義字 exercise 練習
延伸片語 in practice 實際上
practice of 有……的習慣

實境對話
A: You play the piano well. 你鋼琴彈得很好。
B: I **practice** playing it every day. 我每天都練習彈琴。

prepare [priˋpɛr]
動 準備

動詞變化 prepared, prepared, preparing, prepares
延伸片語 prepare for 為……準備
prepare the way 排除障礙

實境對話
A: Why didn't you **prepare** for the math exam? 你為什麼沒準備數學考試？
B: I went shopping with my cousin. 我和表弟去逛街。

pronounce
[prəˋnaʊns]
動 發音

動詞變化 pronounced, pronounced, pronouncing, pronounces
延伸片語 pronounce on 對……發表意見

實境對話
A: The "b" in climb is not **pronounced**. climb的b不發音。
B: I see. 我懂了。

punish [ˋpʌnɪʃ]
動 懲罰

動詞變化 punished, punished, punishing, punishes
同義字 penalise 懲罰
延伸片語 punish for 處罰
punish with 用……懲罰

實境對話
A: Have your parents ever **punished** you? 你的父母處罰過你嗎？
B: Never. 不曾。

read [rid]
動 閱讀

動詞變化 read, read, reading, reads

實境對話
A: What kind of books do you enjoy **reading**? 你喜歡閱讀什麼樣的書？
B: Mysterious novels. 懸疑小說。

repeat [rɪˋpit]
動 重複

動詞變化 repeated, repeated, repeating, repeats
延伸片語 repeat oneself 不自覺的重複

實境對話
A: Sorry. Could you **repeat** that question? 很抱歉。你能重複這個問題嗎？
B: It is not important. 這並不重要。

review [rɪˋvju]
動 複習

動詞變化 reviewed, reviewed, reviewing, reviews
同義字 inspect 回顧

實境對話
A: What did you do last night? 你昨晚做什麼？
B: I **reviewed** my notes. 我複習筆記。

say [se]
動 説

動詞變化 said, said, saying, says
同義字 speak 説話
延伸片語 say to oneself 自言自語
that is to say 換言之

實境對話
A: I don't like Maggie. 我不喜歡瑪姬。
B: Me, either. She always **says** that she is the best. 我也是。她總是說她是最好的。

speak [spik]
動 説話

動詞變化 spoke, spoken, speaking, speaks
同義字 talk 談話
延伸片語 speak of 談到
so to speak 可以說

實境對話
A: Can you **speak** French? 你能講法語？
B: A little bit. 一點點。

spell [spɛl]
動 拼寫

動詞變化 spelled, spelled, spelling, spells
同義字 talk 談話
延伸片語 spell out 講清楚
under a spell 被迷住

實境對話
A: How do you **spell** your name? 你如何拼寫你的名字？
B: A-l-e-x, Alex. A - l - e - x，Alex。

study [ˈstʌdɪ]
動 學習

動詞變化 studied, studied, studying, studies
同義字 learn 學習

實境對話
A: How about going to the movies tonight? 今晚看電影如何？
B: I am afraid I can't go. I have to **study** history. 我恐怕不能去。我要讀歷史。

talk [tɔk]
動 談話

動詞變化 talked, talked, talking, talks
同義字 tell 告訴
延伸片語 talk about 談論
talk on 繼續談論

實境對話
A: We **talked** on the phone over two hours. 我們在電話上談了兩個多小時。
B: You are talkative. 你很健談。

teach [titʃ]
動 教、講授

動詞變化 taught, taught, teaching, teaches
同義字 enlighten 教導
延伸片語 teach oneself 自學

實境對話
A: The accident has **taught** him a lesson. 這次事故給了他上了一課。
B: He has paid for it. 他付出代價了。

underline [ˌʌndɚˈlaɪn]
動 劃線

動詞變化 underlined, underlined, underlining, underlines
同義字 emphasize 強調

實境對話
A: Where are the key words? 關鍵字在哪裡？
B: They are **underlined**. 它們有劃底線。

Part 1 生活情境單字

understand
[ˌʌndɚˈstænd]
動 理解

動詞變化 understood, understood, understanding, understands
同義字 seize 理解

 A: If you don't **understand**, raise your hand.　如果你不**理解**，請舉手。
B: I have one more question.　我有一個問題。

write [raɪt]
動 書寫

動詞變化 wrote, written, writing, writes
延伸片語 write about 寫到
write down 寫下

 A: Who **wrote** Harry Potter?　哈利波特是誰寫的？
B: A British author, J.K. Rowling.　英國作家J.K.羅琳。

alphabet
[ˈælfəˌbɛt]　**名** 字母表

 A: What kind of **alphabet** is it?　這是何種**字母表**？
B: It is manual **alphabet**.　這是聾啞手語**字母表**。

conversation
[kɑnvɚˈseʃən]
名 談話

名詞複數 conversations
同義字 dialogue 對話

 A: Dr. Brown had a long **conversation** with Kate last night.
布朗博士昨晚和凱特進行了長時間的談話。
B: What's wrong?
這是怎麼回事？

exam [ɪgˈzæm]
名 考試

名詞複數 exams　同義字 test 測試
延伸片語 final exam 期末考試
take an exam 參加考試

 A: What did you do last night?　你昨晚做什麼？
B: I prepared for the math **exam**.　我準備數學考試。

example
[ɪgˈzæmpl̩]　**名** 範例

名詞複數 examples　同義字 sample 例子
延伸片語 for example 例如
set an example 舉例子

 A: I don't get it.　我不瞭解。
B: I can give you an **example** of what I just said.　我可以舉例來解釋我剛說的。

exercise
[ˈɛksɚˌsaɪz]
名 練習

名詞複數 exercises
同義字 practice 練習
延伸片語 take exercise 做練習
do exercise 鍛鍊

實境對話
A: My English is not good. 我的英語不好。
B: Maybe you should do more grammar **exercises**. 也許你應該做更多的文法練習。

final [ˈfaɪnl̩]
名 期末考、決賽 形 最後的

同義字 last 最後的
延伸片語 cup final 總決賽
in the final analysis 歸根結底

實境對話
A: When is our **final** exam? 我們期末考試是何時？
B: It is on June 25. 6月25日。

grade [gred]
名 成績、年級、年紀

名詞複數 grades 同義字 degree 等級
延伸片語 at grade 在同一水平面上
top grade 最高級

實境對話
A: Alice got good **grades** in her exams. 愛莉絲考試成績很好。
B: She studied really hard. 她很用功。

homework
[ˈhomˌwɝk]
名 家庭作業

同義字 schoolwork 作業
延伸片語 do homework 寫作業

實境對話
A: Can you finish your **homework** before supper? 你能在晚飯前完成你的功課嗎？
B: I am afraid I can't. 我恐怕不能。

knowledge
[ˈnɑlɪdʒ] 名 知識

同義字 awareness 意識

實境對話
A: Do you like Willy? 你喜歡威利嗎？
B: Yes. He has a wide **knowledge** of art. 是的。他藝術知識廣博。

lesson [ˈlɛsn̩]
名 課程

名詞複數 lessons 同義字 class 課程
延伸片語 learn a lesson 受到教訓

實境對話
A: **Lesson** 4 is difficult. 第四課很難。
B: **Lesson** 5 is more difficult. 第五課更難。

poem [ˈpoɪm]
名 詩歌

名詞複數 poems
同義字 poetry 詩歌

實境對話
A: Is this a lyric **poem**? 這是抒情詩嗎？
B: No, it is a narrative **poem**. 不，這是敘事詩。

Part 1 生活情境單字

problem
['prɑbləm]
名 問題

名詞複數 problems　同義字 question 問題
延伸片語 no problem　沒問題
big problem　大問題、大麻煩

實境對話
A: Would you please pick me up at the train station tonight?
請你今晚到火車站接我？
B: No problem.
沒問題。

question
['kwɛstʃən]
名 問題

名詞複數 questions
同義字 problem 問題
延伸片語 out of the question　不可能
out of question　毫無疑問

實境對話
A: Raise your hand if your have any questions.　如果你有任何問題請舉手。
B: Please explain question 1.　請解釋第一題。

quiz [kwɪz]
名 測驗

名詞複數 quizzes　同義字 test 測驗
延伸片語 quiz show　智力問答

實境對話
A: I failed my quiz.　我測驗不及格。
B: You should have studied hard.　你應該努力學習。

record ['rɛkəd]
名 記錄、唱片

名詞複數 records　同義字 test 測驗
延伸片語 on record　記錄在案的
of record　有案可查的

實境對話
A: I am unable to make ends meet.　我入不敷出。
B: You have to keep a record of your expenses.　你必須記錄你的開銷。

score [skor]
名 分數

名詞複數 scores　同義字 marks 分數
延伸片語 score for　為……得分

實境對話
A: What is the final score?　最後分數是什麼？
B: The final score is 10 – 6.　最後的得分是10 - 6。

story ['storɪ]
名 故事

名詞複數 stories　同義字 tale 故事
延伸片語 tell a story　講故事
the whole story　原委

實境對話
A: The story you told is interesting.　你說的故事很有趣。
B: Actually, it is a true story.　其實，這是一個真實的故事。

test [tɛst]
名 測驗

名詞複數 tests　同義字 quiz 測試
延伸片語 test for　探測
test on　在……做實驗

實境對話
A: I have three tests tomorrow.　我明天有三個測驗。
B: You may have to stay up late.　你可能要熬夜。

學校及學習活動 School　Chapter 12

143

vocabulary
[vəˈkæbjəˌlɛrɪ]
名 字彙

名詞複數 vocabularies
同義字 lexis 辭彙

A: What should I do if I want to increase my **vocabulary**?
　　如果我想增加我的詞彙，我應該怎樣做？
B: Reading is the best way.
　　閱讀是最好的方式。

semester
[səˈmɛstɚ]
名 學期

名詞複數 semesters
同義字 session 學期

A: The fall **semester** will begin on September 10.　秋季學期將於 9月10日開始。
B: No. It is on September 9.　不，是9月9日。

用簡單的小測驗，驗收一下，單字記住了嗎？

( ) 1 university   ( ) 11 law

( ) 2 library   ( ) 12 music

( ) 3 chalk   ( ) 13 friend

( ) 4 diary   ( ) 14 answer

( ) 5 eraser   ( ) 15 listen

( ) 6 magazine   ( ) 16 pronounce

( ) 7 notebook   ( ) 17 speak

( ) 8 picture   ( ) 18 conversation

( ) 9 course   ( ) 19 grade

( ) 10 history   ( ) 20 quiz

A. 圖書館 B 課程   C 橡皮擦 D 談話   E 大學   F 筆記本 G 法律
H 粉筆   I 聽   J 回答   K 歷史   L 朋友   M 日記   N 圖片
O 雜誌   P 成績   Q 測驗   R 音樂   S 説   T 發音

答案

1(E)　2(A)　3(H)　4(M)　5(C)　6(O)　7(F)　8(N)　9(B)　10(K)　11(G)　12(R)　13(L)　14(J)
15(I)　16(T)　17(S)　18(D)　19(P)　20(Q)

here [hɪr]
副 這裡

延伸片語 here by 在這裡
come here 來這裡

實境對話
A: What time will the bus arrive? 公車什麼時候會抵達？
B: It will arrive **here** in five minutes. 在五分鐘內抵達這裡。

there [ðɛr]
副 那裡

延伸片語 over there 在那裡

實境對話
A: Do you know where Frank is? 你知道法蘭克在哪裡嗎？
B: He is over **there**. 在那裡。

position [pəˋzɪʃən]
名 位置、職位

名詞複數 positions
延伸片語 in position 就位
pole position 開始的領先位置

實境對話
A: What **position** did the interviewee apply? 面試者申請什麼職位？
B: An assistant. 助理。

back [bæk]
名 後面 形 後面的 副 向後地

同義字 rear 後面
延伸片語 back on 背靠
at the back of 在……的後面

實境對話
A: Where is the bakery? 麵包店在哪裡？
B: It is in **back** of the library. 圖書館後面。

backward
[ˋbækwəd]
形 向後的 副 向後地

實境對話
A: Go **backward**. 向後走。
B: I don't want to do that. 我不想這麼做。

central [ˋsɛntrəl]
形 中心的

延伸片語 central bank 中央銀行
central government 中央政府

實境對話
A: There are many travelers in the **central** park. 中央公園有很多旅客。
B: It is a hot spot. 那是熱門景點。

forward [ˈfɔrwəd]
副 向前 形 向前的

延伸片語 look forward to 期盼
put forward 提出

 實境對話
A: Please move **forward**.　請往前移動。
B: Alright.　好。

front [frʌnt]
名 前方

延伸片語 in the front of 在……前面
on the front 前線

 實境對話
A: The restaurant is in **front** of the bank.　餐廳在銀行前面。
B: Which bank?　哪間銀行？

left [lɛft]
形 左邊的

延伸片語 on the left 在左邊
left hand 左手

 實境對話
A: Can you tell me how to go to the bookstore?
你能告訴我如何去書店？
B: Turn right on the corner. You will see it on your **left** side.
角落右轉。你會看到它在你的**左手邊**。

middle [ˈmɪdl̩]
形 中間的

延伸片語 in the middle of 在……中間
middle class 中產階級

 實境對話
A: How old is your piano teacher?　妳鋼琴老師幾歲？
B: She is in her **middle thirties**.　她約三十五六歲。

right [raɪt]
形 右邊的 副 向右 名 權利

延伸片語 right now 馬上
all right 好

 實境對話
A: Where is the supermarket?　超市在哪裡？
B: Turn **right** at the corner.　角落右轉。

east [ist]
形 東方的 副 向東方 名 東方

同義字 orient 東方的
延伸片語 in the east 在東方
far east 遠東

 實境對話
A: Where is Taitung?　台東在哪裡？
B: It's in the **East** of Taiwan.　在台灣東部。

west [wɛst]
形 西方的 副 向西方 名 西方

延伸片語 in the west of 在……的西方

實境對話
A: What is never going to change?　什麼是永遠不會變的？
B: That the sun rises in the east and sets in the **west**.　太陽從東邊升起西邊落下這件事。

south [sauθ]
形 南方的 副 向南方 名 南方

同義字 austral 南方的
延伸片語 in the south 在南方

實境對話
A: Where are you going in your summer vacation? 你暑假去哪裡？
B: I am going to the **South** of France. 我要到法國南部。

north [nɔrθ]
形 北方的 副 向北方 名 北方

同義字 boreal 北方的
延伸片語 in the north 在……的北方

實境對話
A: I haven't seen Sean for weeks. 我好幾星期沒看到尚恩。
B: He has moved to the **North**. 他已經搬到北部了。

top [tɑp]
名 頂端 形 最高的

延伸片語 on top of 另外
at the top 在頂端

實境對話
A: Where should I write my address? 我地址要寫在哪裡？
B: Put it at the **top**. 最上方。

area [ˈɛrɪə]
名 地區

名詞複數 areas 同義字 district 地區
延伸片語 in the area of 在……的地區
rural area 鄉村地區

實境對話
A: The manager knows the local **area** well. 經理對當地很熟。
B: Sure. He used to live there for a year. 那當然。他曾在那裡生活了一年。

bakery [ˈbekərɪ]
名 麵包店

名詞複數 bakeries
同義字 tommy-shop 麵包店

實境對話
A: Buy some bread at a **bakery** on your way home. 回家路上去麵包店買一些麵包回來。
B: I didn't have any money with me. 我沒帶錢。

bank [bæŋk]
名 銀行

名詞複數 banks
延伸片語 bank account 銀行存款

實境對話
A: The **bank** manger is still single. 銀行經理仍是單身。
B: Really? He looks over forty. 真的嗎？他看上超過四十。

beach [bitʃ]
名 海灘

名詞複數 beaches
延伸片語 on the beach 在海灘上
at the beach 在海邊

實境對話
A: What do you like to do in summer? 妳夏天喜歡做什麼？
B: I like to swim at the **beach**. 我喜歡去沙灘游泳。

Part 1 生活情境單字

bookstore
[ˈbʊkˌstor] 名 書店

名詞複數 bookstores

 A: The **bookstore** has a big sale. 書店舉行大打折。
B: Great. Let's go there on the weekend. 太棒了。我們週末去那裡。

buffet [ˈbʌfɪt]
名 自助餐

 A: I always have a **buffet** lunch. 我午餐總吃自助餐。
B: It costs a lot of money. 那花很多錢呢。

cafeteria
[ˌkæfəˈtɪrɪə]
名 自助餐廳、咖啡廳

名詞複數 cafeterias

 A: Let's have our lunch at that **cafeteria**. 我們在那間自助餐廳吃午餐吧。
B: Why not! 好啊！

church [tʃɜtʃ]
名 教堂

名詞複數 churches
延伸片語 in church 在教堂

 A: What do you do on Sundays? 妳星期天都做什麼？
B: I usually go to the **church**. 我通常去教堂。

convenience store
[kənˈvinjəns stor]
名 便利商店

名詞複數 convenience stores

 A: He looks tired. 他很累。
B: He got a part-time job in a **convenience store**. 他在便利商店得到了一份兼職工作。

Culture Center
[ˈkʌltʃə ˈsɛntə]
名 文化中心

名詞複數 culture centers

 A: Where will the party be held? 派對在哪裡舉行？
B: It will be held in the **Cultural Center**. 將在文化中心舉行。

bank [bæŋk]
名 銀行

名詞複數 banks

 A: It is twenty after three. 現在是三點二十分。
B: The **bank** will be closed in ten minutes. 銀行將於十分鐘內關門。

Chapter 13 場所、位置 Places & Locations

department store [dɪˈpɑrtmənt stor]
名 百貨公司

名詞複數 department stores

 實境對話
A: This tie is very special.　這條領帶很特別。
B: I bought it in the **department store**.　我在百貨公司買的。

drugstore [ˈdrʌɡˌstor]　名 藥局

名詞複數 drugstores

 實境對話
A: I just accidentally cut my finger.　我剛剛不小心割傷手指頭了。
B: I will get some ointment from the **drugstore** now.　我現在就去藥局買藥膏。

factory [ˈfæktərɪ]
名 工廠

名詞複數 factories

 實境對話
A: What does your uncle do?　你叔叔做什麼的？
B: He works in a **factory**.　他在一家工廠工作。

fast food restaurant [fæst fud ˈrɛstərənt]
名 速食店

名詞複數 fast food restaurants

 實境對話
A: I'm hungry.　我肚子餓了。
B: Let's grab some burgers from the **fast food restaurant**.　我們去速食店吃點漢堡吧。

fire station [faɪr ˈsteʃən]
名 消防站、消防局

名詞複數 fire stations

 實境對話
A: There is a **fire station** in my neighborhood.　我家附近有一間消防局。
B: That's great.　那太好了。

flower shop [ˈflauɚ ʃɑp]　名 花店

名詞複數 flower shops

 實境對話
A: What time does the **flower shop** open?　花店幾點開？
B: It opens at 11 a.m.　上午11時開。

hospital [ˈhɑspɪtl̩]
名 醫院

名詞複數 hospitals
延伸片語 be in hospital　住院
in the hospital　在醫院裡

 實境對話
A: Rita was sent to the **hospital**.　莉塔被送往醫院。
B: What happened?　發生了什麼事？

hotel [hoˋtɛl]
名 旅館

名詞複數 hotels

 實境對話
A: What time should we check out at the **hotel**? 我們要在幾點前結帳離開**旅館**？
B: Before 11:00 AM. 早上十一點前。

mall [mɔl]
名 購物中心

名詞複數 malls

 實境對話
A: Where is your sister? 你姐姐在哪裡？
B: She is shopping in the **mall**. 她正在**商場**購物。

market [ˋmɑrkɪt]
名 市場

名詞複數 markets

 實境對話
A: I usually buy vegetables in the supermarket. How about you? 我平時在超市購買蔬菜。你呢？
B: I usually buy them at the **market**. 我通常去**市場**買。

men's room
[mɛnz rum]
名 男廁所

 實境對話
A: Can you tell me how to go to the **men's room**?
你能告訴我如何去**男廁所**嗎？
B: Go straight. It is near the elevator.
直走。在電梯附近。

women's room [wɪmɪnz rum]
名 女廁所

 實境對話
A: There are many people in the **women's room**.
女廁有很多人。
B: That's OK. I have plenty of time.
沒關係。我有充足的時間。

movie theater
[ˋmuvɪ ˋθɪətɚ]
名 電影院

名詞複數 movie theaters

 實境對話
A: You really love movies. 你真的愛電影。
B: Yes. I go to the **movie theater** once a month. 是的。我每月去電影院一次。

museum
[mjuˋzɪəm]
名 博物館

名詞複數 museums

 實境對話
A: There is a special exhibition at the **museum**. 博物館有個特別的展覽。
B: What is it about? 是關於什麼的展覽呢？

office [ˈɔfɪs]
名 辦公室

名詞複數 offices
延伸片語 in office 執政、在位
head office 總公司

A: The manager is waiting for you in his **office**. 經理正在**辦公室**等你。
B: But I need to make an important call now. 但我需要打一通重要電話。

park [pɑrk]
名 公園

名詞複數 parks

A: What do you plan to do this weekend? 你週末打算做什麼？
B: Fly a kite in the **park**. 去公園放風箏。

pool [pul]
名 游泳池

名詞複數 pools

A: Is there a swimming **pool** in the hotel? 旅館裡有**游泳池**嗎？
B: Yes. We can relax by the **pool**. 是的。我們可以在**泳池**旁放鬆身心。

post office
[post ˈɔfɪs] 名 郵局

名詞複數 post offices

A: I'm going to the **post office** to send this letter. 我要去**郵局**寄封信。
B: But it is closed. 但它關門了。

police station
[pəˈlis ˈsteʃən] 名 警察局

名詞複數 police stations

A: Jill's uncle works in a **police office**. 吉兒的叔叔在一家**警察局**工作。
B: So he is a policeman. 所以他是一名員警。

restroom
[rɛstrum]
名 廁所、化妝室

名詞複數 restrooms

A: Where is the nearest **restroom**? 最近的**廁所**在哪裡？
B: Next to the exit. 在出口旁邊。

restaurant
[ˈrɛstərənt] 名 餐館

名詞複數 restaurants

A: How will you celebrate Mother's Day? 你母親節將如何慶祝？
B: We will celebrate it at a **restaurant**. 我們將在**餐廳**慶祝。

Chapter

13

場所、位置 Places & Locations

---

shop [ʃɑp]
名 商店

名詞複數 shops

 A: Let's buy some souvenirs at the gift **shop**.　我們去禮品店買一些紀念品吧。
B: Let's go.　走吧。

---

stationery store
[ˈsteʃənˌɛrɪ stor]
名 文具店

名詞複數 stationery stores

 A: How many pens did you buy?　你買多少筆？
B: A dozen. The **stationery store** has a big sale.　一打。文具店舉行大拍賣。

---

store [stor]
名 商店

名詞複數 stores

 A: Is there a shoe **store** near your house?　你家附近有鞋店嗎？
B: I guess not.　似乎沒有。

---

supermarket
[ˈsupɚˌmarkɪt] 名 超市

名詞複數 supermarkets

 A: Beth goes to the **supermarket** once a week.　貝絲每週去超市一次。
B: She is a working mother.　她是職業婦女。

---

temple [ˈtɛmpl̩]
名 寺廟

名詞複數 temples

 A: I feel peaceful when I stay in a **temple**.　我待在寺廟時感到平靜。
B: Me, too.　我也是。

---

theater [ˈθiətɚ]
名 戲院、戲劇

名詞複數 theaters

 A: Let's go to the **theater** after work.　我們下班後去戲院吧。
B: But I have a date tonight. How about tomorrow?　但是我今晚有個約會。明天怎麼樣？

---

waterfalls
[ˈwɔtɚˌfɔlz]
名 瀑布

 A: Which **waterfall** is the most famous in the world?
　世界上哪個瀑布最有名？
B: I think Niagara Falls is.
　我覺得是尼亞加拉大瀑布。

zoo [zu]
名 動物園

名詞複數 zoos

實境對話
A: There are many kinds of wild animals in the **zoo**. 動物園裡有許多種野生動物。
B: My favorites are hippos and tigers. 我最喜歡的是河馬和老虎。

city [ˋsɪtɪ]
名 城市

名詞複數 cities

實境對話
A: Where is New York **City**? 紐約市在哪裡？
B: It is a major **city** in southeastern New York. 紐約東南部的主要城市。

country [ˋkʌntrɪ]
名 鄉村

名詞複數 countries

實境對話
A: Mr. Jordan will move to a **country** after he retires. 喬丹先生退休後將搬到鄉下。
B: He really loves **country** life. 他真的熱愛鄉村生活。

downtown [ˋdaʊnˋtaʊn]
名 市區中心

名詞複數 downtowns

實境對話
A: Do you have any plans after graduation? 你畢業後有什麼打算？
B: I will work **downtown**. 我會去市區中心工作。

farm [fɑrm]
名 農場

名詞複數 farms

實境對話
A: Tom invites us to his house. 湯姆邀請我們到他家。
B: I remember he lives at a **farm**. 我記得他住在農場。

place [ples]
名 地方

名詞複數 places
延伸片語 in place 適當
take place 發生

實境對話
A: This would be a good **place** for fishing. 這是釣魚的好地方。
B: Are you kidding? 你在開玩笑吧？

town [taʊn]
名 城鎮

名詞複數 towns

實境對話
A: You live in a secluded place. 你生活在一個僻靜地方。
B: Exactly. The nearest **town** is twenty kilometers away. 沒錯。到最近的城鎮要二十公里。

Part 1 生活情境單字

|154|

village [`vɪlɪdʒ]
名 農村

名詞複數 villages

實境對話
A: What is the film about? 電影是關於什麼呢？
B: It is about **village** life. 和農村生活有關。

local [`lokl]
形 當地的

實境對話
A: I need to make a **local** call. 我要打本地電話。
B: You can use my phone. 你可以用我的電話。

international [ˌɪntɚˋnæʃənl]
形 國際的

延伸片語 international trade 國際貿易
international market 國際市場

實境對話
A: Does Taiwan have any **international** airports? 台灣有沒有任何國際飛機？
B: Yes. Taiwan Taoyuan **International** Airport. 有。桃園國際機場。

country [`kʌntrɪ]
名 國家

名詞複數 countries
延伸片語 in the country 在鄉下
all over the country 全國

實境對話
A: Which **country** is Neil from? 奈爾從哪個國家來？
B: He is from the USA. 他是來自美國。

nation [`neʃən]
名 國家、民族

名詞複數 nations
同義字 country 國家

實境對話
A: Australia is an independent **nation**. 澳洲是獨立國家。
B: How about New Zealand? 那紐西蘭呢？

world [wɝld]
名 世界

名詞複數 worlds　同義字 universe 世界
延伸片語 in the world 在世界上
all over the world 全世界

實境對話
A: I think Vancouver is the most beautiful city in the **world**.
我認為溫哥華是世界上最美麗的城市。
B: I agree with you.
我同意。

America [əˋmɛrɪkə]
名 美國

實境對話
A: Alice will travel in **America** for her winter vacation.
愛莉絲將前往美國過寒假。
B: Wow, I envy her.
哇，我真羨慕她。

| 155 |

China [ˋtʃaɪnə]

名 中國、瓷器

實境對話
A: Look at the **china vase**. 看看這個青花瓷。
B: It is very charming. 非常迷人。

Taiwan [ˋtaɪwən]

名 臺灣

實境對話
A: Where is Yangmingshan? 陽明山哪裡？
B: It is in northern **Taiwan**. 臺灣北部。

用簡單的小測驗，驗收一下，單字記住了嗎？

( ) 1 back

( ) 2 central

( ) 3 forward

( ) 4 west

( ) 5 area

( ) 6 church

( ) 7 bank

( ) 8 drugstore

( ) 9 hospital

( ) 10 market

( ) 11 museum

( ) 12 restaurant

( ) 13 shop

( ) 14 supermarket

( ) 15 zoo

( ) 16 farm

( ) 17 village

( ) 18 country

( ) 19 restroom

( ) 20 beach

A 農場　　B 西方　　C 商店　　D 後面　　E 餐館　　F 向前　　G 市場
H 動物園　I 教堂　　J 地區　　K 中心的　L 博物館　M 銀行　　N 農村
O 國家　　P 海灘　　Q 醫院　　R 化妝室　S 藥局　　T 超市

答案

1(D)　2(K)　3(F)　4(B)　5(J)　6(I)　7(M)　8(S)　9(Q)　10(G)　11(L)　12(E)　13(C)　14(T)　15(H)　16(A)　17(N)　18(O)　19(R)　20(P)

Track 138

---

airplane (plane) [ˈɛrˌplen]
名 飛機

名詞複數 airplanes
同義字 plane 飛機
延伸片語 by airplane 搭飛機

 實境對話
A: The **airplane** is faster than the train.　飛機比火車快。
B: But it is more expensive.　但更昂貴。

---

ambulance [ˈæmbjələns] 名 救護車

名詞複數 ambulances

實境對話
A: The man was hit by a car.　男子被車撞了。
B: Call an **ambulance**, please.　請叫救護車。

---

bicycle (bike) [ˈbaɪsɪk!] 名 自行車

名詞複數 bicycles
同義字 bike 自行車
延伸片語 by bicycle 騎腳踏車

實境對話
A: Riding **bicycle** is interesting.　騎自行車很有趣。
B: Maybe we can go bike-riding together next time.　也許我們下一次可以一起騎。

---

boat [bot]
名 船

名詞複數 boats
同義字 ship 船隻

 實境對話
A: We often go **boating** in summer vacation.　我們暑假經常去划船。
B: It sounds exciting.　這聽起來很刺激。

---

bus [bʌs]
名 公車

名詞複數 buses
延伸片語 by bus 搭乘公車
bus stop 公車站

 實境對話
A: What time is the earliest **bus**?　最早的公車是幾點？
B: Six o'clock in the morning.　早上六點。

---

car [kɑr]
名 汽車

名詞複數 cars　同義字 motor 汽車
延伸片語 car park 停車場
by car 乘汽車

 實境對話
A: Do you drive a **car** to work?　你開車上班？
B: No, I take a bus.　不，我坐公車。

helicopter

[ˈhɛlɪˌkɑptɚ]

名 直升機

名詞複數 helicopters
同義字 whirlybird 直升機

 實境對話
A: He wants to be a **helicopter** pilot when he grows up.
常他長大時，他想成為一名**直升機**飛行員。
B: It is not easy. 這是不容易的。

jeep [dʒip]

名 吉普車

名詞複數 jeeps

 實境對話
A: We can drive a **jeep** over the rough ground. 吉普車可以開在凹凸不平的路上。
B: It can also be used by the military. 它也可以用於軍事。

motorcycle

[ˈmotɚˌsaɪkl̩]

名 摩托車

名詞複數 motorcycles

 實境對話
A: How do you go to school, by **motorcycle** or by bus? 你如何去上學，騎摩托車或坐公車？
B: By **motorcycle**. 騎摩托車。

scooter [ˈskutɚ]

名 小輪摩托車

名詞複數 scooters

 實境對話
A: Many people ride **scooters** in Taiwan. 台灣很多人騎摩托車。
B: Because it is convenient. 因為它很方便。

ship [ʃɪp]

名 船

名詞複數 ships

 實境對話
A: How will they travel to Tokyo? 他們要怎麼到東京去？
B: They will go by **ship**. 他們將搭船去。

tank [tæŋk]

名 坦克

名詞複數 tanks

 實境對話
A: I can't believe that you can drive a **tank**. 我不相信你會開坦克。
B: I was just kidding. 我只是在開玩笑。

taxi [ˈtæksɪ]

名 計程車

名詞複數 taxis

 實境對話
A: You are early today. 你今天早來了。
B: Because I took a **taxi**. 因為我坐計程車。

train [tren]
名詞複數 trains
名 火車

實境對話
A: I like to travel by **train**. How about you?　我喜歡坐火車旅行。你呢？
B: Me, too. It is fun.　我也一樣。這很有趣。

truck [trʌk]
名詞複數 trucks
名 卡車

實境對話
A: The **truck** driver is drunk.　卡車司機喝醉了。
B: It is dangerous to drive.　這是危險駕駛。

airlines [ˈɛrˌlaɪnz]
名詞複數 airlines
名 航空公司

實境對話
A: I often travel by Eva Air.　我經常搭乘長榮航空。
B: I prefer China **Airlines**.　我喜歡中華航空。

airport [ˈɛrˌport]
名詞複數 airports
名 機場

實境對話
A: Who will pick Tim up at the **airport**?　誰將去機場接提姆？
B: I don't know.　我不知道。

bus stop
[bʌs stɑp] 名 公車站
名詞複數 bus stops

實境對話
A: Why were you late this morning?
　今天早上為什麼遲到？
B: I woke up late. When I arrived at the **bus stop**, the bus had left.
　我晚起床。當我來到公車站，公車已經離開。

parking lot
[ˈpɑrkɪŋ lɑt]
名 停車場
名詞複數 parking lots

實境對話
A: It is difficult to find a **parking lot** here.　這裡很難找到停車場。
B: You are right.　沒錯。

station [ˈsteʃən]
名詞複數 stations
名 車站

實境對話
A: Aunt Molly has arrived at the **bus station**.　莫莉阿姨已經抵達巴士站。
B: Let's go there immediately.　讓我們馬上去那裡。

train station
[tren ˋsteʃən] 名 火車站

名詞複數 train stations

實境對話
A: How long does it take to drive to the **train station**? 開車到火車站要多久？
B: About ten minutes. 約十分鐘吧。

block [blɑk]
名 街區 動 阻塞

動詞變化 blocked, blocked, blocking, blocks
名詞複數 blocks

實境對話
A: The bank is two **blocks** from here. 銀行離這裡兩個街區。
B: I will go there on foot. 我將要走路去。

bridge [brɪdʒ]
名 橋

名詞複數 bridges

實境對話
A: I am afraid of suspension **bridges**. 我很怕吊橋。
B: How come! It is exciting to walk on them. 怎麼會！走吊橋很刺激呀。

flat tire [flæt taɪr]
名 爆胎、漏了氣的輪胎

實境對話
A: He got a **flat tire** on the way home.
他回家路上遇到爆胎。
B: He should be more careful.
他應該要多加小心。

highway [ˋhaɪ͵we]
名 高速公路

名詞複數 highways

實境對話
A: Why don't you take the **highway**? 你為何不走高速公路呢？
B: It must be jammed at this time. 這個時候一定很塞。

MRT
名 大眾捷運系統

實境對話
A: It is convenient to travel by **MRT**. 搭捷運很方便。
B: Especially in Taipei. 特別是在臺北。

overpass
[͵ovɚˋpæs]
名 天橋

名詞複數 overpasses

實境對話
A: We should use an **overpass**. 我們應該走天橋。
B: Right, it is safer. 嗯，它更安全。

passenger
[ˈpæsṇdʒɚ]
名 乘客

名詞複數 passengers

A: The passenger was rude to the driver. 乘客對駕駛很粗魯。
B: He was an impolite man. 他是一個沒禮貌的人。

path [pæθ]
名 小路

名詞複數 paths

A: I am full. 我好飽。
B: Let's take a walk on the garden **path**. 讓我們去花園小路散步。

platform
[ˈplætˌfɔrm]
名 月臺

名詞複數 platforms

A: Where should I take the train? 我該在哪兒搭火車？
B: At **platform** 2. 第二月臺。

railroad [ˈreⅬrod]
名 鐵路

名詞複數 railroads

A: It is dangerous to play on the **railroad**. 在鐵路上玩很危險。
B: The train is coming any time. 火車隨時會來。

railway [ˈreⅬwe]
名 鐵路

名詞複數 railways

A: What does your new neighbor do? 你新鄰居從事哪行？
B: He owns a **railway** company. 他擁有鐵路公司。

sidewalk
[ˈsaⅠdˌwɔk]
名 人行道

名詞複數 sidewalks

A: Some people always park their motorcycles on the **sidewalk**.
有些人總是把摩托車停在人行道。
B: It is very dangerous. 這是非常危險的。

subway [ˈsʌbˌwe]
名 地鐵

名詞複數 subways

A: We usually take the **subway** in New York City. 我們在紐約市通常搭地鐵。
B: It is the most convenient transportation. 這是最便捷的交通工具。

Part **1** 生活情境單字

traffic [ˈtræfɪk]
名 交通

名詞複數 traffics　　同義字 transportation 交通
延伸片語 traffic jam 塞車

實境對話
A: You are five minutes late. 你遲到了5分鐘。
B: I was stuck in a **traffic** jam. 我遇到塞車（交通阻塞）。

underpass [ˈʌndɚˌpæs]
名 地下通道

名詞複數 underpasses

實境對話
A: What is **underpass**? 地下通道是什麼？
B: It is a path that passes under another road. 那是穿越另一條道路的路徑。

wheel [hwil]
名 車輪

名詞複數 wheels

實境對話
A: What happened to Ken? 肯發生了什麼事？
B: His front **wheels** skidded. 他的前輪打滑。

arrive [əˈraɪv]
動 到達

動詞變化 arrived, arrived, arriving, arrives
同義字 reach 到達
延伸片語 arrive in/at 到達

實境對話
A: What time will the professor **arrive** at the restaurant? 教授什麼時候會到達餐廳？
B: About 6 p.m. 約6點。

cross [krɔs]
動 穿過

動詞變化 crossed, crossed, crossing, crosses
同義字 reach 到達
延伸片語 on the cross 不光明正大地
cross over 橫渡

實境對話
A: How do we **cross** the road? 我們要怎麼過馬路？
B: Let's take the overpass. 我們走天橋吧。

drive [draɪv]
動 駕駛

動詞變化 drove, driven, driving, drives
同義字 reach 到達
延伸片語 drive in 釘入
drive from 從……趕走……

實境對話
A: Don't drink before you **drive.** 開車前不要喝酒。
B: I won't. 我不會的。

fly [flaɪ]
動 飛、放（風箏） 名 蒼蠅

動詞變化 flied, flied, flying, flies
名詞複數 flies
延伸片語 on the fly 在飛行中
fly in 降落

實境對話
A: We **flew a** kite yesterday. 我們昨天放風箏。
B: But it was rainy. 但昨天下雨。

land [lænd]
動 降落、著陸 名 陸地

動詞變化 landed, landed, landing, lands
名詞複數 lands
延伸片語 on land 在陸地上

實境對話
A: Why did you buy the **land**? 你為何買這塊土地？
B: Because it is an agricultural **land**. 因為這是農業用地。

ride [raɪd]
動 騎車 名 搭乘、兜風

動詞變化 rode, rid, riding, rides
名詞複數 rides
延伸片語 ride on 依靠
go for a ride 騎車兜風

實境對話
A: Can you give me a **ride**? 你能不能載我一程？
B: Of course. 當然。

sail [sel]
動 航行

動詞變化 sailed, sailed, sailing, sails
延伸片語 set sail 啟航
sail for 船開向……

實境對話
A: Going **sailing** is more exciting than going boating. 航行比划船更刺激。
B: Not me. 我不認為。

turn [tɝn]
動 轉向 名 輪到某人

動詞變化 turned, turned, turning, turns
名詞複數 turns
延伸片語 in turn 輪流
turn on 打開、發動

實境對話
A: Do you mind **turning on** the radio? 你介意打開收音機嗎？
B: No, I don't. 不介意。

fast [fæst]
形 快的

形容詞變化 faster, fastest
同義字 quick 快速的
延伸片語 fast food 速食
as fast as 和……一樣快

實境對話
A: He has dinner in a **fast** food restaurant very often. 他常去速食店吃晚餐。
B: That's why he looks heavy. 那是為何他看起來很重。

quick [kwɪk]
形 迅速的

形容詞變化 quicker, quickest
同義字 fast 快速的
延伸片語 to the quick 觸及要害
quick profit 暴利

實境對話
A: The cookies are **quick** to make. 餅乾做起來很快。
B: I am not good at it. 我不擅長這點。

slow [slo]
形 慢的

形容詞變化 slower, slowest
同義字 dull 遲鈍的
延伸片語 slow down 減速
go slow 怠工

實境對話
A: He is a **slow** reader. 他讀得很慢。
B: Maybe he is a careful reader. 也許他是個細心的讀者。

Track 145

centimeter
['sɛntəˌmitɚ] 名 公分

名詞複數 centimeters

延伸片語 square centimeter 平方公分
cubic centimeter 立方公分

 實境對話
A: How tall are you? 你有多高？
B: I am 170 **centimeters** tall. 我170公分高。

foot [fʊt]
名 英呎、腳

名詞複數 feet

 實境對話
A: How tall is Jenny? 珍妮身高多高？
B: She is five **foot** two. 她是五呎二吋。

gram [græm]
名 公克

名詞複數 grams

 實境對話
A: There are one thousand **grams** in one kilo. 一公斤一千公克。
B: It is common sense. 那是常識。

inch [ɪntʃ]
名 英吋

名詞複數 inches

 實境對話
A: Helen is one **inch** taller than you. 海倫比你高一英吋。
B: I think I am taller than her. 我認為我比她高。

kilogram
['kɪləˌgræm] 名 公斤

名詞複數 kilograms

 實境對話
A: How much does Wendy weigh? 溫蒂多重？
B: She weighs forty **kilograms**. 她體重40公斤。

kilometer
['kɪləˌmitɚ] 名 公里

名詞複數 kilometers

 實境對話
A: Where do you live? 你住在哪裡？
B: Ten **kilometers** from my office. 距離我辦公室十公里處。

liter ['litɚ]
名 公升

名詞複數 liters

 實境對話
A: He drinks a **liter** of water a day. 他每天喝一公升的水。
B: I drink two. 我喝兩公升。

meter [`mitɚ]
名 公尺

名詞複數 meters

實境對話
A: The snake is over 10 **meters**.　那條蛇超過10公尺長。
B: It looks scary.　看起來很可怕。

mile [maɪl]
名 英里

名詞複數 miles
延伸片語 run a mile　避而遠之
miles away　相隔千里

實境對話
A: How about going there on foot?　走路去那裡如何？
B: Are you kidding? It's 8 **miles** from here.　你在開玩笑吧？它距離這裡8英里耶。

pound [paʊnd]
名 （重量單位）磅、英鎊

名詞複數 pounds
延伸片語 pound of flesh　合乎法律的無禮要求

實境對話
A: Sue looks slim.　蘇看起來很纖細。
B: I guess she only weighs one hundred **pounds**.　我猜她只有一百磅。

circle [`sɝkl̩]
名 週期、圓形

名詞複數 circles
延伸片語 in circles　毫無進展、兜圈子

實境對話
A: We're going round in **circles**.　我們老在同一個地方兜圈子。
B: It is a waste of time.　真是浪費時間。

dot [dɑt]
名 點

名詞複數 dots
延伸片語 on the dot　準點
dot with　用……點綴於

實境對話
A: The bus showed up **on the dot**.　公車準點抵達。
B: I am surprised.　我很訝異。

line [laɪn]
名 線

名詞複數 lines
延伸片語 in line with　符合
in line　協調

實境對話
A: Draw a **line** with a ruler.　用尺劃一條線。
B: But I lost my ruler.　但是我的尺不見了。

Part 1 生活情境單字

point [pɔɪnt]
名 標點、小數點

名詞複數 points
延伸片語 at this point 這時候
starting point 出發點

 實境對話
A: What is the answer? 答案是什麼？
B: Two **point** one. 2點1。

rectangle [ˋrɛktæŋgl̩] 名 矩形

名詞複數 rectangles

 實境對話
A: Can you fold the newspaper into a **rectangle**? 你能把報紙摺成長方形嗎？
B: Not necessary. 不需要。

row [ro]
名 列、排 動 划船

動詞變化 rowed, rowed, rowing, rows
名詞複數 rows
延伸片語 in a row 連續
in row 行內的

 實境對話
A: Why not go for a **row**? 何不去划船？
B: I'd love to, but I have a headache. 我想去，但是我頭痛。

shape [ʃep]
名 形狀

名詞複數 shapes
延伸片語 in shape 在外形上
out of shape 走樣、身體狀況不佳

 實境對話
A: The tub is in the **shape** of a heart. 浴缸形狀是心型的。
B: It is really romantic. 真浪漫。

square [skwɛr]
名 正方形、廣場

名詞複數 squares
延伸片語 on the square 正角
least square 最小二乘方

 實境對話
A: Who is your manager? 你們經理是哪位？
B: The one who's sitting at the **square** desk. 坐在正方型的桌子旁的那位。

triangle [ˋtraɪæŋgl̩]
名 三角形

名詞複數 triangles

 實境對話
A: Can you cut the sandwich into **triangles**? 你能把三明治切成三角形嗎？
B: I have no time. 我沒有時間。

big [bɪg]
形 大的

形容詞變化 bigger, the biggest 反義字 small 小的
延伸片語 make big 飛黃騰達
big problem 大問題

實境對話
A: Kelly made a **big** mistake. 凱莉犯了大錯。
B: No wonder her mother was mad. 難怪她的母親很生氣。

deep [dip]
形 深的

形容詞變化 deeper, the deepest
反義字 shallow 淺的
延伸片語 in deep 深陷其中
　　　 deep in 深陷於

 實境對話
A: How **deep** do you love me? 你愛我有多深？
B: As **deep** as the ocean. 深如海洋。

distant [ˈdɪstənt]
形 遠的

同義字 remote 遙遠的
延伸片語 in the distant past 遠古
　　　 distant view 遠景

實境對話
A: When can I see you again? 我何時才能再看到你？
B: In the not too **distant** future. 在不遠的將來。

extra [ˈɛkstrə]
形 額外的
名 附加的人或錢、號外

 實境對話
A: The dress looks too large. 洋裝看起來太大。
B: This is **extra** large. 這是**特**大號的。

far [fɑr]
形 遠的

形容詞變化 farther, the farthest　　反義字 near 近的
延伸片語 far and wide 到處
　　　 far from 遠離……

 實境對話
A: Where is your company? 你公司多遠？
B: It is not **far** from the MRT station. 離捷運站不遠處。

high [haɪ]
形 高的

形容詞變化 higher, the highest
反義字 low 低的
延伸片語 high speed 高速
　　　 high quality 高品質

 實境對話
A: Why didn't you buy the wallet? 你為什麼不買皮夾？
B: The price was too **high**. 價格太高。

large [lɑrdʒ]
形 大的

形容詞變化 larger, the largest　　同義字 big 大的
延伸片語 at large 詳盡的
　　　 large amount 大量

 實境對話
A: He rents a **large** apartment. 他租一間大公寓。
B: It must be expensive. 它一定很昂貴。

little [ˈlɪt!]
形 少的、小的

形容詞變化 less, the least　　同義字 few 少的
延伸片語 little bit 一點點
　　　 for a little 一會兒

 實境對話
A: The **little** girl is very cute. 小女孩很可愛。
B: She is my cousin. 她是我表妹。

Part 1 生活情境單字

long [lɔŋ]
形 長的

形容詞變化 longer, the longest　反義字 short 短的
延伸片語　no longer 不再
　　　　　as long as 只要

實境對話
A: The woman with **long** hair is an actress.　留長髮的女孩是演員。
B: She is attractive.　她很有吸引力的。

low [lo]
形 低的

形容詞變化 lower, the lowest　反義字 high 高的
延伸片語　low price 廉價
　　　　　low cost 低成本

實境對話
A: The table is too **low**.　桌子太低了。
B: That's OK. I can sit on the floor.　沒問題。我可以坐在地板上。

maximum [`mæksəməm]
形 最大限度的 名 最大極限

反義字 minimum 最小限度的

實境對話
A: Can you turn up the radio a little bit?　你能把收音機音量調高一些嗎？
B: But it's already the **maximum** volume.　但是現在已經是最高音量了。

medium [`midɪəm]
形 中等的、M號的

實境對話
A: How would you like your steak?　您的牛排要幾分熟？
B: **Medium**, please.　五分熟。

minus [`aɪnəs]
名 減號、負數 介 減去

實境對話
A: Thomas looks frustrated.　湯瑪士看起來很沮喪。
B: He got a C **minus** on his final paper.　他期末報告得到C減。

narrow [`næro]
形 狹窄的

形容詞變化 narrower, the narrowest
反義字 wide 寬的
延伸片語　narrow gap 窄隙

實境對話
A: To walk on a **narrow** street is not comfortable.　走在一條狹窄的街道是不舒服的。
B: I feel uncomfortable, too.　我也覺得不舒服。

plus [plʌs]
名 加號、正數 介 加上

實境對話
A: One hundred **plus** nine is 109.　一百加九是109。
B: It is correct.　這是正確的。

short [ʃɔrt]
形 短的

形容詞變化 shorter, the shortest
反義字 long 長的
延伸片語 short of 缺乏
in short 總之

實境對話
A: The girl in a **short** skirt is from Paris. 穿短裙的女孩來自巴黎。
B: She is very popular. 她很受歡迎。

small [smɔl]
形 小的

形容詞變化 smaller, the smallest
反義字 big 大的

實境對話
A: There are ten people living in the **small** apartment. 10個人住在小公寓。
B: Are you serious? 你說真的嗎？

straight [stret]
形 直的

形容詞變化 straighter, the straightest
反義字 curly 彎曲的
延伸片語 go straight 改過自新
straight up 直率地

實境對話
A: The line is not **straight**. 這條線不直。
B: I didn't draw it with a ruler. 我沒有用尺畫。

tiny [ˈtaɪnɪ]
形 微小的

形容詞變化 tinier, the tiniest
反義字 large 大的

實境對話
A: It is just a **tiny** problem. 這只是一個小問題。
B: I don't think so. 我不這麼認為。

wide [waɪd]
形 寬的

形容詞變化 wider, the widest
反義字 narrow 狹窄的
延伸片語 a wide range of 大範圍的
far and wide 廣泛地

實境對話
A: The actress is cute. 女演員很可愛。
B: But I think she has a **wide** mouth. 但我覺得她嘴巴很寬。

round [raʊnd]
形 圓的

延伸片語 in the round 全面地
all round 周圍

實境對話
A: Look at the baby's big **round** eyes. 你看那寶寶又大又圓的眼睛。
B: They are so beautiful. 它們真美啊。

light [laɪt]
形 輕的 **名** 光線

形容詞變化 lighter, the lightest
反義字 heavy 沉重的
延伸片語 in the light of 根據
light on 偶然遇見

實境對話
A: The camera is **light** and small. 相機重量輕薄短小。
B: It is cheap, too. 價格也很便宜。

Part 1 生活情境單字

bottle [ˈbɑtl̩]
名 瓶子

名詞複數 bottles
延伸片語 a bottle of 一瓶
on the bottle 嗜酒

實境對話
A: I am thirsty.　我很渴。
B: Do you need a **bottle** of water?　你需要一瓶水嗎？

cup [kʌp]
名 杯子

名詞複數 cups
延伸片語 cup of tea 命運
cup of coffee 短暫逗留

實境對話
A: I want to order a **cup** of tea.　我想點一杯茶。
B: Anything else?　還要點其他的東西嗎？

dozen [ˈdʌzn̩]
名 一打

名詞複數 dozens
延伸片語 dozens of 許多
daily dozen 每日健身操

實境對話
A: How many eggs do you need?　你需要多少個雞蛋？
B: I need a **dozen**.　我需要一打。

glass [glæs]
名 玻璃杯

名詞複數 glasses
延伸片語 glass in 四周嵌上玻璃
a glass of 一杯

實境對話
A: He has drunk four **glasses** of juice.　他已經喝四杯果汁了。
B: What's wrong with him?　他怎麼了？

loaf [lof]
名 一條（麵包）

實境對話
A: How much is a **loaf of** bread?　一條麵包多少錢？
B: Fifty dollars.　50元。

pack [pæk]
名 一小包

名詞複數 packs
延伸片語 pack up 整理
pack in 停止

實境對話
A: A **pack** of chocolates costs three hundred dollars.　一包巧克力300元。
B: It is costly.　很貴。

package [ˈpækɪdʒ]
名 包裹

名詞複數 packages

實境對話
A: Here is your **package**.　這是你的包裹。
B: But I didn't order anything.　但是我沒訂購任何東西啊。

pair [pɛr]
名 (一) 對

名詞複數 pairs

 實境對話
A: It is chilly today.　今天很寒冷。
B: You will need a **pair** of gloves.　你需要一雙手套。

piece [pis]
名 片

名詞複數 pieces
延伸片語 fall in pieces 變得破舊不堪
go to pieces 身心崩潰、沮喪至極

 實境對話
A: What did you have for breakfast?　你早餐吃什麼？
B: I had a **piece** of bread.　我吃了一片麵包。

size [saɪz]
名 尺寸

名詞複數 sizes
延伸片語 that's about the size of it 情況大致就是這樣
size somebody/something up 估量、判斷

 實境對話
A: What **size** do you wear?　你穿什麼尺寸？
B: Size 8.　八號。

height [haɪt]
名 高度

名詞複數 heights
延伸片語 at the height of 在……頂點
in the height of 在……的高潮中

 實境對話
A: How tall is your boss?　你老闆多高？
B: He is of medium **height**.　他身高中等。

distance [ˈdɪstəns]
名 距離

名詞複數 distances
延伸片語 in the distance 在遠處
at a distance 在遠處

 實境對話
A: What's the **distance** between Taipei and Kaohsiung?　臺北到高雄之間的距離多少？
B: I have no idea.　我不知道。

weight [wet]
名 重量

名詞複數 weights
延伸片語 of weight 有權勢的
lose weight 減肥

 實境對話
A: You look different.　你看起來不同。
B: I lost some **weight**.　我減了一些體重。

Part 1

生活情境單字

用簡單的小測驗，驗收一下，單字記住了嗎？

( ) 1 bicycle

( ) 2 taxi

( ) 3 station

( ) 4 bridge

( ) 5 passenger

( ) 6 subway

( ) 7 traffic

( ) 8 drive

( ) 9 ride

( ) 10 quick

( ) 11 centimeter

( ) 12 kilometer

( ) 13 yard

( ) 14 circle

( ) 15 rectangle

( ) 16 extra

( ) 17 dozen

( ) 18 narrow

( ) 19 straight

( ) 20 height

A. 地鐵　　B 庭院　　C 騎車　　D 矩形　　E 車站　　F 自行車　G 額外的
H 直的　　I 計程車　J 高度　　K 一打　　L 乘客　　M 交通　　N 狹窄的
O 迅速的　P 公里　　Q 橋　　　R 公分　　S 駕駛　　T 圓形

答案

1(F)　2(I)　3(E)　4(Q)　5(L)　6(A)　7(M)　8(S)　9(C)　10(O)　11(R)　12(P)　13(B)　14(T)
15(D)　16(G)　17(K)　18(N)　19(H)　20(J)

Track 153

Chinese New Year [tʃaɪˈniz njuˈjir]
名 春節

名詞複數 Chinese New Years
同義字 The Spring Festival 傳統春節
延伸片語 give New Years greetings 拜年
pay New Years call 電話拜年

 A: When is **Chinese New Year** this year? 今年春節是什麼時候？
B: It falls on February 3rd. 二月三號。

New Year's Eve [njuˈjirzˈiv] 名 除夕、跨年夜

名詞複數 New Year's Eves
延伸片語 the New Year's Eve party 跨年晚會

 A: What did you do on **New Year's Eve** last year? 去年的除夕你怎麼過？
B: I had a reunion dinner with my family. 和家人一起吃團圓飯。

Double Tenth Day [ˈdʌblˌtɛnθ de]
名 雙十節

名詞複數 Double Tenth Days
延伸片語 The Origins of Double Ten Day 雙十節的由來

 A: Do you have any plan on **Double Tenth Day**? 雙十節你有什麼計畫嗎？
B: I plan to attend the flag-raising ceremony. 我打算去參加升旗典禮。

Dragon-boat Festival [ˈdrægən botˈfɛstəvl̩]
名 端午節

名詞複數 Dragon-boat Festivals
延伸片語 a dragon boat race 龍舟大賽

 A: What should we do on **Dragon-boat Festival**? 端午節要做什麼呢？
B: Let's watch the dragon boat race. 去看划龍舟比賽吧！

Lantern Festival [ˈlæntənˈfɛstəvl̩] 名 元宵節

名詞複數 Lantern Festivals
延伸片語 exhibit of lanterns 元宵燈會
Lantern Riddle Game 猜燈謎

 A: What do you eat on **Lantern Festival**? 元宵節你都吃些什麼？
B: Sweet dumplings. 甜湯圓。

Moon Festival [munˈfɛstəvl̩] 名 中秋節

名詞複數 Moon Festivals
延伸片語 enjoy the moon on Mid-Autumn Festival 中秋賞月

 A: What do you do on **Moon Festival**? 中秋節你都做些什麼？
B: I enjoy the moon and eat moon cakes with my family. 和家人一邊賞月，一邊吃月餅。

Part **1** 生活情境單字

|174|

Teacher's Day [ˈtitʃɚz de]
名 教師節

名詞複數 Teacher's Days

延伸片語 Happy Teacher's Day　教師節快樂
teacher's day card　教師節謝卡

實境對話
A: I received the card on **Teacher's Day**.　我在**教師節**收到了這張卡片。
B: Wow, how sweet your students are.　哇，你的學生真貼心。

Christmas [ˈkrɪsməs]
名 耶誕節

名詞複數 Christmases

延伸片語 Christmas eve　聖誕夜
Christmas card　聖誕卡片
Christmas tree　聖誕樹

實境對話
A: **Christmas** is around the corner.　聖誕節快到了。
B: Let's decorate the Christmas tree.　我們來佈置聖誕樹吧。

Easter [ˈistɚ]
名 復活節

名詞複數 Easters

延伸片語 Easter egg　復活節彩蛋

實境對話
A: What types of activities do you do for **Easter**?　復活節你會做些什麼活動？
B: I will have an **Easter** egg hunt.　我會去找一顆復活節彩蛋。

Halloween [ˌhæloˈin]
名 萬聖節

名詞複數 Halloweens

延伸片語 Happy Halloween　萬聖節快樂

實境對話
A: What do kids say on **Halloween** to get candy?　小孩在**萬聖節**要糖時會說什麼？
B: Trick or treat.　不給糖就搗蛋。

New Year's Day [nju jirz de]
名 元旦

名詞複數 New Year's Days

延伸片語 New Year's Day Concert　新年音樂會

實境對話
A: My sister was born on **New Years Day**.　我妹妹的生日是元旦。
B: What a coincidence! So do I.　真巧，我也是。

Mother's Day [ˈmʌðɚz de]
名 母親節

名詞複數 Mother's Days

反義字 Father's Day 父親節

延伸片語 Happy Mother's Day　母親節快樂

實境對話
A: Will you go home to celebrate **Mother's Day**?　你**母親節**要回家嗎？
B: I haven't decided yet.　我還沒決定。

Father's Day
[ˈfɑðɚz de]
 名 父親節

名詞複數 Father's Days
反義字 Mother's Day 母親節
延伸片語 Happy Father's Day 父親節快樂

實境對話
A: How will you celebrate **Father's Day**? 你要怎麼慶祝**父親節**？
B: I will treat my dad to a nice meal. 我會請父親吃一頓大餐。

Thanksgiving
[ˌθæŋksˈɡɪvɪŋ]
 名 感恩節

名詞複數 Thanksgivings
延伸片語 Thanksgiving feast 感恩節盛宴

實境對話
A: Do you know the origin of **Thanksgiving**? 你知道感恩節的由來嗎？
B: I don't know. 不知道。

Valentine's Day [ˈvæləntaɪnz de]
 名 情人節

名詞複數 Valentine's Days
延伸片語 Valentine's Day Dinner 情人節大餐
Valentine's Day gift 情人節禮物

實境對話
A: What do you want as a **Valentine's Day** gift? 情人節你想要什麼禮物？
B: I just want you to accompany me. 你陪在我身邊就好。

culture [ˈkʌltʃɚ]
 名 文化

名詞複數 cultures
同義字 civilization（特定時期／地區的）文化
延伸片語 culture shock 文化衝擊

實境對話
A: Are you interested in Japanese **culture**? 你對日本文化有興趣嗎？
B: Yes, this is one of the reasons I study Japanese. 有，這是我學日文的原因之一。

custom [ˈkʌstəm]
 名 習慣、習俗

名詞複數 customs 反義字 tradition 慣例
延伸片語 folk custom 民俗
custom-made 訂製的

實境對話
A: **Custom** is a second nature. 習慣是後天養成的。
B: What do you mean? 我不懂你在說什麼。

festival [ˈfɛstəvl]
 名 節日

名詞複數 festivals 反義字 weekday 工作日
延伸片語 film festival 電影節
Cannes Film Festival 坎城影展

實境對話
A: Mid-Autumn Festival is one of the major **festivals** in Taiwan. 中秋節是台灣重大節日之一。
B: What do people usually do on that day? 那天大家通常會做些什麼？

Part 1 生活情境單字

holiday [ˈhɑlə͵de]
 名 節日、假日

名詞複數 holidays
反義字 workday 工作日、非假日
延伸片語 holiday camp 度假村
holiday getaway 假日出遊

實境對話
A: How many national **holidays** in a year? 一年有幾天國定假日？
B: I'm not quite sure. 我不太曉得。

vacation
[veˋkeʃən]
 名 假期

名詞複數 vacations
同義字 holiday 假日、假期
延伸片語 vacation hangover 度假後遺症
summer vacation 暑假

實境對話
A: Wish you have a nice **vacation**. 祝你有個美好的假期。
B: Thanks. 謝啦。

celebrate
[ˋsɛlə͵bret]
 動 慶祝

動詞變化 celebrated, celebrated, celebrating, celebrates
同義字 observe 慶祝（節日等）
延伸片語 to celebrate one's birthday 幫某人過生日

實境對話
A: Thanks for **celebrating** my birthday. 謝謝你們幫我慶祝生日。
B: We hope you like it. 希望你會喜歡。

Chapter **16** 假日、節慶 Holidays & Festivals

Track 157

actor [ˈæktɚ]
名 男演員

名詞複數 actors
延伸片語 a bad actor 做壞事的人

實境對話
A: The **actor** acts well. 這位**男演員**演技真好。
B: I don't think so. 我倒不這麼覺得。

actress [ˈæktrɪs]
名 女演員

名詞複數 actresses

實境對話
A: Who is that **actress**? 那位**女演員**是誰啊？
B: Do you mean the one in the red dress? 你是說穿紅色洋裝的那位嗎？

artist [ˈɑrtɪst]
名 藝術家

名詞複數 artists
延伸片語 con artist 騙子
piss artist 酒鬼

實境對話
A: What do you want to be when you grow up? 你長大後想要做什麼？
B: I want to be an **artist**. 我想成為一名**藝術家**。

assistant
[əˈsɪstənt] 名 助手

名詞複數 assistants 同義字 aid 助手
延伸片語 assistant manager 副經理
accounting assistant 會計助理

實境對話
A: I want to hire an **assistant**. 我想雇一名**助手**。
B: Can I recommend my friend? 我可以推薦我的朋友嗎？

babysitter
[ˈbebɪsɪtɚ] 名 保姆

名詞複數 babysitters
同義字 childminder 照看小孩的人

實境對話
A: What do you do for a living? 你的工作是什麼？
B: I'm a **babysitter**. 保姆。

barber [ˈbɑrbɚ]
名 理髮師

名詞複數 barbers
同義字 hairdresser 理髮師

實境對話
A: My father is a **barber**. 我爸爸是**理髮師**。
B: Is this the reason why you want to be a **barber**? 這是你想當**理髮師**的原因嗎？

boss [bɔs]
名 老闆

名詞複數 bosses 同義字 leader 領導者
延伸片語 show somebody who's boss 讓某人知道誰說了算

實境對話
A: Who is the **boss** of the store? 這家店的**老闆**是誰？
B: One of my elementary classmates, Lucy. 我的國小同學，露西。

businessman
['bɪznɪsmən]
名 商人

| 名詞複數 | businessmen |
| 同義字 | merchant 商人 |

實境對話
A: He works really hard. 他真的很努力工作。
B: I think he will be a successful **businessman**. 我想他會成為一名成功的商人。

clerk [klɝk]
名 辦事員

名詞複數	clerks	同義字	secretary 秘書
延伸片語	bank clerk 銀行辦事人員
	office clerk 職員

實境對話
A: He got a job as a bank **clerk** after graduation. 畢業後他找到一份銀行**辦事員**的工作。
B: That sounds great. 聽起來還不錯。

cook [kʊk]
名 廚師 動 煮

動詞變化	cooked, cooked, cooking, cooks
同義字	chef 廚師
延伸片語	too many cooks spoil the broth 人多手雜反壞事

實境對話
A: What are you doing? 你在做什麼？
B: I'm **cooking** the fish. 我在煮魚。

cowboy ['kaʊˌbɔɪ]
名 牛仔

| 名詞複數 | cowboys |

實境對話
A: What will you dress up as for Halloween? 萬聖節你要扮成什麼？
B: A **cowboy**. 牛仔。

dentist ['dɛntɪst]
名 牙醫

| 名詞複數 | dentists |
| 同義字 | dental surgeon 牙科醫生 |

實境對話
A: I need to see a **dentist**. 我要去看牙醫。
B: What's wrong? 你怎麼啦？

diplomat
['dɪpləˌmæt]
名 外交官

| 名詞複數 | diplomats |

實境對話
A: How to become a **diplomat**? 要怎麼成為外交官？
B: You can google it. 你可以上網查。

doctor ['dɑktɚ]
名 醫生

| 名詞複數 | doctors |
| 延伸片語 | see a doctor 看醫生 |

實境對話
A: My stomach is aching. 我的胃好痛。
B: You should see a **doctor** right away. 你應該馬上去看醫生。

driver [ˈdraɪvɚ]
名 司機

名詞複數 drivers

實境對話
A: What does he do? 他的工作是什麼？
B: A taxi **driver**. 計程車司機。

engineer
[ˌɛndʒəˈnɪr] 名 工程師

名詞複數 engineers

實境對話
A: Is she an **engineer**? 她是工程師嗎？
B: Yes, she is. 是。

farmer [ˈfɑrmɚ]
名 農民

名詞複數 famers
同義字 peasant 農夫

實境對話
A: My grandfather is a fruit **farmer**. 我的爺爺是果農。
B: What fruits does he grow? 他種哪些水果？

fisherman
[ˈfɪʃəmən] 名 漁夫

名詞複數 fishermen
同義字 peterman 漁夫

實境對話
A: What is the movie about? 這部電影在演些什麼？
B: It is about a **fisherman** who meets a mermaid. 一位漁夫遇到一條美人魚。

guide [gaɪd]
名 導遊 動 引導

動詞變化 guided, guided, guiding, guides
名詞複數 guides
延伸片語 guide dog 導盲犬

實境對話
A: Could you be my **guide** when I visit Japan? 我去日本的時候，你可以當我的導遊嗎？
B: Of course. 當然可以。

hairdresser
[ˈhɛrˌdrɛsɚ] 名 理髮師

名詞複數 hairdressers

實境對話
A: She wants to be a **hairdresser**. 她想當理髮師。
B: Really? I have never heard of it. 是嗎？我從沒聽說過。

housewife
[ˈhausˌwaɪf] 名 家庭主婦

名詞複數 housewives

實境對話
A: What is your mother's job? 你媽媽做什麼工作？
B: She is a **housewife**. 她是家庭主婦。

hunter [ˈhʌntɚ]
名 獵人

名詞複數 hunters

延伸片語 fortune hunter　追求財富者
job hunter　求職者

 實境對話
A: What did the **hunter** shoot?　獵人射中了什麼？
B: A deer.　一頭鹿。

journalist
[ˈdʒɝnḷɪst] 名 新聞工作者

名詞複數 journalists

 實境對話
A: Who is the man holding a camera?　拿著相機的男人是誰？
B: He is a **journalist**.　新聞工作者。

judge [dʒʌdʒ]
動 判斷、審判 名 法官

動詞變化 judged, judged, judging, judges
名詞複數 judges

延伸片語 don't judge a book by its cover　不要以貌取人
judge by　根據……做出判斷

 實境對話
A: He was **judged** innocent.　他被判無罪。
B: It's unfair.　太不公平了。

lawyer [ˈlɔjɚ]
名 律師

名詞複數 lawyers

 實境對話
A: What can I do?　我該怎麼辦？
B: You should consult with a **lawyer**.　你應該去請教律師。

magician
[məˈdʒɪʃən] 名 魔術師

名詞複數 maficians

 實境對話
A: The **magician** is amazing.　這位魔術師太神奇了。
B: No wonder he is so popular.　難怪他這麼受歡迎。

mailman
(mail carrier)
[ˈmelˌmæn] 名 郵差

名詞複數 mailmen

 實境對話
A: Did the **mailman** bring you a letter?　郵差有送信給你嗎？
B: No, I just got a water bill.　沒有，我只收到一張水費帳單。

manager
[ˈmænɪdʒɚ]
名 經理

名詞複數 managers

延伸片語 general manager　總經理
assistant manager　副經理

 實境對話
A: Excuse me, I have an appointment with your **manager**.　不好意思，我和經理有約。
B: May I have your name?　請問您貴姓大名？

mechanic
[mə`kænɪk] 名 技工

名詞複數 mechanics 技工

 實境對話
A: I need a **mechanic** to fix my car. 我需要一位**技工**幫我修車。
B: What's wrong with your car? 你的車怎麼了？

model [`madl̩]
名 模特兒

名詞複數 models
延伸片語 model something on something 模仿
model yourself on somebody 仿效

 實境對話
A: She is so beautiful. 她真是太漂亮了。
B: She is Taiwan's top **model**. 她可是台灣第一名模。

musician
[mju`zɪʃən] 名 音樂家

名詞複數 musicians

 實境對話
A: Will you go to her piano recital? 你會去聽她的鋼琴獨奏會嗎？
B: Of course. She is one of my favorite **musicians**. 當然，她是我最喜歡的音樂家之一。

nurse [nɝs]
名 護士

名詞複數 nurses

 實境對話
A: My sister is a **nurse**. 我的姐姐是護士。
B: Which hospital is she working at? 她在哪一家醫院工作？

owner [`onɚ]
名 主人、擁有者

名詞複數 owners
延伸片語 house-owner 房主

 實境對話
A: Who is the **owner** of the wallet? 這個錢包的物主是誰？
B: No one knows. 沒人知道。

painter [`pentɚ]
名 畫家

名詞複數 painters

 實境對話
A: Are you a **painter**? 你是畫家嗎？
B: No, I'm not. 不是。

police officer
[pə`lis `ɔfəsɚ] 名 警官

名詞複數 police officers

 實境對話
A: Do you want to be a **police officer**? 你想當警官嗎？
B: No. I think the job is dangerous. 不想，我覺得這個工作很危險。

president
[ˈprɛzədənt]
名 總統、校長

名詞複數 presidents
延伸片語 vice president 副總統
president-elect 候任總統

 A: Which **president** do you vote for? 你要投給哪一位總統？
B: I don't know. 不知道。

priest [prist]
名 牧師、神父

名詞複數 priests

 A: What is your brother? 你哥哥的職業是什麼？
B: He is a **priest**. 牧師。

reporter [rɪˈportə]
名 記者

名詞複數 reporters

 A: He told the truth to a **reporter**. 他把真相告訴記者了。
B: How stupid he was! 他太傻了！

sailor [ˈselə]
名 水手

名詞複數 sailors

 A: How many **sailors** are on the ship? 船上有幾位水手？
B: Five. 五位。

salesman
[ˈselzmən] 名 銷售人員

名詞複數 salesmen

 A: He is not a **salesman**. 他不是銷售人員。
B: Really? But he told me that he was! 是嗎？但他說他是。

scientist
[ˈsaɪəntɪst] 名 科學家

名詞複數 scientists

 A: The **scientist** died of lung caner. 這位科學家死於肺癌。
B: What a pity! 真是可惜。

secretary
[ˈsɛkrəˌtɛrɪ] 名 秘書

名詞複數 secretaries

實境對話 A: What is the job that you applied for? 你應徵什麼工作？
B: A **secretary**. 祕書。

servant [ˈsɝvənt]
名 僕人

名詞複數 servants
延伸片語 public servant 公務員

 實境對話
A: How do you think about him? 你覺得他怎麼樣？
B: He is a loyal **servant**. 他是一位忠誠的僕人。

shopkeeper [ˈʃɑpˌkipɚ] 名 店主

名詞複數 shopkeepers

 實境對話
A: Have the **shopkeeper** caught the thief? 店主抓到小偷了嗎？
B: Not yet. 還沒。

singer [ˈsɪŋɚ]
名 歌手

名詞複數 singers

 實境對話
A: Her mother was a director and a **singer**. 她的媽媽是導演也是歌手。
B: That's cool. 好酷喔。

soldier [ˈsoldʒɚ]
名 士兵

名詞複數 soldiers

實境對話
A: How many **soldiers** have been injured? 有幾名士兵受傷？
B: Three. 三名。

waiter [ˈwetɚ]
名 男服務員

名詞複數 waiters

 實境對話
A: The **waiter's** attitude is terrible. 這位服務員的態度太糟了。
B: I want to speak to the manager. 我想和經理談。

waitress [ˈwetrɪs]
名 女服務員

名詞複數 waitresses

 實境對話
A: I used to work as a **waitress**. 我曾當過女侍。
B: I heard it's not an easy job. 我聽說那並不輕鬆。

worker [ˈwɝkɚ]
名 工人

名詞複數 workers

 實境對話
A: The employer decided to layoff a **worker**. 雇主決定要解聘一名工人。
B: How do you know that? 你怎麼知道？

writer [ˈraɪtɚ]
名 作者

名詞複數 writers
同義字 author 作者

 實境對話
A: What do you want to be after graduation? 你畢業以後要做什麼？
B: I plan to be a full-time **writer**. 我計劃當全職作家。

Part 1 生活情境單字

vendor [ˈvɛndɚ]
名 小販、賣主、自動販賣機

名詞複數 vendors
同義字 packman 小販

 實境對話
A: Who is the **vendor**? 誰是賣主？
B: The woman with a ponytail is. 綁著馬尾的女人就是賣主。

business [ˈbɪznɪs]
名 商業、生意

同義字 commerce 商業
延伸片語 in business 經商
business card 名片

 實境對話
A: Why do you want to take the course? 你為什麼想修這門課？
B: I am interested in **business**, especially marketing. 因為我對商業很有興趣，尤其是行銷。

company [ˈkʌmpənɪ]
名 公司

名詞複數 companies
同義字 firm 公司
延伸片語 in company 一起、當眾
for company 陪伴

 實境對話
A: The **company** has gone bankrupt. 這間公司破產了。
B: More people are unemployed. 又有更多人失業了。

employ [ɪmˈplɔɪ]
動 雇用

動詞變化 employed, employed, employing, employs
延伸片語 employ in 被……雇傭
in the employ of 受雇於

 實境對話
A: How many people does the company **employ**? 這間公司雇用了多少人？
B: About three thousand people. 大約三千名。

hire [haɪr]
動 租借、雇用

動詞變化 hired, hired, hireing, hires
同義字 employ 雇傭
延伸片語 hire yourself out 為（某人）工作
pay for hire 招攬顧客

 實境對話
A: What did the boss say? 老闆說什麼？
B: He said that he plans to **hire** more workers. 他說打算雇用更多工人。

job [dʒɑb]
名 工作

名詞複數 jobs 同義字 work 工作
延伸片語 on the job 在上班時
jobs for the boys 為親信安排的工作

實境對話
A: Why do you want to quit your **job**? 為什麼你想辭掉工作？
B: The salary is too low. 薪水太低了。

work [wɜk]
動 工作 名 作品

名詞複數 works 同義字 job 工作
動詞變化 worked, worked, working, works
延伸片語 work out 解決
work around 漸漸轉變

 實境對話
A: Do you have any **working** experience? 你有工作經驗嗎？
B: Yes, I had **worked** in a trade company for two years. 有，我曾在貿易公司工作二年。

weather [ˈwɛðɚ]
名 天氣

延伸片語 in all weather 風雨無阻
under the weather 身體不舒服

實境對話
A: How's the **weather** tomorrow? 明天天氣怎麼樣？
B: According to the weather forecast, it will rain. 氣象預報說明天會下雨。

clear [klɪr]
形 晴朗的

形容詞變化 clearer, the clearest
同義字 fine 晴朗的
延伸片語 make clear 顯示
clear up 清理

實境對話
A: It is **clear** today. 今天天氣真晴朗。
B: Let's go picnicking. 我們去野餐吧。

cloudy [ˈklaʊdɪ]
形 多雲的

實境對話
A: What is the weather like today? 今天天氣怎麼樣？
B: It is **cloudy**. 多雲。

cold [kold]
形 寒冷的 名 感冒

形容詞變化 colder, the coldest 同義字 chill 寒冷的
延伸片語 a cold fish 冷漠無情的人
leave somebody cold 未打動某人

實境對話
A: I've got a **cold**. 我感冒了。
B: Take care. 保重。

cool [kul]
形 涼爽的

形容詞變化 cooler, the coolest
延伸片語 play it cool 沉著應付
as cool as a cucumber 泰然自若

實境對話
A: The weather is quite changeable here. 這裡的天氣真是多變。
B: Yes. It was hot yesterday, but it's **cool** today. 對啊，昨天很熱，今天卻很涼爽。

dry [draɪ]
形 乾燥的

形容詞變化 drier, the driest
延伸片語 run dry 乾涸
dry out 使變乾

實境對話
A: What's the weather like in winter? 冬天的天氣怎麼樣？
B: It is cold and **dry**. 又冷又乾燥。

foggy [ˈfɑgɪ]
形 有霧的

形容詞變化 foggier, the foggiest

實境對話
A: Did you see the robber clearly? 你有看清楚搶匪嗎？
B: No. It was too **foggy** at that time. 沒有。當時霧茫茫的。

Part 1 生活情境單字

freezing [ˈfrizɪŋ]
形 冰凍的

| 延伸片語 | freezing point 冰點 |

實境對話
A: It is **freezing** outside. 外面好冷。
B: Close the door at once. 快關門。

hot [hɑt]
形 炎熱的

形容詞變化	hotter, the hottest
同義字	warm 溫暖的
延伸片語	be in hot water 有麻煩
	go hot and cold 突然感到害怕

實境對話
A: I don't like **hot** weather. 我討厭炎熱的天氣。
B: Neither do I. 我也是。

humid [ˈhjumɪd]
形 潮濕的

| 形容詞變化 | humider, the humidest |
| 同義字 | moist 潮濕的 |

實境對話
A: The air is **humid**. 空氣很潮溼。
B: And there is a musty odor. 還有發黴的味道。

natural [ˈnætʃərəl]
形 自然的

反義字	unnatural 不自然的
延伸片語	natural selection 自然選擇
	natural-born 天生的

實境對話
A: I like to watch **natural** scenes. 我喜歡看自然的美景。
B: So do I. 我也是。

rainy [ˈrenɪ]
形 下雨的

形容詞變化	rainier, the rainiest
反義字	sunny 晴朗的
延伸片語	rainy day 艱難時刻
	save something for a rainy day 未雨綢繆

實境對話
A: My boyfriend and I met in a **rainy** day. 我和男朋友在下雨天相遇。
B: It sounds romantic. 聽起來很浪漫。

snowy [snoɪ]
形 下雪的

| 同義字 | nival 下雪的 |

實境對話
A: Walking on **snowy** roads is dangerous. 在下雪的道路上走路很危險。
B: Don't worry. I will be careful. 別擔心，我會小心點。

stormy [ˈstɔrmɪ]
形 暴雨的

| 形容詞變化 | stormier, the stormiest |
| 延伸片語 | stormy petrel 引起爭端的人 |

實境對話
A: It's really **stormy** outside. 外面真是狂風暴雨的。
B: We'd better stay inside. 我們最好待在屋裡。

Chapter **18** 氣候、大自然 Weather & Nature

sunny [ˈsʌnɪ]
形 晴朗的

形容詞變化 sunnier, the sunniest
同義字 fine 晴朗的

實境對話
A: How's the weather there? 你那邊天氣怎麼樣？
B: It's **sunny**. 很晴朗。

warm [wɔrm]
形 溫暖的 動 使暖和

形容詞變化 warmer, the warmest 同義字 hot 熱的
動詞變化 warmed, warmed, warming, warms
延伸片語 warm up 熱身
warm to somebody 開始喜歡某人

實境對話
A: It will be **warm** tomorrow. 明天會變暖和。
B: That's great. 太好了。

wet [wɛt]
形 潮濕的

形容詞變化 wetter, the wettest
同義字 humid 潮濕的
延伸片語 all wet 完全錯了
get one's feet wet 開始參加

實境對話
A: I'm frozen. 冷死了。
B: Take off your **wet** clothes. 快脫下濕掉的衣服。

windy [ˈwɪndɪ]
形 有風的

形容詞變化 windier, the windiest
同義字 blowy 多風的

實境對話
A: It looks like rain, isn't it? 看起來快下雨了，對吧？
B: No, it's just **windy**. 沒有，只是有風而已。

fog [fɑg]
名 霧

延伸片語 in a fog 困惑的
dense fog 濃霧

實境對話
A: Why did you stop driving? 為什麼不開車了？
B: It's dangerous driving in heavy **fog**. 在濃霧中開車很危險。

lightning [ˈlaɪtnɪŋ]
名 閃電

延伸片語 lightning never strikes twice 倒楣的事情不可能在同一場所重複發生
like lightning 閃電般、飛快地

實境對話
A: Did you see the **lightning**? 你有看到閃電嗎？
B: Yes, let's hurry home. 有，我們快回家吧。

rainbow [ˈrenˌbo]
名 彩虹

實境對話
A: How many colors in a **rainbow**? 彩虹有幾個顏色？
B: Seven. 七個。

shower [ˈʃauɚ]
名 陣雨、淋浴 動 傾注、淋浴

動詞變化 showered, showered, showering, showers
同義字 storm 暴風雨
延伸片語 shower bath 淋浴

實境
對話
A: The forecast says there will be **showers** on Sunday.　氣象報告説將會有暴雨。
B: Then the picnic may be canceled.　那野餐可能會取消。

snow [sno]
名 雪 動 下雪

延伸片語 snow white 白雪公主
as white as snow 雪白的

實境
對話
A: Have you ever seen **snow**?　你看過雪嗎？
B: No, it never **snows** in my country.　沒有，我的國家從不下雪。

snowman
[ˈsnoˌmæn] 名 雪人

名詞複數 snowmen
延伸片語 make a snowman 堆雪人

實境
對話
A: Let's make a **snowman**.　我們來堆雪人吧。
B: Good idea.　好耶。

storm [stɔrm]
名 暴風雨

延伸片語 dust storm 塵暴
weather the storm 渡過難關

實境
對話
A: The meeting has been postponed due to the **storm**.　會議因暴風雨而延期了。
B: OK. I see.　好，我知道了。

thunder [ˈθʌndɚ]
名 雷聲

延伸片語 blood and thunder 暴力打鬥

實境
對話
A: I heard a loud crash of **thunder**.　我聽見雷聲大作。
B: It's going to rain soon.　馬上就要下雨了。

typhoon [taɪˈfun]
名 颱風

同義字 hurricane 颶風

實境
對話
A: It is said a **typhoon** is coming.　據説有一個颱風要來了。
B: Then we'd better fix the window as soon as possible.　那我們最好要快點把窗戶修好。

wind [wɪnd]
名 大風

延伸片語 in the wind 即將發生
put the wind up somebody's sails
出其不意地打擊某人的信心

實境
對話
A: Where is your hat?　你的帽子呢？
B: It was blown off by the **wind**.　被一陣大風吹走了。

blow [blo]
動 吹

動詞變化 blew, blown, blowing, blows
延伸片語 blow your own trumpet 自吹自擂
blow your mind 使某人興奮

實境對話
A: Do you mind that I **blow** the candle out? 我可以吹熄蠟燭嗎？
B: No, I don't mind. 可以。

rain [ren]
動 下雨 **名** 雨

動詞變化 rained, rained, raining, rains
延伸片語 as right as rain 十分健康
rain on somebody's parade 煞風景

實境對話
A: Has it stopped **rain**ing yet? 雨停了嗎？
B: No, it hasn't. 還沒。

shine [ʃaɪn]
動 照耀、發光

動詞變化 shone, shone, shining, shines
延伸片語 shine through 顯現出來
take a shine to somebody 一見鍾情

實境對話
A: Why does the moon **shine**? 為什麼月亮會發光？
B: The sun makes the moon **shine**. 是太陽使月亮照耀的。

nature [ˈnetʃɚ]
名 自然

延伸片語 back to nature 回歸自然
in the nature of things 理所當然地

實境對話
A: What a beautiful landscape!
好漂亮的景色。
B: Don't forget to protect the **nature** as we enjoy the beauty of it.
欣賞**自然**美景的同時，別忘了也要保護它。

air [ɛr]
名 空氣

延伸片語 in the air 在傳播中、流行
up in the air 懸而未決

實境對話
A: Man can't live without **air**. 人沒有**空氣**不能活。
B: It's common sense. 這是常識。

climate [ˈklaɪmɪt]
名 氣候

同義字 weather 天氣

實境對話
A: Who is responsible for **climate** change? 誰該為**氣候**變遷負責？
B: Humans. 人類。

cloud [klaʊd]
名 雲彩

名詞複數 clouds
延伸片語 under a cloud 有嫌疑
on cloud nine 極其快樂

實境對話
A: What do you usually do when you are free? 你空閒的時候都做些什麼？
B: I usually lie on the grass and watch the **clouds**. 我通常躺在草地上看雲。

Part **1** 生活情境單字

degree [dɪˋgri]
名 溫度

名詞複數	degrees
延伸片語	bachelor's degree　學士學位
	master's degree　碩士學位

 實境對話
A: It is so cold today.　今天好冷。
B: The temperature has decreased by ten **degrees**.　氣溫已經下降十度了。

earth [ɝθ]
名 地球

同義字	ground 大地
延伸片語	come back to earth　回到現實
	go to earth　躲藏起來

 實境對話
A: What is the slogan on the poster?　海報上的標語是什麼？
B: We only have one **Earth**.　我們只有一個地球。

moon [mun]
名 月亮、衛星

名詞複數	moons
延伸片語	moon around　閒逛
	moon over somebody　癡癡地思念

 實境對話
A: The **moon** has risen.　月亮升起來了。
B: Wow, it's a full **moon**.　哇，是滿月。

sky [skaɪ]
名 天空

名詞複數	skies
延伸片語	a pie in the sky　難以實現的事情
	the sky's the limit　不可限量

 實境對話
A: What did you see in the **sky** tonight?　今晚你在天空中看到什麼？
B: I saw the stars glittering in the **sky**.　星星在空中閃爍。

sun [sʌn]
名 太陽

名詞複數	suns
延伸片語	under the sun　全世界
	with the sun　日出時

 實境對話
A: Why does the **sun** rise in the east and set in the west?　為什麼太陽東升西落？
B: I have no idea.　不知道。

star [stɑr]
名 星星

名詞複數	stars

實境對話
A: Look! A shooting **star**!　有流星！
B: Let's make a wish.　許願吧！

temperature [ˋtɛmprətʃɚ]
名 氣溫

延伸片語	raise the temperature　升溫
	lower the temperature　降溫

 實境對話
A: What's the **temperature** now?　現在氣溫幾度？
B: It's about 28 degrees Celsius.　大概28度。

✍ 練習試試看 📖

用簡單的小測驗，驗收一下，單字記住了嗎？

( ) 1 Dragon-boat Festival

( ) 2 Halloween

( ) 3 culture

( ) 4 celebrate

( ) 5 assistant

( ) 6 dentist

( ) 7 doctor

( ) 8 guide

( ) 9 manager

( ) 10 nurse

( ) 11 owner

( ) 12 secretary

( ) 13 soldier

( ) 14 employ

( ) 15 weather

( ) 16 foggy

( ) 17 humid

( ) 18 rainbow

( ) 19 thunder

( ) 20 earth

A 主人　　B 經理　　C 助手　　D 護士　　E 文化　　F 雷聲　　G 地球
H 有霧的　I 萬聖節　J 慶祝　　K 端午節　L 彩虹　　M 天氣　　N 潮濕的
O 士兵　　P 導遊　　Q 雇用　　R 祕書　　S 牙醫　　T 醫生

答案

1(K)　2(I)　3(E)　4(J)　5(C)　6(S)　7(T)　8(P)　9(B)　10(D)　11(A)　12(R)　13(O)　14(Q)
15(M)　16(H)　17(N)　18(L)　19(F)　20(G)

beach [bitʃ]
名 海灘

同義字 shore 海濱

實境對話
A: Let's go to the **beach** to see the sunset. 我們去海灘看夕陽吧！
B: Good idea! 好主意。

coast [kost]
名 海岸

名詞複數 coasts

實境對話
A: Where is the tribe? 這個部落在哪裡？
B: The tribe is on the north **coast**. 在北方的海岸。

desert [dɪˋzɝt]
名 沙漠

名詞複數 deserts

實境對話
A: What is the biggest **desert** in the world? 世界上最大的沙漠是哪一個？
B: Sahara **Desert**. 撒哈拉沙漠。

environment
[ɪnˋvaɪrənmənt]
名 環境

名詞複數 environments

實境對話
A: We should protect our **environment**. 我們應該要保護環境。
B: What is the first step? 第一步該怎麼做？

forest [ˋfɔrɪst]
名 森林

名詞複數 forests
延伸片語 rain forest 雨林

實境對話
A: We got lost in the **forest**. 我們在森林裡迷路了。
B: Do you have a compass? 你們有指南針嗎？

hill [hɪl]
名 山

名詞複數 hills
同義字 mountain 山
延伸片語 a hill of beans 沒有多大價值的東西
over the hill 老而不中用的

實境對話
A: Where are you? 你們在哪？
B: We are on the top of the **hill**. 我們在山頂上。

island [ˈaɪlənd]
名 島嶼

名詞複數	islands
延伸片語	traffic island　安全島 desert island　荒島

A: He has lived on the **island** alone for ten years.　他在島上獨自生活了十年。
B: It's amazing.　太不可思議了。

lake [lek]
名 湖泊

名詞複數	lakes

A: The **lake** looks like a mirror.　這片湖看起來像面鏡子。
B: Yeah, I can even see fish swimming in it.　對啊，我還看到魚呢！

mountain [ˈmaʊntn̩]
名 山峰

名詞複數	mountains
同義字	hill 山
延伸片語	make a mountain out of a molehill　小題大作

A: I plan to climb a **mountain** this Sunday.　星期天我打算去爬山。
B: Can I go with you?　我可以和你一起去嗎？

ocean [ˈoʃən]
名 海洋

名詞複數	oceans　同義字　sea 海洋
延伸片語	a drop in the ocean　滄海一粟 Atlantic Ocean　大西洋

A: The Pacific Ocean is the largest **ocean** in the world.　太平洋是全世界最大的海洋。
B: What is the second largest **ocean**?　那第二大的海洋呢？

plain [plen]
名 平原

名詞複數	plains　同義字　lowland 低地
延伸片語	flood plain　氾濫平原

A: What are the children doing?　孩子們在做什麼？
B: They are flying kites on the **plain**.　他們在平原上放風箏。

pond [pɑnd]
名 池塘

名詞複數	ponds
同義字	pool 池塘

A: What did you see in the **pond**?　你在池塘裡看到什麼？
B: I saw frogs and tadpoles.　我看到青蛙和蝌蚪。

pool [pul]
名 水池、泳池

名詞複數	pools　同義字　mere 小湖
延伸片語	dirty pool　不道德行為 swimming pool　游泳池

A: Excuse me, where is the swimming **pool**?　不好意思，請問游泳池在哪裡？
B: It's in the basement.　在地下室。

river [ˈrɪvɚ]
名 河流

| 名詞複數 | rivers |
| 同義字 | stream 溪流 |

實境對話
A: Did you see them? 你有看到他們嗎？
B: Yes, they walked along the **river** bank. 有，他們沿著河岸走。

sea [si]
名 海洋

名詞複數	seas
同義字	ocean 海洋
延伸片語	go to sea 去當水手
	at sea 在海上

實境對話
A: Where is Tom? 湯姆在哪？
B: He is standing over there looking at the **sea**. 他站在那裡看海。

spring [sprɪŋ]
名 春天、泉水

名詞複數	springs
延伸片語	spring from 突如其來地從（某處）出現
	spring up 迅速出現

實境對話
A: How do you like the village life? 你覺得鄉村生活如何？
B: I like the fresh air and **spring** water there. 我喜歡那邊的新鮮空氣和泉水。

stream [strim]
名 小溪

名詞複數	streams
同義字	river 河流
延伸片語	go with the stream 順應潮流
	be on stream 投產

實境對話
A: Turn left and you will see a **stream**. 左轉你就會看到一條溪流。
B: OK. I see it. 好，我看到了。

valley [ˈvælɪ]
名 山谷

| 名詞複數 | valleys |
| 同義字 | mountain 大山 |

實境對話
A: Did you hear the echo from the **valley**? 你有聽見從山谷傳來的回音嗎？
B: No, I heard nothing. 沒有，我什麼也沒聽到。

woods [wʊdz]
名 樹林

同義字	forest 森林
延伸片語	neck of the woods 某地方
	not out of the woods 尚未擺脫困境

實境對話
A: Kids often play in the **woods**. 孩子們常在樹林裡玩。
B: Is it safe to play in the **woods**? 在樹林玩安全嗎？

Chapter **19** 地理用語 Geography

Chapter 20 動物、昆蟲

animal [ˈænəml̩]
名 動物

名詞複數 animals
延伸片語 animal magnetism　人格吸引力
animal spirits　精力充沛

 實境對話
A: What **animals** are from Africa?　什麼動物來自非洲？
B: Elephants and hippos.　大象和河馬。

bear [bɛr]
名 熊

名詞複數 bears
延伸片語 polar bear　北極熊

 實境對話
A: There is a **bear** behind the tree.　有一隻熊在樹後面。
B: Let's go inside.　讓我們進屋內。

cat [kæt]
名 貓

名詞複數 cats
延伸片語 cats and dogs　（下雨）猛烈地
bell the cat　為大家的利益承擔危險

 實境對話
A: He has two pet **cats**.　他有兩隻寵物貓。
B: I prefer dogs.　我比較喜歡狗。

chicken [ˈtʃɪkɪn]
名 雞

延伸片語 chicken feed　一筆微不足道的錢
spring chicken　年輕人

 實境對話
A: What would you like to order?　請問您想點什麼？
B: Roast **chicken**, please.　請給我烤雞。

cow [kaʊ]
名 母牛

名詞複數 cows

 實境對話
A: There are a herd of **cows** on the farm.　農場上有一群牛。
B: We can have fresh milk.　我們可以喝到新鮮的牛奶。

deer [dɪr]
名 鹿

 實境對話
A: Where are red **deers** from?　紅鹿來自哪裡？
B: From North Africa.　北非。

dinosaur
[ˈdaɪnəˌsɔr] **名** 恐龍

名詞複數 dinosaurs

 實境對話
A: We can't see **dinosaurs** now. 我們現在看不到恐龍。
B: They became extinct. 他們滅亡了。

dog [dɔg]
名 狗

名詞複數 dogs
延伸片語 let sleeping dogs lie 沒惹是非
pet dog 寵物

 實境對話
A: **Dogs** are faithful animals. 狗是忠實的動物。
B: They sometimes protect people. 他們有時保護人類。

donkey [ˈdɑnkɪ]
名 驢

名詞複數 donkeys
延伸片語 donkey work 單調的苦差事
donkey's years 很長時間

 實境對話
A: The little **donkey** rolled on the ground. 小驢在地上打滾。
B: So cute. 好可愛

duck [dʌk]
名 鴨子

名詞複數 ducks
延伸片語 like a duck to water 輕而易舉
a dead duck 註定要失敗

 實境對話
A: What is your favorite dish? 你喜歡哪道菜？
B: I like roast **duck**. 我喜歡烤鴨。

eagle [ˈigl̩]
名 鷹

名詞複數 eagles

實境對話
A: There is an **eagle** soaring overhead. 有一個老鷹在頭頂翱翔。
B: I can't believe it. 我不相信。

elephant
[ˈɛləfənt] **名** 大象

名詞複數 elephants
延伸片語 white elephant 無價值的束西

實境對話
A: **Elephants** are one of the biggest animals in the world. 大象是世上最大的動物。
B: They are heavy but friendly. 他們很重的，但很友善。

fox [fɑks]
名 狐狸

名詞複數 foxes
延伸片語 play fox 耍狡猾

 實境對話
A: Neil is dishonest. 奈爾不誠實。
B: He is an old **fox**. 他像是老狐狸。

frog [frɑg]
名 青蛙

名詞複數 frogs
延伸片語 frog in one's throat 聲音嘶啞

 實境對話
A: Prince **Frog** is a famous story. 青蛙王子是有名的故事。
B: It is very funny. 很有趣。

goat [got]
名 山羊

名詞複數 goats
延伸片語 get somebody's goat 使某人惱怒
old goat 討厭的老傢夥

 實境對話
A: The **goat's** cheese tastes delicious. 山羊乳酪味道鮮美。
B: Really? I want to try it. 真的嗎？我想嚐一下。

goose [gus]
名 鵝

名詞複數 geese
延伸片語 goose egg 零分

實境對話
A: What would you like to order, sir? 請問您要點什麼菜，先生？
B: Roast **goose** and an onion soup. 燒鵝和洋蔥湯。

hen [hɛn]
名 母雞

名詞複數 hens
延伸片語 mother hen 愛操心的女人
hen party 準新娘聚會

實境對話
A: What does "mother hen" mean? 「mother hen」是什麼意思？
B: It means the women who care about others too much. 是指愛操心的女人。

hippo ['hɪpo]
名 河馬

名詞複數 hippos

實境對話
A: Where are **hippos** from? 河馬來自哪裡？
B: They are from Africa and Asia. 牠們來自非洲和亞洲。

horse [hɔrs]
名 馬

名詞複數 horses
延伸片語 horses for courses 知人善任
hold your horses 且慢、請三思

實境對話
A: Did you see Tommy? 你看到湯米了嗎？
B: Yes. He just rode his **horse** off. 是的。他剛騎馬走了。

kangaroo [ˌkæŋgəˈru] 名 袋鼠

名詞複數 kangaroos

 實境對話
A: **Kangaroos** are cute. 袋鼠很可愛。
B: I saw them in Australia last year. 我去年在澳洲看過牠們。

kitten [ˈkɪtṇ]
名 小貓

名詞複數 kittens

實境對話
A: Look at the **kittens**. 看看這些小貓。
B: Wow, they are small and cute. 哇，牠們靈巧可愛。

koala [kəˈɑlə]
名 無尾熊

名詞複數 koalas

實境對話
A: Tell me something about **koalas**. 告訴我一些關於**無尾熊**的事情。
B: They love eating leaves and live in trees. 牠們喜歡吃葉子，生活在樹上。

lamb [læm]
名 小羊

名詞複數 lambs

實境對話
A: This is the first time that I have **lamb** chops. 這是我第一次吃羊小排。
B: Do you like them? 喜歡嗎？

lion [ˈlaɪən]
名 獅子

名詞複數 lions

實境對話
A: The **Lion** King is a famous and interesting film. 獅子王是著名的和有趣的電影。
B: In fact, I have seen it for ten times. 其實，我已經看過十遍了。

monkey [ˈmʌŋkɪ]
名 猴子

名詞複數 monkeys
延伸片語 brass monkeys 極冷的天氣
get sb.'s monkey up 使某人生氣

實境對話
A: **Monkeys** are smart and active. 猴子是聰明又好動的。
B: It is said that they are related to human beings. 有人說牠們與人類有關係。

monster
[ˈmɑnstɚ] 名 怪物

名詞複數 monsters

實境對話
A: My new neighbor looks like a **monster**. 我的新鄰居看起來像**怪物**。
B: Don't be rude. 不得無禮。

mouse [maʊs]
名 老鼠

名詞複數 mice
延伸片語 play cat and mouse with somebody 耍弄
Mickey Mouse 品質不高的、太容易的

實境對話
A: I am afraid of **mice**. 我怕老鼠。
B: Why? Don't you think they are cute? 為什麼？難道你不覺得牠們很可愛？

Chapter 20 動物、昆蟲 Animals & Insects

ox [ɑks]
名 公牛

名詞複數 oxen
同義字 bull 公牛

實境對話
A: **Oxen** work hard on the farm. 公牛在農場上辛勤工作。
B: Harder than the other animals. 比其他動物更辛勤。

panda [ˋpændə]
名 熊貓

名詞複數 pandas
延伸片語 panda car 巡邏警車

實境對話
A: What kind of food do **pandas** usually have? 熊貓通常吃什麼樣的食物？
B: They are fed on bamboo. 牠們吃竹子。

parrot [ˋpærət]
名 鸚鵡

名詞複數 parrots
延伸片語 sick as a parrot 大失所望
parrot-fashion 盲從地

實境對話
A: I am as **sick as a parrot**. 我大失所望。
B: What's wrong? 發生什麼事情？

pet [pɛt]
名 寵物

名詞複數 pets
延伸片語 pet name 昵稱
somebody's pet hate 特別厭惡的東西

實境對話
A: Do you keep a **pet**? 你養寵物嗎？
B: No, I am too busy. 不，我太忙了。

pig [pɪg]
名 豬

名詞複數 pigs
延伸片語 make a pig's ear 盲目購買
a pig of a something 撓頭的事情

實境對話
A: I think **pigs** look dirty. 我認為豬看其來很髒。
B: Actually, they are clean animals. 其實，牠們是乾淨的動物。

pigeon [ˋpɪdʒən]
名 鴿子

名詞複數 pigeons
延伸片語 be somebody's pigeon 是某人的職責

實境對話
A: Where is Ted? 泰德在哪裡？
B: He's feeding the **pigeons** on the balcony. 他在陽台餵鴿子。

puppy [ˋpʌpɪ]
名 小狗

名詞複數 puppies

實境對話
A: Emma's dog has had a litter of **puppies** last night. 艾瑪的狗昨晚生了一堆小狗。
B: Really? She must be very busy. 真的嗎？她一定很忙。

Part 1 生活情境單字

rabbit [ˋræbɪt]
名 兔子

名詞複數 rabbits
延伸片語 rabbit on 沒完沒了地說話、閒扯
pull a rabbit out of the hat 突然提出解決辦法

A: Can **rabbits** jump over a wall? 兔子可以跳過牆嗎？
B: It is impossible. 這是不可能的。

rat [ræt]
名 鼠

名詞複數 rats
延伸片語 rug rat 小孩
rat on somebody 洩露祕密

A: **Rats** may carry diseases. 老鼠可能帶來疾病。
B: Hence, people don't like them. 因此，人們不喜歡牠們。

sheep [ʃip]
名 羊

名詞複數 sheep
延伸片語 a black sheep 害群之馬
like sheep 盲從

A: **Sheep** are grazing over there. 羊在那邊吃草。
B: They look hungry. 牠們看起來很餓。

swan [swɑn]
名 天鵝

名詞複數 swans
延伸片語 swan song 最後的詩篇、絕筆

A: What is a white and graceful bird? 哪種鳥是白色且優雅的？
B: A **swan** is. 是天鵝。

tiger [ˋtaɪgɚ]
名 老虎

名詞複數 tigers

A: The man fought like a **tiger**. 男人像老虎一樣搏鬥。
B: He was very brave. 他很勇敢。

turkey [ˋtɝkɪ]
名 火雞

名詞複數 turkeys
延伸片語 talk turkey 鄭重其事地談
cold turkey 吸毒成癮者突然解毒時的痛苦

A: What do you usually have on Thanksgiving Day? 你們感恩節都吃什麼呢？
B: We usually have roast **turkey**. 我們通常都會吃烤火雞。

wolf [wʊlf]
名 狼

名詞複數 wolves
延伸片語 keep the wolf form the door 勉強度日
throw somebody to the wolves 見死不救

A: There is a pack of **wolves** in the forest. 有一個群狼在森林中。
B: The hunters are in danger. 獵人們有危險了。

zebra [ˈzibrə]
名 斑馬

名詞複數 zebras
延伸片語 zebra crossing 斑馬線

實境對話
A: The **zebra** crossing is for pedestrians, not motorcycles.
斑馬線是給行人走的,不是摩托車。
B: Sorry.
對不起。

insect [ˈɪnsɛkt]
名 昆蟲

名詞複數 insects

實境對話
A: He was bitten by an **insect**.　他被昆蟲叮咬。
B: Here is an **insect** repellent.　這裡有些驅蟲劑。

ant [ænt]
名 螞蟻

名詞複數 ants
延伸片語 have ants in your pants 坐立不安

實境對話
A: Watch out! There is an **ants**' nest in the garden.　當心!花園裡有螞蟻窩。
B: Thank you.　謝謝。

bat [bæt]
名 蝙蝠

名詞複數 bats
延伸片語 off your own bat 自覺地
not bat an eyelid 不動聲色

實境對話
A: There are many types of **bats**.　蝙蝠有很多種類。
B: Can you give me an example?　你能舉例嗎?

bee [bi]
名 蜜蜂

名詞複數 bees
延伸片語 the bee's knees 出類拔萃的人
have a bee in your bonnet 念念不忘

實境對話
A: Meg is as busy as a **bee**.　梅格像蜜蜂一樣忙。
B: She works overtime every day.　她每天都加班。

bird [bɝd]
名 鳥

名詞複數 birds
延伸片語 birds of a feather 同類的人
a bird's-eye view 鳥瞰

實境對話
A: Do you know what **bird** this is?　你知道這是什麼鳥嗎?
B: This is a sparrow.　這是隻麻雀。

bug [bʌg]
名 小蟲

名詞複數 bugs
延伸片語 bug off 滾開

實境對話
A: What's difference between **bugs** and insects?　小蟲和昆蟲之間有何區別?
B: I am not sure.　我不知道。

Chapter 20 動物、昆蟲 Animals & Insects

butterfly
[ˈbʌtɚˌflaɪ]
名 蝴蝶

名詞複數 butterflies
延伸片語 have butterflies in your stomach 心慌、緊張

A: She is really good at swimming. 她真的很會游泳耶。
B: Yes, she is especially good at **butterfly** stroke. 是啊，她尤其擅長蝶泳。

cockroach
[ˈkɑkˌrotʃ] 名 蟑螂

名詞複數 cockroaches

A: There are **cockroaches** in your kitchen. 你的廚房裡有蟑螂。
B: What? 什麼！

dragon [ˈdrægən]
名 龍

名詞複數 dragons
延伸片語 Dragon Boats Contest 龍舟競賽
Dragon Boat Festival 端午節

A: Did **dragons** have wings? 龍有翅膀嗎？
B: I guess so. 我猜有。

mosquito
[məˈskito] 名 蚊子

名詞複數 mosquitoes

A: You got a **mosquito** bite. 你被蚊子叮咬。
B: Can you close the window for me? 你能替我關窗戶嗎？

snail [snel]
名 蝸牛

名詞複數 snails
延伸片語 at a snail's pace 非常緩慢

A: Are **snails** edible? 蝸牛可以吃嗎？
B: Yes, some types of **snails**. 是的，某些種類的蝸牛。

snake [snek]
名 蛇

名詞複數 snakes
延伸片語 a snake in the grass 陰險的人

A: Be careful. 請小心。
B: Oh, there is a **snake** in the grass. 哦，有一條蛇在草叢中。

spider [ˈspaɪdɚ]
名 蜘蛛

名詞複數 spiders

A: **Spider** man is brave. 蜘蛛人很勇敢的。
B: It is just a movie. 這只是一部電影。

crab [kræb]
名 螃蟹

名詞複數 crabs

 實境對話
A: What did you have for dinner? 你晚餐吃什麼？
B: Some dressed crab. 一些加工過的螃蟹。

dolphin [ˈdɑlfɪn]
名 海豚

名詞複數 dolphins

 實境對話
A: Dolphins are very friendly. 海豚很友善。
B: They are smart, too. 牠們也很聰明。

fish [fɪʃ]
名 魚

名詞複數 fishes
延伸片語 fish for something 旁敲側擊地打聽
fish something/somebody out 取出

 實境對話
A: What are you going to do this Saturday? 你週六打算做什麼？
B: I am going fishing. 我去釣魚。

shark [ˈʃɑrk]
名 鯊魚

名詞複數 sharks
延伸片語 loan shark 放高利貸者

 實境對話
A: Some sharks will attack people. 有些鯊魚會攻擊人。
B: Swimmers should be careful. 泳客應小心。

shrimp [ʃrɪmp]
名 蝦

名詞複數 shrimps

 實境對話
A: Why don't you eat those shrimps? 你為何不吃蝦？
B: I'm allergic to shrimps. 我對蝦子過敏。

turtle [ˈtɝtl̩]
名 烏龜

名詞複數 turtles
延伸片語 turn turtle 傾覆

 實境對話
A: Turtles lay eggs on the beach. 海龜海灘上產卵。
B: How do you know that? 你怎麼知道的？

whale [hwel]
名 鯨魚

名詞複數 whales
延伸片語 have a whale of a time 玩得很愉快

 實境對話
A: What are the largest animal on earth? 地球上最大的動物是什麼嗎？
B: The Blue Whale. 藍鯨。

Part **1** 生活情境單字

bark [bɑrk]
動 吠叫

動詞變化 barked, barked, barking, barks

延伸片語 with the bark on 因缺乏教養而舉止粗魯的
somebody's bark is worse than their bite 表面上兇猛

 實境對話
A: Whom is the dog **barking** at? 狗在對著誰狂叫啊？
B: My cousin. 我表妹。

bite [baɪt]
動 咬

動詞變化 bite, bite, biting, bites

延伸片語 be bitten by something 對某事物著迷
bite the dust 失敗

 實境對話
A: Did you get hurt? 你受傷了嗎？
B: Yes. I was **bitten** by a dog. 是的。我被狗咬傷。

swallow [ˋswɑlo]
名 燕子 **動** 吞下

動詞變化 swallowed, swallowed, swallowing, swallows
名詞複數 swallows

延伸片語 bitter pill to swallow 不得不忍受的苦事
swallow up 吞沒

 實境對話
A: I have a sore throat. 我喉嚨痛。
B: Does it hurt when you **swallow**? 吞嚥時喉嚨會痛嗎？

tail [tel]
名 尾巴

名詞複數 tails

延伸片語 on somebody's tail 尾隨
turn tail 轉身逃跑

 實境對話
A: The dog is wagging its **tail**. 狗在搖尾巴。
B: It likes you. 牠喜歡你。

wing [wɪŋ]
名 翅膀

名詞複數 wings

延伸片語 in the wings 準備接替工作
take wing 飛走

 實境對話
A: The bird is flapping its **wings**. 鳥拍動翅膀。
B: It is noisy. 很吵雜。

✎ 練習試試看 📖

用簡單的小測驗，驗收一下，單字記住了嗎？

( ) 1 desert

( ) 2 mountain

( ) 3 ocean

( ) 4 river

( ) 5 woods

( ) 6 animal

( ) 7 deer

( ) 8 dinosaur

( ) 9 elephant

( ) 10 goat

( ) 11 hippo

( ) 12 koala

( ) 13 monster

( ) 14 pet

( ) 15 puppy

( ) 16 rabbit

( ) 17 insect

( ) 18 bat

( ) 19 spider

( ) 20 bark

A 海洋　　B 鹿　　　C 山羊　　D 昆蟲　　E 沙漠　　F 河馬　　G 小狗
H 吠叫　　I 蝙蝠　　J 怪物　　K 山峰　　L 大象　　M 蜘蛛　　N 樹林
O 恐龍　　P 無尾熊　Q 河流　　R 兔子　　S 寵物　　T 動物

答案
1(E)　2(K)　3(A)　4(Q)　5(N)　6(T)　7(B)　8(O)　9(L)　10(C)　11(F)　12(P)　13(J)　14(S)
15(G)　16(R)　17(D)　18(I)　19(M)　20(H)

Part

2

依詞性分類的
生活單字

Part 2 音檔雲端連結

因各家手機系統不同，若無法直接掃描，
仍可以至以下電腦雲端連結下載收聽。
（https://tinyurl.com/bdzapf5e）

Track 184

a [ə]
冠 一個

延伸片語 a pain in the neck 極討厭的人
a storm in a teacup 大驚小怪

實境對話
A: Sorry, I broke **a** cup. 對不起，我打破了一個杯子。
B: Never mind. 沒關係。

every [ˈɛvrɪ]
形 每個

延伸片語 every other day 每隔一天
every bit as 就如

實境對話
A: How often do the buses run? 公車多久來一班？
B: Once **every** fifteen minutes. 每十五分鐘一班。

the [ðə]
冠 這、那

實境對話
A: Which skirt do you think she likes?
你覺得她喜歡哪件裙子？
B: **The** red one.
紅色的那件。

this [ðɪs]
形 這個 代 這、這個

延伸片語 all this while 有好久
at this rate 這樣

實境對話
A: What is **this**? 這是什麼？
B: Suntan lotion. 防曬乳。

that [ðæt]
形 那個 代 那、那個

延伸片語 that's that 就這樣定了
that is 也就是說

實境對話
A: Where did you see **that** boy? 你在哪裡看到那個男孩？
B: At the train station. 火車站。

these [ðiz]
形 這些的 代 這些

實境對話
A: Are **these** all yours? 這些都是你的嗎？
B: No, **these** are not all mine. 不，這些不全是我的。

those [ðoz]
形 那些的 代 那些

實境對話
A: **Those** people are crazy. 那些人太瘋狂了。
B: What's going on? 怎麼了？

my [maɪ]
代 我的

延伸片語 for my money 依我看
to my mind 以我之見

實境對話 A: Do you happen to see **my** friend, John? 你有遇到我的朋友約翰嗎？
B: I'm not sure. What does he look like? 我不確定。他長什麼樣子？

our [aʊr]
代 我們的

實境對話 A: Who is **our** new director? 我們的新任主管是哪一位？
B: The one wearing glasses. 帶著眼鏡的那位。

your [jʊɚ]
代 你的

實境對話 A: This is **your** postcard. 這是你的明信片。
B: Thank you. 謝謝。

his [hɪz]
代 他的

實境對話 A: Do you know **his** sister?
你認識他的妹妹嗎？
B: Yes, **his** sister is my classmate.
認識，他的妹妹是我的同學。

her [hɛ]
代 她的

實境對話 A: Did you get **her** gift? 你收到她的禮物了嗎？
B: Yes. I like it. 收到了，我很喜歡。

its [ɪts]
代 牠的

實境對話 A: The dog is waving **its** tail. 這隻狗正搖著牠的尾巴。
B: It's so cute. 好可愛喔。

their [ðɛr]
代 他們的

實境對話 A: I think **their** idea is great. 我覺得他們的主意很棒。
B: I beg to differ. 我不這麼認為。

Chapter **1** 冠詞&限定詞 Articles & Determiners

Track 186

I (me/my/ mine/myself)
[aɪ] 代 我

 A: May I help you? 有什麼需要我幫忙的嗎？
B: Yes, I'd like to reserve a room. 我想訂一間房間。

you (you/your/ yours/ yourself/ yourselves)
[ju] 代 你、你們

A: How much do **you** need? 你需要多少？
B: One hundred is enough. 一百美元就夠了。

he (him/his/ himself) [hi]
代 他

A: How do you think about **him**? 你覺得他怎麼樣？
B: A little arrogant. 有一點自大。

she (her/hers/ herself) [ʃi]
代 她

A: **She** can't speak Chinese, can **she**?
她不會說中文，對吧？
B: I'm not sure.
我不確定。

it (it/its/itself)
[ɪt] 代 它

A: Can you see the word? 你看得到字嗎？
B: No. **It** is too small. 不行，它太小了。

we (usour/ ours/ ourselves)
[wi] 代 我們

A: **We** really appreciate your help.
我們真的很感謝您的幫忙。
B: It's nothing.
別客氣。

they (them/ their/theirs / themselves)
[ðe] 代 他們

實境對話
A: Why were **they** late? 他們為什麼遲到？
B: Cause **they** were stuck in traffic jam. 因為他們路上塞車。

---

all [ɔl]
形 所有的 代 全部

延伸片語 all in all 從各方面考慮
all or nothing 孤注一擲

實境對話
A: **All** of them wear perfume. 所有人都有擦香水。
B: That's interesting. 真有趣。

---

another [ə`nʌðə]
代 另一個 形 另一個的

延伸片語 one another 互相
another story 另一回事

實境對話
A: I don't like this one. Please show me **another**. 我不喜歡這一個，請給我看**另一個**。
B: How about the pink one? 粉紅色的怎麼樣？

---

any [`ɛnɪ]
形 任何的 代 任何

延伸片語 at any cost 在任何情況下
at any moment 不知何時地、隨時地

實境對話
A: Do you need **any** help? 你有**任何**需要幫忙的嗎？
B: No, I can manage. Thanks. 不用，我可以自己來，謝謝。

---

anyone (anybody)
[`ɛnɪˌwʌn] 代 任何人

延伸片語 anybody's guess 誰也拿不準的事情

實境對話
A: I don't want to talk to **anyone**. 我不想跟任何人說話。
B: Are you OK? 你還好吧？

---

anything
[`ɛnɪˌθɪŋ] 代 任何事

延伸片語 anything but 決不
not for anything 根本不

實境對話
A: You can do **anything** you want. 你可以做任何想做的事。
B: Am I dreaming? 我在做夢嗎？

---

both [boθ]
形 兩個的 代 兩者都

延伸片語 make both ends meet 勉強維持生計
have a foot in both camps 腳踩兩隻船

實境對話
A: Which do you want? 你想要哪一個？
B: I want **both**. 兩個都要。

each [itʃ]
形 各自的 代 各自

延伸片語　each other　彼此
at each other's throats　互相攻擊

 實境對話
A: We **each** took the exam.　我們各自考了試。
B: Who got the best grade?　誰的成績最高？

everyone (everybody)
[`ɛvrɪˌwʌn]　代 所有人

延伸片語　on everyone's lips　大家都在討論
everyone has their price　重賞之下，必有勇夫

 實境對話
A: It is impossible to please **everyone**.　要討好所有人是不可能的。
B: You can say that again.　沒錯。

everything
[`ɛvrɪˌθɪŋ]
代 所有事

延伸片語　everything in the garden is rosy　樣樣稱心如意
everything but the kitchen sink　過多的東西

 實境對話
A: Don't worry. **Everything** will be ok.　別擔心，所有事都會沒問題的。
B: Really?　真的嗎？

many [`mɛnɪ]
形 很多的 代 許多

形容詞變化　more, the most
延伸片語　a good many　很多
many hands make light work　人多好辦事、眾人拾柴火焰高

 實境對話
A: **Many** students are absent today.　今天很多學生缺席。
B: How come?　為什麼？

most [most]
形 大部分的

延伸片語　at most　至多
make the most of something/somebody/yourself
充分利用

 實境對話
A: What is the result of this research?　研究結果得出什麼？
B: It shows **most** people have the experience of traveling abroad.　大部分的人都有出國的經驗。

nobody [`noˌbɑdɪ]
代 沒有人

延伸片語　like nobody's business　非常、很多
be nobody's fool　精明機智

 實境對話
A: Why are you crying?　你怎麼哭了？
B: **Nobody** wants to help me.　沒有人想幫我。

none [nʌn]
代 沒有的

延伸片語　none but　僅僅
have none of something　拒絕接受

 實境對話
A: Is there any gasoline left?　還有汽油嗎？
B: No, **none** at all.　沒有，一滴都沒了。

Part **2** 依詞性分類的生活單字

| 214 |

nothing [ˈnʌθɪŋ]
代 無

延伸片語 nothing but 只有
have nothing on somebody 遠比不上某人

實境對話
A: Do you really want to do that? 你真的要那樣做？
B: Yes. **Nothing** can change my mind. 沒錯，沒有任何事可以改變我的心意。

other [ˈʌðɚ]
形 其他的、另外的
代 另外一個

實境對話
A: Where are the **other** girls? 其他的女孩在哪？
B: They are on the playground. 她們在操場。

part [pɑrt]
形 部分的

延伸片語 on the part of somebody/on somebody's part 有某人所為
bit part （電影中的）小角色

實境對話
A: I'm exhausted. 我好累。
B: This is just a small **part** of our work. 這只是我們工作的一小部分呢。

some [ˈsʌm]
形 一些 代 一些

延伸片語 and then some 至少
some day 總有一天

實境對話
A: Could you give me **some** suggestions? 你可以給我一些建議嗎？
B: Of course. 當然可以。

someone (somebody)
[ˈsʌmˌwʌn]
代 某些人

延伸片語 put someone on 欺騙、捉弄
take someone for 錯人某認為

實境對話
A: Can you find **someone** to cover for you? 你可以找人幫你代班嗎？
B: I'm afraid I can't. 恐怕不行。

something
[ˈsʌmθɪŋ]
代 某些事

實境對話
A: What happened?
怎麼了？
B: There is **something** wrong with my car.
我的車出了些問題。

how [haʊ]
代 如何

 A: **How** did you go to the airport? 你是如何來機場的？
B: By taxi. 搭計程車。

what [hwɑt]
代 什麼

 A: **What** is your favorite food? 你最喜歡什麼食物？
B: Shrimps. 蝦子。

which [hwɪtʃ]
代 哪一個

 A: **Which** one do you like? 你喜歡哪一個？
B: The left one. 左邊那一個。

who [hu]
代 誰

 A: **Who** is that woman? 那女人是誰？
B: She is my **mother**. 她是我媽媽。

whose [huz]
代 誰的

 A: **Whose** dictionary is it? 這是誰的字典？
B: It's George's. 喬治的。

when [hwɛn]
代 什麼時候

 A: **When** did you come back? 你什麼時候回來的？
B: Two weeks ago. 兩週前。

where [hwɛr]
代 哪裡

 A: **Where** is my umbrella? 我的雨傘在哪裡？
B: It's in the drawer. 在抽屜裡。

whether [ˈhwɛðɚ]
連 是否

 A: I don't know **whether** she loves me or not.
我不知道她是否愛我。
B: You should ask her directly.
你應該直接問她。

while [hwaɪl]
連 當……時候

 A: Can you tell me the situation?
你可以告訴我當時的情況嗎？
B: **While** I entered the room, the phone was ringing.
當我進門的時候，電話就在響了。

why [waɪ]
副 為什麼

 A: **Why** are you still awake?　你為什麼還醒著？
B: I can't sleep.　我睡不著。

Chapter
3
疑問詞 Wh-Words

Chapter 4 Be動詞 & 助動詞

---

be (am are is was were been) [bi]

be動 在、是

 A: Where **is** your dog?　你的狗在哪裡？
B: It **is** in the yard.　在院子裡。

---

do (does did done) [du]

助動 做

 A: What are you **doing**?　你在做什麼？
B: I'm **doing** my homework.　我在做功課。

---

have (has had) [hæv]

助動 有

 A: **Have** you ever been to France?　你有去過法國嗎？
B: No, I **haven't**.　沒有。

---

can (could) [kæn]　助動 能

 A: **Can** you do me a favor?　你能幫我一個忙嗎？
B: Sure. What do you need help with?　當然好，怎麼了？

---

will (would) [wɪl]　助動 將、會

 A: I can't find my purpose of life.　我找不到人生的目標。
B: You **will** find it one day.　總有一天你會找到的。

---

may (might) [me]　助動 可能

 A: That **may** not be true.　那可能不是真的。
B: What makes you say that?　怎麼說？

---

must [mʌst]
助動 必須

實境對話
A: **Must** you go so soon?　你必須那麼早走嗎？
B: Yes, I **must**.　是的，我必須。

shall [ʃæl]
助動 會

實境對話
A: Good bye.　再會。
B: Good bye. We **shall** miss you.　再見，我們會想你的。

should [ʃʊd]
助動 應當

實境對話
A: What **should** I do?　我應該怎麼辦？
B: You **should** apologize to her.　你應該跟她道歉。

Chapter 4 Be 動詞 & 助動詞 Be & Auxiliaries

|219|

✎ 練習試試看 📖

用簡單的小測驗，驗收一下，單字記住了嗎？

( ) 1 every
( ) 2 these
( ) 3 her
( ) 4 their
( ) 5 she
( ) 6 another
( ) 7 both
( ) 8 each
( ) 9 everything
( ) 10 most

( ) 11 none
( ) 12 nothing
( ) 13 part
( ) 14 whose
( ) 15 whether
( ) 16 why
( ) 17 can
( ) 18 may
( ) 19 must
( ) 20 should

A 他們的	B 誰的	C 每個	D 能	E 各自的 F 無 G 是否
H 沒有的	I 可能	J 這些	K 必須	L 她 M 所有事 N 兩個的
O 應當	P 她的	Q 任何的	R 大部分的	S 部分的 T 為什麼

答案
1(C) 2(J) 3(P) 4(A) 5(L) 6(Q) 7(N) 8(E) 9(M) 10(R) 11(H) 12(F) 13(S) 14(B)
15(G) 16(T) 17(D) 18(I) 19(K) 20(O)

Chapter 5 介系詞

about [əˈbaʊt]
介 大約

延伸片語 that's about all　我的話說完了
be in two minds about something　猶豫不決

實境對話
A: How often do you play tennis?　你多久打一次網球？
B: **About** twice a week.　大約一週二次。

above [əˈbʌv]
介 在……之上

延伸片語 above water　沒有經濟上的困難
above price　極其珍貴的

實境對話
A: What happened?　怎麼了？
B: A bird is flying **above** my head.　有隻鳥在我頭上飛。

across [əˈkrɔs]
介 穿過

延伸片語 across the board　全體
cut across　徑直穿過

實境對話
A: What is the couple doing?　那對情侶在做什麼？
B: They are walking **across** the road.　他們正在過馬路。

after [ˈæftɚ]
介 在……之後

延伸片語 after all　畢竟
after-sales service　售後服務

實境對話
A: Come to my office **after** lunch.　午餐後到我的辦公室。
B: Yes, sir!　好的，長官。

against [əˈgɛnst]
介 反對

延伸片語 against the clock　爭分奪秒
hedge against something　採取保護措施

實境對話
A: The public was **against** the proposal.　大眾反對這項提議。
B: What will the government do next?　那政府下一步會怎麼做？

along [əˈlɔŋ]
介 沿著

延伸片語 along with　與……在一起
carry along　吸引

實境對話
A: What did you see from the window?　你從窗戶看過去看到什麼？
B: A couple where walking **along** the road.　一對夫婦沿著馬路走。

among [əˋmʌŋ]
介 在……之中

> 延伸片語 among others 尤其
> put the cat among the pigeons 引起麻煩

實境對話
A: Who is the tallest **among** them? 在他們之中誰最高？
B: Linda is. 琳達。

around [əˋraʊnd]
介 圍繞

> 延伸片語 rally around 一群人團結在一起
> turn around 轉身

實境對話
A: What are we going to do next? 接下來我們要做什麼？
B: Go for a run **around** the river bank. 繞著河岸跑一圈。

at [æt]
介 在

> 延伸片語 be at the end of your tether 筋疲力盡
> at the table 吃飯時

實境對話
A: Where is the meeting room? 會議室在哪裡？
B: **At** B201. 在B201.

before [bɪˋfor]
介 在……之前

> 延伸片語 before long 不久以後
> look before you leap 三思而後行

實境對話
A: Did anything happen **before** I came? 在我來之前有發生什麼事嗎？
B: No. Everything was fine. 沒有，一切都很好。

behind [bɪˋhaɪnd]
介 在……之後

> 延伸片語 behind the curtain 祕密地
> drop behind 落後

實境對話
A: Is this the line for tickets? 這是排隊買票的地方嗎？
B: Yes, please stand **behind** the yellow line. 是的，請站在黃線後。

below [bəˋlo]
介 在……之下

> 延伸片語 below par 不舒服
> below the belt 說話不公正的

實境對話
A: The temperature will falls **below** zero at night. 晚上氣溫會降到零度以下。
B: Let's turn on the heater then. 那我們開暖氣吧。

beside [bɪˋsaɪd]
介 在……旁邊

> 延伸片語 beside the mark 沒有擊中目標
> beside oneself 情緒失控

實境對話
A: My crush is **beside** me. 我的暗戀對象就在我旁邊。
B: It's a good chance to talk to him. 這是和他說話的好機會。

between
[bə'twin] 介 在……中間

 延伸片語 go-between　中間人
between a rock and a hard place　進退兩難

實境對話
A: It's a secret only **between** us.　這是我們兩個之間的祕密。
B: OK. I will keep the secret.　好，我不會説出去。

beyond [bɪ'jɑnd]
介 在……之外

 延伸片語 beyond compare　無與倫比
beyond question　毫無疑問

實境對話
A: I got 100 on my test!　It was totally **beyond** my expectation.
我考了一百分！這完全在我預期之外。
B: Congratulations!
恭喜！

by [baɪ]
介 通過、被

延伸片語 hard by　臨近
by heart　單憑記憶

實境對話
A: Why was he punished **by** the teacher?　為什麼他被老師處罰？
B: He did not do the homework.　因為他沒做作業。

down [daʊn]
介 向下

 延伸片語 sit down　坐下
calm down　使平靜

實境對話
A: Where is Mom?　媽媽在哪？
B: She is walking **down** the stairs.　她正走下樓梯。

during ['djʊrɪŋ]
介 在……期間

實境對話
A: You must exercise **during** pregnancy.
懷孕期間你必須要做運動。
B: What kinds of exercise can I do?
我可以做哪些運動？

except [ɪk'sɛpt]
介 除了

 延伸片語 except for　除了……之外

實境對話
A: How was the result?　結果如何？
B: All passed **except** me.　除了我之外，大家都過了。

for [fɔr]
介 為了

 延伸片語 be in for it　會惹出麻煩
for good　永遠

實境對話
A: This is prepared **for** you.　這是為你準備的。
B: You are so sweet.　你真貼心。

from [frɑm]

介 從

延伸片語 apart from 除了……外
hear from 收到信件

實境對話 A: Where do you come **from**? 你從哪裡來？
B: I come **from** America. 從美國。

in [ɪn]
介 在……裡

延伸片語 come in 進來
in and out 時常出入

實境對話 A: Who is **in** the car? 誰在車裡？
B: My brother. 我哥哥。

in back of
[ɪn bæk ɑv]
介 在……後面

實境對話 A: I can't find that restaurant. 我找不到那間餐廳。
B: It is just **in back of** the school. 就在學校後面啊。

in front of
[ɪn frʌnt ɑv]
介 在……前面

實境對話 A: Where is the post office? 郵局在哪裡？
B: It's is **in front of** the bookstore. 在書局的前面。

inside [ˈɪnˋsaɪd]
介 在……內

延伸片語 inside of 少於
inside out 裡面朝外

實境對話 A: Where is my doll, daddy? 爸爸，我的洋娃娃呢？
B: It is **inside** the box. 在盒子裡。

into [ˈɪntu]
介 到……裡

延伸片語 get into something 使陷入
ease into something 熟悉

實境對話 A: May I go **into** the hall? 我可以到大廳裡嗎？
B: Please wait a minute. 請等一下。

like [laɪk]
介 像

延伸片語 look like 看起來像
like father, like son 有其父必有其子

實境對話 A: What does the cloud look **like**? 這朵雲看起來像什麼？
B: It looks **like** a dog. 像一條狗。

near [nɪr]
介 接近

延伸片語 far and near 到處
near miss 僥倖脫險

實境對話 A: It's convenient living **near** the MRT. 住在**接近**捷運的地方真方便。
B: But the rent is expensive. 但是租金很貴。

of [ɑv]
介 ……的

延伸片語 hear of 聽說
get rid of 擺脫

實境對話 A: Who is the girl in black? 穿黑色衣服的女生是誰？
B: She is one **of** my friends. 我的一個朋友。

off [ɔf]
介 離開

延伸片語 get off 動身、從……下來
turn off 關閉

實境對話 A: I must be **off** now. 我得離開了。
B: Take good care of yourself. 請保重。

on [ɑn]
介 在……上

延伸片語 go on 繼續
get on 上車

實境對話 A: Where is the vase? 花瓶在哪裡？
B: It's **on** the dressing table. 在化妝臺上。

out [aut]
介 向、離去

延伸片語 look out 小心
give out 分發

實境對話 A: Where is manager? 經理呢？
B: She is **out**, not in the office. 她**離開**了，不在辦公室。

out of [aut ɑv]
介 自……離開

實境對話 A: What is he doing? 他在做什麼？
B: He is walking **out of** the elevator. 他正要從電梯走出來。

outside [ˋautˋsaɪd]
介 在……外面

延伸片語 at the outside 至多
on the outside 從表面

實境對話 A: Who is standing **outside** the house? 站在屋外的是誰？
B: Bella's boyfriend. 貝拉的男朋友。

over [ˋovɚ]
介 超過

延伸片語 all over the place　到處
hand over　交出

實境對話
A: How old is he?　他幾歲了？
B: He is **over** sixty.　超過六十歲了。

next to [nɛkst tu]
介 挨著

實境對話
A: Who's the boy **next to** you?　緊挨著你的小男孩是誰？
B: My nephew.　我的姪子。

since [sɪns]
介 自從　連 自從

延伸片語 ever since　從那時到現在
long since　很久以前

實境對話
A: Where have you been **since** we last met?　自從上次見面以後，你去哪裡了啊？
B: I went to London to study.　我去倫敦讀書。

than [ðæn]
介 比

延伸片語 no more than　只是、僅僅
no other than　只有、就是

實境對話
A: What do you think?　你覺得怎麼樣？
B: I think purple is better **than** blue.　我覺得紫色比藍色好。

through [θru]
介 通過

延伸片語 go through　參加
all through　一直

實境對話
A: Why were they so fast?　為什麼他們這麼快？
B: They took a shortcut **through** the forest.　他們走一條通過森林的捷徑。

till [tɪl]
介 直到

實境對話
A: I will wait **till** you come.　我會一直等，直到你來。
B: Leave me alone.　少煩我。

to [tu]
介 到

實境對話
A: Please go **to** the movie theater at 7:00p.m.
請在晚上七點到電影院。
B: OK. I'll be there on time.
好，我一定會準時。

toward [təˋwɔrd]
介 向著

延伸片語
go toward　朝……方向走去
make toward　向……延伸

實境對話
A: What does he want to do?　他想做什麼？
B: No idea. He is just walking **toward** the sea.　不知道。他只是向著海走去。

under [ˋʌndɚ]
介 在……之下

延伸片語
go under　破產

實境對話
A: Did you see my pillow?　你有看到我的枕頭嗎？
B: It's **under** the bed.　在床底下。

until [ənˋtɪl]
介 直到

實境對話
A: He didn't know that she still loved him **until** now.
他直到現在才知道她還愛他。
B: What a poor girl.
那個女孩真可憐。

up [ʌp]
介 向上

延伸片語
up with　拿起
up and down　上上下下

實境對話
A: Excuse me, where is the restroom?　不好意思，請問廁所在哪裡？
B: Please go straight **up**.　請往上直走。

upon [əˋpɑn]
介 根據

實境對話
A: Why did you do that?　你為什麼要那樣做？
B: I just acted **upon** directions.　我只是根據命令行事。

upper [ˋʌpɚ]
形 上面的

延伸片語
upper part　上部
upper end　上端

實境對話
A: Which is your book?　哪一本書是你的？
B: The **upper** one.　上面的那一本。

with [wɪð]
介 和……一起

延伸片語
do with　處理
up with　拿起

實境對話
A: I want to be **with** you forever.　我想要永遠和你在一起。
B: Are you serious?　你是認真的嗎？

without [wɪðˋaut]
介 沒有

實境對話
A: I can't live **without** you.　沒有你我活不下去。
B: Wise up.　別傻了。

Chapter 6 連接詞

and [ænd]
連 和

實境對話
A: What did you buy?
你買了什麼？
B: I bought a bar of chocolate **and** a loaf of toast.
一條巧克力和一條吐司。

---

as [æz]
連 像、隨著

延伸片語 as if 好像
as well 也、同樣

實境對話
A: Why is he dressed **as** a woman? 為什麼他打扮得像個女人？
B: Who knows? 誰知道。

---

because [bɪˈkɔz]
連 因為

延伸片語 because of 因為

實境對話
A: **Because** of you, I was late for school this morning. 因為你，所以我早上上學遲到。
B: I'm sorry. 對不起。

---

besides [bɪˈsaɪdz]
連 除……之外

實境對話
A: What did you do **besides** mapping the floor?
除了拖地之外，你還做了什麼？
B: I threw the garbage.
倒垃圾。

---

but [bʌt]
連 但是

延伸片語 but now 剛剛
but for 要不是

實境對話
A: I have tried **but** in vain. 我試過了但沒用。
B: Don't be sad. 別難過了。

---

however
[haʊˈɛvɚ]
連 無論如何

實境對話
A: I'll come **however** busy I am. 無論有多忙，我都會來的。
B: Thank you very much. 真是太感謝您了。

if [ɪf]
連 如果

延伸片語 if only　要是……就好了
as if　好像

實境對話 A: What will happen **if** I am late for my exam?　考試如果遲到會怎麼樣？
B: You will flunk out.　會被當掉。

or [ɔr]
連 或者

同義字 either 或者

實境對話 A: What do you want to eat, steak **or** pasta?　你想吃什麼？牛排**或**義大利麵？
B: Pasta.　義大利麵。

that [ðæt]
連 以至於

實境對話 A: Why is he alone?　為什麼他獨自一人？
B: He is so selfish **that** no one wants to talk to him.
他太自私了，**以致於**沒人想跟他講話。

therefore
[ˈðɛr͵for]
連 因此

實境對話 A: Where is the hostess?
女主人呢？
B: She was sick, and **therefore** couldn't come.
她生病了，**因此**不能來。

though (although) [ðo]
連 儘管

延伸片語 even though　雖然
as though　好像

實境對話 A: **Though** he is poor, he is happy.　儘管他很窮，但生活過得很快樂。
B: Happy is he who is content.　知足常樂。

Track 203

hello [hə'lo]
感 你好

 實境對話
A: **Hello**, nice to meet you.　你好，很高興認識你。
B: Nice to meet you, too.　很高興認識你。

hey [he]
感 嘿

 實境對話
A: **Hey!**　嘿！
B: You are... Catherine?　你是……凱薩琳？

hi [haɪ]
感 嗨

 實境對話
A: **Hi.**　嗨！
B: **Hi.** What's up?　嗨！你好嗎？

good-bye (goodbye bye) [gʊd'baɪ]
感 再見

 實境對話
A: It is time for me to leave.　我該走了。
B: **Good-bye.**　再見。

Track 204

accident
[ˈæksədənt]
 名 事故

名詞複數 accidents
延伸片語 by accident 偶然
car accident 車禍

實境對話
A: I had a slight **accident** on the way to school yesterday.
　　昨天我去學校的路上發生了一點小事故。
B: Are you OK?　你還好吧？

action [ˈækʃən]
名 動作

名詞複數 actions
延伸片語 take action 採取行動
action on 對……的作用

實境對話
A: His quick **action** saved the kid's life.　他及時的動作救了這名小孩。
B: He was brave, wasn't he?　他很勇敢，對吧？

activity [ækˈtɪvətɪ]
 名 活動

名詞複數 activities

實境對話
A: Who is the sponsor of the **activity**?　這個活動的贊助商是誰？
B: Microsoft.　微軟。

advertisement
[ˌædvɚˈtaɪzmənt]
 名 廣告

名詞複數 advertisements

實境對話
A: What do you think of the **advertisement**?　你覺得這個廣告怎麼樣？
B: It is creative.　很有創意。

advice [ədˈvaɪs]
 名 建議

名詞複數 advices
延伸片語 give advice 勸告

實境對話
A: If you had followed her **advice**, you would have passed the exam.
　　如果你聽她的建議，你就會通過那次考試的。
B: I know I was wrong.　我知道錯了。

age [edʒ]
 名 年齡

延伸片語 at the age of 在……歲
of age 成年

實境對話
A: How old are you?　你幾歲？
B: It's rude to ask a woman's **age**.　問女人的年齡是很失禮的。

aim [em]
名 目的

名詞複數 aims
延伸片語 aim of 旨在
aim at 針對

 實境對話
A: What is your final **aim**? 你最終的**目的**是什麼？
B: Being a billionaire. 成為億萬富翁。

alarm [əˋlɑrm]
名 警報

名詞複數 alarms
延伸片語 alarm clock 鬧鐘
fire alarm 火警

實境對話
A: The **alarm** is going off! 警報器響了！
B: Run! 快逃！

album [ˋælbəm]
名 相冊

名詞複數 albums
延伸片語 photo album 相冊

實境對話
A: Whose **album** is that? 那是誰的**相冊**？
B: It's Cathy's. 凱西的。

American [əˋmɛrɪkən]
名 美國、美國人

名詞複數 Americans

實境對話
A: What is your nationality? 你是哪一國人？
B: I am **American**. 美國人。

angel [ˋendʒəl]
名 天使

名詞複數 angles

實境對話
A: She is kind and considerate. 她既友善又體貼。
B: Yeah, she is just like an **angel**. 沒錯，就像一位**天使**。

anger [ˋæŋg]
名 生氣

延伸片語 in anger 生氣地
show anger 顯示憤怒

實境對話
A: Why did he speak in **anger**? 為什麼他**氣沖沖**地說話？
B: He was dumped. 他被甩了。

army [ˋɑrmɪ]
名 軍隊

名詞複數 armies
延伸片語 join the army 在陸軍中
in the army 在陸軍中

實境對話
A: The enemy **army** surrendered. 敵**隊**投降了。
B: The war is over. 戰爭結束了。

Chapter 8 其他名詞 Other Nouns

attention
[əˈtɛnʃən]
名 注意

名詞複數 attentions
延伸片語 pay attention 專心
pay more attention to 更加注意

實境對話
A: Do you hear something? 你有聽到什麼聲音嗎？
B: No. Pay **attention** to what you're doing. 沒有，注意你手邊的事。

balloon [bəˈlun]
名 氣球

名詞複數 balloons

實境對話
A: Have you ever ridden in a hot-air **balloon**? 你有坐過熱氣球嗎？
B: No, I haven't. 沒有。

band [bænd]
名 樂隊

名詞複數 bands

實境對話
A: Who is the man in a tuxedo? 穿著燕尾服的男士是誰？
B: He is the conductor of the **band**. 這個樂隊的指揮。

base [bes]
名 基礎

名詞複數 bases
延伸片語 at base 本質上
base in 基於

實境對話
A: The **base** of the building is strong enough to bear a 7-degree earthquake.
這棟建築物的根基夠紮實，可以承受七級的地震。
B: I'm relieved to hear that. 聽到這樣我就放心了。

beauty [ˈbjutɪ]
名 美麗

名詞複數 beauties

實境對話
A: She is **beauty** itself. 她真得好美。
B: I totally agree with you. 對啊。

beginner
[bɪˈɡɪnɚ]
名 初學者

名詞複數 beginners
同義字 learner 學習者

實境對話
A: Can I use this one? 我可以使用這個嗎？
B: This is not for **beginners**. 這個不適合初學者使用。

beginning
[bɪˈɡɪnɪŋ] 名 開頭

名詞複數 beginnings
延伸片語 at the beginning 首先
from the beginning 開始

實境對話
A: I've read the paper from **beginning** to end. 我把報告從頭到尾看完了。
B: Then you can take the exam. 那你可以參加考試了。

bell [bɛl]
名 鐘

名詞複數	bells
延伸片語	ring the bell　鳴鐘 bell the cat　為大家的利益承擔風險

A: How often does the **bell** chime?　鐘多久響一次？
B: It chimes every hour on the hour.　每整點一次。

birthday [ˈbɝˌθˌde]
名 生日

A: When is your **birthday**?　你的生日是幾月幾號？
B: July 6th.　六月六號。

blank [blæŋk]
名 空白

名詞複數	blanks
延伸片語	in blank　在空格裡 go blank　變成空白

A: Do you have a **blank** sheet of paper?　你有白紙嗎？
B: Yes, I do.　有。

blood [blʌd]
名 血液

延伸片語	in blood　充滿活力的 high blood　勇氣

A: What is diabetes?
　什麼是糖尿病？
B: It is a condition where the **blood** sugar level is higher than normal.
　糖尿病是指血糖值超過正常標準的情況。

bomb [bɑm]
名 炸彈

名詞複數	bombs

A: The **bomb** has been defused.　炸彈已經被拆解了。
B: It is safe now, right?　那現在安全了吧？

bottom [ˈbɑtəm]
名 底部

延伸片語	at the bottom　在底部 from top to bottom　完完全全

A: Where is the number of the store?　那家店的電話號碼在哪？
B: It's on the **bottom** of the cup.　杯子底部。

branch [bræntʃ]
名 樹枝

名詞複數	branches
延伸片語	branch company　分公司 branch line　支線

A: What is the gardener doing?　園丁在做什麼？
B: He is trimming the tree **branches**.　他正在修剪樹枝。

bundle [ˈbʌndl̩]
名 束

名詞複數 bundles

 實境對話
A: What do you want for Valentine's Day? 情人節你想要什麼？
B: A **bundle** of flowers. 一束花。

cable [ˈkebl̩]
名 電纜

名詞複數 cables

 實境對話
A: The **cable** has been cut off. 電纜被切斷了。
B: Who did that? 是誰做的好事啊？

cage [kedʒ]
名 籠子

名詞複數 cages

 實境對話
A: The **cage** is too small for my dog. 這個籠子裝不下我的狗。
B: How about this one? 那這一個如何？

can [kæn]
名 罐頭

名詞複數 cans

 實境對話
A: The **can** has expired. 這個罐頭過期了。
B: Throw it away. 丟掉吧。

captain [ˈkæptɪn]
名 隊長

名詞複數 captains

 實境對話
A: Who is the **captain**? 誰是隊長？
B: I am the **captain**. 我就是隊長。

case [kes]
名 情況、實情

名詞複數 cases 同義字 situation 情況
延伸片語 in that case 既然那樣
in case of 假設

 實境對話
A: He's not coming. 他不會來了。
B: **In that case**, I won't come, either. 既然那樣，我也不會來。

castle [ˈkæsl̩]
名 城堡

名詞複數 castles
延伸片語 castle in the air 空中樓閣

 實境對話
A: I have dreamed of living in a **castle**. 我曾幻想自己住在**城堡**。
B: Me, too. 我也是。

cause [kɔz]
名 原因

名詞複數 causes
延伸片語 cause of 起因
in the cause of 為了

實境對話
A: What was the **cause** of the fire? 起火的原因是什麼？
B: It is still under investigation. 還在調查中。

cell phone [sɛl fon]
名 手機

名詞複數 cell phones

實境對話
A: Can I borrow your **cell phone**? 可以跟你借手機嗎？
B: Sure. 好。

center [ˈsɛntɚ]
名 中心

名詞複數 centers
延伸片語 in the center 服務中心
business center 商業中心

實境對話
A: Excuse me, where is the information **center**? 請問遊客服務中心在哪裡？
B: It's on the 2nd floor. 二樓。

century [ˈsɛntʃərɪ]
名 世紀

名詞複數 centuries
延伸片語 turn of the century 世紀之交

實境對話
A: What **century** are we in now? 現在是幾世紀？
B: 21st **century**. 21世紀。

chance [tʃæns]
名 機會

名詞複數 chances
延伸片語 by chance 偶然
by any chance 萬一

實境對話
A: Please give me another **chance**. 請再給我一次機會。
B: No way. 不可能。

channel [ˈtʃænl̩]
名 通道

名詞複數 channels

實境對話
A: Where is the **channel**? 通道在哪裡？
B: At the end of the cave. 在洞穴的最裡面。

character [ˈkærɪktɚ]
名 特點

名詞複數 characters

實境對話
A: What are the **characters** of successful leaders? 成功的領導人有什麼特點？
B: They are smart and understanding. 既聰明又善解人意。

Part 2 依詞性分類的生活單字

chart [tʃɑrt]
名 圖表

名詞複數 charts
同義字 graph 圖表

實境對話
A: Can you show me the **chart**? 可以讓我看圖表嗎？
B: It's on the last page. 圖表在最後一頁。

childhood
[ˈtʃaɪldˌhʊd] 名 童年

延伸片語 early childhood 幼兒教育

實境對話
A: How was your **childhood**? 你的童年過得怎麼樣？
B: I was happy. 很快樂。

choice [tʃɔɪs]
名 選擇

名詞複數 choices 同義字 selection 選擇
延伸片語 for choice 根據選擇
of choice 特別的

實境對話
A: Why did you allow him to do that? 為什麼你讓他那樣做？
B: I had no **choice**. 我沒有選擇的餘地。

club [klʌb]
名 俱樂部

名詞複數 clubs
同義字 society 社團

實境對話
A: We formed a **club**. 我們成立了一個俱樂部。
B: Really? Can I join it? 是嗎？我可以加入嗎？

coach [kotʃ]
名 教練

名詞複數 coaches 同義字 selection 選擇
延伸片語 head coach 主教練
assistant coach 助理教練

實境對話
A: My **coach** is wearing a pair of glasses. 我的教練戴著一副眼鏡。
B: He is good-looking. 他還蠻帥的。

command
[kəˈmænd]
名 指揮

名詞複數 commands
同義字 instruction 指揮
延伸片語 in command 領導

實境對話
A: Who is **in command** of the army? 誰指揮陸軍？
B: General Smith. 史密斯將軍。

congratulation
[kənˌgrætʃəˈleʃən]
名 祝賀

名詞複數 congratulations

實境對話
A: I passed the exam. 我通過考試了。
B: **Congratulation!** I'm happy for you. 恭喜你！真替你開心。

contact
['kɑntækt]
名 接觸

名詞複數 contacts
延伸片語 contact with 與……聯繫
　　　　 in contact with 接觸

 實境對話
A: What if cockroaches come **in contact with** the powder? 蟑螂接觸到這個粉末會怎麼樣？
B: They will die soon. 很快就會死掉。

corner ['kɔrnɚ]
名 拐角

名詞複數 corners
延伸片語 in the corner 在角落
　　　　 around the corner 在拐角處

實境對話
A: Where is the restaurant? 餐廳在哪裡？
B: It is situated on the **corner** of the street. 就在街道的**拐角**處。

courage ['kɝɪdʒ]
名 勇氣

延伸片語 take courage 鼓起勇氣
　　　　 get up the courage 鼓起勇氣

實境對話
A: He plucked up **courage** to propose to her. 他鼓起**勇氣**向她求婚了。
B: Did she say "Yes"？ 她有答應嗎？

court [kort]
名 法院

名詞複數 courts
延伸片語 in court 在法庭上
　　　　 high court 高等法院

實境對話
A: He was brought to **court** for trial. 他上**法院**受審了。
B: I still believe that he is innocent. 我仍然相信他是清白的。

crime [kraɪm]
名 犯罪

名詞複數 crimes

實境對話
A: He committed a serious **crime**. 他犯了重罪。
B: Do you think he will be sentenced to life imprisonment? 你覺得他會被判終身監禁嗎？

crowd [kraʊd]
名 群眾

名詞複數 crowds
延伸片語 a crowd out 擠出
　　　　 follow the crowd 人云亦云

 實境對話
A: A large **crowd** gathers on the street. 大批**群眾**聚集在街上。
B: What are they doing? 他們在做什麼？

curve [kɝv]
名 曲線

名詞複數 curves

 實境對話
A: Did you see the **curve**? 有看到那條曲線嗎？
B: Yes, what's next? 有，接下來呢？

Part 2 依詞性分類的生活單字

damage
[ˈdæmɪdʒ]
名 破壞

名詞複數 damages
同義字 harm 傷害

實境對話
A: It is said that the **damage** brought by the typhoon is hard to estimate.
據說這次颱風帶來的破壞難以估計。
B: The typhoon was strong. 這次的颱風真的很強。

danger [ˈdendʒɚ]
名 危險

延伸片語 in danger 在危險中
out of danger 脫離危險

實境對話
A: Is her life in **danger**? 她有生命**危險**嗎？
B: No, she is now out of **danger**. 沒有，已經脫離**險**境了。

debate [dɪˈbet]
名 爭論

名詞複數 debates 同義字 dispute 爭論
延伸片語 debate on 關於……進行辯論
under debate 在爭論中

實境對話
A: What are they **debating**? 他們在**爭論**什麼？
B: They are arguing about who the best player is. 爭論誰是最佳球員。

decision
[dɪˈsɪʒən]
名 決定

名詞複數 decisions 同義字 determination 決定
延伸片語 make a decision 做決定
final decision 最後決定

實境對話
A: Do I have to make a **decision** now? 我必須現在做**決定**嗎？
B: Yes, you do. 是的。

department
[dɪˈpɑrtmənt]
名 部門

名詞複數 departments
同義字 division 部門

實境對話
A: Which **department** do you work for? 你在哪一個部門工作？
B: Human Resource **Department**. 人力資源部門。

desire [dɪˈzaɪr]
名 欲望

名詞複數 desires 同義字 requirement 欲望、要求
延伸片語 desire for 渴望
sincere desire 誠心誠意

實境對話
A: How to reduce material **desire**? 如何減少物質**欲望**？
B: First, cut your credit card. 首先，剪掉你的信用卡。

difference
[ˈdɪfərəns] 名 不同

名詞複數 differences 同義字 diversity 差異
延伸片語 difference in 在……方面的差別

實境對話
A: What is the **difference** between them? 他們有什麼不同？
B: I don't know. 不知道。

difficulty
[ˈdɪfəˌkʌltɪ] 名 困難

名詞複數 difficulties
同義字 poverty 困難
延伸片語 with difficulty 困難地
in difficulty 處境困難

實境對話
A: I think I have a learning **difficulty**. 我覺得我有學習上的困難。
B: Why? 為什麼？

direction
[dəˈrɛkʃən] 名 方向

名詞複數 directions
同義字 orientation 方向
延伸片語 in the direction 朝……方向
in all directions 四面八方

實境對話
A: I have no sense of **direction**. 我沒有方向感。
B: Me, neither. 我也是。

discussion
[dɪˈskʌʃən] 名 討論

名詞複數 discussions
同義字 argumentum 討論
延伸片語 under discussion 正在討論中
group discussion 小組討論

實境對話
A: What is our topic of **discussion** today? 我們今天討論的主題是什麼？
B: Financial crisis. 金融危機。

dream [drim]
名 夢想

名詞複數 dreams
延伸片語 dream of 夢想
dream about 夢想

實境對話
A: What is your **dream**? 你的夢想是什麼？
B: Being a professional translator. 當一名專業的譯者。

duty [ˈdjutɪ]
名 責任

名詞複數 duties 同義字 liability 責任
延伸片語 on duty 值班
stamp duty 印花稅

實境對話
A: Why do you want to join the army? 為什麼你想從軍？
B: I have a sense of **duty** to my country. 我對國家有責任感。

edge [ɛdʒ]
名 邊緣

名詞複數 edges 同義字 margin 邊緣
延伸片語 on the edge of 幾乎

實境對話
A: A woman is standing at the **edge** of the platform. 有一個女人站在月臺邊緣。
B: That's dangerous. 真危險。

education
[ˌɛdʒʊˈkeʃən] 名 教育

同義字 cultivation 教育

實境對話
A: Is **education** compulsory in your country? 你們國家有實施義務教育嗎？
B: Yes, it is compulsory. 有，這是義務。

effort [`ɛfət]
名 努力

名詞複數 efforts　同義字 achievement 努力
延伸片語 in an effort to 企圖
make every effort 盡一切努力

實境對話
A: He made a great **effort**, but ultimately failed.　他很**努力**但終究失敗了。
B: What a pity.　真可惜。

e-mail [i`mel]
名 電子郵件

名詞複數 e-mails

實境對話
A: Did you receive my **e-mail**?　你收到我的電子郵件了嗎？
B: Yes, I got it.　收到了。

emotion [ɪ`moʃən]
名 感情、情感

名詞複數 emotions　同義字 feeling 感情
延伸片語 with emotion 激動地
intense emotion 激情

實境對話
A: Do you think fish have **emotions**?　你覺得魚有情感嗎？
B: Yes, I think so.　嗯，我認為有。

enemy [`ɛnəmɪ]
名 敵人

名詞複數 enemies　同義字 foe 敵人
延伸片語 sworn enemy 不共戴天的敵仇
natural enemy 天敵

實境對話
A: What is your motto in life?　你的人生座右銘是什麼？
B: Every man is his own worst **enemy**.　人最大的**敵人**就是自己。

energy [`ɛnədʒɪ]
名 能量

同義字 vitality 能量

實境對話
A: What food gives you **energy**?　什麼食物供給人體**能量**？
B: Meat and nuts.　肉和堅果。

engine [`ɛndʒən]
名 引擎

名詞複數 engines

實境對話
A: The car stopped itself.　車子自動熄火了。
B: Maybe something is wrong with the **engine**.　可能是**引擎**出了問題。

entrance [`ɛntrəns]
名 入口

名詞複數 entrances

實境對話
A: Where is the **entrance**?　入口在哪裡？
B: It is on your right side.　在你的右手邊。

error [ˈɛrɚ]
名 錯誤

名詞複數 errors　同義字 mistake 錯誤
延伸片語 in error 錯誤地

實境對話
A: Is it a typing **error**?　這是打字錯誤嗎？
B: Yes, please delete it.　對，請把它刪除。

event [ɪˈvɛnt]
名 事件

名詞複數 events　同義字 incident 事件
延伸片語 in the event　如果
　　　　 in any event　無論如何

實境對話
A: When did the **event** happen?　這起事件何時發生？
B: In 2001.　2001年。

excuse [ɪkˈskjuz]
名 藉口

名詞複數 excuses　同義字 reason 藉口
延伸片語 excuse for 藉口
　　　　 in excuse of 為……辯解

實境對話
A: He was fired.　他被解雇了。
B: He deserved it. He always made **excuses** for being late.　活該，他總是編一堆遲到的藉口。

exit [ˈɛgzɪt]
名 出口

名詞複數 exits

實境對話
A: Can you find the **exit**?　你找得到出口嗎？
B: No, I am stuck in the maze.　找不到，我被困在迷宮裡了。

experience
[ɪkˈspɪrɪəns]
名 經驗

延伸片語 experience in　有……的經驗
　　　　 rich experience　豐富的經驗

實境對話
A: Do you have working **experience**?　你有工作經驗嗎？
B: No, I just graduated from the university.　沒有，我才剛從大學畢業。

fact [fækt]
名 實際

名詞複數 facts　同義字 truth 事實
延伸片語 in fact　事實上
　　　　 matter of fact　事實

實境對話
A: In **fact**, I don't trust him.　實際上我並不相信他。
B: Then why do you help him?　那你為什麼還要幫他？

fault [fɔlt]
名 錯誤

名詞複數 faults
同義字 error 困難

實境對話
A: I am sorry. I messed up everything.　抱歉，我搞砸了一切。
B: No, this is my own **fault**.　不，這是我自己的錯。

fear [fɪr]
名 害怕

同義字	worry 害怕
延伸片語	for fear 以免
	in fear 害怕

實境對話
A: Where is your sister? 你妹妹在哪裡？
B: She is standing there in **fear**. 她**害怕**的站在那裡。

fee [fi]
名 費用

| 名詞複數 | fees |
| 同義字 | charge 費用 |

實境對話
A: How much is the registration **fee**? 手續費多少？
B: NT$100. 台幣一百元。

feeling ['filɪŋ]
名 感覺

名詞複數	feelings	同義字	mood 情緒
延伸片語	good feeling 好感
	own one's feelings 接受、承認個人的真實情感

實境對話
A: Why do you want to be a teacher? 為什麼你想當老師？
B: Teaching gives me a **feeling** of joy. 教學讓我感覺愉快。

fire [faɪr]
名 火

| 延伸片語 | on fire 著火 |
| | under fire 受到嚴厲批評、遭到攻擊 |

實境對話
A: What's going on? 怎麼了？
B: The factory is on **fire**! 工廠失火了！

flag [flæg]
名 旗幟

名詞複數	flags
延伸片語	white flag 白旗（表示降旗）
	under the flag of 受到……保護

實境對話
A: How many stars are on the US **flag**? 美國國旗有幾顆星星？
B: Fifty. 五十顆。

flight [flaɪt]
名 飛行

| 同義字 | fly 飛行 |
| 延伸片語 | in flight 在飛行中 |

實境對話
A: Can you explain to me the theory of the **flight** of airplanes?
你可以跟我解釋飛機飛行的原理嗎？
B: No problem. 沒問題。

foreigner ['fɔrɪnə]
名 外國人

| 名詞複數 | foreigners |

實境對話
A: More and more **foreigners** come to Taiwan to study Chinese.
越來越多外國人來台學中文。
B: Yeah, my roommate from Canada is studying Chinese.
對啊，我來自加拿大的室友就正在學。

flower [ˈflauɚ]
名 花朵

名詞複數 flowers
延伸片語 in flower 開著花

 實境對話
A: What kind of **flower** do you like? 你喜歡哪一種花？
B: Jasmine. 茉莉花。

freedom [ˈfridəm]
名 自由

延伸片語 freedom from 免於

 實境對話
A: Everyone has the **freedom** of speech. 每個人都有言論的自由。
B: That's right. We should respect other's opinions. 沒錯，我們應該尊重他人的意見。

friendship [ˈfrɛndlɪ]
名 友情

同義字 fellowship 友誼

 實境對話
A: I value the **friendship** between us. 我很重視我們的友情。
B: Then why did you lie to me? 那為什麼要說謊？

fun [fʌn]
名 快樂

名詞複數 funs　同義字 joy 樂趣
延伸片語 have fun 玩得開心
for fun 開玩笑地

實境對話
A: Did you have a **fun** holiday? 假期過得愉快嗎？
B: So-so. 還好。

garbage [ˈgɑrbɪdʒ]
名 垃圾

同義字 rubbish 垃圾

實境對話
A: What housework did you do today? 你今天做了什麼家事？
B: I took out the **garbage**. 丟垃圾。

gas [gæs]
名 汽油

 實境對話
A: The car runs out of **gas**. 車子沒油了。
B: There is a **gas** station nearby. 附近有間加油站。

gesture [ˈdʒɛstʃɚ]
名 姿勢

同義字 motion 姿勢
延伸片語 make a gesture 做手勢

 實境對話
A: She shakes her head in a refusal **gesture**. 她搖頭做出拒絕的姿勢。
B: What does she want from me? 她到底要我怎麼樣？

ghost [gost]
名 鬼

名詞複數 ghosts
同義字 shadow 幽靈

實境
對話
A: Are you afraid of **ghosts**? 你怕鬼嗎？
B: No, I am not afraid at all. 一點也不怕。

gift [gɪft]
名 禮物

名詞複數 gifts
同義字 present 禮物

實境
對話
A: Can I use the **gift** voucher? 我可以使用這張禮券嗎？
B: Sorry, it is unavailable. 對不起，這一張不能使用了。

goal [gol]
名 目標

名詞複數 goals　　同義字 target 目的
延伸片語 primary goal 首要目標
long-term goal 長期目標

實境
對話
A: What is your **goal** in life? 你的人生目標是什麼？
B: Beats me. 你問倒我了。

God [gɑd]
名 上帝

實境
對話
A: Oh! My **God**! 天啊！
B: What's going on? 怎麼了？

goodness
[ˋgʊdnɪs]
名 善良

同義字 kindness 善良
延伸片語 thank goodness 謝天謝地

實境
對話
A: How do you think of Tom? 你覺得湯姆這個人怎麼樣？
B: He is **goodness** itself. 他的心地很善良。

government
[ˋgʌvənmənt]
名 政府

名詞複數 governments

實境
對話
A: What do you think? 你有什麼看法？
B: I think the **government** should take measures to solve the problem.
我認為政府應該採取措拖來解決問題。

grass [græs]
名 草地

同義字 lawn 草地
延伸片語 on the grass 在草地上

實境
對話
A: Where is Harry? 哈利在哪裡？
B: He is lying on the **grass** watching the stars. 他正躺在草地上看星星。

ground [graʊnd]
名 地面

同義字 earth 土地

延伸片語 on the ground 在地上、當場
to the ground 徹底地

 A: What's up? 怎麼了？
B: A glass fell to the **ground** and shattered. 杯子掉在地上，碎了一地。

group [grup]
名 組

名詞複數 groups

延伸片語 group 成組
a group of 一組、一群

 A: How many people are there in each **group** at most? 每一組最多有幾個人？
B: Five. 五個人。

gun [gʌn]
名 槍枝

名詞複數 guns

A: It is legal to own a **gun** in the US. 在美國持有槍枝是合法的。
B: But it is banned in some countries. 但在有些國家是禁止的。

habit [ˈhæbɪt]
名 習慣

名詞複數 habits 同義字 custom 習慣

延伸片語 in the habit of 有……的習慣
form the habit of 養成……的習慣

 A: How to get out of the **habit** of smoking? 要怎麼改掉抽菸的習慣？
B: I have the same problem. 我也有同樣的煩惱。

haircut [ˈhɛrˌkʌt]
名 理髮

延伸片語 get a haircut 剪頭髮
have a haircut 理髮

 A: Do I need to get a **haircut**? 我該去理髮嗎？
B: Yes, it is too long. 去吧，你的頭髮太長了。

heat [hit]
名 熱量

 A: What does the sun give off? 太陽會釋放出什麼？
B: **Heat** and light. 熱和光。

honesty [ˈɑnɪstɪ]
名 誠實

同義字 integrity 正直

 A: **Honesty** is the best policy. 誠實為上策。
B: What do you mean? 我不懂你的意思。

Chapter 8 其他名詞 Other Nouns

honey [ˈhʌnɪ]
名 蜂蜜

實境對話
A: What animal likes to eat **honey**? 什麼動物喜歡吃蜂蜜？
B: Bears. 熊。

human [ˈhjumən]
名 人類

實境對話
A: Who created **human** beings? 誰創造人類？
B: I have no clue. 不知道。

humor [ˈhjumɚ]
名 幽默

延伸片語 sense of humor 幽默
black humor 黑色幽默

實境對話
A: She has a good sense of **humor**. 她很有幽默感。
B: Yeah, and she loves to laugh. 對啊，而且很愛笑。

hunger [ˈhʌŋgɚ]
名 饑餓

延伸片語 from hunger 極差的
hunger for 渴望

實境對話
A: Lots of kids die from **hunger** each day in Africa. 每天非洲有很多小孩死於饑餓。
B: How can we help them? 我們要如何幫助他們？

idea [aɪˈdiə]
名 主意

名詞複數 ideas 同義字 concept 想法
延伸片語 have no idea 不知道
good idea 好主意

實境對話
A: Do you have any **idea**? 你有任何主意嗎？
B: No, I don't. 沒有。

importance [ɪmˈpɔrtṇs]
名 重要性

延伸片語 of great importance 有著重要意義
attach importance to 重視

實境對話
A: The matter is of little **importance** to us. 這件事對我們沒什麼重要性。
B: Why would you think that? 你怎麼會這樣想？

income [ˈɪn.kʌm]
名 收入

同義字 salary 工資
延伸片語 low income 低收入
income gap 收入差距

實境對話
A: How much is his annual **income**? 他的年收入有多少？
B: Five million US dollars. 五百萬美元。

influence
['ɪnfluəns]

名 影響

 同義字 effect 影響

延伸片語 influence on 對……影響
under the influence 酒醉的

實境對話
A: He was under the **influence** of alcohol when he crashed the car.
他在喝醉（酒精的影響）的情況下撞到車。
B: It is dangerous to drive after drinking.
酒後開車是很危險的。

information
[ˌɪnfəˋmeʃən]

名 信息

實境對話
A: Can you give me any **information** on this matter?
關於此事你能給我任何**資訊**嗎？
B: Sorry, I can't reveal anything.
抱歉，我不能透露任何消息。

Internet
[ˋɪntɚˌnɛt]

名 網際網路

實境對話
A: Do you have any questions?
你有什麼問題嗎？
B: Yes, I want to know how to access to the **Internet**.
有，我想知道如何連上**網路**。

interview
[ˋɪntɚˌvju]

名 面試

名詞複數 interviews

延伸片語 job interview 求職面試
exclusive interview 獨家採訪

實境對話
A: I have an **interview** tomorrow. 我明天有一場**面試**。
B: Good luck. 祝你好運。

invitation
[ˌɪnvəˋteʃən]

名 邀請

名詞複數 invitations
同義字 calling 邀請

延伸片語 by invitation 憑請柬
invitation letter 邀請函

實境對話
A: Did you get the **invitation**? 你有收到**邀請**函嗎？
B: No, I didn't. 沒有。

joke [dʒok]

名 玩笑

名詞複數 jokes
同義字 fun 玩笑

延伸片語 make a joke 開玩笑
in joke 開玩笑

實境對話
A: Are you making fun of me? 你在嘲笑我嗎？
B: No, I'm just **joking**. 不，我只是開個**玩笑**。

joy [dʒɔɪ]
名 歡樂

同義字 fun 歡樂
延伸片語 with joy 高興地
tears of joy 喜極而泣

 實境對話
A: I wish you **joy** and happiness. 祝你快樂幸福。
B: Thanks. 謝謝。

kind [kaɪnd]
名 種類

名詞複數 kinds
同義字 type 類型

實境對話
A: What **kind** of flower is it? 這是哪一種花？
B: It is daisy. 雛菊。

kingdom ['kɪŋdəm]
名 王國

名詞複數 kingdoms
同義字 domain 王國

 實境對話
A: Who will be the next ruler of the **kingdom**? 這個王國的下一位統治者是誰？
B: The king's son. 國王的兒子

lack [læk]
名 缺少

同義字 shortage 缺少
延伸片語 lack of 缺乏
lack in 缺少

 實境對話
A: Many countries face the problem of **lack** of water. 許多國家面臨缺水的問題。
B: How do they deal with the problem? 他們如何應對？

leader ['lidɚ]
名 領導

名詞複數 leaders **同義字** captain 領導
延伸片語 market leader 市場領袖
political leader 政治領袖

 實境對話
A: Who is the current **leader** of the Labor Party? 工黨的現任領導是誰？
B: Ed Miliband. 米勒班。

leaf [lif]
名 葉子

名詞複數 leaves

實境對話
A: Spring is coming. 春天要來了。
B: The trees begin to grow **leaves**. 樹要開始長葉子了。

level ['lɛvl]
名 水準

名詞複數 levels **同義字** standard 標準
延伸片語 level of ……的水準
on the level 誠實的

 實境對話
A: Crude oil prices have remained at a high **level**. 原油價格一直維持在高價位的水準。
B: That's a big problem. 那可真是糟糕。

lid [lɪd]
名 眼瞼

名詞複數 lids　　同義字 target 目的
延伸片語　put a lid on　取締
　　　　　blow the lid off　揭發（醜聞）

實境對話
A: My eye**lid** is itching.　我的眼瞼好癢。
B: You should go to see an eye-doctor.　你應該去看眼科醫生。

link [lɪŋk]
名 連接

名詞複數 links　　同義字 target 目的
延伸片語　link up　連接
　　　　　link with　與……有關

實境對話
A: Do you think there is a **link** between these two events?　你覺得這兩件事有關連嗎？
B: Yes, I think so.　有。

locker [ˋlɑkɚ]
名 櫃子

名詞複數 lockers
延伸片語　locker room　衣帽間

實境對話
A: What do you put in the **locker**?　你在櫃子裡放什麼東西？
B: My clothes.　我的衣服。

mail [mel]
名 郵件

名詞複數 mails

實境對話
A: Are there any **mails** today?　今天有郵件嗎？
B: No mails today.　沒有。

manner [ˋmænɚ]
名 方法

名詞複數 manners
延伸片語　in a manner　在某種意義上
　　　　　all manner of　各種各樣的

實境對話
A: In this **manner**, you will be able to save more money.　用這種方法就可以存更多錢。
B: Really?　真的嗎？

mass [mæs]
名 （一）塊

名詞複數 masses

實境對話
A: A **mass** of rock rolled down from a mountain.　有一塊岩石從山上掉下來了。
B: Was anyone hurt?　有人受傷嗎？

matter [ˋmætɚ]
名 物質

延伸片語　no matter　不論怎樣
　　　　　a matter of　大約

實境對話
A: Is it organic **matter**?　這是有機物質嗎？
B: Yes, it is.　是的。

Part **2** 依詞性分類的生活單字

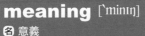
Chapter 8 其他名詞 Other Nouns

meaning [ˈminɪŋ]
名 意義

名詞複數 meanings　　同義字 significance 意義
延伸片語 meaning of life　生活的意義
no meaning　沒意義

實境對話
A: What is the **meaning** of the sentence?　這個句子是什麼意思？
B: I don't know.　不知道。

meeting [ˈmitɪŋ]
名 會議

名詞複數 meetings　　同義字 conference 會議
延伸片語 at the meeting　在會議上

實境對話
A: I'm looking for Mr. White. 我找懷特先生。
B: He is in **meeting**.　他正在會議中。

member
[ˈmɛmbɚ]　名 成員

名詞複數 members　　同義字 fellow 成員
延伸片語 family member　家庭成員
party member　黨員

實境對話
A: How many **member**s are there in your team?　你們那一隊有幾名成員？
B: Seven.　七個。

message
[ˈmɛsɪdʒ]　名 信息

名詞複數 messages
延伸片語 leave a message　留信

實境對話
A: Would you like to leave a **message**?　你要留信息嗎？
B: No, thanks. I will try again later.　不用了，謝謝。我等一下再打來。

metal [ˈmɛtl]
名 金屬

實境對話
A: What is it made of?　這個是用什麼做的？
B: It is made of **metal**.　金屬。

method [ˈmɛθəd]
名 方法

名詞複數 methods
同義字 way 方法

實境對話
A: What **methods** of payment do you accept?　你們接受哪些付款**方法**？
B: Cash only.　只接受現金。

mind [maɪnd]
名 精神、心理

延伸片語 in mind　記住
state of mind　精神狀態

實境對話
A: He is out of his **mind**.　他精神錯亂了。
B: What happened to him?　為什麼會這樣？

| 251 |

mistake [mə`stek]
名 錯誤

名詞複數 mistakes	**同義字** fault 錯誤
延伸片語	make a mistake 犯錯誤
	mistake for 把……錯認為

A: What's the matter? 怎麼了？
B: I made a big **mistake**. 我犯了一個大錯。

motion [`moʃən]
名 動作

名詞複數 motions	**同義字** action 動作
延伸片語	in motion 在運轉中
	wave motion 波動

A: Her **motion** is graceful. 她的動作真優雅。
B: Yeah, she looks like a beautiful swan. 對啊，看起來就像隻美麗的天鵝。

movement [`muvmənt]
名 運動

名詞複數 movements
同義字 activity 運動

A: He stands there without **movement**. 他一動也不動地站在那裡。
B: What's wrong with him? 他怎麼了？

mud [mʌd]
名 泥

同義字 soil 土

A: My shoes stuck in the **mud**. 我的鞋子陷進泥巴裡了。
B: Yank it out! 用力拉出來。

nest [nɛst]
名 巢

名詞複數 nests

A: What are you looking at? 你在看什麼？
B: A bird's **nest** in the tree. 樹上的鳥巢。

news [njuz]
名 新聞

A: What's wrong with her?
她怎麼了？
B: She burst out crying when she heard the **news**.
聽到這則新聞，她就突然大哭。

newspaper [`njuzˌpepɚ]
名 報紙

A: Would you like a **newspaper**? 需要報紙嗎？
B: That's OK. 不用了。

noise [nɔɪz]
名 噪音

同義字 sound 聲音

實境對話
A: Don't make such a loud **noise**! 不要發出那麼大的噪音。
B: I'm sorry. 對不起。

note [not]
名 筆記

名詞複數 notes
延伸片語 of note 著名的
take note 注意到

實境對話
A: Can you teach me how to take **notes**? 你可以教我如何做筆記嗎？
B: First, don't write everything you hear. 首先，不要把聽到的全寫下來。

object [ˋɑbdʒɪkt]
名 物體

名詞複數 objects

實境對話
A: What is the name of the **object**? 這個物體的名稱是什麼？
B: Kettle. 水壺。

operation
[ˌɑpəˋreʃən]
名 操作

名詞複數 operations
同義字 work 操作
延伸片語 in operation 操作

實境對話
A: How to start the **operation** system? 如何啟動操作系統？
B: Push the red bottom. 按紅色鈕。

opinion [əˋpɪnjən]
名 意見

名詞複數 opinions 同義字 idea 主意
延伸片語 in my opinion 依我看來
opinion about 有關……意見

實境對話
A: What is your **opinion** about the affair? 對於這件事，你有什麼意見？
B: No comments. 無可奉告。

order [ˋɔrdɚ]
名 命令

名詞複數 orders 同義字 command 命令
延伸片語 in order 狀況良好
order of 大約

實境對話
A: You must obey the **order**. 你必須遵守命令。
B: Don't push me. 別逼我。

party [ˋpɑrtɪ]
名 聚會

名詞複數 parties

實境對話
A: Will you come to my birthday **party**? 你會來參加我的生日聚會嗎？
B: Of course. 當然會啊。

pattern [ˈpætən]
名 樣式

名詞複數 patterns
同義字 mode 模式

實境對話
A: I like this **pattern**. 我喜歡這個樣式。
B: Same here. 我也是。

peace [pis]
名 和平

同義字 harmony 和睦
延伸片語 in peace 和平地
at peace 處於和平狀態

實境對話
A: What wish did you make? 你許了什麼願望？
B: I wish **peace** in the world. 世界和平。

period [ˈpɪrɪəd]
名 時期

名詞複數 periods
延伸片語 period of time 一段時間
long period 長時間

實境對話
A: What did he do during that **period**? 那段時期他做了什麼？
B: He wrote lots of novels. 他寫了很多本小說。

photo [ˈfoto]
名 照片

名詞複數 photos   同義字 picture 圖片
延伸片語 take a photo 照相

實境對話
A: Could you take a **photo** of me? 能幫我照張相片嗎？
B: Sure. 當然可以。

pile [paɪl]
名 堆

名詞複數 piles
延伸片語 a pile of 一堆
pile in 塞進

實境對話
A: There is a **pile** of books on the desk. 桌上有一堆書。
B: Whose books are those? 那些書是誰的？

pin [pɪn]
名 大頭針

名詞複數 pins   同義字 needle 針
延伸片語 pins and needles 如坐針氈
pin down 確定

實境對話
A: Please attach it with **pins**. 請把這個用大頭針固定。
B: Okay. 好。

pipe [paɪp]
名 管。

名詞複數 pipes

實境對話
A: The water **pipe** was broken. 水管破了。
B: I'll try to fix it. 我來修修看。

Chapter 8 其他名詞 Other Nouns

planet [ˈplænɪt]
名 行星

名詞複數 planets

實境對話
A: How many **planets** are there in the universe? 宇宙有幾顆行星？
B: Eight? 八顆嗎？

player [ˈpleə]
名 運動員

名詞複數 players
同義字 athlete 運動員

實境對話
A: He is chosen as the best **player**. 他被選為最佳運動員。
B: He deserves it. 這是他應得的。

pleasure [ˈplɛʒə]
名 快樂

同義字 joy 快樂
延伸片語 with pleasure 愉快地
for pleasure 為了取樂

實境對話
A: It gives me great **pleasure** to be with you. 和你在一起我很快樂。
B: Me, too. 我也是。

poison [ˈpɔɪzṇ]
名 毒藥

名詞複數 poisons
延伸片語 deadly poison 致命毒藥

實境對話
A: What is the cause of his death? 他的死因為何？
B: He committed suicide by taking **poison**. 服毒自殺。

pollution [pəˈluʃən]
名 污染

同義字 contamination 污染
延伸片語 environment pollution 環境污染

實境對話
A: Cars will cause serious air **pollution**. 車輛會造成嚴重的空氣污染。
B: Then let's ride bikes. 那我們騎腳踏車吧。

population [ˌpɑpjəˈleʃən]
名 人口

名詞複數 populations

實境對話
A: What is the **population** of the city? 這個城市有多少人口？
B: More than one million. 超過一百萬。

powder [ˈpaudə]
名 粉

實境對話
A: What should I do first? 我該先做什麼？
B: Mix the **powder** with eggs. 把粉和蛋混在一起。

power [`pauɚ]
名 力量

同義字 strength 力量
延伸片語 in power 執政的、掌權的

實境對話 A: Sorry, it is beyond my **power** to do this. 抱歉，我沒有能力幫你。
B: That's all right. 沒關係。

pressure [`prɛʃɚ]
名 壓力

名詞複數 pressures
延伸片語 under pressure 面臨壓力
blood pressure 血壓

實境對話 A: What is your advantage? 你有什麼優點？
B: I work well under **pressure**. 我在有壓力的情況下工作很出色。

prize [praɪz]
名 表揚

名詞複數 prizes
同義字 award 獎品

實境對話 A: He is awarded a **prize** for his invention. 他因發明而受獲獎表揚。
B: He is something else. 真了不起。

production
[prəˋdʌkʃən]
名 生產

名詞複數 productions

實境對話 A: The product will go into mass **production** in 2013. 該產品將在2013年大量生產。
B: Is the product eco-friendly? 這個產品環保嗎？

program
[`progræm]
名 程式

名詞複數 programs
同義字 procedure 過程

實境對話 A: I want to learn how to write a **program**. 我想學如何寫電腦程式。
B: Welcome to our lab this afternoon. 歡迎你今天下午來我們的實驗室。

progress
[`prɑgrɛs]
名 進步

名詞複數 progresses
同義字 development 發展
延伸片語 progress in 在……上有進展
in progress 正在進行

實境對話 A: You made a big **progress**. 你進步很多。
B: Thanks. 謝謝。

project [`prɑdʒɛkt]
名 計畫

名詞複數 projects
同義字 plan 計畫

實境對話 A: The company will form a **project** to improve the quality of service.
公司將擬訂一份計畫以提升服務品質。
B: That sounds great. 聽起來還不錯。

Part 2 依詞性分類的生活單字

Chapter 8 其他名詞 Other Nouns

purpose [ˋpɝpəs]
名 目的

名詞複數 purposes
同義字 goal 目標
延伸片語 for the purpose 為了某目的
on purpose 故意地

 實境對話
A: What is the **purpose** of the project? 這個計畫的目的是什麼？
B: To control inflation. 抑制通貨膨脹。

reason [ˋrizn̩]
名 原因

名詞複數 reasons 同義字 excuse 理由
延伸片語 reason for 原因
by reason of 由於

 實境對話
A: Is there any **reason** why you are late? 你遲到有任何原因嗎？
B: No, I just overslept. 沒有，我只是睡過頭了。

report [rɪˋport]
名 報導

名詞複數 reports 同義字 advisory 報告
延伸片語 report on 就……作報告
report of 說出對……的印象

 實境對話
A: Did you see the **report** about the accident? 你有看到那則事故的報導嗎？
B: No. What's up? 沒有，怎麼了嗎？

result [rɪˋzʌlt]
名 結果

名詞複數 results 同義字 outcome 結果
延伸片語 as a result 結果
result in 導致

 實境對話
A: When will they announce the **result** of the exam? 什麼時候會公佈考試結果？
B: The day after tomorrow. 後天。

robot [ˋrobət]
名 機器人

名詞複數 robots

 實境對話
A: What is in the gift box? 禮物盒裡是什麼東西？
B: A **robot**. 一個機器人。

rock [rɑk]
名 岩石

延伸片語 on the rocks 觸礁、毀壞

 實境對話
A: The house is as solid as a **rock**. 這棟房子如岩石般堅固。
B: How much is it? 一棟多少錢？

role [rol]
名 角色

名詞複數 roles
延伸片語 play an important role 起到重要作用

 實境對話
A: Who is the leading **role** in this film? 這部電影的主角是誰？
B: Julia Roberts. 茱莉亞羅勃茲。

root [rut]
名 根源

名詞複數 roots　　同義字 origin 起源
延伸片語 root in　來源於

實境對話
A: Is money the **root** of all evils?　金錢是萬惡的**根源**嗎？
B: No, I think money itself is not evil.　不，我想金錢的本質不是壞的。

rope [rop]
名 繩索

名詞複數 ropes　　同義字 line 線
延伸片語 on the ropes　瀕於失敗
　　　　 rope in　說服

實境對話
A: Hold the **rope** tightly in case I fall.　要是我掉下去，就握緊**繩索**。
B: Got it!　知道了。

rose [roz]
名 玫瑰花

名詞複數 roses

實境對話
A: Is that a **rose**?　那是**玫瑰花**嗎？
B: Yes, it is.　對。

rule [rul]
名 規則

名詞複數 rules　　同義字 regulation 規則
延伸片語 rule out　排除
　　　　 as a rule　通常

實境對話
A: What if I break the **rule**?　如果不遵守**規則**會怎麼樣？
B: You will be fined.　你會被罰錢。

safety [ˈseftɪ]
名 安全

延伸片語 in safety　安全地
　　　　 with safety　放心地

實境對話
A: For your **safety**, please fasten your seat belt.　為了您的**安全**，請繫上安全帶。
B: Where is the seat belt?　安全帶在哪裡？

sale [sel]
名 銷售

名詞複數 sales
同義字 sell 售賣
延伸片語 for sale　出售
　　　　 on sale　廉價出售

實境對話
A: Is the necklace for **sale**?　這條項鍊有**銷售**嗎？
B: No, it is not for **sale**.　沒有，那是非賣品。

sample [ˈsæmpl̩]
名 樣品

名詞複數 samples
同義字 example 樣品

實境對話
A: We will send you a **sample** in 3 days.　我們會在三天內寄送**樣品**。
B: Thank you very much.　謝謝。

sand [sænd]
名 沙子

實境對話
A: Where are the kids?
孩子們呢？
B: They are playing with **sand** in a sandbox.
在沙堆裡玩沙子。

---

scene [sin]
名 場面

名詞複數 scenes
延伸片語 on the scene　在場
behind the scene　幕後

實境對話
A: Have you ever seen the **scene** of robbery?　你看過搶劫的場面嗎？
B: Never.　從來沒有。

---

scenery [ˋsinərɪ]
名 風景

名詞複數 sceneries
同義字 landscape 景色

實境對話
A: The mountain **scenery** is breathtaking.　山景真是美不勝收。
B: Yeah, and the air is fresh.　對啊，而且空氣又新鮮。

---

screen [skrin]
名 螢幕

名詞複數 screens

實境對話
A: My laptop **screen** is broken.　我的筆電螢幕壞了。
B: Wanna buy a new one?　想買一個新的嗎？

---

secret [ˋsikrɪt]
名 祕密

名詞複數 secrets　同義字 privacy 隱私
延伸片語 in secret　祕密地
keep a secret　保守祕密

實境對話
A: Please keep the **secret**.　請保密。
B: I will.　我會的。

---

seat [sit]
名 座位

名詞複數 seats

實境對話
A: Is this **seat** taken?　這個座位有人坐嗎？
B: No. Have a seat.　沒有，請坐。

---

section [ˋsɛkʃən]
名 部分

名詞複數 sections　同義字 division 部分
延伸片語 cross section　橫截面

實境對話
A: Cut the cake into four **sections**.　把蛋糕切成四等分。
B: What is next?　接下來呢？

seed [sid]
名 種子

名詞複數 seeds
延伸片語 in seed 播過種的
seed selection 選種

實境對話
A: What will the **seed** grow into? 這個種子會長成什麼？
B: Tulips. 鬱金香。

sense [sɛns]
名 意義

名詞複數 senses　同義字 concept 概念
延伸片語 make sense 有意義
in a sense 在某種意義上

實境對話
A: What he says is right in a **sense**. 就某種意義而言，他是對的。
B: But I still can't forgive him. 但我還是不能原諒他。

sentence [ˈsɛntəns]
名 句子

名詞複數 sentences

實境對話
A: Please make a **sentence** with the word "boy". 請用「男孩」造一個句子。
B: The boy is sleeping. 男孩在睡覺。

service [ˈsɝvɪs]
名 服務

名詞複數 services
延伸片語 of service 有說明的

實境對話
A: The **service** of this restaurant is terrible. 這間餐廳的**服務**很差。
B: At least the food is good. 至少食物很好吃。

set [sɛt]
名 （一）套、（一）組、（一）副

名詞複數 sets
延伸片語 set up 建立
set out 出發

實境對話
A: What did you win? 你抽到什麼獎？
B: A tea **set**. 一套茶具。

shore [ʃor]
名 海濱

名詞複數 shores
延伸片語 off shore 離開岸邊
on shore 在岸上

實境對話
A: What is it? 那是什麼？
B: It's a ring I found on the **shore**. 我在海濱上找到的戒指。

side [saɪd]
名 方面

名詞複數 sides
延伸片語 on the side 另外
on the other side 另一方面

實境對話
A: What is your opinion? 你有什麼看法？
B: I think we should seek comments from all **sides**. 我想我們應該尋求各方意見。

sight [saɪt]
名 視力

延伸片語 at first sight 乍一看
out of sight 看不見

實境對話
A: I have poor **sight**. 我的視力不好。
B: What's your eyeglass prescription? 你近視幾度？

silence [`saɪləns]
名 沉默

同義字 still 沉默
延伸片語 in silence 沉默地
keep silence 保持沉默

實境對話
A: What should I do next? 我下一步該怎麼做？
B: You have the right to keep **silence**. 你有權保持沉默。

skill [skɪl]
名 技能

名詞複數 skills　同義字 technique 技能
延伸片語 skill in 對……熟練
skill training 技能訓練

實境對話
A: I want to learn new **skills**. 我想要學習新技能。
B: What **skills**? 什麼技能？

smile [smaɪl]
名 微笑

名詞複數 smiles
延伸片語 smile to oneself 暗笑
big smile 笑容滿面

實境對話
A: You are all **smiles**. What's up? 看你笑容滿面，發生了什麼好事？
B: It's my secret. 不告訴你。

society [sə`saɪətɪ]
名 社會

延伸片語 in society 在社會上
civil society 公民社會

實境對話
A: The rich should contribute to the **society**. 富人應該貢獻社會。
B: I agree with you completely. 我完全同意你的看法。

soul [sol]
名 靈魂

名詞複數 souls　同義字 spirit 精神
延伸片語 with heart and soul 熱心地
have no soul 沒有生氣、無人性

實境對話
A: He died. 他死了。
B: May his **soul** rest in Heaven. 願他的靈魂在天安息。

space [spes]
名 空間

名詞複數 spaces　同義字 room 空間
延伸片語 in space 在空間
living space 生存空間

實境對話
A: Is there enough **space** for thirty chairs? 這裡有足夠的空間放三十張椅子嗎？
B: Yes, there is. 有。

speech [spitʃ]
名 演講

名詞複數 speeches
同義字 lecture 講座

實境對話
A: Who is the speaker of the **speech**? 這場演講的講者是誰？
B: A professor from Harvard. 哈佛的教授。

speed [spid]
名 速度

名詞複數 meanings
延伸片語 high speed 高速
speed up 加速

實境對話
A: It's dangerous to drive a car at high **speed** during rush hour. 在尖峰時段高速行駛很危險。
B: Yeah, I strongly agree. 沒錯。

spirit [ˋspɪrɪt]
名 精神

名詞複數 spirits 同義字 emotion 情感
延伸片語 in the spirit of 本著……的精神
team spirit 團隊精神

實境對話
A: I shall be with you in **spirit**. 我的精神將與你同在。
B: Glad to hear you say that. 很高興聽到你這麼說。

state [stet]
名 國家

名詞複數 states 同義字 country 國家
延伸片語 in state 莊重地
in a state 不整潔

實境對話
A: Who is the head of the **state**? 誰是這個國家的元首？
B: The queen. 女王。

steam [stim]
名 蒸汽

實境對話
A: Have you ever ridden on a train with a **steam** locomotive?
你坐過蒸汽火車嗎？
B: No, I haven't.
沒有。

step [stɛp]
名 臺階

名詞複數 steps
延伸片語 step by step 逐步地
step in 介入

實境對話
A: Watch the **step**! 小心臺階！
B: Okay. 好。

stone [ston]
名 石頭

名詞複數 stones
延伸片語 leave no stone unturned 千方百計

實境對話
A: A rolling **stone** gathers no moss. 滾石不生苔。
B: What does the proverb mean? 這句諺語是什麼意思？

Part 2 依詞性分類的生活單字

story [ˈstorɪ]
名 故事

名詞複數 stories　　同義字 tale 故事
延伸片語 the whole tale 原委
　　　　 tell a story 講故事

 實境對話
A: What is that on the desk?　桌上那是什麼東西？
B: It's a children's **story** book.　一本兒童故事書。

style [staɪl]
名 模式

名詞複數 styles　　同義字 mode 風格
延伸片語 in style 流行
　　　　 out of style 過時的

 實境對話
A: This is the latest **style** in hairdressing.　這是最新的髮型樣式。
B: I don't think it fits me.　我覺得不適合我。

subject
[səbˈdʒɛkt]
名 主題

名詞複數 subjects　　同義字 theme 主題
延伸片語 on the subject of 涉及……時
　　　　 on the subject 就某話題

 實境對話
A: What is your **subject**?　你的主題是什麼？
B: The relationship between culture and religion.　文化與宗教的關係。

success [səkˈsɛs]
名 成功

名詞複數 successes　　同義字 victory 勝利
延伸片語 success in 在……方面成功
　　　　 with success 成功地

 實境對話
A: Finally, I met with **success**.　我終於獲得成功了。
B: You should have it.　這是你應得的。

swing [swɪŋ]
名 搖擺

名詞複數 swings
延伸片語 in full swing 活躍
　　　　 go with a swing 順利進行

 實境對話
A: Stop the **swing** of the ship.　讓船停止搖擺。
B: I can't control it.　我無法控制。

symbol [ˈsɪmbl̩]
名 象徵

名詞複數 symbols
同義字 significant 象徵

 實境對話
A: What is the **symbol** of peace?　什麼是和平的象徵？
B: White dove.　白鴿。

system [ˈsɪstəm]
名 系統

名詞複數 systems　　同義字 institution 制度
延伸片語 power system 電網
　　　　 economic system 經濟體制

 實境對話
A: The **system** is out of order.　系統故障了。
B: We need to identify the problem as soon as possible.　我們必須盡快找出問題。

Chapter 8　其他名詞　Other Nouns

|263|

talent [ˈtælənt]
名 才能

名詞複數 talents　　同義字 capability 才能
延伸片語 talent for 天才、有……的天賦
　　　　 talent show 才藝表演會

A: He has a **talent** for painting.　他有繪畫才能。
B: Did you tell his parents?　你有告訴他的父母嗎？

tear [tɪr]
名 淚水

名詞複數 tears
延伸片語 in tears 流著淚

A: Her eyes filled with **tears**.　她的眼睛充滿了淚水。
B: Why?　為什麼？

term [tɝm]
名 學期

名詞複數 terms　　同義字 session 學期
延伸片語 in terms 明確地
　　　　 in terms of 依據

A: Did you have part-time jobs during the **term**?　你在學期中有打工嗎？
B: Yes. I have two part-time jobs.　有，我打了兩份工。

thief [θif]
名 小偷

名詞複數 thieves
同義字 pilferer 小偷

A: When did the police catch the **thief**?　員警什麼時候抓到小偷？
B: Last Saturday.　上週六。

thing [θɪŋ]
名 事情

名詞複數 things
同義字 affair 事件

A: Could you give me some suggestions?　你可以給我一些建議嗎？
B: Sometimes, you take **things** too seriously.　有時候你把事情看得太嚴重了。

thought [θɔt]
名 想法

名詞複數 thoughts　　同義字 idea 主意
延伸片語 in thought 在沉思
　　　　 at the thought of 一想起

A: It was just my **thought**.　這只是我個人的想法。
B: Thanks for sharing your opinion with us.　謝謝您與我們分享意見。

ticket [ˈtɪkɪt]
名 票

名詞複數 tickets

A: Please show me your **ticket**.　請出示您的票。
B: I lost it.　我的票不見了。

Part 2 依詞性分類的生活單字

Chapter **8** 其他名詞 Other Nouns

title [ˈtaɪt!]
 名 題目

名詞複數 titles　　同義字 heading 標題

延伸片語 title page 扉頁
official title 官銜

實境對話 A: What is the **title** of your thesis?　你的論文題目是什麼？
B: I haven't decided yet.　我還沒決定。

tool [tul]
 名 工具

名詞複數 tools
同義字 instrument 設備 equipment 設備

實境對話 A: What **tools** do you have?　你有什麼工具？
B: A screwdriver and some screws.　一把螺絲起子和一些螺絲釘。

topic [ˈtɑpɪk]
 名 主題

名詞複數 topics　　同義字 theme 主題

延伸片語 hot topic 熱門話題
special topic 特殊話題

實境對話 A: What's the **topic** of this seminar?　這場研討會的主題是什麼？
B: It's English Literature.　英國文學。

tower [ˈtaʊɚ]
 名 塔

名詞複數 towers　　同義字 minar 塔

延伸片語 tower over/above somebody/something
高於，超過某人或某物
ivory tower 象牙塔

實境對話 A: Tokyo **Tower** is a famous landmark of Tokyo.　東京鐵塔是東京有名的地標。
B: I see.　我知道。

trade [tred]
 名 交易　動 交換

名詞複數 towers

實境對話 A: Can I **trade** my apple for your oranges?　我可以用蘋果跟你換橘子嗎？
B: No, you can't.　不，不行。

tradition
[trəˈdɪʃən]
 名 傳統

名詞複數 traditions　　同義字 convention 慣例

延伸片語 by tradition 照傳統

實境對話 A: Giving red envelope is a Chinese **tradition**.　包紅包是中國傳統。
B: Should children give red envelopes, too?　小孩也要包紅包嗎？

trash [træʃ]
名 垃圾

同義字	rubbish 垃圾
延伸片語	white trash 窮苦白人

A: Where is the **trash** can? 垃圾桶在哪裡？
B: Here it is. 在這裡。

treasure ['trɛʒɚ]
名 財富、金銀財寶

同義字	wealth 財富
延伸片語	treasure trove 無主珍寶

A: I know pirates buried their **treasure** on that island. 我知道海盜把金銀財寶埋在那座島。
B: Why are you so sure? 你這麼肯定？

treat [trit]
名 對待、特別款待 **動** 對待

名詞複數	treats
動詞變化	treated, treated, treating, treats
延伸片語	Dutch treat 各自付賬的聚餐

A: For a birthday **treat**, I took my son to his favorite restaurant.
為了慶祝我兒子的生日，我帶他去了他最愛的餐廳。
B: He must be very happy.
他一定很開心。

tree [tri]
名 樹木

名詞複數	trees	同義字	wood 木材
延伸片語	in the tree 在樹上		

A: Look at the divine **tree**! 看那棵神木！
B: Wow, that's spectacular! 哇！真是太壯觀了！

trick [trɪk]
名 詭計

名詞複數	tricks	同義字	scheme 詭計
延伸片語	dirty trick 卑鄙手段		
	play a trick 捉弄		

A: **Trick** or treat! 不給糖就搗蛋！
B: Here's your candy. 你的糖果在這裡。

trouble ['trʌbl̩]
名 問題

名詞複數	troubles	同義字	problem 問題
延伸片語	in trouble 在監禁中		
	get into trouble 使自己或他人陷入困擾之境		

A: My car had got some **trouble**. 我的車子有點問題。
B: Let me see. 讓我看看。

truth [truθ]
名 真相

同義字	integrity 真理、事實
延伸片語	tell the truth 説實話
	moment of truth 關鍵時刻

A: Please don't lie to me. 請別對我説謊。
B: Fine, I'll tell you the **truth**. 好，我會告訴你真相。

tunnel [ˈtʌnl̩]
名 管道

| 名詞複數 | tunnels | 同義字 | tube 隧道 |

延伸片語 light at the end of the tunnel 曙光在即

 實境對話
A: How many **tunnels** are there in Taiwan? 台灣有幾條隧道？
B: I don't know. 我不知道。

universe
[ˈjunəˌvɝ s]
名 宇宙

延伸片語 universe of discourse 討論或辯論的範圍

 實境對話
A: What's your dream? 你的夢想是什麼？
B: When I grow up, I want to explore the **universe**. 我長大以後想要探索宇宙。

value [ˈvælju]
名 價值

同義字 price 價格
延伸片語 of value 貴重的

 實境對話
A: Can you tell me what the **value** of this research is? 你能告訴我這份研究的價值是什麼嗎？
B: Sure I can. 當然可以。

victory [ˈvɪktərɪ]
名 勝利

名詞複數 victories 同義字 success 成功
延伸片語 victory over 戰勝
Pyrrhic victory 得不償失的勝利

 實境對話
A: The team's **victory** was just a fluke. 那一隊會贏純屬僥倖。
B: I don't think so. 我不這麼認為。

voice [vɔɪs]
名 聲音

同義字 sound 聲音
延伸片語 make your voice heard 發表意見
with one voice 異口同聲

 實境對話
A: I can't hear your **voice**. 我聽不到你的聲音。
B: Sorry, I'll repeat it again. 對不起，我再説一次。

war [wɔr]
名 戰爭

名詞複數 wars 同義字 battle 戰役
延伸片語 civil war 內戰
cold war 冷戰

 實境對話
A: Have you ever read articles about American Civil **War**?
你有讀過任何有關美國南北戰爭的文章嗎？
B: Yes, I have.
有，我讀過。

way [we]
名 方法

名詞複數 ways 同義字 method 方法
延伸片語 all the way 自始至終
by the way 順便提一下

實境對話
A: Is there any **way** to fix it? 有任何方法可以修好嗎？
B: I'm afraid there's no **way** to fix it. 恐怕沒辦法修好。

wedding [ˈwɛdɪŋ]
名 婚禮

名詞複數 weddings	同義字 marriage 結婚
延伸片語 wedding breakfast 婚宴	

> **實境對話**
> A: I'm getting married!　我要結婚了！
> B: Congratulations! When is the **wedding**?　恭喜！婚禮是什麼時候？

wood [wʊd]
名 木材

名詞複數 woods
同義字 timber 木材

> **實境對話**
> A: Is the chair made of **wood**?　椅子是**木頭製**的嗎？
> B: Yes, it is. So is the desk.　是的，桌子也是。

word [wɝd]
名 詞語

名詞複數 words
延伸片語 in a word　總之
in other word　換句話說

> **實境對話**
> A: Did he say anything?　他有說什麼嗎？
> B: I can't remember the exact **words** he said.　我不記得他確切說了什麼話。

用簡單的小測驗，驗收一下，單字記住了嗎？

(   ) 1 between

(   ) 2 since

(   ) 3 army

(   ) 4 blood

(   ) 5 captain

(   ) 6 channel

(   ) 7 debate

(   ) 8 energy

(   ) 9 fault

(   ) 10 garbage

(   ) 11 goal

(   ) 12 honesty

(   ) 13 invitation

(   ) 14 kind

(   ) 15 leader

(   ) 16 matter

(   ) 17 nest

(   ) 18 pile

(   ) 19 result

(   ) 20 trick

A 軍隊　　B 能量　　C 爭論　　D 領導　　E 目標　　F 種類　　G 巢
H 堆　　　I 通道　　J 詭計　　K 血液　　L 自從　　M 結果
N 在……中間　　O 錯誤　　P 垃圾　　Q 隊長　　R 邀請　　S 誠實
T 物質

答案
1(N)　2(L)　3(A)　4(K)　5(Q)　6(I)　7(C)　8(B)　9(O)　10(P)　11(E)　12(S)　13(R)　14(F)
15(D)　16(T)　17(G)　18(H)　19(M)　20(J)

Track 242

feel [fil]
動 感覺

動詞變化 felt, felt, feeling, feels
延伸片語 feel about　摸索
　　　　feel better　感覺好點了

實境對話
A: How do you **feel** right now?　你現在感覺如何？
B: I **feel** awful.　我覺得糟透了。

hear [hɪr]
動 聽見

動詞變化 heard, heard, hearing, hears　　同義字 listen 聽
延伸片語 hear from　收到……的信
　　　　hear of　聽說

實境對話
A: Can you **hear** me?　你聽得到我的聲音嗎？
B: Yes, I can.　是的，我聽得到。

listen [ˈlɪsn̩]
動 聽

動詞變化 listened, listened, listening, listens
同義字 hear 聽見
延伸片語 listen for　傾聽
　　　　listen in　收聽

實境對話
A: Is she reading?　她在看書嗎？
B: No, she's **listening** to music.　不，她在聽音樂。

look [lʊk]
動 看

動詞變化 looked, looked, looking, looks
同義字 see 看見
延伸片語 look out　小心
　　　　look for　尋找

實境對話
A: She **looks** sad.　她看起來好傷心。
B: Yes, indeed.　是啊，沒錯。

see [si]
動 看到

動詞變化 saw, saw, seeing, sees
同義字 look 看見
延伸片語 see in　帶領……進去
　　　　see for oneself　親眼看

實境對話
A: Did you **see** my brother?　你有看到我哥哥嗎？
B: No, I didn't.　不，我沒看到。

smell [smɛl]
動 聞到

動詞變化 smelled, smelled, smelling, smells
延伸片語 smell of　有……的氣味

實境對話
A: I **smell** something burning.　我聞到燒焦味。
B: Me, too.　我也是。

Part 2 依詞性分類的生活單字

sound [saʊnd]
動 聲音、聽起來

動詞變化 sounded, sounded, sounding, sounds
同義字 noise 噪音
延伸片語 sound like 説起來像……
sound quality 品質優良

實境對話
A: Can you understand him? 你聽得懂他説的話嗎？
B: No, but it **sounds** like Spanish. 不懂，但是聽起來像西班牙文。

taste [test]
動 品嚐

動詞變化 tasted, tasted, tasting, tastes
延伸片語 taste for 對……的喜愛
taste of 體驗

實境對話
A: How's your meal? 你的餐點如何？
B: It **tastes** great! 很好吃！

watch [wɑtʃ]
動 觀看

動詞變化 watched, watched, watching, watches
同義字 observe 觀察
延伸片語 watch out 小心
keep a close watch on somebody 密切注視

實境對話
A: What are you doing? 你在做什麼？
B: I'm **watching** TV. 我在看電視。

check [tʃɛk]
動 檢查

動詞變化 checked, checked, checking, checks
同義字 examine 檢查
延伸片語 check up 檢查
check in 登記

實境對話
A: Are you **checking** on me? 你在查看我嗎？
B: Well, not really. 呃，也不是啦。

complete
[kəm`plit] 動 完成

動詞變化 completed, completed, completing, completes
同義字 accomplish 完成
延伸片語 complete with 包括

實境對話
A: The mission is **completed**. 任務完成了。
B: Good job. 做得好。

end [ɛnd]
動 結束

動詞變化 ended, ended, ending, ends
同義字 complete 完成
延伸片語 in the end 終於
at the end 最終

實境對話
A: This lecture is so boring! 這場演講好無聊！
B: Yeah, when will it **end**? 對啊，什麼時候結束啊？

finish [`fɪnɪʃ]
動 完成

動詞變化 finished, finished, finishing, finishes
同義字 complete 完成
延伸片語 finish off 吃完
finish up with 以……告終

實境對話
A: Have you **finished** the book? 你看完那本書了嗎？
B: Not yet. 還沒。

其他動詞 Other Verbs
Chapter 9

|271|

succeed [sək`sid]
動 成功

動詞變化 succeeded, succeeded, succeeding, succeeds
同義字 complete 完成
延伸片語 succeed in 成功
succeed at 在……成功

實境對話
A: Hope you **succeed** in your business. 希望你事業成功。
B: Thank you. 謝謝。

survive [sə`vaɪv]
動 生存

動詞變化 survived, survived, surviving, survives
延伸片語 survive on 靠……活下來

實境對話
A: Anything new? 有新消息嗎？
B: Only one little girl **survived** from that disaster. 只有一個小女孩在那場災難中倖存。

affect [ə`fɛkt]
動 影響

動詞變化 affected, affected, affecting, affects
同義字 influence 影響

實境對話
A: What should I do? 我該怎麼辦？
B: Just don't let him **affect** you. 別讓他影響你就好了。

believe [bɪ`liv]
動 相信

動詞變化 believed, believed, believing, believes
同義字 trust 信任
延伸片語 believe it or not 信不信由你
believe in 信任

實境對話
A: Do you **believe** me? 你相信我嗎？
B: Yes, I do. 是的，我相信。

blame [blem]
動 責怪

動詞變化 blamed, blamed, blaming, blames
同義字 reproach 責備
延伸片語 blame for 因為……責備
take the blame 承擔過錯

實境對話
A: Please don't **blame** me. 請別責怪我。
B: I won't. That's not your fault. 我不會的。那不是你的錯。

bother [`baðə]
動 打擾

動詞變化 bothered, bothered, bothering, bothers
同義字 disturb 打擾
延伸片語 not bother yourself 不操心
hot and bothered 不安的、氣衝衝的

實境對話
A: Why don't you ask him? 你怎麼不問他？
B: I don't want to **bother** him. 我不想打擾他。

confuse [kən`fjuz]
動 使混亂

動詞變化 confused, confused, confusing, confuses
同義字 perplex 使困惑
延伸片語 confuse with 混淆

實境對話
A: What's going on? 怎麼了？
B: His behavior **confused** me. 他的行為讓我很混亂。

Chapter 9 其他動詞 Other Verbs

consider
[kən`sɪdə] **動** 考慮

動詞變化	considered, considered, considering, considers
同義字	think 思考
延伸片語	consider as　認為 all things considered　從全面考慮

 實境對話
A: How about this project?　這個計劃怎麼樣？
B: I'll **consider** it.　我會考慮一下。

develop [dɪ`vɛləp]
動 發展

動詞變化	developed, developed, developing, develops
同義字	exploit 開發
延伸片語	develop into　發展成為

 實境對話
A: Is Taiwan a **developing** country or a **developed** one?
　台灣是開發中國家還是已開發國家？
B: In my opinion, Taiwan is a **developed** country.　我認為台灣是已開發國家。

divide [də`vaɪd]
動 分開

動詞變化	divided, divided, dividing, divides
同義字	separate 分開
延伸片語	divide into　把……分為 divide by　除以

 實境對話
A: He **divided** us into 3 groups.　他把我們分成三組。
B: Which group am I in?　我在哪一組？

doubt [daʊt]
動 懷疑

動詞變化	doubted, doubted, doubting, doubts
同義字	question 質疑
延伸片語	in doubt　可懷疑的 no doubt　毫無疑問

 實境對話
A: He said he has finished his homework.　他說他已經做完功課了。
B: I **doubt** it.　我很懷疑。

ease [iz]
動 去除

動詞變化	eased, eased, easing, eases
同義字	remove 去除
延伸片語	ease of　使解脫

 實境對話
A: Do you feel better now?　你感覺好一點了嗎？
B: Yes, the drug **eased** my pain.　是的，藥物減輕我的痛苦。

embarrass
[ɪm`bærəs] **動** 使侷促不安

動詞變化	embarrassed, embarrassed, embarrassing, embarrasses
同義字	abash 使侷促

實境對話
A: He looks **embarrassed**.　他看起來侷促不安。
B: Does he?　有嗎？

forgive [fə`gɪv]
動 原諒

動詞變化	forgave, forgave, forgiven, forgives
同義字	excuse 原諒

 實境對話
A: Will you **forgive** me?　你會原諒我嗎？
B: I'll consider it.　我會考慮。

forget [fə`ɡɛt]
動 忘記

動詞變化 forgot, forgotten , forgetting, forgets
同義字 fail 忘記、忽略
延伸片語 forget about　忘記
　　　　 forgive and forget　既往不咎

實境對話
A: Where is your textbook?　你的課本呢？
B: I **forget** to bring it.　我忘了帶。

frighten [`fraɪtn̩]
動 使受驚嚇

動詞變化 frightened, frightened, frightening, frightens
同義字 scare 驚嚇

實境對話
A: You **frightened** those children!　你嚇到那些小孩了！
B: No, I didn't!　不，我才沒有。

gather [`ɡæðɚ]
動 聚集

動詞變化 gathered, gathered, gathering, gathers
同義字 collect 收集
延伸片語 gather up　收集起
　　　　 gather in　收集

實境對話
A: I'm so glad that we **gathered** here.　我很高興我們今天聚集在此。
B: Me, too.　我也是。

guess [ɡɛs]
動 猜測

動詞變化 guessed, guessed, guessing, guesses
同義字 suppose 猜想
延伸片語 guess at　猜測
　　　　 by guess　憑猜測

實境對話
A: Why hasn't he come yet?　為什麼他還沒來？
B: I **guess** we should wait for a couple of minutes.　我猜我們得再等幾分鐘。

hate [het]
動 恨、嫌惡

動詞變化 hated, hated, hating, hates　同義字 loathe 討厭
延伸片語 somebody's pet hate　特別厭惡的東西
　　　　 hate somebody's guts　對某人恨之入骨

實境對話
A: Why do you **hate** each other?　為什麼你們互相討厭？
B: It's a long story.　說來話長。

hope [hop]
動 希望

動詞變化 hoped, hoped, hoping, hopes　同義字 wish 希望
延伸片語 hope for　希望
　　　　 in the hope of　懷著……的希望

實境對話
A: I **hope** I can go to Egypt someday.　我希望有天能去埃及。
B: Why do you want to go to Egypt?　你為什麼想去埃及？

imagine
[ɪ`mædʒɪn]
動 想像

動詞變化 imagined, imagined, imagining, imagines
同義字 suppose 猜想

實境對話
A: Can you **imagine** how beautiful the ring is?　你能想像那個戒指有多美嗎？
B: Actually, I can't.　其實，我無法想像。

inspire [ɪnˈspaɪr]
動 激發

動詞變化 inspired, inspired, inspiring, inspires
同義字 stimulate 激發

實境對話
A: A girl **inspired** that famous designer. 一位女孩激發那位名設計師的靈感。
B: Wow, who was that girl? 哇，那個女孩是誰？

know [no]
動 知道、認識

動詞變化 knew, known, knowing, knows
同義字 understand 知道、瞭解
延伸片語 know about 瞭解
know as 稱為

實境對話
A: Do you **know** him? 你認識他嗎？
B: Yes, he's my roommate. 認識，他是我室友。

like [laɪk]
動 喜歡

動詞變化 liked, liked, liking, likes
同義字 love 愛
延伸片語 feel like 想要
look like 看起來像……

實境對話
A: Do you **like** animals? 你喜歡動物嗎？
B: Yes, I **like** dogs. 是的，我喜歡狗。

love [lʌv]
動 愛

動詞變化 loved, loved, loving, loves
同義字 like 喜歡
延伸片語 fall in love with 和某人相愛

實境對話
A: Do you **love** me? 你愛我嗎？
B: Of course! My dear. 親愛的，當然！

mind [maɪnd]
動 介意

動詞變化 minded, minded, minding, minds
同義字 care about 介意
延伸片語 in mind 記住
state of mind 心理狀態

實境對話
A: Do you **mind** if I take this job? 你介意我接下這份工作嗎？
B: No, I don't. Just do whatever you want to do! 不，我不介意。做你想做的事吧！

need [nid]
動 需要

動詞變化 needed, needed, needing, needs
同義字 ask 需要
延伸片語 need for 對……的需要
in need 在危難中

實境對話
A: Do you **need** a hand? 你需要幫忙嗎？
B: Yes. Can you do the laundry for me? 是的。你能幫我洗衣服嗎？

notice [ˈnotɪs]
動 注意

動詞變化 noticed, noticed, noticing, notices
同義字 observe 觀察、留心
延伸片語 take notice 注意　　prior notice 事先通知

實境對話
A: I think Jeff is cheating on you. 我覺得傑夫在劈腿。
B: I **noticed** that. I just need a proper time to break up with him.
我注意到了。我只是需要一個好時機跟他分手。

realize [ˋriəˏlaɪz]
動 意識到

動詞變化 realized, realized, realizing, realizes
同義字 be aware of 意識到
延伸片語 realize on 變賣產業
come to realize 認識到

實境對話
A: Do you **realize** what you have done? 你有意識到你做了什麼好事嗎？
B: Yes, I do. That's why I came here and try to apologize. 我有。這就是為什麼我來這裡試著道歉。

regret [rɪˋgrɛt]
動 後悔

動詞變化 regretted, regretted, regretting, regrets
同義字 repent 後悔
延伸片語 regret doing 後悔做某事
with regret 遺憾地

實境對話
A: Do you **regret** for what you have said? 你對你說過的話感到**後悔**嗎？
B: I don't **regret** at all. 我一點也不後悔。

remember
[rɪˋmɛmbɚ] **動** 記住

動詞變化 remembered, remembered, remembering, remembers
同義字 learn by heart 記住
延伸片語 remember of 記得
remember oneself 約束自己

實境對話
A: Do you **remember** her telephone number? 你記得她的電話號碼嗎？
B: No, I don't. Why don't you ask Lisa? 不記得。你怎麼不問麗莎？

remind [rɪˋmaɪnd]
動 提醒

動詞變化 reminded, reminded, reminding, reminds
同義字 jack 提醒
延伸片語 remind of 提醒

實境對話
A: I have to go buy my ticket tomorrow. 我明天得去買票。
B: Okay. I will **remind** you tomorrow morning. 好的，我明天早上會**提醒**你。

surprise
[səˋpraɪz]
動 使吃驚 **名** 驚奇

動詞變化 surprised, surprised, surprising, surprises
延伸片語 by surprise 出其不意地
big surprise 大吃一驚

實境對話
A: Here, your new laptop! 來，這是你的新筆電！
B: What a **surprise**! 真是太驚喜了！

think [θɪŋk]
動 認為

動詞變化 thought, thought, thinking, thinks
同義字 consider 思考
延伸片語 think of 記起

實境對話
A: I **think** he should improve his writing ability. 我認為他應該加強寫作能力。
B: That is what I **thought**. 我也這麼覺得。

want [wɑnt]
動 想要

動詞變化 wanted, wanted, wanting, wants
同義字 claim 要求
延伸片語 want of 缺乏

實境對話
A: I'm hungry. I **want** to eat something. 我餓了。我想吃些東西。
B: No, you can't. You are on a diet! 不行，你正在減肥耶！

Part 2 依詞性分類的生活單字

wish [wɪʃ]
動 願望、希望

動詞變化 wished, wished, wishing, wishes
同義字 hope 願望
延伸片語 wish for 盼望
as you wish 隨心所欲

實境對話
A: I **wish** I had never talked to her. 我真**希望**我從沒跟她講過話。
B: Me, too. 我也是。

worry [ˈwɝɪ]
動 擔心

動詞變化 worried, worried, worrying, worries
同義字 concern 擔心
延伸片語 worry about 擔心
no worry 無需煩惱

實境對話
A: I'm so **worried** about my final exam. 我好**擔心**我的期末考。
B: Don't **worry**. You'll get a good grade. 別**擔心**，你會得到好成績的。

act [ækt]
動 表演

動詞變化 acted, acted, acting, acts
同義字 play 扮演
延伸片語 act on 對……起作用
act in 扮演

實境對話
A: She **acted** a doctor in the drama. 她在那齣戲**扮演**醫生。
B: I thought she would **act** lawyer. 我還以為她會**演**律師。

bathe [beð]
動 洗澡

動詞變化 bathed, bathed, bathing, bathes
同義字 wash 洗
延伸片語 to take a bath 入浴
to give a bath to 給……洗澡

實境對話
A: Do you need a hand? 你需要幫忙嗎？
B: Yes. Please help me **bathe** the baby. 的。請幫我給寶寶**洗澡**。

beat [bit]
動 敲擊

動詞變化 beat, beat, beating, beats **同義字** strike 打擊
延伸片語 beat down 打倒、殺價
beat all 意想不到

實境對話
A: What's that noise? 那是什麼噪音啊？
B: It's Mr. Hopkins **beating** his drum. 是霍普金斯先生在打鼓。

blow [blo]
動 吹

動詞變化 blew, blew, blowing, blows
延伸片語 blow up 爆發
blow out 吹熄

實境對話
A: Where is our clothes? 我們的衣服呢？
B: I think the wind **blew** them away. 我想風把他們吹走了。

bow [bau]
動 鞠躬、低（頭）

動詞變化 bowed, bowed, bowing, bows
延伸片語 bow down 鞠躬
bow in 恭敬

實境對話
A: Why did he **bow** his head? 他為什麼要低頭？
B: Maybe he felt embarrassed. 也許他覺得尷尬。

break [brek]
動 休息

動詞變化 broke, broke, breaking, breaks　同義字 rest 休息
延伸片語 break up 打碎
break through 突破

A: I have been working for 10 hours!　我已經工作十個小時了！
B: Maybe you should take a **break**.　也許你應該休息一下。

bring [brɪŋ]
動 帶來

動詞變化 brought, brought, bringing, brings
延伸片語 bring about 引起
bring up 教育

A: Can you **bring** me my key?　你可以幫我拿鑰匙過來嗎？
B: Sure. Where should I meet you?　當然可以。我們要在哪裡見面？

brush [brʌʃ]
動 刷

動詞變化 brushed, brushed, brushing, brushes
延伸片語 brush up 復習

A: **Brush** your teeth before you go to sleep.　睡前要刷牙。
B: Okay, I will.　好，我會的。

carry [ˈkærɪ]
動 搬動

動詞變化 carried, carried, carrying, carries
延伸片語 carry out 執行
carry on 繼續

A: Where is my luggage?　我的行李呢？
B: I saw Tom **carrying** it into your house.　我看到湯姆把它搬進你家。

catch [kætʃ]
動 抓住、接住

動詞變化 caught, caught, catching, catches
同義字 grasp 抓住
延伸片語 catch up 趕上
catch on 理解

A: Let's play **catch** and throw!　我們來玩丟接球！
B: Give me a break. I just came back from yoga class!　放過我吧。我才剛上完瑜珈課耶！

chase [tʃes]
動 追趕

動詞變化 chased, chased, chasing, chases
同義字 pursue 追求
延伸片語 chase after 追逐
chase down 找出

A: How did he do that?　他是怎麼做到的啊？
B: He never gives up **chasing** his dream.　他從不放棄追逐夢想。

cheat [tʃit]
動 欺騙

動詞變化 cheated, cheated, cheating, cheats
同義字 lie 說謊
延伸片語 cheat on 對……不忠

A: Why is he in prison?　他為什麼被關進監獄？
B: He **cheated** an old lady for her money.　他騙了一位老婦人的錢。

choose [tʃuz]
動 選擇

動詞變化 chose, chosen, choosing, chooses
延伸片語 choose from 挑選
　　　　 as you choose 隨你的便

實境對話
A: Who did you **choose**? Keith or Zack? 你選了誰？凱斯還是查克？
B: I **chose** Zack. 我選了查克。

clap [klæp]
動 鼓掌

動詞變化 clapped, clapped, clapping, claps
同義字 applaud 鼓掌
延伸片語 clap eyes on 看見、注視
　　　　 a clap of thunder 一聲霹靂

實境對話
A: They **clapped** for Jenna heartily. 他們熱情地為珍娜鼓掌。
B: She must be very happy. 她一定很開心。

close [kloz]
動 關閉

動詞變化 closed, closed, closing, closes
同義字 shut 關閉

實境對話
A: When will the store **close**? 店何時要打烊？
B: In ten minutes. 十分鐘後。

come [kʌm]
動 來

動詞變化 came, come, coming, comes
延伸片語 come true 實現
　　　　 come from 來自

實境對話
A: Why don't you **come** to my place? 你怎麼不來我家？
B: I thought you were busy. 我以為你在忙。

control [kənˋtrol]
動 控制

動詞變化 controlled, controlled, controlling, controls
同義字 manage 控制
延伸片語 control of 對……的控制
　　　　 out of control 失去控制

實境對話
A: You can't **control** her heart. 你控制不了她的心。
B: I know. I just don't want to break up with her. 我知道。我只是不想跟她分手。

collect [kəˋlɛkt]
動 收集

動詞變化 collected, collected, collecting, collects
同義字 gather 收集

實境對話
A: Are you **collecting** these dolls? 你在收集這些娃娃嗎？
B: Yes, I love them. 對啊，我很喜歡它們。

comment [ˋkɑmɛnt]
動 評論

動詞變化 commented, commented, commenting, comments
延伸片語 comment on 對……評論
　　　　 no comment 無可奉告

實境對話
A: What do you feel about your ex-wife getting married again? 你對前妻再婚有什麼感覺嗎？
B: I have no **comments**. 我不予置評。

correct [kəˈrɛkt]
動 糾正

動詞變化 corrected, corrected, correcting, corrects
同義字 rectify 糾正

實境對話
A: I don't know how to be a good mother. 我不知道怎麼當個好媽媽。
B: First, when children make mistakes, you should **correct** them.
首先，小孩做錯事的時候，你應該糾正他們。

copy [ˈkɑpɪ]
動 複製　名 副本

動詞變化 copied, copied, copying, copies
同義字 repeat 重複

實境對話
A: Can you **copy** this document for me? 你可以幫我影印這份檔案嗎？
B: Sure. Where's the copier? 當然可以。影印機在哪裡？

count [kaʊnt]
動 計數

動詞變化 counted, counted, counting, counts
同義字 figure 計算
延伸片語 count on　指望
　　　　 count for　有價值

實境對話
A: You can't move until I **count** to ten. 在我數到十之前，你不能動。
B: Got it! 知道了！

cover [ˈkʌvɚ]
動 包括

動詞變化 covered, covered, covering, covers
同義字 include 包括
延伸片語 cover up　掩蓋
　　　　 cover for　代替

實境對話
A: His interests **cover** language, sports, travel and other new things.
他的興趣包括語言、運動、旅行和其他新奇事物。
B: I think that's why he can be such an excellent interpreter.
我想這就是為什麼他能成為一個優秀的口譯。

cry [kraɪ]
動 哭泣

動詞變化 cried, cried, crying, cries　　同義字 weep 哭泣
延伸片語 cry for　迫切需要
　　　　 cry out　懇求

實境對話
A: Why are you **crying**? 你怎麼在哭？
B: Nothing. I don't want to talk about it. 沒事，我不想談。

cut [kʌt]
動 割、剪

動詞變化 cut, cut, cutting, cuts
延伸片語 cut off　中斷

實境對話
A: Did you **cut** your hair? 你剪頭髮嗎？
B: Yes, I did it yesterday. 是啊，昨天剪的。

dial [ˈdaɪəl]
動 撥號

動詞變化 dialed, dialed, dialing, dials
延伸片語 dial up　撥號

實境對話
A: Did you call Mr. Lee? 你打給李先生了嗎？
B: I **dialed** the number you gave me, but no one answered. 我撥了你給我的號碼，但是沒人接。

dig [dɪg]
動 挖

動詞變化 dug, dug, digging, digs
同義字 tunnel 挖
延伸片語 dig out 掘出
dig up 挖出

實境對話
A: Why is there a hole? 為什麼那裡有個洞？
B: I think my dog **dug** it. 我想是我的狗**挖**的。

deliver [dɪˋlɪvɚ]
動 傳送

動詞變化 delivered, delivered, delivering, delivers
同義字 transfer 傳遞
延伸片語 deliver up 交出
deliver from 從……處釋放出來

實境對話
A: He wakes up so early! 他起得真早。
B: Because he has to **deliver** newspapers. 因為他要去送報紙。

drop [drɑp]
動 落下

動詞變化 dropped, dropped, dropping, drops
同義字 decline 下降
延伸片語 drop in 順便走訪
at the drop of 一看到

實境對話
A: I think I **dropped** my keys. 我想我把鑰匙弄丟了。
B: No, you didn't. Your keys are in my bag. 你沒有弄丟。你的鑰匙在我包包裡。

elect [ɪˋlɛkt]
動 做出選擇

動詞變化 elected, elected, electing, elects
同義字 choose 選擇

實境對話
A: How's the election going? 選舉結果如何？
B: They **elected** Obama as their president. 他們選了歐巴馬當總統。

enter [ˋɛntɚ]
動 進入

動詞變化 entered, entered, entering, enters
延伸片語 enter in 進入
enter for 參加

實境對話
A: Do you know where Tom is? 你知道湯姆在哪裡嗎？
B: I saw him **entering** the room. 我看到他進去那個房間。

exit [ɪgˋzɪst]
動 離開、出口

動詞變化 exited, exited, exiting, exits
延伸片語 make one's exit 離開

實境對話
A: I can't find the **exit**. 我找不到出口。
B: Me neither. Let's just ask the staff over there. 我也是。去問那邊的工作人員吧！

feed [fid]
動 餵 **名** 飼料

動詞變化 fed, fed, feeding, feeds
名詞變化 feeds
延伸片語 feed on 以……為食
feed back 回饋

實境對話
A: What are you doing? 你在做什麼？
B: I'm **feeding** my dog. 我在餵我的狗。

fight [faɪt]
動 打仗

動詞變化 fought, fought, fighting, fights
同義字 combat 搏鬥
延伸片語 fight for 為……而戰
　　　　　 fight back 回擊

實境對話
A: You have to **fight** for his trust! 你必須爭取他的信任。
B: But how? 怎麼爭取？

follow [ˈfɑlo]
動 跟隨

動詞變化 followed, followed, following, follows
延伸片語 follow up 跟蹤
　　　　　 follow in 跟進

實境對話
A: Please **follow** the recipe. 請跟著食譜做。
B: Okay, I will. 好，我會的。

fry [fraɪ]
動 炸

動詞變化 fried, fried, frying, fries

實境對話
A: Are you hungry? 你餓了嗎？
B: Yes, I want some **fried** chicken. 是啊，我想來點炸雞。

go [go]
動 去、往

動詞變化 went, gone, going, goes
延伸片語 go up 增長
　　　　　 go on 繼續

實境對話
A: Where are you **going**? 你要去哪裡？
B: I'm heading to my girlfriend's house and pick her up. 我正要去我女朋友家接她。

greet [grit]
動 迎接

動詞變化 greeted, greeted, greeting, greets

實境對話
A: Is she doing great? 她還可以嗎？
B: I think so. She is **greeting** her guests with smile. 我覺得不錯。她笑著接待賓客。

grow [gro]
動 成長

動詞變化 grew, grew, growing, grows
延伸片語 grow up 成長
　　　　　 grow on 加深影響

實境對話
A: When I **grow** up, I want to be a doctor. 我長大想當醫生。
B: Then you have to study hard right now. 那你現在就得用功讀書。

guide [gaɪd]
動 擔任、嚮導、帶領

動詞變化 guided, guided, guiding, guides

實境對話
A: Where is the interpreter? 口譯在哪裡？
B: Lisa **guided** him to the conference room. 莉莎帶他去會議室了。

Part **2** 依詞性分類的生活單字

hand [hænd]
動 用手拿

動詞變化 handed, handed, handing, hands
同義字 pass 傳遞
延伸片語 hand in 交上

實境對話
A: **Hand** me those bottles, please. 請把那些瓶子拿給我。
B: Here you are. 給你。

hang [hæŋ]
動 懸掛

動詞變化 hung, hung, hanging, hangs
延伸片語 hang on 堅持下去
hang out 掛出

實境對話
A: Please **hang** these coats for me. 請幫我把這些大衣吊起來。
B: Sure. **Hand** them over. 好。我把它們掛起來。

help [hɛlp]
動 幫助

動詞變化 helped, helped, helping, helps **同義字** aid 援助
延伸片語 help oneself 自用
help with 幫忙某人做

實境對話
A: Can you **help** me clean the house? 你可以幫我清理房子嗎？
B: I'm afraid I can't. I have other things to do. 恐怕不行。我還有其他事要做。

hit [hɪt]
動 打擊

動詞變化 hit, hit, hitting, hits **同義字** beat 打擊
延伸片語 hit on 偶然發現
hit the ball 順利、成功

實境對話
A: Is he okay? 他還好嗎？
B: A robber **hit** him. But he's doing fine. 一個搶匪打了他。但他還好。

hold [hold]
動 控制

動詞變化 held, held, holding, holds **同義字** control 控制
延伸片語 hold on 等一下
hold in 抑制

實境對話
A: I can't **hold** my feelings for him anymore! 我再也無法控制我對他的感覺了！
B: Then tell him! 那就告訴他啊！

hop [hɑp]
動 跳躍

動詞變化 hopped, hopped, hopping, hops
同義字 jump 跳

實境對話
A: See that little girl! She's **hopping** like a little rabbit! 看那個小女孩！她像小兔子一樣**跳來跳去**。
B: How cute is she! 好可愛喔！

hunt [hʌnt]
動 打獵、搜尋

動詞變化 hunt, hunt, hunting, hunts
延伸片語 hunt for 搜尋
hunt down 窮追直至抓獲

實境對話
A: So, what are you doing lately? 所以你最近在做什麼？
B: I'm still **hunting** a job. 我還在找工作。

hurry [ˈhɝɪ]
動 匆忙

動詞變化 hurried, hurried, hurrying, hurries
同義字 hasten 趕緊
延伸片語 in a hurry 立即
　　　 hurry up 趕快

實境對話
A: Can you stop by and pick me up? 你可以順道來接我嗎？
B: No, I can't. I'm in a **hurry**. 不，我不行。我趕時間。

jump [dʒʌmp]
動 跳躍

動詞變化 jumped, jumped, jumping, jumps
延伸片語 jump in 投入
　　　 jump over 跳過

實境對話
A: Stop **jumping** on my bed! 別在我床上跳！
B: Come on, why so serious! 唉唷，別這樣嘛！

kick [kɪk]
動 踢

動詞變化 kicked, kicked, kicking, kicks
同義字 boot 踢
延伸片語 kick off 中線開球
　　　 kick oneself 自責

實境對話
A: Mom, Jack **kicked** me. 媽媽，傑克踢我。
B: But Lisa hit me first! 但是麗莎先打我的！

knock [nɑk]
動 敲

動詞變化 knocked, knocked, knocking, knocks
同義字 strike 擊打
延伸片語 knock on 撞擊
　　　 knock off 停工

實境對話
A: Please **knock** the door before you come in. 請先敲門再進來。
B: Okay, I will **knock** next time. 好的，我下次會先敲門。

kill [kɪl]
動 殺、引起死亡

動詞變化 killed, killed, killing, kills
同義字 murder 謀殺
延伸片語 kill off 消滅
　　　 shoot to kill 一擊斃命

實境對話
A: Was the earthquake a big one? 那個地震很大嗎？
B: Yes, it was, and it **killed** 105 people. 對啊，而且有一百零五人死亡。

kiss [kɪs]
動 親吻

動詞變化 kissed, kissed, kissing, kisses

實境對話
A: How was your date? 你的約會如何？
B: She **kissed** me after she drove me home! 她載我回家後親了我！

laugh [læf]
動 笑

動詞變化 laughed, laughed, laughing, laughs
同義字 smile 微笑
延伸片語 laugh at 嘲笑
　　　 laugh off 用笑擺脫

實境對話
A: Are you **laughing** at me? 你們在笑我嗎？
B: No, we are not. Dan just told a joke. 不，我們沒有。丹恩剛剛講了一個笑話。

Part 2 依詞性分類的生活單字

lay [le]
動 躺

動詞變化 laid, laid, lying, lays
延伸片語 lay in 貯存
lay down 放下

實境對話
A: If you are tired, you can **lay** on my knees. 如果你累了，可以躺在我膝蓋上。
B: Thank you. 謝謝。

leave [liv]
動 離開

動詞變化 left, left, leaving, leaves
同義字 quit 離開
延伸片語 leave for 動身去
leave on 留住

實境對話
A: Are you **leaving** without saying goodbye? 你不說再見就要走了嗎？
B: No, I just want to check my mailbox. 不，我只是要去檢查一下信箱。

lick [lɪk]
動 舔

動詞變化 licked, licked, licking, licks
延伸片語 lick up 吞噬

實境對話
A: Is your baby **licking** my window? 你的寶寶在舔我的窗戶嗎？
B: Gosh, I have to stop her! 天啊，我得阻止她。

lift [lɪft]
動 舉起

動詞變化 lifted, lifted, lifting, lifts
延伸片語 lift up 舉起
lift from 從……提起

實境對話
A: I can't **lift** the box. It's too heavy. 我抬不起這個箱子。它太重了。
B: Let me help you. 我來幫你。

list [lɪst]
動 列表

動詞變化 listed, listed, listing, lists

實境對話
A: Things you have to buy are **listed** below. 你必須買的東西都列在底下。
B: Okay, I'll check it. 好，我會確認。

lock [lɑk]
動 鎖

動詞變化 locked, locked, locking, locks
延伸片語 lock up 把……鎖起來
lock in 把……關在裡面

實境對話
A: Did you **lock** the door? 你有鎖門嗎？
B: I think I did. Let me check it one more time. 我想有。我再去檢查一次好了。

make [mek]
動 製造

動詞變化 made, made, making, makes
延伸片語 make sure 確信
make up 彌補

實境對話
A: The famous company **made** a new smart phone.
那家知名公司製造了一款新型智慧型手機。
B: I know! I saw the news yesterday.
我知道！我昨天有看到新聞。

meet [mit]
動 見面

動詞變化 met, met, meeting, meets
延伸片語 meet with　符合
　　　　　 meet the needs of　滿足……的需要

實境對話
A: Where should I **meet** you?　我們要在哪裡見面？
B: How about the park next to post office?　郵局旁邊的公園如何？

miss [mɪs]
動 錯過

動詞變化 missed, missed, missing, misses
同義字 lose 錯過
延伸片語 miss out　遺漏
　　　　　 miss out on　錯過機會

實境對話
A: What did I **miss**?　我錯過什麼了嗎？
B: Not much. Come join us!　沒有很多。快來加入我們。

mix [mɪks]
動 混合

動詞變化 mixed, mixed, mixing, mixes
同義字 confuse 混合
延伸片語 mix in　混合
　　　　　 mix with　和……混合

實境對話
A: She **mixes** milk with black tea.　她把牛奶混到紅茶裡。
B: I want that, too!　我也想要那樣！

move [muv]
動 移動

動詞變化 moved, moved, moving, moves
延伸片語 move on　往前走
　　　　　 move in　生活於

實境對話
A: I think the house is **moving**.　我覺得房子在移動。
B: No, it's not! That's impossible!　才沒有呢！這怎麼可能！

nod [nɑd]
動 點頭

動詞變化 nodded, nodded, nodding, nods
延伸片語 nod off　打盹
　　　　　 on the nod　默許

實境對話
A: Did you see Serena? She's back.　你有看到瑟琳娜嗎？她回來了。
B: Yes, I did. She **nodded** to me.　有，我有看到。她跟我點頭。

offer [ˈɔfɚ]
動 提供

動詞變化 offered, offered, offering, offers
同義字 supply 供應
延伸片語 offer for　對……報價
　　　　　 on offer　出售中

實境對話
A: Will you **offer** me help?　你會提供協助嗎？
B: I'm not sure yet. I'll let you know.　我現在還不清楚。我會再通知你。

open [ˈopən]
動 打開

動詞變化 opened, opened, opening, opens
延伸片語 open up　打開
　　　　　 in the open　在戶外

實境對話
A: Can you **open** the door for me, please?　你能幫我開門嗎？
B: Sure!　當然！

pack [pæk]
動 包裝

動詞變化 packed, packed, packing, packs
延伸片語 pack in 停止
pack up 整理

實境對話
A: Are you **packing** your clothes? 你在**打包**你的衣服嗎？
B: Yes, I'm **packing** my clothes and accessories. 是啊，我在打包我的衣服和首飾。

park [pɑrk]
動 停車

動詞變化 parked, parked, parking, parks

實境對話
A: If you **park** your car here, you'll be fined. 如果你把車停在這裡，會被罰款。
B: Really? Then I have to move it away. 真的嗎？那我要移走。

paste [pest]
動 貼

動詞變化 pasted, pasted, pasting, pastes
同義字 post 張貼

實境對話
A: There's a poster **pasted** on the wall. 那裡有一張海報貼在牆上。
B: Who did that! 誰貼的啊！

pause [pɔz]
動 暫停

動詞變化 paused, paused, pausing, pauses
同義字 stop 停止

實境對話
A: Can you **pause** a while? 你可以暫停一下嗎？
B: Is there something wrong? 怎麼了嗎？

pick [pɪk]
動 挑

動詞變化 picked, picked, picking, picks
同義字 select 挑選
延伸片語 pick up 撿起
pick out 挑選出

實境對話
A: I think I **picked** a great book. 我想我挑了一本好書。
B: What's name of the book? 書名是什麼？

plant [plænt]
動 種植

動詞變化 planted, planted, planting, plants
同義字 cultivate 培育
延伸片語 plant oneself 站立不動
in plant 在生長發育中

實境對話
A: Do you want to **plant** any flowers? 你有想種什麼花嗎？
B: I'd love to **plant** some lilies. 我想要種百合花。

print [prɪnt]
動 印刷

動詞變化 printed, printed, printing, prints
延伸片語 in print 已出版
print out 列印出

實境對話
A: These pictures are amazing! 這些照片太棒了！
B: That's why I wanted to **print** them out. 這就是我把它們印出來的原因。

pull [pʊl]
動 拉

動詞變化 pulled, pulled, pulling, pulls
同義字 draw 拖
延伸片語 pull out 離開
pull down 推毀

實境對話
A: Why can't I open the door? 為什麼我打不開門？
B: You have to **pull** it, not push it. 你要用拉的，不是用推的。

pump [pʌmp]
動 抽水

動詞變化 pumped, pumped, pumping, pumps

實境對話
A: What are they doing? 他們在做什麼？
B: They are **pumping** water out of the house. 他們在抽房子裡的水。

produce
[`prɑdjus] 動 製造

動詞變化 produced, produced, producing, produces
同義字 make 製造

實境對話
A: What does the factory **produce**? 那家工廠製造什麼？
B: They mainly **produce** shoes and boots. 他們主要製造鞋子和靴子。

protect [prə`tɛkt]
動 保護

動詞變化 protected, protected, protecting, protects
同義字 prevent 保護
延伸片語 protect from 保護

實境對話
A: Stop controlling your child. 別再控制你的孩子了。
B: I'm not controlling him. I'm trying to **protect** him. 我沒有控制他。我是在保護他。

push [pʊʃ]
動 推

動詞變化 pushed, pushed, pushing, pushes
同義字 enhance 推動
延伸片語 push for 奮力爭取
push on 推進

實境對話
A: Hey, don't **push** me! 喂，別推我！
B: Sorry, my bad. 對不起，是我不好。

put [pʊt]
動 放置

動詞變化 put, put, putting, puts
同義字 set 放置
延伸片語 put forward 提出
put in 提交

實境對話
A: Where did I **put** my glasses? 我把眼鏡放到哪去了？
B: I don't know. I didn't see them. 我不知道。我沒看到。

recycle [ri`saɪk!]
動 回收

動詞變化 recycled, recycled, recycling, recycles
同義字 rebirth 再生

實境對話
A: Do you know how to **recycle**? 你知道怎麼回收嗎？
B: Yes, I do. 是的，我知道。

Part 2 依詞性分類的生活單字

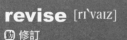
Chapter **9** 其他動詞 Other Verbs

revise [rɪ`vaɪz]
動 修訂

動詞變化 revised, revised, revising, revises
同義字 amend 修訂
延伸片語 revise for 復習功課

實境對話
A: I think this part should be **revised**. 我覺得這部分應該要修改。
B: Can you tell me why? 你可以告訴我為什麼嗎？

rise [raɪz]
動 升起

動詞變化 rose, risen, rising, rises
同義字 raise 上升
延伸片語 rise up 上升
rise and fall 漲落

實境對話
A: Look! The sun is **rising**. 看！太陽升起了！
B: Wow, how beautiful is that! 哇，真是太漂亮了。

roll [rol]
動 捲起

動詞變化 rolled, rolled, rolling, rolls
延伸片語 roll out 鋪開
roll in 蜂擁而來

實境對話
A: What is Aunt Sally doing? 莎莉阿姨在做什麼？
B: She is **rolling** up her sleeves in order to clean her room. 她正捲起袖子好整理房間。

rub [rʌb]
動 摩擦

動詞變化 rubbed, rubbed, rubbing, rubs
延伸片語 rub off 擦掉
rub in 用力擦入、反復講

實境對話
A: My dog is **rubbing** its back against the carpet. 我的狗用背部摩擦地毯。
B: I think it means it's itchy. 我想那表示牠很癢。

run [rʌn]
動 跑

動詞變化 ran, run, running, runs 同義字 set 放置
延伸片語 in the long run 長遠
run away 逃跑

實境對話
A: Look at Charles! 你看查爾斯！
B: Wow, he is **running** so fast! 哇，他跑得真快！

rush [rʌʃ]
動 衝

動詞變化 rushed, rushed, rushing, rushes
延伸片語 in a rush 急急忙忙地

實境對話
A: Did he catch his train? 他有搭上火車嗎？
B: I'm not sure, but I saw him **rushed** to the train. 我不確定，但是我有看到他往火車衝去。

rob [rɑb]
動 搶劫

動詞變化 robbed, robbed, robbing, robs
同義字 hijack 搶劫

實境對話
A: What happened? 發生什麼事？
B: They **robbed** the poor old lady. 他們搶劫了那個可憐的老太太。

rest [rɛst]
動 休息

動詞變化 rest, rest, resting, rests
同義字 relax 休息
延伸片語 rest in 依賴於
at rest 靜止

實境對話
A: I think I have jet lag. 我想我有時差。
B: You should **rest** now. 你該休息了。

shake [ʃek]
動 搖動

動詞變化 shook, shook, shaking, shakes
同義字 rock 搖動
延伸片語 shake off 擺脫
shake up 搖勻

實境對話
A: Is the house **shaking**? 房子在**搖**嗎？
B: Yeah, I think it's earthquake. 對，我想是地震。

shoot [ʃut]
動 射擊

動詞變化 shot, shot, shooting, shoots
延伸片語 shoot at 力爭
shoot at 向……射擊

實境對話
A: How did you get hurt? 你怎麼受傷的？
B: A man came from that door and **shot** me. 一個男人從那扇門出來，向我**射**了一槍。

shout [ʃaut]
動 喊叫

動詞變化 shouted, shouted, shouting, shouts
同義字 yell 喊叫
延伸片語 shout at 對……大喊
shout out 突然呼喊

實境對話
A: Why are you **shouting** at your computer? 你為什麼對著電腦大叫？
B: I just can't fix it! 我就是修不好它！

shut [ʃʌt]
動 關閉

動詞變化 shut, shut, shutting, shuts 同義字 close 關閉
延伸片語 shut up 住口
shut off 切斷

實境對話
A: Can I come in? 我可以進來嗎？
B: Sure, please **shut** the door after you come in. 當然可以，進來之後請關門。

smoke [smok]
動 抽菸

動詞變化 smoked, smoked, smoking, smokes

實境對話
A: Can I **smoke** here? 我可以在這裡**抽菸**嗎？
B: No, you have to go to **smoking** area. 不行，你必須到**吸菸區**。

sign [saɪn]
動 簽署

動詞變化 signed, signed, signing, signs
延伸片語 sign up 簽約雇傭
sign on 開始廣播

實境對話
A: Did he **sign** the contract? 他有**簽**合約嗎？
B: No, he said he had to think about it. 沒有，他說他得想再想想。

Part 2 依詞性分類的生活單字

stand [stænd]
動 站立

動詞變化 stood, stood, standing, stands
延伸片語 stand up 起立
stand for 象徵

實境對話
A: Why is he **standing** there? 為什麼他站在那裡？
B: He's waiting someone. 他在等人。

steal [stil]
動 偷盜

動詞變化 stole, stolen, stealing, steals
延伸片語 steal in 潛入
steal out 偷溜走

實境對話
A: I think someone has **stolen** my cell phone. 我想有人偷了我的手機。
B: Maybe you just dropped it in your house. 也許只是掉在你家了。

strike [straɪk]
動 罷工

動詞變化 struck, struck, striking, strikes
延伸片語 strike in 插嘴
strike at 襲擊

實境對話
A: Why is the hospital closed? 為什麼這家醫院關了？
B: Their employees **stroke** for better working environment.
他們的員工罷工，要求更好的工作環境。

take [tek]
動 拿走

動詞變化 took, taken, taking, takes
同義字 carry 拿
延伸片語 take off 脫下
take part in 參加

實境對話
A: Did you **take** my notebook? 你拿走了我的筆記本嗎？
B: No, I didn't. 不，我沒有。

tell [tɛl]
動 告訴

動詞變化 told, told, telling, tells
同義字 talk 談話

實境對話
A: I really want to **tell** him my real feelings. 我真的很想告訴他我真正的感覺。
B: I'm not sure if it's a good idea. 我不確定這個主意好不好。

throw [θro]
動 投擲

動詞變化 threw, thrown, throwing, throws
同義字 cast 投擲
延伸片語 throw away 扔掉
throw out 扔掉

實境對話
A: I'm a pitcher. 我是投手。
B: Wow, you must be very good at **throwing** balls. 哇，你一定很擅長投球吧。

touch [tʌtʃ]
動 觸摸

動詞變化 touched, touched, touching, touches
延伸片語 in touch 聯繫
keep in touch 保持聯絡

實境對話
A: Don't **touch** my book! 別碰我的書！
B: Sorry. 抱歉。

trace [tres]
動 跟蹤

動詞變化 traced, traced, tracing, traces
延伸片語 trace back 追溯

實境對話
A: It seems the police are **tracing** the criminal. 看來警方正在**追蹤**犯人。
B: I hope they can find him soon. 我希望他們能盡快找到他。

trap [træp]
動 誘捕

動詞變化 trapped, trapped, trapping, traps
同義字 ensnare 誘捕

實境對話
A: They **trapped** the crazy elephant. 他們**捕獲**那隻發狂的大象了。
B: Thank God! 感謝上帝！

type [taɪp]
動 打字

動詞變化 typed, typed, typing, types

實境對話
A: What are you doing? 你在做什麼？
B: I'm **typing**. 我在**打字**。

use [juz]
動 使用

動詞變化 used, used, using, uses
延伸片語 in use 在使用中
make use of 使用

實境對話
A: You can **use** my phone if you want. 如果你想要的話，可以**用**我的電話。
B: Thank you. 謝謝你。

vote [vot]
動 投票

動詞變化 voted, voted, voting, votes
同義字 poll 投票
延伸片語 vote for 投票贊成
vote on 就……表決

實境對話
A: Who are you going to **vote** for? 你要把票**投**給誰？
B: I haven't decided yet. 我還沒決定。

walk [wɔk]
動 走路

動詞變化 walked, walked, walking, walks
延伸片語 walk in 走進去
walk along 散步

實境對話
A: When I was **walking** on the street, the dog suddenly attacked me.
我**走**在路上的時候，那隻狗突然攻擊我。
B: That's terrible!
那真是太可怕了！

wave [wev]
動 揮手

動詞變化 waved, waved, waving, waves
同義字 roll 卷

實境對話
A: Look! Martin is **waving** at us! 你看！馬丁在向我們**揮手**！
B: Where is he? 他在哪裡？

Part 2 依詞性分類的生活單字

accept [ək`sɛpt]
動 接受

動詞變化 accepted, accepted, accepting, accepts

實境對話
A: I'm not sure if I can **accept** the result. 我不確定我有沒有辦法**接受**結果。
B: Just take a deep breath. 深呼吸吧。

add [æd]
動 增加

動詞變化 added, added, adding, adds
同義字 accelerate 增加
延伸片語 add up 合計
add in 添加

實境對話
A: How is that? 好吃嗎？
B: I think you should **add** some salt. 我覺得你應該**加**點鹽。

admire [əd`maɪr]
動 欽佩

動詞變化 admired, admired, admiring, admires
延伸片語 admire for 讚賞

實境對話
A: I **admire** her courage. 我**欽佩**她的勇氣。
B: Me, too. She's so brave. 我也是，她真勇敢。

advise [əd`vaɪz]
動 建議

動詞變化 advised, advised, advising, advises
同義字 suggest 建議
延伸片語 advise of 通知

實境對話
A: So, what's your decision? 所以你決定如何？
B: My friend **advised** me be patient. So I'm trying to hold my feelings.
我朋友**建議**我要有耐心。所以我正試著克制自己的感情。

agree [ə`gri]
動 同意

動詞變化 agreed, agreed, agreeing, agrees
同義字 accept 贊成
延伸片語 agree with 同意
agree in 在……方面意見一致

實境對話
A: I think his performance is excellent! 我覺得他的表現真是太優秀了！
B: I can't **agree** with you more. 我真是太**同意**你了。

allow [ə`lau]
動 允許

動詞變化 allowed, allowed, allowing, allows
同義字 permit 允許
延伸片語 allow for 考慮到
allow of 容許

實境對話
A: Will you **allow** me to go out with Kevin? 你會**允許**我和凱文出去嗎？
B: Well, it depends. 嗯，這要看情況。

apologize
[ə`pɑləˌdʒaɪz]
動 道歉

動詞變化 apologized, apologized, apologizing, apologizes
延伸片語 apologize for 道歉

實境對話
A: I have to **apologize** to him. 我必須跟他**道歉**。
B: You really should do that. 你真的應該這麼做。

appear [əˋpɪr]
動 出現

動詞變化 appeared, appeared, appearing, appears
同義字 occur 出現
延伸片語 appear in 出現在
appear on 在……上出現

 A: Will he **appear**? 他會**出現**嗎？
B: I'm sure he will. 我很確定他會出現。

appreciate [əˋpriʃʌet]
動 讚賞、感激

動詞變化 appreciated, appreciated, appreciating, appreciates
同義字 enjoy 欣賞

 A: So, how did it go? 事情進行得如何？
B: It went perfectly! We really **appreciated** her help. 進行得很順利！我們真的很感謝她的幫忙。

argue [ˋɑrgjʊ]
動 爭論

動詞變化 argued, argued, arguing, argues
同義字 debate 爭論
延伸片語 argue about 爭論
argue for 贊成

 A: No, you can't do that! 不，你不能那樣做！
B: Don't **argue** with me! 別跟我**爭論**！

arrange [əˋrendʒ]
動 安排

動詞變化 arranged, arranged, arranging, arranges
同義字 schedule 安排
延伸片語 arrange for 安排

 A: Can you help me with these things? 你可以幫我做這些事情嗎？
B: Sure, I will **arrange** everything you need. 當然，我會幫你**安排**所有需要的事項。

assume [əˋsum]
動 假定

動詞變化 assumed, assumed, assuming, assumes
同義字 suppose 假設

 A: Where is your Mom? 你媽媽呢？
B: I **assume** that she had gone to the market. 我猜她去市場了。

attack [əˋtæk]
動 攻擊

動詞變化 attacked, attacked, attacking, attacks
延伸片語 attack on 攻擊

A: What happened? 發生了什麼事？
B: Those crazy monkeys **attacked** me! 那些瘋狂的猴子**攻擊**我！

avoid [əˋvɔɪd]
動 避免

動詞變化 avoided, avoided, avoiding, avoids
同義字 escape 逃避

 A: You have to **avoid** this kind of mistake. 你必須**避免**這樣的錯誤。
B: OK, I see. 好，我知道了。

Part 2 依詞性分類的生活單字

become [bɪˋkʌm]
動 變成

動詞變化 became, become, becoming, becomes
同義字 turn 變成

實境對話
A: What did she do after leaving the company? 她離開公司之後在做什麼？
B: She **became** a freelance. 她成了自由工作者。

begin [bɪˋgɪn]
動 開始

動詞變化 began, began, beginning, begins
同義字 start 開始
延伸片語 begin with 以……開始
begin at 從……開始

實境對話
A: Has the lecture **begun**? 演講開始了嗎？
B: Yes, it started 10 minutes ago. 對，十分鐘前開始的。

belong [bəˋlɔŋ]
動 屬於

動詞變化 belonged, belonged, belonging, belongs
延伸片語 belong to 應歸於

實境對話
A: Is this Jenna's notebook? 這是珍娜的筆記本嗎？
B: No. I think it **belongs** to Lisa. 不，我想那屬於麗莎。

broadcast [ˋbrɔdˌkæst]
動 廣播

動詞變化 broadcast, broadcast, broadcasting, broadcasts

實境對話
A: She **broadcasted** your secrets to her friends. 她把你的祕密講給她的朋友聽。
B: Why did she do that to me! 她為什麼要那樣對我！

burst [bɝst]
動 爆發

動詞變化 burst, burst, bursting, bursts
同義字 outbreak 爆發
延伸片語 burst into 闖入
burst into tears 突然哭起來

實境對話
A: What' that noise? 那是什麼聲音？
B: A balloon **burst**. 一顆氣球爆炸了。

call [kɔl]
動 召集

動詞變化 called, called, calling, calls
延伸片語 call for 要求
call on 訪問

實境對話
A: Please **call** a taxi for me. 請幫我叫一台計程車。
B: No problem! 沒問題！

calm [kɑm]
動 使平靜

動詞變化 calmed, calmed, calming, calms
同義字 compose 使平靜
延伸片語 calm down 平靜下來
keep calm 保持冷靜

實境對話
A: What should I do? 我該怎麼辦？
B: Just **calm** down. 冷靜點。

cancel [ˈkænsḷ]
動 取消

動詞變化　canceled, canceled, canceling, cancels
同義字　abolish 取消
延伸片語　cancel out　取消

實境對話
A: I think I'm having a fever.　我想我發燒了。
B: Should I **cancel** the meeting for you?　我應該幫你取消開會嗎？

care [kɛr]
動 關懷

動詞變化　cared, cared, caring, cares
同義字　concern 關心
延伸片語　take care　注意

實境對話
A: Was Ann happy about her birthday party?　安滿意她的生日派對嗎？
B: I don't know and I don't **care**.　我不知道，也不關心。

check [tʃɛk]
動 檢查

動詞變化　checked, checked, checking, checks
同義字　examine 檢查

實境對話
A: I need to double **check**.　我需要再檢查一次。
B: Take your time.　慢慢來。

compare
[kəmˈpɛr]　**動** 比較

動詞變化　compared, compared, comparing, compares
延伸片語　compare with　與……相比較
compare to　把……比作

實境對話
A: **Compared** with Joe's project, I think Linda's better.
和喬的計畫比較之下，我覺得琳達的比較好。
B: I agree.
我同意。

complain
[kəmˈplen]　**動** 抱怨

動詞變化　complained, complained, complaining, complains
同義字　beef 抱怨
延伸片語　complain of　抱怨
complain about　抱怨

實境對話
A: He **complained** to me about his new job.　他向我抱怨新工作的事。
B: What's wrong with his new job?　他的新工作怎麼了？

concern [kənˈsɝn]
動 關心

動詞變化　concerned, concerned, concerning, concerns
同義字　care 關心
延伸片語　concern about　對……表示擔心
concern with　使關心

實境對話
A: John is very **concerned** about his girlfriend.　約翰很關心他的女朋友。
B: He's such a nice guy.　他真的人很好。

continue
[kən`tɪnjʊ] 動 繼續

動詞變化 continued, continued, continuing, continues

A: Are we going to **continue** this subject? 我們還要**繼續**這個主題嗎？
B: Yes, we are. 對，要繼續。

create [krɪ`et]
動 創造

動詞變化 created, created, creating, creats
同義字 invent 創造

A: I want to **create** new memories with you. 我想要和你**創造**新的回憶。
B: But I'm tired. 但是我累了。

date [det]
動 約會

動詞變化 dated, dated, dating, dates
延伸片語 up to date 最新的
out of date 過時的

A: I think Laura is **dating** Chris. 我覺得蘿拉在和克里斯**約會**。
B: Really? I thought they were friends. 真的嗎？我以為他們是朋友。

deal [dil]
動 交易、經管

動詞變化 dealt, dealt, dealing, deals
延伸片語 deal with 處理
deal in 經營

A: What do they do? 他們是做什麼的？
B: Their shop **deals** in jewelry. 他們的店經營珠寶。

decide [dɪ`saɪd]
動 決定

動詞變化 decided, decided, deciding, decides
同義字 determine 決定
延伸片語 decide on 決定
decide for 作對……有利的事情

A: Have you **decided** yet? 你**決定**了嗎？
B: Not yet. I just can't **decide** it. 還沒。我就是**決定**不了。

decrease
[dɪ`kris] 動 減少

動詞變化 decreased, decreased, decreasing, decreases
同義字 reduce 減少
延伸片語 on the decrease 在減少中
decrease by 減少了

A: We need to **decrease** our expenses. 我們必須**減少**開銷。
B: Yeah, if we don't do that, we will face a financial problem.
是啊，如果我們不那樣做的話，就會面臨財務問題。

depend [dɪ`pɛnd]
動 取決於

動詞變化 depended, depended, depending, depends
延伸片語 depend on 取決於
depend upon 依賴

A: What kind of cake should we buy? 我們該買哪種蛋糕？
B: It **depends** on what she wants. 這**取決於**她想要哪一種。

describe
[dɪˋskraɪb]
動 描述

動詞變化 described, described, describing, describes
延伸片語 describe as 描述為
describe with 用……描述

實境對話 A: Can you **describe** what happened? 你能**描述**發生了什麼事嗎？
B: No, I can't remember what happened. 不，我記不起來發生了什麼事。

detect [dɪˋtɛkt]
動 察覺

動詞變化 detected, detected, detecting, detects
同義字 perceive 覺察

實境對話 A: What's wrong with her? 她怎麼了？
B: I don't know. But I **detected** fear in her voice. 我不知道。但是我從她的聲音**察覺**到恐懼。

die [daɪ]
動 死亡

動詞變化 died, died, dying, dies
延伸片語 die for 渴望
die of 因……死

實境對話 A: Why do you look so sad? 你看起來怎麼這麼傷心？
B: My dog **died** yesterday. 我的狗昨天**死掉**了。

direct [dəˋrɛkt]
動 指導

動詞變化 directed, directed, directing, directs
同義字 guide 指導

實境對話 A: Why is she still working? 為什麼她還在工作？
B: Her boss **directed** her to write an article about the disease, so she is busy right now.
她的老闆**指示**她寫一篇有關那種疾病的文章，所以她現在很忙。

disappear
[ˏdɪsəˋpɪr] **動** 消失

動詞變化 disappeared, disappeared, disappearing, disappears
同義字 vanish 消失

實境對話 A: When did he leave? 他什麼時候走的？
B: I don't know. He just **disappeared**. 我不知道。他就這樣**消失**了。

discover
[dɪˋskʌvɚ] **動** 發現

動詞變化 discovered, discovered, discovering, discovers
同義字 detect 發現

實境對話 A: She **discovered** that man is a stalker. 她**發現**那個男人是個跟蹤狂。
B: That's terrible! 真是可怕！

discuss [dɪˋskʌs]
動 討論

動詞變化 discussed, discussed, discussing, discusses
同義字 debate 討論
延伸片語 discuss with 商洽

實境對話 A: Should we **discuss** what happened just now? 我們應該**討論**剛剛發生了什麼事嗎？
B: No, I don't want to talk about it. 不，我不想談。

Part **2** 依詞性分類的生活單字

emphasize
[ˈɛmfəˌsaɪz] **動** 強調

動詞變化 emphasized, emphasized, emphasizing, emphasizes
同義字 stress 強調

實境對話
A: I think I should **emphasize** the importance of being on time.
　我覺得我應該**強調**準時的重要。
B: Yeah, you totally should. 　是啊，你真的應該那麼做。

enjoy [ɪnˈdʒɔɪ]
動 享受

動詞變化 enjoyed, enjoyed, enjoying, enjoys
同義字 appreciate 欣賞

實境對話
A: **Enjoy** your weekend! 　盡情**享受**週末吧！
B: I will. 　我會的。

envy [ˈɛnvɪ]
動 嫉妒

動詞變化 envied, envied, envying, envies
延伸片語 envy of 　嫉妒

實境對話
A: Sally's going to United Kingdom next week. 　莎莉下禮拜要去英國。
B: I really **envy** her good luck. 　我真**嫉妒**她的好運。

excite [ɪkˈsaɪt]
動 使興奮

動詞變化 excited, excited, exciting, excites

實境對話
A: We are going to Paris tomorrow! 　我們明天要去巴黎了耶！
B: I'm so **excited**! 　我好**興奮**！

expect [ɪkˈspɛkt]
動 期望

動詞變化 expected, expected, expecting, expects
同義字 promise 希望
延伸片語 expect of 　對……期望

實境對話
A: I shouldn't **expect** that he will change. 　我不該**期待**他會改變的。
B: Yeah, me, either. 　對啊，我也是。

express [ɪkˈsprɛs]
動 表達

動詞變化 expressed, expressed, expressing, expresses

實境對話
A: I don't know how to **express** how I feel. 　我不知道該如何**表達**我的感覺。
B: Maybe you can write it down. 　也許你可以寫下來。

fall [fɔl]
動 跌落

動詞變化 fell, fallen, falling, falls
延伸片語 fall in 　到期、集合
　　　　　fall in love with 　愛上某人

實境對話
A: How did he get hurt? 　他怎麼受傷的？
B: He **fell** from his bed. 　他從床上**摔**下來。

Chapter **9** 其他動詞 Other Verbs

fill [fɪl]
動 滿足

動詞變化 filled, filled, filling, fills
同義字 satisfy 滿足
延伸片語 fill up 填補
fill in 填寫

實境對話
A: Can you refill my glass? 可以加滿我的杯子嗎？
B: Sure, I will **fill** it with beer. 當然，我會幫你加滿啤酒。

find [faɪnd]
動 尋找

動詞變化 found, found, finding, finds
同義字 search 尋找
延伸片語 find out 找出
find fault 吹毛求疵

實境對話
A: I can't **find** my glasses. 我找不到我的眼鏡。
B: Here they are. 在這裡。

fit [fɪt]
動 使適應

動詞變化 fit, fit, fitting, fits **同義字** suit 適合
延伸片語 fit for 適於
fit in 適應

實境對話
A: I just can't **fit** to the new school. 我就是無法適應這間新學校。
B: It takes time to get used to a new environment. 習慣一個新環境要花一點時間。

focus [ˈfokəs]
動 焦點

動詞變化 focused, focused, focusing, focuses
同義字 point 焦點
延伸片語 focus on 集中於
focus in 焦點

實境對話
A: I can't **focus** today. 我今天無法集中精神。
B: Me, either. We drank too much yesterday. 我也是。我們昨天喝太多了。

form [fɔrm]
動 形成 **名** 形式

動詞變化 formed, formed, forming, forms
延伸片語 in the form of 以……的形式
in form 在形式上

實境對話
A: We **formed** a study group. 我們成立了一個讀書會。
B: Can I join you? 我能加入嗎？

gain [gen]
動 收穫、增加

動詞變化 gained, gained, gaining, gains
同義字 acquire 獲得
延伸片語 gain in 增長

實境對話
A: I need to get rid of the weight that I **gained** lately. 我得減掉最近增加的體重。
B: You can go to the gym with me! 你可以跟我一起上健身房！

get [gɛt]
動 得到

動詞變化 got, gotten, getting, gets
延伸片語 get rid of 擺脫

實境對話
A: What did you **get**? 你拿到什麼？
B: I **got** some candies. 我拿到一些糖果。

Chapter **9** 其他動詞 Other Verbs

give [gɪv]
動 給予

動詞變化 gave, given, giving, gives
延伸片語 give up 放棄
　　　 give in 屈服

 實境對話
A: When did you buy that book? 你什麼時候買了那本書？
B: I didn't buy it. John **gave** it to me. 我沒有買，是約翰給給我的。

handle [ˈhændl]
動 處理、操作

動詞變化 handled, handled, handling, handles
同義字 deal 處理
延伸片語 handle with 處理
　　　 handle with care 小心輕放

 實境對話
A: Can you **handle** this machine? 你會操作這台機器嗎？
B: Yes, I can. 是的，我會。

sleep [slip]
動 睡覺

動詞變化 slept, slept, sleeping, sleeps
延伸片語 sleep in 睡過頭
　　　 sleep on 留下

 實境對話
A: It's a bit late. I feel really **sleepy**. 有點晚了，我很想睡。
B: Then you should go to **sleep** right away. We all need to get up early.
那麼你應該快點去睡覺，我們都要早起。

start [stɑrt]
動 開始

動詞變化 started, started, starting, starts
同義字 begin 開始
延伸片語 start with 從……開始
　　　 start from 從……開始

實境對話
A: Do you know when this movie is going to **start**? 你知道這部電影幾點開演嗎？
B: Let me check the ticket. 讓我看一下票根。

stay [ste]
動 停留

動詞變化 stayed, stayed, staying, stays
延伸片語 stay in 呆在家裡
　　　 stay on 繼續停留

實境對話
A: You have to **stay** home today until you finish your homework.
你今天要待在家直到你寫完你的回家作業。
B: Oh! Not again. 噢！又來了。

stop [stɑp]
動 停止

動詞變化 stopped, stopped, stopping, stops
同義字 pause 停止
延伸片語 stop short 中途停下
　　　 stop in 順便訪問

 實境對話
A: Please **stop** yelling at me. 請停止對我吼叫。
B: Then you should stop making me angry. 那你應該別再讓我生氣。

suggest
[səgˈdʒɛst] **動** 建議

動詞變化 suggested, suggested, suggesting, suggests
同義字 advise 建議

實境對話
A: He **suggests** that we eat less at night. 他建議我們晚上吃少一點。
B: It's better for our health. 這樣對我們的健康比較好。

support [sə`port]
動 支持

動詞變化 supported, supported, supporting, supports
同義字 encourage 鼓勵
延伸片語 support for 對……的支援
support of 支持

實境對話
A: My parents always **support** me no matter what I do. 不管我做什麼我父母親都會支持我。
B: You are so lucky! 你真的很幸運！

thank [θæŋk]
動 感謝

動詞變化 thanked, thanked, thanking, thanks
同義字 appreciate 感激
延伸片語 thank you for 為某事感激

實境對話
A: You should **thank** Ray for his help. 你應該要感謝瑞的幫忙。
B: Going right away. 馬上就去。

treat [trit]
動 對待

動詞變化 treated, treated, treating, treats
延伸片語 treat with 處理
treat of 論及

實境對話
A: Her manager **treats** her quite well. 她的主管待她還不錯。
B: It's because she works pretty hard. 那是因為她很努力工作。

trust [trʌst]
動 相信

動詞變化 trusted, trusted, trusting, trusts
同義字 believe 相信
延伸片語 trust in 信任

實境對話
A: I don't **trust** strangers easily. 我不輕易相信陌生人。
B: Neither do I. 我也是。

try [traɪ]
動 嘗試

動詞變化 tried, tried, trying, trys
延伸片語 try my best 盡最大努力
try hard 努力

實境對話
A: I'll **try** my best to reach my goal. 我會試著盡我最大的努力去達到我的目標。
B: Don't push yourself too hard. 別給自己太多壓力。

visit [`vɪzɪt]
動 拜訪

動詞變化 visited, visited, visiting, visites　**同義字** call 訪問
延伸片語 pay a visit 進行訪問
visit on 遷怒於某人

實境對話
A: Mary will come **visit** us tomorrow. 瑪莉明天會來拜訪我們。
B: We must clean up our house then. 那我們一定要來打掃一下家裡。

wait [wet]
動 等待

動詞變化 waited, waited, waiting, waits
延伸片語 wait for 等候

實境對話
A: The students are **waiting for** the teacher to dismiss the class. 學生們正等著老師下課。
B: But it's not nearly break time. 但現在還不到下課時間。

Part **2** 依詞性分類的生活單字

wake [wek]
動 叫醒

動詞變化 woke, waken, waking, wakes
同義字 arouse 醒來
延伸片語 wake up 起床

實境對話
A: I'm going to take a nap. **Wake** me up an hour later.　我要去睡個午覺，一小時後把我叫醒。
B: Sure.　好的。

waste [west]
動 浪費

動詞變化 wasted, wasted, wasting, wastes
同義字 lose 浪費

實境對話
A: You are **wasting** too much time on this project.　你**浪費**太多時間在這企劃上。
B: But I'm almost finished.　但我就快完成了。

welcome
[ˈwɛlkəm]
動 歡迎

動詞變化 welcomed, welcomed, welcoming, welcomes
延伸片語 welcome in　款待
　　　　 welcome back　歡迎歸來

實境對話
A: They **welcome** us to visit their new apartment.　他們**歡迎**我們去參觀他們的新公寓。
B: I can't wait.　我等不及了。

Chapter 9 其他動詞 Other Verbs

用簡單的小測驗，驗收一下，單字記住了嗎？

(   ) 1 complete

(   ) 2 survive

(   ) 3 forgive

(   ) 4 guess

(   ) 5 inspire

(   ) 6 remind

(   ) 7 beat

(   ) 8 cheat

(   ) 9 deliver

(   ) 10 guide

(   ) 11 hold

(   ) 12 kick

(   ) 13 lock

(   ) 14 meet

(   ) 15 paste

(   ) 16 roll

(   ) 17 shout

(   ) 18 throw

(   ) 19 decide

(   ) 20 welcome

A 捲起	B 傳送	C 激發	D 見面	E 控制	F 歡迎	G 決定
H 完成	I 提醒	J 投擲	K 喊叫	L 欺騙	M 原諒	N 嚮導
O 猜測	P 踢	Q 鎖	R 生存	S 敲擊	T 貼	

答案

1(H)　2(R)　3(M)　4(O)　5(C)　6(I)　7(S)　8(L)　9(B)　10(N)　11(E)　12(P)　13(Q)　14(D)
15(T)　16(A)　17(K)　18(J)　19(G)　20(F)

Track 276

able [ˈebl̩]
形 有能力的

形容詞變化 abler, the ablest
同義字 capable 有能力的

實境對話
A: I'll be **able** to pay for my daily expenses when I find a job.
我找到工作後就**有能力**支付我的生活開銷了。
B: Don't worry. You will. 放心。你可以的。

absent [ˈæbsn̩t]
形 缺席的

延伸片語 absent from 缺席
absent from work 曠工

實境對話
A: Is Ken **absent** from work today? 肯今天缺席嗎？
B: He doesn't feel well, so he can't come to the office today.
他不舒服，所以今天沒辦法來公司上班。

afraid [əˈfred]
形 害怕的

形容詞變化 more afraid, the most afraid
同義字 scared 害怕的
延伸片語 afraid of 害怕

實境對話
A: Mom will be very angry if she founds out what you've done to her kitchen.
媽要是發現你把她廚房弄成這樣一定會很生氣。
B: Please don't tell her. I'm so **afraid**. 拜託你不要跟她說，我好害怕。

alike [əˈlaɪk]
形 相似的

同義字 similar 相似的

實境對話
A: The twins look much **alike.** 這對雙胞胎長得極為相似。
B: You can distinguish them by their personalities. 你可以從他們的個性上來分辨他們。

alive [əˈlaɪv]
形 活著的

形容詞變化 more alive, the most alive
同義字 lively 活著的、活潑的
延伸片語 alive with 充滿

實境對話
A: I don't know why some people want to commit suicide. 我不瞭解為什麼有些人要自殺。
B: Everything has its way to be solved. It's better to be **alive**.
每件事都有解決的辦法。能活著是最好的。

alone [əˈlon]
形 獨自的

同義字 isolated 孤獨的
延伸片語 let alone 更不必說

實境對話
A: My dog hates being **alone** at home. 我的狗不喜歡獨自待在家。
B: It sounds like human being. 感覺好像人喔。

American
[əˋmɛrɪkən]
形 美國的

 實境對話
A: **American** food usually contains a lot of fat.
美國食物通常含有很高的脂肪。
B: It reminds me of the fast food culture.
這讓我想到速食文化。

ancient [ˋenʃənt]
形 古代的

形容詞變化 more ancient, the most ancient
同義字 aged 古老的
延伸片語 in ancient times 在古代

 實境對話
A: I'm quite interested in the **ancient** Egyptian history. 我對古代埃及文化相當有興趣。
B: Me, too! It's full of mystery. 我也是耶！它充滿了神祕感。

asleep [əˋslip]
形 睡著的

延伸片語 fall asleep 入睡
sound asleep 熟睡

實境對話
A: Kate fell **asleep** during the class today. 凱特今天在課堂上睡著了。
B: I can imagine how angry the teacher was. 我可以想像老師有多生氣。

available
[əˋveləb!]
形 有效的、有空的

形容詞變化 more available, the most available
同義字 effective 有效的
延伸片語 available for 可用於……的
available from 可向……購買

 實境對話
A: The special discount is only **available** in this sale season.
這特別優惠只在這次拍賣季生效。
B: We should be hurry otherwise there will be nothing left.
那我們得快點去買，不然就什麼都買不到了。

basic [ˋbesɪk]
形 基礎的

形容詞變化 more basic, the most basic
同義字 fundamental 基礎的

 實境對話
A: I need to improve my English. 我需要改善我的英文。
B: Why don't you start from **basic** conversation? 何不從基礎對話開始呢？

bright [braɪt]
形 明亮的

形容詞變化 brighter, the brightest
反義字 dark 黑暗的

 實境對話
A: She looks so pretty. 她看起來好美。
B: It's because her eyes shine so **bright** when she smiles.
那是因為她笑的時候眼睛很明亮動人。

Part 2 依詞性分類的生活單字

broad [brɔd]
形 寬闊的

形容詞變化 broader, the broadest
反義字 narrow 狹窄的

實境對話
A: What's so special about your new home?　你的新家有什麼特別特殊的地方？
B: There happens to be a **broad** river running through the backyard of our villa.
　我們別墅後院剛好有條寬闊的河流過。

classical
[ˋklæsɪkl] 形 古典的

同義字 traditional 傳統的

實境對話
A: What kind of music do you like?　你喜歡什麼樣的音樂？
B: I like **classical** music.　我喜歡古典樂。

colorful [ˋkʌləfəl]
形 多彩的

形容詞變化 more colorful, the most colorful

實境對話
A: The sky looks so **colorful** today.　今天的天空顏色好多彩。
B: It reminds me of Monet's painting.　它讓我聯想到莫內的畫。

common
[ˋkɑmən]　形 共同的

形容詞變化 commoner, the commonest
同義字 mutual 共同的
延伸片語 in common　共同的

實境對話
A: We have a lot **in common**.　我們有許多共同點。
B: That's why you two are very close friends.　那就是為什麼你們這麼要好。

complete
[kəmˋplit]　形 完整的

同義字 whole 完整的

實境對話
A: I need your **complete** information to help you apply for the college.
　我需要你完整的資料才能幫你申請大學。
B: Let me complete this form right away.
　我馬上填完這份表格。

convenient
[kənˋvinjənt]　形 方便的

形容詞變化 more convenient, the most convenient

實境對話
A: Traveling in Taipei by MRT is really **convenient**.　在臺北移動搭捷運真的很方便。
B: You can say that again.　你說的沒錯。

correct [kəˋrɛkt]
形 正確的

同義字 right 正確的

實境對話
A: My watch isn't telling the **correct** time.　我的手錶顯示的不是正確時間。
B: I think you need a new battery.　我想你需要一個新電池了。

crowded
[ˈkraʊdɪd] 形 擁擠的

同義字 jammed 擁擠的

 實境對話
A: Why don't we go out today? 我們今天為什麼不出門？
B: Because it's weekend. Everywhere is **crowded**. 因為現在是週末，上哪兒都很擁擠。

dangerous
[ˈdendʒərəs] 形 危險的

形容詞變化 more dangerous, the most dangerous
反義字 safe 安全的

 實境對話
A: It's very **dangerous** to run through a red light. 闖紅燈是很危險的。
B: Sorry, I won't do it again. 對不起，我不會再犯了。

dark [dɑrk]
形 黑暗的

形容詞變化 darker, darkest　　反義字 bright 明亮的
延伸片語 in the dark 在黑暗中

 實境對話
A: I can't see anything. It's too **dark**. 我什麼都看不見，太暗了。
B: Let me light up a candle. 我來點根蠟燭。

dead [dɛd]
形 死的、無效的、無生命的

延伸片語 dead on 完全正確的
　　　　 dead end 死路

 實境對話
A: This tree is **dead** because of serious air pollution. 這樹因為嚴重的空氣污染而死亡。
B: We should reduce the emission of carbon dioxide. 我們應該降低二氧化碳的排放。

dear [dɪr]
形 親愛的

形容詞變化 dearer, the dearest
延伸片語 for dear life 拼命地

 實境對話
A: This baby is my **dear** darling. 這小嬰兒是我親愛的寶貝。
B: She looks so naïve. 她看起來很天真無邪。

different
[ˈdɪfərənt] 形 不同的

形容詞變化 more different, the most different
反義字 same 相同的
延伸片語 different from 與……不同

 實境對話
A: New Jersey is very **different from** where I live. 紐澤西州和我住的地方非常不同。
B: I quite like the atmosphere there. 我還蠻喜歡那裡的氣氛。

difficult [ˈdɪfəˌkʌlt]
形 困難的

形容詞變化 more difficult, the most difficult
反義字 easy 簡單的

 實境對話
A: It's not easy for me to finish this task. 這項任務對我來說不太容易完成。
B: Don't worry. Everything is **difficult** from the beginning. 別擔心。萬事起頭難。

dirty [ˈdɝtɪ]
形 骯髒的

形容詞變化 dirtier, the dirtiest
反義字 clean 乾淨的

 實境對話
A: You need to clean up your **dirty** room.　你應該把你骯髒的房間打掃一下。
B: Ok, Mom.　好的，媽。

double [ˈdʌbl̩]
形 雙倍的

同義字 dual 雙重的

 實境對話
A: What do you like to order, sir?　先生，想點些什麼？
B: I'd like to have a cup of **double** shot coffee, thank you.　我想要一杯雙倍濃縮咖啡，謝謝。

easy [ˈizɪ]
形 簡單的

形容詞變化 easier, the easiest
反義字 difficult 困難的

 實境對話
A: Looks like this exam is quite **easy** for her. she got pretty high score.
看來這次的測驗對她來說很容易，她得了很高分。
B: She studied really hard this time.　她這次很認真唸書。

electric [ɪˈlɛktrɪk]
形 電的

 實境對話
A: The boy likes to play the **electric** toys.
那男孩喜歡玩電動玩具。
B: Even though I'm not a kid, I like it, too.
雖然我不是小孩，但我也很喜歡。

else [ɛls]
形 其他的

延伸片語 or else 否則
someone else 其他人

 實境對話
A: Do you know where this place is?　你知道這地方在哪嗎？
B: Sorry, I'm not sure. Can you ask someone **else**?　對不起，我不確定，你可以問問看其他人。

enough [əˈnʌf]
形 足夠的

同義字 adequate 足夠的
延伸片語 enough for 足夠地
more than enough 綽綽有餘

 實境對話
A: I never have **enough** allowance.　我從來沒有足夠的零用錢。
B: Stop complaining.　別抱怨了。

equal [ˈikwəl]
形 平等的

同義字 equivalent 相等的
延伸片語 be equal to 等於

 實境對話
A: I don't know if I have the right to reject him.　我不知道我是否有權利拒絕他。
B: Of course you have. All men are **equal** before the law.
你當然有，在法律前人人都是平等的。

excellent
[ˈɛkslənt]
形 卓越的

形容詞變化 more excellent, the most excellent
同義字 wonderful 卓越的

實境對話
A: You did an **excellent** job today. 你今天做得太棒了！
B: Thanks to your help. 幸虧有你的幫助。

false [fɔls]
形 錯誤的

反義字 same 相同的

實境對話
A: Your information about the meeting is **false**. 你所得到的會議資訊是錯的。
B: Where can I get the correct information then? 那麼我要到哪兒取得正確的資訊呢？

fancy [ˈfænsɪ]
形 幻想的

形容詞變化 fancier, the fanciest　同義字 ideal 想像的
延伸片語 take a fancy to 喜歡

實境對話
A: I had a **fancy** dream last night. 我昨晚做了一個異想天開的夢。
B: What was it about? 關於什麼？

fantastic
[fænˈtæstɪk] 形 奇異的

形容詞變化 more fantastic, the most fantastic
同義字 weird 怪異的

實境對話
A: My trip to Tibet was a **fantastic** experience. 我的西藏之行是個很奇妙的經驗。
B: Tell me about it! 跟我說說吧！

fair [fɛr]
形 公平的

同義字 equal 平等的
延伸片語 fair play　公平競爭
　　　　 fair trade　公平貿易

實境對話
A: What you did to him wasn't **fair**. 你對他做的事是不公平的。
B: I'll apologize to him. 我會去跟他道歉。

fashionable
[ˈfæʃənəbl] 形 流行的

形容詞變化 more fashionable, the most fashionable
同義字 popular 流行的

實境對話
A: She is always wearing those most **fashionable** clothes to work.
她總是穿著最流行的服飾去工作。
B: Yes, those clothes look good on her.
對啊，那些衣服穿在她身上很好看。

favorite [ˈfevərɪt]
形 最喜愛的

實境對話
A: What is your **favorite** place to travel?
你最喜愛的旅遊地點是哪裡？
B: Canada.
加拿大。

Part 2 依詞性分類的生活單字

fine [faɪn]
形 好的

形容詞變化 finer, the finest　　同義字 nice 好的
延伸片語 in fine　最後

實境對話
A: It's such a **fine** restaurant.
這真是一家**好**餐廳。
B: Yes, it is. I always celebrate some special occasions there with my family.
對啊。我總是和家人去那裡慶祝一些特別節日。

foreign [ˈfɔrɪn]
形 外國的

實境對話
A: Can you speak any **foreign** languages?
你會說任何**外語**嗎？
B: Yes, I can speak Spanish and German.
會，我會說西班牙語和德語。

formal [ˈfɔrml̩]
形 正式的

形容詞變化 more formal, the most formal
同義字 official 正式的

實境對話
A: Can you teach me how to write a **formal** business letter?
你可以教我如何寫一封**正式的**商業信函嗎？
B: Sure!
當然！

former [ˈfɔrmɚ]
形 從前的

實境對話
A: He is a **former** employee of our company.
他是我們公司**以前的**員工。
B: No wonder he looks so familiar.
難怪他看起來很面熟。

free [fri]
形 自由的

形容詞變化 freer, the freest　　同義字 liberal 自由的
延伸片語 for free　免費
free from　使擺脫

實境對話
A: I feel **free** and easy when I am here.　我在這裡感到**自由自在**。
B: You can come here whenever you want.　你想來隨時都可以來。

fresh [frɛʃ]
形 新鮮的

形容詞變化 fresher, the freshest
同義字 new 新的

實境對話
A: This lemonade is really **fresh**.　這杯檸檬汁很**新鮮**。
B: I know you'll like it.　我就知道你喜歡。

general [ˈdʒɛnərəl]
形 一般的

實境對話
A: Is it very difficult?
這很難嗎？
B: No, it's a very **general** subject.
不會，這是很**一般的**科目。

glad [glæd]
形 高興的

形容詞變化 gladder, the gladdest　同義字 happy 高興的
延伸片語 glad of 對……感到高興

實境對話
A: It's **glad** to have you as a friend. 很高興有你這個朋友。
B: I feel the same way. 我也這樣覺得。

great [gret]
形 偉大的

形容詞變化 greater, the greatest　同義字 important 重大的
延伸片語 a great deal 大量

實境對話
A: How do you like the book? 你覺得這本書怎麼樣？
B: It's a **great** literary work. 這是部偉大的文學作品。

hard [hɑrd]
形 難的

形容詞變化 harder, the hardest
同義字 difficult 困難的
延伸片語 hard on 嚴厲對待

實境對話
A: It's **hard** for me to understand what you are trying to say.
真的有點難瞭解你想試著說什麼。
B: I'll say it again then.
那我再說一次。

helpful [ˈhɛlpfəl]
形 有用的

形容詞變化 more helpful, the most helpful
同義字 useful 有說明的

實境對話
A: This information is quite **helpful**. 這資訊蠻有用的。
B: Yes, you can learn a lot from it. 對啊，你可以從那學到很多東西。

homesick
[ˈhomˌsɪk]
形 想家的

實境對話
A: Teddy looks quite down lately.
泰迪最近看起來很沮喪。
B: It's because he is getting **homesick**.
那是因為他最近開始想家。

horrible [ˈhɑrəbl]
形 可怕的

形容詞變化 more horrible, the most horrible
同義字 terrible 可怕的

實境對話
A: The food taste so **horrible** here. 這裡的食物嚐起來怪可怕的。
B: I guess the chief is in a bad mood today. 我想廚師今天心情不太好。

important
[ɪmˈpɔrtn̩t]
形 重要的

形容詞變化 more important, the most important
同義字 crucial 重大的

實境對話
A: Nothing is more **important** than your family. 沒有什麼比家庭更重要了。
B: True. 沒錯。

Part **2** 依詞性分類的生活單字

impossible

[ɪmˈpɑsəbḷ]

形 不可能的

實境對話 A: It's **impossible** to have you as the chairman.
不可能讓你當主席。
B: Why not?
為什麼不行？

independent

[ˌɪndɪˈpɛndənt]

形 獨立的

形容詞變化 more independent, the most independent
同義字 free 自由的
延伸片語 independent of 不依賴……的

實境對話 A: Sally is such an **independent** girl. 莎莉是個很獨立的女孩。
B: She does everything by herself. 她什麼都自己來。

instant [ˈɪnstənt]

形 立即的

同義字 immediate 立即的

實境對話 A: I need your **instant** reply. 我需要你給我立即的回覆。
B: I'll tell you right away. 我會馬上告訴你。

interesting

[ˈɪntərɪstɪŋ] 形 有趣的

形容詞變化 more interesting, the most interesting

實境對話 A: I'm playing hide and seek with my kids right now. 我正在和我的小孩玩躲迷藏。
B: It looks pretty **interesting**. 看起來很有趣。

latest [ˈletɪst]

形 最新的

實境對話 A: The writer's **latest** book is great!
那個作家的最新作品真是太棒了。
B: Really? I'll definitely read it today.
真的嗎？我今天絕對會拜讀！

latter [ˈlætɚ]

形 後者

實境對話 A: Do you prefer the former or the **latter**?
你比較想要前者還是後者？
B: The former.
前者。

likely [ˈlaɪklɪ]

形 可能的

形容詞變化 more likely, the most likely
同義字 possible 可能的
延伸片語 is likely to 有可能

實境對話 A: It's **likely** that you'll have a chance to study abroad. 你有可能有機會可以出國唸書。
B: I've been waiting for this for so long. 我等這一刻等好久。

Chapter 10 其他形容詞 Other Adjectives

|313|

loud [laʊd]
形 大聲的

形容詞變化 louder, the loudest

實境對話
A: Can you turn down your music? It's quite **loud**. 你可以把音樂關小聲一點嗎？它有點**大聲**。
B: I'm sorry. I will. 對不起，我會的。

lucky [ˈlʌkɪ]
形 幸運的

形容詞變化 luckier, the luckiest
同義字 fortunate 幸運的

實境對話
A: I'm **lucky** to have you with me. 我很**幸運**有你在我身旁。
B: You are so sweet. 你好貼心喔。

magic [ˈmædʒɪk]
形 神奇的

同義字 mysterious 不可思議的
延伸片語 black magic 巫術
　　　　as if by magic 不可思議地

實境對話
A: What the doctor did to him was **magic**. 那醫生為他做的事真是**神奇**。
B: He saved his life. 他救了他的命。

main [men]
形 主要的

同義字 chief 主要的

實境對話
A: Our **main** course today is spaghetti with meatballs. 我們今天的主菜是肉丸義大利麵。
B: I'll have one. 我點一份。

major [ˈmedʒɚ]
形 主要的 動 主修

同義字 crucial 主要的
延伸片語 major in 主修
　　　　major factor 主要因素

實境對話
A: My **major** subject in college was English. 我大學主修英文。
B: Me, too! 我也是！

marvelous [ˈmɑrvələs]
形 了不起的、令人驚嘆的

形容詞變化 more marvelous, the most marvelous
同義字 remarkable 卓越的

實境對話
A: You did a **marvelous** job! 你做得很棒！
B: Thank you. 謝謝。

minor [ˈmaɪnɚ]
形 較小的 動 副修

延伸片語 minor in 輔修

實境對話
A: She only got the **minor** part of the teacher's wedding cake. 她只拿到老師結婚蛋糕的一小部份。
B: It's because she doesn't like sweet. 那是因為她不喜歡甜食。

Part 2 依詞性分類的生活單字

modern [ˋmɑdɚn]
形 現代的

形容詞變化 more modern, the most modern

實境對話 A: New York is a very **modern** city.　紐約是一個很**現代的**城市。
B: I love that place.　我愛那地方。

national [ˋnæʃənl]
形 國家的

實境對話 A: The Moon Festival is a **national** holiday.
中秋節是一個**全國性**假日。
B: It's my birthday, too.
那天也是我生日。

necessary
[ˋnɛsəˏsɛrɪ] 形 必要的

形容詞變化 more necessary, the most necessary
同義字 essential 必要的

實境對話 A: It's **necessary** for you to understand how to operate the machine.
你**必須**知道如何操作這機器。
B: I'll try my best.
我會盡力的。

new [nju]
形 新的

形容詞變化 newer, the newest

實境對話 A: Who is the owner of this **new** book?　這本新書的主人是誰。
B: I think it belongs to Mary.　我想應該是瑪莉。

negative
[ˋnɛgətɪv] 形 消極的

形容詞變化 more negative, the most negative
反義字 positive 積極的

實境對話 A: Don't be so **negative** about everything.　對所有事情不要太過**消極**。
B: I'll try.　我會試試。

noisy [ˋnɔɪzɪ]
形 吵鬧的

形容詞變化 noisier, the noisiest

實境對話 A: It is very **noisy** outside.　外面很吵。
B: Then close the windows.　那把窗戶關起來。

only [ˋonlɪ]
形 唯一的

同義字 sole 唯一的
延伸片語 only for　要是沒有
only if　只要……就

實境對話 A: Do you know any other method to solve this problem?
你知道有什麼其他能解決這問題的辦法嗎？
B: No, it's the **only** way.
沒有，這是**唯一的**辦法。

|315|

ordinary
[ˋɔrdnˏɛrɪ]
形 平凡的

形容詞變化 more ordinary, the most ordinary
同義字 usual 普通的
延伸片語 in ordinary 常任的

實境對話
A: He is just an **ordinary** guy that plays the guitar. 他只是個會彈吉他的平凡人。
B: You are just jealous. 你只是在忌妒罷了。

other [ˋʌðɚ]
形 其他的

延伸片語 each other 彼此
or other 或者説

實境對話
A: Is there any **other** transportation I can take to get there?
要去那裡有什麼**其他**交通工具可以搭嗎？
B: You can take the bus.
你可以搭巴士。

overseas
[ˏovɚˋsiz]
形 海外的

實境對話
A: We should expand our **overseas** markets.
我們應當拓展**海外**市場。
B: Yes. That's definitely our priority.
對，那絕對是我們的當務之急。

own [on]
形 自己的

延伸片語 of your own 你自己的
on your own 獨立地

實境對話
A: I got my **own** car to drive. 我有自己的車可以開。
B: So good. 好好哦。

peaceful [ˋpisfəl]
形 和平的

形容詞變化 more peaceful, the most peaceful
同義字 pacific 和平的

實境對話
A: I hope the world can be a **peaceful** place. 我希望這世界可以變成一個和平的地方。
B: It's quite impossible. 這可能很難。

perfect [ˋpɝfɪkt]
形 完美的

同義字 ideal 完美的
延伸片語 perfect oneself in 精通

實境對話
A: The concert is really **perfect**! 這演唱會真完美！
B: I finally can see my idols. 我終於可以看到我的偶像了。

personal [ˋpɝsn̩l]
形 個人的

同義字 individual 個人的

實境對話
A: It's not polite to ask **personal** questions. 問太過個人的問題不太禮貌。
B: I'll remember it. 我會記住的。

Part **2**

依詞性分類的生活單字

pleasant [ˈplɛzn̩t]
形 令人愉快的

形容詞變化 more pleasant, the most pleasant
同義字 lovely 令人愉悅的

實境對話
A: What a **pleasant** evening! 真是個令人愉快的夜晚啊！
B: We should come out more. 我們應該常出來走走。

popular [ˈpɑpjələ]
形 流行的

形容詞變化 more popular, the most popular
同義字 fashionable 流行的

實境對話
A: Iphone is very **popular** now. Iphone 現在很流行。
B: I got one, too. 我也有一隻。

positive [ˈpɑzətɪv]
形 積極的

形容詞變化 more positive, the most positive
反義字 negative 消極的

實境對話
A: You should be more **positive**. 你應該要更積極。
B: I know. 我知道。

possible [ˈpɑsəbl̩]
形 可能的

形容詞變化 more possible, the most possible
同義字 probable 可能的
延伸片語 if possible 如果可能的話
as much as possible 盡可能

實境對話
A: Is it **possible** that you put our seats together? 有可能幫我們把座位劃在一起嗎？
B: Let me check it. 讓我查一下。

precious [ˈprɛʃəs]
形 寶貴的

形容詞變化 more precious, the most precious
同義字 valued 寶貴的

實境對話
A: Water is one of the most **precious** resources on earth. 水是地球最珍貴的資源之一。
B: Unfortunately water pollution is getting serious now. 很不幸地水污染是越來越嚴重了。

present [ˈprɛzn̩t]
形 現在的

同義字 current 現在的
延伸片語 at present 目前

實境對話
A: You need to focus on the **present** life rather than the past.
你應該專注於**現在的**生活，而不是過去。
B: I know.
我知道。

primary
[ˈpraɪˌmɛrɪ]
形 主要的

同義字 main 主要的
延伸片語 primary school 小學

實境對話
A: Your **primary** task is to finish this assignment. 你**主要的**任務是要完成這個工作。
B: I'm doing it right now. 我現在就正在做了。

Chapter 10 其他形容詞 Other Adjectives

|317|

private [`praɪvɪt]
形 私人的

形容詞變化 more private, the most private
延伸片語 in private 私下地

實境對話
A: I need to talk to you in **private**. 我需要私下跟你談談。
B: What's wrong? 怎麼了嗎？

public [`pʌblɪk]
形 公共的

形容詞變化 more public, the most public
延伸片語 in public 公開地
public opinion 民意

實境對話
A: You can't smoke in **public** space. 你不能在公共區域吸菸。
B: Sorry. 對不起。

quiet [`kwaɪət]
形 安靜的

形容詞變化 quieter, the quietest
同義字 peaceful 安靜的
延伸片語 on the quiet 私下地
keep quiet 保持安靜

實境對話
A: Claire is a **quiet** girl. 克萊兒是個安靜的女孩。
B: I know. She's tamed. 我知道。她好乖。

rare [rɛr]
形 稀有的

形容詞變化 rarer, the rarest
同義字 unique 稀罕的

實境對話
A: Panda is a **rare** animal. 熊貓是一種稀有動物。
B: It's also very cute. 牠們也很可愛。

ready [`rɛdɪ]
形 準備好的

形容詞變化 readier, the readiest
延伸片語 get ready 準備好
all ready 全部準備

實境對話
A: Are you **ready**? 你準備好了嗎？
B: Not yet! 還沒！

real [`riəl]
形 真的

形容詞變化 more real, the most real
同義字 true 真實的
延伸片語 for real 真的

實境對話
A: Is his testimony **real**? 他的證言是真的嗎？
B: I'm not sure. 我不確定。

regular [`rɛgjələ]
形 規律的

形容詞變化 more likely, the most likely

實境對話
A: What does Johnny do? 強尼做什麼的？
B: I think he doesn't have a **regular** job. 我認為他沒有正常工作。

responsible
[rɪˋspɑnsəbl̩]
形 負責的

形容詞變化 more responsible, the most responsible
同義字 reliable 可靠的
延伸片語 responsible for 是……的緣由
be responsible to sb. 對某人負責

A: Who is **responsible** for this mistake? 誰該為這個錯誤**負責**？
B: I am. 是我。

right [raɪt]
形 正確的

同義字 correct 正確的
延伸片語 right now 馬上
right away 立刻

A: Is my answer **right**? 我的答案**正確**嗎？
B: Yes, it is. 是的，正確。

safe [sef]
形 安全的

形容詞變化 safer, the safest
反義字 dangerous 危險的
延伸片語 safe from 免於
safe mode 安全模式

A: Where did you hide your jewelry? 你把你的珠寶藏在哪裡？
B: A **safe** place. 一個**安全的**地方。

same [sem]
形 一樣的

反義字 different 不同的
延伸片語 at the same time 同時
same as 和……一樣

A: The two boys look exactly the **same**. 這兩個男孩看起來一模一樣。
B: They are twins. 他們是雙胞胎。

scared [skɛrd]
形 害怕的

形容詞變化 more scared, the most scared
同義字 afraid 害怕的
延伸片語 be scared of 害怕……
scared to death 嚇得要死

A: I'm going to tell you a ghost story. 我要跟你們說一個鬼故事。
B: Don't do that! They are already **scared**. 別這樣！他們已經很**害怕**了。

secondary
[ˋsɛkənˌdɛrɪ]
形 第二的

A: Where are **secondary** schools?
中等學校在哪裡？
B: All the **secondary** schools are in town.
所有的中等學校都在鎮上。

serious [ˋsɪrɪəs]
形 嚴重的

形容詞變化 more serous, the most serious
同義字 acute 嚴重的
延伸片語 serious about 嚴肅、認真對待
serious injury 重傷

A: Is his injury **serious**? 他受的傷嚴重嗎？
B: Well, it's fine. 還好。

sharp [ʃɑrp]

形 尖鋭的

形容詞變化	sharper, the sharpest
延伸片語	look sharp 注意 sharp rise 激增

實境對話
A: Where should I put this **sharp** knife? 我該把這尖鋭的刀放在哪兒？
B: Just make sure it is out of reach of children. 只要確定放在小孩拿不到的地方就好。

silent [ˈsaɪlənt]

形 沉默的

形容詞變化	more silent, the most silent
同義字	still 沉默的
延伸片語	keep silent 保持沉默

實境對話
A: The old house was **silent**. 那間老房子一片寂靜。
B: That's terrifying. 好可怕。

similar [ˈsɪmələ]

形 相似的

形容詞變化	more similar, the most similar
同義字	alike 相似的

實境對話
A: His hair style is **similar** to yours. 他的髮型跟你的好像。
B: No, it's not! 才沒有呢！

simple [ˈsɪmpl̩]

形 簡單的

形容詞變化	simpler, the simplest
同義字	easy 簡單的

實境對話
A: This is a **simple** math question. 這是一個簡單的數學題。
B: Not to me. 對我來説不簡單。

single [ˈsɪŋgl̩]

形 單身的

實境對話
A: Is he **single** or married? 他單身還是已婚？
B: I think he has a girlfriend. 我想他有個女朋友。

skillful [ˈskɪlfəl]

形 熟練的 動 有技術的

形容詞變化	more skillful, the most skillful
同義字	experienced 熟練的
延伸片語	be skillful in 精於

實境對話
A: He is a **skillful** pianist. 他是位有技巧的鋼琴家。
B: I agree. 我同意。

sleepy [ˈslipɪ]

形 欲睡的

形容詞變化	sleepier, the sleepiest
同義字	slumberous 昏昏欲睡的
延伸片語	feel sleepy 困倦

實境對話
A: I'm so **sleepy**. 我好想睡。
B: Did you stay up late last night? 你昨晚熬夜嗎？

sorry [ˈsɔrɪ]

形 對不起的

形容詞變化	sorrier, the sorriest	同義字	regretful 遺憾的
延伸片語	sorry for oneself 垂頭喪氣		

實境對話
A: I'm so **sorry**. I don't know what to say. 我很抱歉。我不知道該説什麼。
B: It's OK. Don't worry about it. 沒關係的，別擔心。

Part **2** 依詞性分類的生活單字

special [ˈspɛʃəl]
形 特殊的

形容詞變化 more special, the most special
延伸片語 in special　特殊的

實境對話
A: This place is so **special**!　這個地方好特別！
B: I agree.　我同意。

strange [strendʒ]
形 陌生的

形容詞變化 stranger, the strangest
同義字 unknown 陌生的

實境對話
A: Remember, don't speak to **strange** people.　記住，別和陌生人說話。
B: OK, I won't.　好，我不會。

such [sʌtʃ]
形 這樣的

延伸片語 such as　比如
all such　所有這些

實境對話
A: How can you do **such** things!　你怎麼能這樣做！
B: Sorry, I ruined it.　對不起，我搞砸了。

sudden [ˈsʌdn]
形 突然的

延伸片語 of a sudden　突然

實境對話
A: In a **sudden**, the baby started to cry.　寶寶突然開始哭。
B: So what did you do next?　那你接下來做了什麼？

super [ˈsupɚ]
形 特級的

實境對話
A: The bag cost me 50,000 NT dollars.
　我花了五萬元買這個包包。
B: Wow, that's **super** expensive!
　哇！那超貴的。

sure [ʃur]
形 確定的

形容詞變化 surer, the surest　　同義字 confident 確信的
延伸片語 make sure　確信
for sure　確實

實境對話
A: Are you **sure** about this?　你確定嗎？
B: Yes, I'm pretty **sure**.　對，我滿確定的。

surprised
[səˈpraɪzd]　形 感到驚訝的

形容詞變化 more surprised, the most surprised

實境對話
A: This is for you.　這是給你的。
B: I'm **surprised** that you bring me a gift.　我好驚訝你送禮物給我。

terrible [ˈtɛrəbl]
形 可怕的

形容詞變化 more terrible, the most terrible
同義字 horrible 可怕的

實境對話
A: How was your date?　你的約會怎麼樣？
B: It was **terrible**!　糟透了！

Chapter 10 其他形容詞 Other Adjectives

terrific [təˋrɪfɪk]
形 極好的

形容詞變化 more terrific, the most terrific
同義字 excellent 極好的

實境對話 A: I won the first prize in the competition. 我在那場比賽得到第一名。
B: That's **terrific**! 真是太棒了！

thick [θɪk]
形 厚的

形容詞變化 thicker, the thickest　　反義字 thin 薄的
延伸片語 thick with 充滿著
through thick and thin 不畏艱險

實境對話 A: The beef steak is so **thick**! 牛排好厚喔！
B: Can you eat it all? 你能全部吃完嗎？

tidy [ˋtaɪdɪ]
形 整齊的

形容詞變化 tidier, the tidiest　　同義字 ordered 整齊的
延伸片語 tidy up 收拾、整理

實境對話 A: Your room is so **tidy**! 你的房間好整齊！
B: Yes, it is. 對啊。

traditional [trəˋdɪʃənl]
形 傳統的

形容詞變化 more traditional, the most traditional
同義字 conventional 傳統的
延伸片語 traditional culture 傳統文化

實境對話 A: Eating rice dumplings on Dragon Boat Festival is a tradition. 吃粽子是端午節的傳統。
B: I'd like to experience the **traditional** holiday. 我很想參與這個傳統節日。

true [tru]
形 真實的

形容詞變化 truer, the truest　　同義字 real 真實的
延伸片語 come true 實現
true to oneself 忠於自己的理想

實境對話 A: Is that **true**? 那是真的嗎？
B: I don't think so. 我不這麼認為。

unique [juˋnik]
形 獨特的

形容詞變化 more unique, the most unique
同義字 sole 唯一的

實境對話 A: Your jacket is so **unique**! 你的外套好特別！
B: Isn't it? I bought it yesterday. 對吧！我昨天買的。

useful [ˋjusfəl]
形 有用的

形容詞變化 more useful, the most useful
同義字 helpful 有用的
延伸片語 be useful for 對……有用

實境對話 A: I will tell you some **useful** skills in studying. 我會告訴你一些有用的讀書技巧。
B: That's great! 太好了！

Part 2 依詞性分類的生活單字

usual [ˈjuʒʊəl]
形 通常的

同義字 common 平常的
延伸片語 as usual 像往常一樣
out of the usual 與眾不同

實境對話 A: Why do you come home later than **usual**? 你怎麼比平常晚回來？
B: I had to finish my work. 我得完成我的工作。

valuable [ˈvæljʊəbl]
形 有價值的

形容詞變化 more valuable, the most valuable
同義字 worthy 有價值的

實境對話 A: That is definitely a **valuable** accessory. 那絕對是個有價值的飾品。
B: I'm not sure about it. 我不確定耶。

social [ˈsoʃəl]
形 社會的

實境對話 A: She doesn't have a lot of **social** experience.
她沒有很多社會經驗。
B: Because she's still a student.
因為她還是個學生。

whole [hol]
形 完整的

同義字 complete 完整的
延伸片語 as a whole 總的來說
in whole 整個地

實境對話 A: The **whole** thing is terrible. 這整件事太可怕了。
B: Yeah, how could she do that to me! 對啊！她怎麼能那樣對我！

wild [waɪld]
形 野生的

形容詞變化 wilder, the wildest   同義字 field 野生的
延伸片語 in the wild 在野外
run wild 失去控制

實境對話 A: Do you want to go to the **Wild** Animal Park with me? 你想跟我一起去野生動物園嗎？
B: Sounds fun! 聽起來很有趣！

wonderful [ˈwʌndəfəl]
形 精彩的

形容詞變化 more wonderful, the most wonderful
同義字 excellent 極好的
延伸片語 have a wonderful time 玩得快活極了

實境對話 A: Your performance was just **wonderful**! 你的演出真是太精采了！
B: Thank you for your compliments. 謝謝你的讚美。

wrong [rɔŋ]
形 錯誤的

同義字 false 錯誤的
延伸片語 go wrong 出毛病
What's wrong? 怎麼了？

實境對話 A: You picked the **wrong** one. 你挑到錯的了。
B: Oh, I didn't notice that. 噢，我沒注意到。

Chapter **10** 其他形容詞 Other Adjectives

|323|

Chapter 11 其他副詞

Track 295

always [`ɔlwɪz]
副 總是

實境對話
A: Where is John? 約翰去哪裡了？
B: He is **always** at the park at this time.
這個時間他總是在公園。

ever [`ɛvɚ]
副 永遠

同義字 forever 永遠
延伸片語 as ever 一直
never ever 絕不

實境對話
A: I won't talk to him **ever** again! 我永遠不會跟他說話了！
B: What happened? 發生了什麼事？

never [`nɛvɚ]
副 從不

實境對話
A: How was your trip to Thailand? 你的泰國之旅如何？
B: I will **never** go there again. 我再也不會去那裡了。

often [`ɔfən]
副 經常

同義字 frequently 經常
延伸片語 as often as 每當
how often 多長時間一次

實境對話
A: Do you go to the museum **often**? 你經常去博物館嗎？
B: Not really. 不常去。

seldom [`sɛldəm]
副 很少

延伸片語 seldom and never 簡直不、幾乎不

實境對話
A: My mom **seldom** cooks. 我媽媽很少煮飯。
B: Mine, either. We usually eat out. 我媽媽也是。我們通常在外面吃飯。

sometimes
[`sʌmˌtaɪmz] 副 有時

同義字 occasionally 間或

實境對話
A: **Sometimes** he talks to me gently. 有時候他會溫柔地跟我說話。
B: But usually he shouts at you. 但他經常向你大吼大叫。

usually [`juʒʊəlɪ]
副 通常

同義字 frequently 經常

實境對話
A: After school, I **usually** hang out with my friend. 放學之後，我通常和朋友一起出去。
B: Maybe we should hang out sometime. 也許我們哪天也可以一起出去。

Part 2 依詞性分類的生活單字

actually
[ˈæktʃʊəlɪ]
副 實際上

同義字 really 實際上

 A: Are you satisfied with your grade? 你滿意你的成績嗎？
B: **Actually**, I'm not. 事實上，我不滿意。

again [əˈgɛn]
副 再一次

同義字 moreover 再一次
延伸片語 again and again 再三地
over again 再一次

 A: Do you want to play the game **again**? 你想再玩一次遊戲嗎？
B: Of course! 當然！

also [ˈɔlso]
副 也

同義字 too 也
延伸片語 as also 同樣
see also 參見

 A: Danny is an English teacher. 丹尼是個英文老師。
B: He is **also** a translator. 他也是個翻譯。

away [əˈwe]
副 離去

延伸片語 far away 遙遠的
right away 立刻

 A: He just walked **away**. 他就那樣離開了。
B: You can't blame him. 你不能怪他。

too [tu]
副 也

同義字 also 也

 A: I have been to Seattle once. 我曾經去過一次西雅圖。
B: Me, **too**. 我也是。

almost [ˈɔlˈmost]
副 幾乎

同義字 nearly 幾乎
延伸片語 almost all 幾乎處處

 A: Did you see Elena yesterday? 你昨天有看到愛琳娜嗎？
B: Yes, I did. I **almost** couldn't recognize her. 有，我有看到。我**幾乎**認不出她。

altogether
[ˌɔltəˈgɛðɚ]
副 一起、合計

同義字 totally 總共

A: She bought 5 pairs of shoes **altogether**! 她一共買了五雙鞋子！
B: That was crazy! 那太瘋狂了！

especially
[əˋspɛʃəlɪ] 副 特別

同義字 peculiarly 特別

實境對話
A: Do you like those kids? 你喜歡那些孩子嗎？
B: I do. I like Miranda **especially**. 我喜歡他們，**尤其是**米蘭達。

even [ˋivən]
副 甚至

延伸片語 even if 即使
even as 正如

實境對話
A: I bet she doesn't **even** know what she's talking about. 我賭她**甚至**不知道她在說什麼。
B: I agree with you. 我同意。

finally [ˋfaɪn̩lɪ]
副 最後、終於

同義字 eventually 最後

實境對話
A: **Finally**, my work has done. 我的工作**終於**完成了。
B: Now you can take some rest. 現在你可以休息一下了。

hardly [ˋhɑrdlɪ]
副 幾乎不

同義字 scarcely 幾乎不
延伸片語 hardly ever 幾乎不

實境對話
A: I'm so tired that I can **hardly** stand. 我太累了，幾乎沒辦法站。
B: What did you do? 你做了什麼呀？

least [list]
副 最少

延伸片語 at least 至少
in the least 一點、絲毫

實境對話
A: How long does it take to get there? 到那邊要多久？
B: At **least** two hours by car. 開車至少要兩小時。

maybe [ˋmebi]
副 可能、或許

 實境對話
A: I'm moving to San Diego. Will you come visit me?
我要搬去聖地牙哥了。你會來拜訪我嗎？
B: **Maybe** someday.
也許有一天吧。

nearly [ˋnɪrlɪ]
副 差不多

同義字 almost 幾乎

實境對話
A: How old is he? 他幾歲了？
B: He's **nearly** 30 now. 他現在差不多三十歲。

 Part **2** 依詞性分類的生活單字

perhaps
[pəˋhæps] 副 可能

同義字 possibly 可能

A: Will Peter come to our party? 彼得會來我們的宴會嗎？
B: **Perhaps** not. 可能不會。

probably
[ˋprɑbəblɪ] 副 大概

同義字 perhaps 可能

A: Will he show up? 他會出現嗎？
B: **Probably**. 大概吧。

rather [ˋræðɚ]
副 相當、有點兒

延伸片語 would rather 寧願
or rather 倒不如說

A: I'm feeling **rather** drowsy right now. 我現在覺得有點昏昏欲睡。
B: Are you ok? 你還好吧？

really [ˋrɪəlɪ]
副 真地

同義字 actually 真實地
延伸片語 really and truly 千真萬確地

A: He is **really** a great violinist. 他真的是個很棒的小提琴家。
B: Absolutely! 當然！

so [so]
副 這麼

延伸片語 so on 等等
so far 到目前為止

A: I'm **so** happy to see you! 我好高興看到你。
B: Me, too! 我也是。

still [stɪl]
副 仍然

A: Is she **still** single? 她還是單身嗎？
B: No, she's married. 不，她結婚了。

then [ðɛn]
副 然後

延伸片語 since then 從那時以來
by then 到那時候

A: What happened, **then**? 然後發生什麼事了？
B: I just can't remember. 我就是記不起來。

together
[təˈgɛðɚ] 副 一起

延伸片語　together with　和
　　　　　　get together　一起

 實境對話
A: I want to grab some food from the convenience store. How about you?
我想去超商買點吃的。你呢？
B: I'm hungry, too. Let's go **together**.
我也餓了，我們一起去吧。

quite [kwaɪt]
副 相當

 實境對話
A: I think your report is **quite** good.　我覺得你的報告相當好。
B: Is it? I'm so happy.　真的嗎？我好開心。

yet [jɛt]
副 但是

延伸片語　as yet　至今仍
　　　　　　and yet　可是

 實境對話
A: My house is small **yet** comfortable.　我的房子雖然小但很舒適。
B: It really is a comfortable place.　這真的是一個很舒服的地方。

aloud [əˈlaʊd]
副 大聲地

同義字　loudly 大聲地
延伸片語　think aloud　邊想邊說出、自言自語

 實境對話
A: What's that noise?　那是什麼聲音？
B: Ellie's baby is crying **aloud**.　愛莉的寶寶在大聲哭鬧。

abroad [əˈbrɔd]
副 海外

延伸片語　go broad　去國外

 實境對話
A: I really want to go **abroad** and have a new life.　我真的很想去國外展開新生活。
B: Me, too. I hope we can go together someday.　我也是。我希望我們哪天可以一起去。

ahead [əˈhɛd]
副 向前

延伸片語　ahead of　在……之前
　　　　　　go ahead　前進

 實境對話
A: The road **ahead** seems to be under construction.　前面的路好像在施工中。
B: Then we shouldn't go over there.　那我們不應該過去那邊。

Part

2

依詞性分類的生活單字

everywhere
[ˈɛvrɪˌhwɛr]
副 每個地方

 實境對話
A: Have you found your glasses?
你找到你的眼鏡了嗎?
B: I've looked **everywhere**, but I can't find them.
我找了**每個地方**,但就是找不到。

anywhere
[ˈɛnɪˌhwɛr]
副 任何地方

 實境對話
A: Where is my cell phone?
我的手機在哪裡?
B: I don't know. It could be **anywhere**.
我不知道。可能在**任何地方**。

somewhere
[ˈsʌmˌhwɛr]
副 某些地方

 實境對話
A: I just need **somewhere** tranquil for me to think.
我只是需要某個安靜的**地方**讓我思考。
B: Maybe you can go to our garret.
也許你可以去我們的閣樓。

either [ˈiðɚ]
副 也

同義字 too 也

實境對話
A: I don't like those flowers. 我不喜歡那些花。
B: Me, **either**. 我也是。

neither [ˈniðɚ]
副 兩個都不

 實境對話
A: Robert doesn't know how to ride a bicycle.
羅伯特不知道怎麼騎腳踏車。
B: **Neither** do I.
我也不知道。

no [no]
副 不

延伸片語 no longer 不再
no more 不再

 實境對話
A: Is their baby a girl? 他們的寶寶是女孩嗎?
B: **No**, it's a boy. 不,是男孩。

nor [nɔr]
副 也不

 實境對話
A: Will you and John go to the party? 你和約翰會去派對嗎?
B: No. Neither John **nor** I will go. 不,約翰和我都不會去。

not [nɑt]
副 不是

 實境對話
A: Is she Julia?　她是茱莉亞嗎？
B: No, she's **not**. She's Judy.　不，她不是。她是茱蒂。

yes (yeah) [jɛs]
副 是的

實境對話
A: Do you know the background knowledge of World War II?
你知道第二次世界大戰的背景知識嗎？
B: **Yes**, I do.
是的，我知道。

Part

2

依詞性分類的生活單字

用簡單的小測驗，驗收一下，單字記住了嗎？

( ) 1 available   ( ) 11 popular

( ) 2 convenient   ( ) 12 quiet

( ) 3 different   ( ) 13 sleepy

( ) 4 enough   ( ) 14 sudden

( ) 5 fancy   ( ) 15 usually

( ) 6 great   ( ) 16 away

( ) 7 important   ( ) 17 finally

( ) 8 marvelous   ( ) 18 rather

( ) 9 other   ( ) 19 aloud

( ) 10 perfect   ( ) 20 neither

A 偉大的　B 安靜的　C 有效的　D 完美的　E 突然的　F 相當　　G 幻想的
H 不同的　I 離去　　J 通常　　K 最後　　L 了不起的
M 兩個都不　　　　N 大聲地　O 流行的　P 重要的　Q 足夠的　R 其他的
S 欲睡的　T 方便的

答案

1 (C)　2(T)　3(H)　4(Q)　5(G)　6(A)　7(P)　8(L)　9(R)　10(D)　11(O)　12(B)　13(S)　14(E)
15(J)　16(I)　17(K)　18(F)　19(N)　20(M)

語研力 E077

國中單字2000得分王：
會考、英檢初級必考單字全收錄，關連性記憶取代背誦，答題快狠準！

作　　　者	凱信英研所講師團隊
顧　　　問	曾文旭
出版總監	陳逸祺、耿文國
主　　　編	陳蕙芳
執行編輯	翁芯俐
美術編輯	李依靜
法律顧問	北辰著作權事務所

印　　　製	世和印製企業有限公司
初　　　版	2023 年 01 月
初版二刷	2023 年 11 月
出　　　版	凱信企業集團 - 凱信企業管理顧問有限公司
電　　　話	（02）2773-6566
傳　　　真	（02）2778-1033
地　　　址	106 台北市大安區忠孝東路四段 218 之 4 號 12 樓
信　　　箱	kaihsinbooks@gmail.com

定　　　價	新台幣 360 元 / 港幣 120 元
產品內容	1 書

總 經 銷	采舍國際有限公司
地　　　址	235 新北市中和區中山路二段 366 巷 10 號 3 樓
電　　　話	（02）8245-8786
傳　　　真	（02）8245-8718

國家圖書館出版品預行編目資料

國中單字2000得分王：會考、英檢初級必考單字
全收錄，關連性記憶取代背誦，答題快狠準！／凱
信英研所講師團隊著. — 初版. — 臺北市：凱信企業
集團凱信企業管理顧問有限公司, 2023.01
　面；　公分
ISBN 978-626-7097-53-3(平裝)

1.CST: 英語 2.CST: 詞彙

805.12　　　　　　　　　　　　111020431

凱信企管

用對的方法充實自己，
讓人生變得更美好！

凱信企管

用對的方法充實自己，
讓人生變得更美好！

凱信企管

用對的方法充實自己，
讓人生變得更美好！

凱信企管

用對的方法充實自己，
讓人生變得更美好！